LAVENDER DREAMS

LAVENDER DREAMS

DIANA SUE WELLSPRING

SAPPHIRE BOOKS

SALINAS, CALIFORNIA

Lavender Dreams
Copyright © 2017 by Diana Sue Wellspring All rights reserved.

ISBN - 978-1-943353-59-0

This is a work of fiction - names, characters, places, and incidents are the product of the author's imagination or are used fictitiously. Any resemblance to actual persons living or dead, business, events or locales is entirely coincidental.

All rights reserved. No part of this publication may be reproduced, distributed, or transmitted in any form or by any means, including photocopying, recording, or other electronic or mechanical methods, without written permission of the publisher.

Editor - Kaycee Hawn
Book Design - LJ Reynolds
Cover Design - Michelle Brodeur

Sapphire Books Publishing, LLC
P.O. Box 8142
Salinas, CA 93912
www.sapphirebooks.com

Printed in the United States of America
First Edition – March 2017

This and other Sapphire Books titles can be found at
www.sapphirebooks.com

Dedication

To my beloved wife, Gay Dawn Wellspring, to my mentor, Charlotte Brown Hammond (I miss you every day) and to Kathy Keller, creative writing teacher and editor extraordinaire.

Acknowledgment

Thanks to all those who have given me support through this ten-year journey: Diane Rautio, Patty Becker, Cindy Walston, Yvonne Mickey, Dara Knowles, Illania Edwards, and so many other friends and soul sisters.

PART I

The huge ferry honked its departure signal and began to back out of the slip as Sarah jerked the van to a screeching halt in front of the boarding ramp.

"Damn," she muttered to herself. Now she would have to wait an hour for the next ferry to Bainbridge Island. She hated getting stuck in the ever-increasing Seattle traffic, she hated to be late, and she hated missing the boat. Especially when that boat was supposed to be taking her to a new job and maybe a new life.

She settled back with a sigh and patted the yowling cat carrier on the seat beside her. "I'm sorry, Margret, we just have to wait a little longer," she said. She rolled the window down and let the breeze blowing in from Puget Sound fill the van and ruffle her short, dark hair.

It was one of those incredibly beautiful days Seattle residents don't discuss with tourists, especially those from California. Sunlight glinted off the jagged skyline of green-glassed buildings and crisp white sails skimming across the water. Dark mountains with lightly frosted peaks formed a backdrop in the distance. Gulls screamed and circled, swooping down to seize french fries thrown by people eating on the deck at Ivar's Acres of Clams. Grudgingly, she allowed her mood to lift. After all, she was starting on a new adventure. She hoped that missing the boat was not a bad omen.

Twelve years ago, when she graduated from nursing school, she never would have considered a live-in nursing job. She belonged in a hospital, where the action was, up to her elbows in high-tech drama. Now she felt burned out and more than a little weary. Then, when Nancy announced that she "needed her space," she suddenly had no real reason to hang around. When she saw the ad for a private nurse posted on the bulletin board at work, it sounded like just what she needed. So she put her stuff in storage and packed up Miss Margret.

Cars lined up in the boarding lanes all around her as she watched the huge ferry moving toward them in the distance. She wondered how long it would be before she got to come across the water to Seattle again. If this new job didn't work out, it might be very soon, indeed.

She pulled slowly up the ramp at the deck hand's signal. Sarah's gaydar antennae began to wave at the sight of her. She was definitely a dyke, with her spiky hair, crooked grin, and that certain something that Sarah could not define. She could certainly recognize it, though. Too cute. And very, very hot. She smiled back as she pulled past her and positioned the van inches from the car in front of her.

She reached into her bag on the floor and grabbed her wallet. "Sorry, Margret, I have to go. I'll be back real soon. Don't cry," she said, tapping lightly on the vibrating basket. She grabbed the handle and pushed her shoulder against the door.

"Ow! Hey!" she heard, and froze, half in and half out. The deck hand stood beside the van, rubbing her arm where the door had smacked her. She held a wooden chock she had been bending to place by Sarah's tire.

"Oh no, I am so sorry! I didn't see you!" Sarah babbled as she slid the remainder of her body out of the van. "Here, let me take a look at it. I'm a nurse. Can you move it?"

"Oh, I'm okay," the woman replied, flexing her arm. A very strong-looking arm, Sarah noted. "No big deal." She bent and shoved the chock behind the wheel.

"No, really, I want to make sure you're all right. I didn't even look before I opened the door," Sarah apologized. "Maybe we can put some ice on it."

"I'm just fine," she answered. "All part of the job." Quickly, she looked Sarah up and down and the crooked grin reappeared. "Making an emergency espresso run, huh?"

"Yes," Sarah said, stuffing her keys in her pocket. She smiled at the woman. "I think I'm about a quart low."

"Sounds good," she answered. "Enjoy!"

Sarah watched her back as she moved away down the row of cars. A very strong-looking back, she noted. She smiled to herself as she joined the crowd heading up the stairwell to the passenger deck. That was interesting, she thought. Stupid, but interesting.

Several people stood in line ahead of her at the snack bar. Suddenly, she realized she was hungry. She hadn't eaten since the farewell breakfast she'd treated herself to in the Cow Room at Mae's Phinney Ridge Cafe. She had put away a frightening amount because she didn't know if there would be great coffee cake and hash browns on Bainbridge Island—or when she would have time to find them, if they were there. But breakfast was a long time ago, and it was almost two o'clock now.

She picked up a bagel with cream cheese from the counter and moved along to the espresso line. She was sure she would find espresso on the island—the people of the Puget Sound area could not live without their fragrant brown brew.

"Grande vanilla latte, please," she ordered. Suddenly, a thought struck her. "No, wait, make that two, please," she said. Maybe she could apologize again to the deck hand for attacking her with the van door. Yes, definitely, another apology was in order.

She stuck the bagel in her pocket and made her way back down to the car deck, carefully balancing the two huge cups of coffee. At the foot of the stairs, she looked around quickly, but the woman was nowhere in sight.

"Oh, well, nice thought," she said to herself. She let herself back into the van.

"Hi, Miss Margret, how are you doing? Are you seasick?" Margret hissed and shook the carrier. Sarah unwrapped the bagel, took a bite, and chased it with a sip of steaming liquid. She swiped her finger across the cream cheese then stuck it into the front of the carrier. "Here, kitty, kitty," she said. She laughed as she felt the cold nose touch her finger, followed by the warm rough tongue. At least she was able to apologize to someone, she thought ruefully.

She cranked up an Indigo Girls CD and settled back in her seat, watching the darkly forested islands slide by. Soon she could see the dock at Bainbridge Island in the distance. They would be landing in about ten minutes.

A quick movement caught her eye. It was the deck hand, making her way through the cars, picking up the tire chocks in preparation for docking. Sarah rolled down her window quickly. "Hey!" she said as the woman came alongside the van. "Excuse me!"

"Yes? Can I help you?" the woman said, peering

into the van. She caught sight of Sarah and "Oh, hi. Have a nice ride?"

"Yes, thanks," Sarah said. She grabbed the and handed it out the window. "Here, I got this for you. For hitting you with the door. I mean, to apologize," she babbled on.

"Thanks a lot—or a latte, I guess," the woman said with a grin. "That's the nicest thing that's happened to me today." She reached out to take the drink from Sarah's hand. As their fingers touched, Sarah felt an electric tingle shoot up her arm. Their eyes were almost level—dark blue, Sarah noted. *My, my,* she said to herself.

"I hope you're okay," Sarah murmured. "Are you sure you don't want me to take a look?"

"Oh, no, I'm fine. Thanks again," she said. "Are you visiting the island for the day? I don't remember seeing you on the boat before."

"Actually, I'm moving out here today. At least for a while. I think. I'm out here for a job," Sarah said.

"Hurry up, Jen," one of the other deck hands yelled. "Get those chocks! We're ready to dock!"

"Sorry, have to run," she said. "What's your name?"

"Sarah Chase," she said quickly.

"See you around, Sarah Chase," Jen said. She grabbed the chock from behind the tire, turned, and shot a last grin in her direction, then trotted off.

Sarah touched her hand where it had met Jen's fingers. She hadn't felt that kind of chemistry in quite a while. She wondered if the other woman had felt it, too. "Well, Margret," Sarah said, "that was fun. Wonder if she lives on the island." The cars around her revved their engines. The boat had docked.

She drove slowly up the ramp, following the car in front of her. Jen stood at the end of the ramp, holding her latte in one hand, waving the cars along with the other. As Sarah passed her, Jen raised the cup and winked. Sarah felt a little twinge in her midsection. She was definitely cute.

She drove slowly through the town, checking out the stores and houses. The town had grown quite a bit in the last few years since the technology boom had hit Seattle. Long-term residents who worked in the area and busy people with cell phones, laptops, and IPods now made up the population of the town. The bistros, boutiques, and galleries bespoke affluence, but the town still retained much of its original flavor. She had a brief flash of herself sitting at one of the sidewalk cafes, having a brilliant and witty conversation with— someone? Then she laughed at herself. You're really something, she thought.

The buds on the alders and oaks were just starting to show gray and green, and the evergreens were just starting to get little bright green candles on the end of each branch. The van strained a bit as the road swirled away from the town, growing steeper with each turn.

As she got further from town, the distance between the houses increased, and some of them had fenced fields where horses, goats, and an occasional llama grazed. Deer watched her pass by from the side of the road, unafraid. She caught glimpses of water far below as the road climbed and changed directions.

She had spent a day on a studio and garden tour a couple of years ago, and had attended a couple of concerts on the island, but she had forgotten how nice it was. "What a beautiful place, Margret!" she said. She turned left and began to check the addresses on the mailboxes alongside the road. At last, she saw one with painted purple flowers and The Meadows stenciled neatly on the side. She turned the van onto a winding gravel drive.

She drove for a couple of minutes before she saw a big white house that looked like a steamboat floating across the wide lawn. A railed porch encircled the first floor and several of the upstairs windows had balconies big enough to satisfy Shakespeare. Tall terra cotta urns overflowed with daffodils and ivy on each side of the tall front door.

Suddenly, a black and white rocket came hurtling toward her, barking and barking, then pawed at the van door. She hesitated for a moment before opening the door, then noticed that the dog was wagging its tail so hard it looked like it was dancing. "Well hello," she said. "My, you're friendly!" The dog sniffed her and covered her hand with kisses. "Not much of a watch dog, are you?" Together, they walked up to the steps of the house.

The door flew open as she reached for the gleaming knocker. A tiny, gray-haired woman peered at her over wire-rim glasses. For a moment, she looked as if she'd seen a ghost, then she shook her head. "Miss Chase?"

"Yes," Sarah said. "I'm sorry I'm late. I missed the ferry."

"Hmmmph. We were wondering," she said, frowning. "I see you've met our boy. Back up, now, Ralph! Let the girl in!" She made a grab for his collar. "I'm Marie Fitch," she said, holding out a little bird-like hand. Sarah took it and was surprised to feel a thick ridge of scar tissue in her palm. Marie pulled her hand out of her grasp and stuck it in her pocket. "Come this way. Miss Grace is waiting for you." She stepped back to admit Sarah into the hall.

"Wow, what a beautiful place," Sarah said, taking in the Oriental rugs and light-filled paintings on the walls. A wide stairway with a brand new chair lift led to the second floor. She glimpsed book-lined walls through a set of double doors.

She followed Marie up the stairs. She turned right and tapped briskly at a half-open door. "Grace? Miss Chase is here." She stepped back to let Sarah pass.

A beautiful, white-haired woman on a flowered chaise lounge looked up from her book, then smiled. Sarah felt as if someone had switched on a light in the room. "Welcome, Miss Chase. Or can I call you Sarah? We're so glad you're here."

※ ※ ※ ※

Grace looked up at Marie's knock and for a moment, the breath caught in her throat. But no, on closer inspection, there was not a real resemblance. The way she held herself was so familiar, though, head high and shoulders straight. She smiled. "Welcome, Miss Chase. Or can I call you Sarah? We're so glad you're here."

"Please call me Sarah, Miss Meadows," she said. She came across the room and stuck out her hand.

"Please call me Grace," she said. "And you've met Marie."

"Yes, thanks. Your home is so beautiful," she said, looking around appreciatively. A big four-poster bed piled high with pillows faced east over the garden to catch the first light. A large carved armoire took up most of one wall, and a pair of matching dressers took up another. A wheelchair was pushed into against a door that looked like it connected to a room. A small table next to the chaise lounge held a crystal decanter of water and a flowered mug. A gnarled wooden cane leaned against it, close to Grace's hand.

"Thank you, my dear. We've lived here long enough to make it quite cozy, haven't we, Marie?"

"Yes indeed. Do you need anything right now, Grace?" Marie pulled a crocheted afghan in many shades of blue up over Grace's lap. "No? Then maybe we can let Sarah settle in."

"Good idea," Grace said. "The people at the agency said that you had a cat. Did you bring her with you?"

"Oh, yes, she's in the van. Thank you so much for letting me bring her," Sarah said. "Her name is Margret."

"We lost our Mouser not too long ago," Grace said with a sigh. "It'll be lovely to have a cat in the house again. Oh, and we have a dog as well. I think you've already met him. Ralph loves cats. He was very upset when he lost his friend." She held out her hand and Sarah took it in her own warm one. "Marie will show you your room. Take your time getting settled. And once again, welcome."

Grace waited until she saw the door close behind them before she let the tears fall.

≈≈≈≈

Marie opened the next door in the hall. "This is your room," she said. "Do you need some help with your things?"

"Oh, no thanks, I can manage. I don't have a lot of stuff," Sarah said.

Quickly, she looked around the room. It was generously proportioned, like Grace's room, but it had a very different feel. The furniture was dark wood with clean, uncluttered lines. There was a tall bed with a slatted headboard, an armoire, a chest of drawers, and a lovely big desk. A wing chair covered with tapestry flowers and a small round table with a Craftsman-style reading lamp took up one corner. An open door led to a spacious bath. Bright curtains striped in green and burgundy rustled in the breeze. She was pleased to see that her room opened onto one of the balconies. She could hear water flowing, and the hoarse *grock* of frogs. She looked forward to exploring the grounds.

"Oh, it's a wonderful room," she said.

Marie gave her a small smile. "I've always liked this room myself," she said. "Here is the door that connects to Grace's room. You can hear her if she needs something during the night. Not that she's any trouble," she added hastily. "I've been taking care of her myself since she came home from the hospital, you know."

"It must have been hard for you," Sarah said sympathetically.

"Well, Grace is no trouble. I did worry that she would need something and I wouldn't hear her. And I'm not a trained nurse, so I don't know how to do everything," she said, frowning. "The doctor said she would need to go to a rehab facility if we couldn't get a nurse and a therapist to come out here. That would have been terrible for Grace. She needs to be here, in her home."

Sarah sensed that it was hard for Marie to relinquish her role as caretaker. She was obviously very fond of Grace. "I know you did a great job. She looks very well cared for. I hope I can ask for your help and advice."

Marie smiled, with relief, Sarah thought. "Of course. Any time," she said. "Here are the keys to the house." She handed Sarah a silver key ring. "Let me know if you need anything. We'll have dinner around seven." She turned and closed the door softly behind her.

Sarah sat on the bed and bounced gently. It was perfect, not too hard or soft, just right, like Goldilocks' bed. There were great down pillows and a hand-stitched quilt in purples and greens. It was just her kind of room.

A wave of tiredness washed over her, and she lay back on the bed. So many things had happened in the past few days. She had a different job, a different home. Grace and Marie certainly seemed nice enough, but she had never done home nursing before. She didn't know how it would be to have one patient, and to be on duty most of the time except for her day off. She didn't know how it would be to live so far from her friends in Seattle. She didn't know how it would be sleeping alone in that empty bed, missing Nancy. Suddenly she felt misty-eyed and homesick, like she had the first time she went to summer camp. Well, at least she had Margret to keep her company. She would always be home if Margret were with her.

Then she remembered that Margret was still down in the van, probably wailing her head off. Quickly, she gathered up the van keys and stuffed the silver key ring Marie had given her into her pocket. She headed downstairs to free Margret from her carrier and introduce her to her new home.

Ralph was happy to escort her back to the van,

wagging his tail and bowing. "My, you're handsome." She rubbed the dog's soft head. "One dog ear and one pig ear," she said, admiring the dog's asymmetrical look. She slid Margret's carrier out and Ralph immediately stuck his face against the grate for a look and a sniff. If anything, he was more thrilled, wiggling and moaning. Margret hissed and retreated to the back corner of the carrier. "It's okay, girl." She hoped it really would be.

❧❧❦❦

It was a long time since Marie had set three places for dinner. For the last four years, it had been only Grace and her. Now a new person would be sitting at that third place.

Marie had been opposed to the idea of getting a live-in nurse for Grace. After all, the two of them had managed just fine, thank you very much. But after Grace fell and broke her hip, things had changed. For one thing, she needed all those physical therapy treatments. Of course, Carol Bigelow came three times a week to do the major treatments, but Marie had to get Grace up, walk her, get her in and out of bed, and help her up and down the stairs on the new chair lift. And there were all the medications and other details to see about for Grace's blood pressure and arthritis. And then there was the house to see about. Grace couldn't help her with that anymore, or with the cooking. It was hard enough when they had to hire Lindy, a high-school girl from town, to help with the cleaning. Marie knew she was intimidating to Lindy, who flitted from room to room like a slender ghost, but she wanted things to be just so, as they had been since she came to live here. It was hard for her to realize that she was slowing down a bit, needed a bit of help.

Finally, Grace sat her down for a talk. "Marie, you take better care of me than anyone else in the world could. But it's too much for you and Lindy to do by yourselves. We need some other help. My insurance will pay for a nurse, and you won't have to worry about me anymore."

"Not worry about you! You think I can just let some stranger in here to see about you? Someone who doesn't know you?" Marie sputtered.

"Well, it's certainly not what I would choose. But that's the point—we don't have a choice," Grace said gently. "You know I don't want to go into Viking Manor for rehab. Of course, she'll need you to help her."

Well, Sarah Chase looked like a nice person, no hard edges, and she smiled easily. But Marie would be watching her carefully. She wouldn't tolerate anyone mistreating her Grace.

※※※※

Margret was relieved to be out of the cat carrier, and after a brief look around her new room, she curled up at the foot of the bed for a snooze. Sarah checked herself out in the bathroom mirror and combed her hair. She didn't know if her shirt and jeans were okay to wear to dinner. Finally, she decided to change. She pulled on a long Indian-style gauze skirt and a short-sleeved black knit top and headed out the door.

She tapped on Grace's door. "Hi, Grace," she said, peering into the darkening room. "Can I help you with anything before dinner?"

"Oh, hello, dear," Grace answered. "Is it that late

already? I was just sitting here thinking about old times and old friends. Typical old lady, huh?" She grasped her cane and scooted forward. "Marie should be up in a minute, but if you like, you can walk me to the stairs." Sarah took her elbow and helped her to her feet. "My goodness, I'm stiff from all this sitting around. I just can't get used to it."

"It must be a difficult adjustment, especially if you were pretty active before your accident," Sarah said. They moved slowly.

Marie caught sight of them leaving the room and started quickly up the stairs. "Wait, now, you two, I'm coming!"

"We're doing just fine, Marie," Grace said. "Don't worry!"

She wedged herself between them and took Grace's arm from Sarah. "Here, Grace, you sit down here now," she said, guiding her toward the seat. "Be careful," she fussed. "I guess I should show you how to work this contraption," she said to Sarah. She pointed to the controls. "Here is the down switch. You have to make sure that Grace is positioned right so she doesn't fall out of the chair. Then you can just walk down beside her and help her get up at the bottom," Marie said. A bit curtly, Sarah thought.

"Okay, I think I understand," she said. The device was certainly self-explanatory. "Thanks for your help."

After a slow and stately ride, the three of them moved through the foyer to the dining room. Sarah noted the massive table that could easily seat twelve. There were three places set. Marie and Grace were obviously in the habit of eating together. They seemed more like family than employer and servant, Sarah thought. "It smells wonderful in here," she said.

"Hmmmph," Marie said. "It's just plain cooking." She helped Grace settle in her chair at the head of the table. "Sit there," she said, pointing Sarah towards the chair farthest from the kitchen. She turned and disappeared through the swinging door.

Sarah sat down and checked out the room. "I can't get over this place," she said. "It's just beautiful, like an old New England inn."

Grace smiled. "Funny you should say that," she said. "That's what the first owner wanted when he built this house. He was from Stockbridge, Massachusetts, originally." She paused. "Actually, we ran a guest house here for many years. We bought this house not long after World War II. We moved here from Massachusetts, too, and that was one of the reasons we fell in love with the place. It looked like home to us."

"You and your husband?" Sarah asked.

"Oh, no," Grace said. "George was killed in the war. I came out here with Annie, George's sister." Grace sighed. "She died four years ago."

"I'm so sorry. I didn't mean to pry," Sarah said.

"Oh, no, dear, you're not prying. It's still hard for me to realize that she's gone," Grace said with another sigh. "The house is huge, of course. You'll have to look around. Eight bedrooms in all, six up and two down. There are also some little cottages around back, and a house where the caretaker and his family used to live."

Marie placed a steaming tureen of mushroom and wild rice soup and a bowl of salad on the table. Sarah didn't realize how hungry she was until she smelled the soup. It had certainly never seen the inside of a can.

Grace and Marie clasped hands and bowed their heads. "Happy happy, joy joy," they said. Sarah looked at them, shocked, then started to laugh. It was the last place she ever would have thought to hear Ren and Stimpy quoted. "Excuse me," she said. Grace smiled at her and winked.

"Would you like some wine?" Grace asked, pointing to the glasses on the table. "Marie and I like to have a bit with dinner."

"Oh, thanks," she said. She watched Marie expertly open the green bottle and pour each of them a glass. She had never had a drink while she was working, but it seemed to be part of their routine. She made a conscious effort not to bolt her food. "This is just delicious." She smiled at Marie, who was concentrating on the movement of Grace's spoon. By the time Marie brought in the roast chicken and vegetables, she was able to relax and resume the conversation.

"How did you break your hip?" she asked.

"Well, it was so silly. I was walking down to the water with Ralph, and I stepped into something squishy. I think it might have been goose poop. Did you know geese poop about every six minutes?"

"Uh, no," Sarah said, taken aback. "Yuck!"

"It was totally undignified. And quite painful. I was glad nobody was there to see it happen. But I couldn't stand up, and then I had to sit there, goose poop all over me, until Marie came looking for me."

"I was ready to cook some geese that day, I tell you!" Marie said.

"Now, you know it wasn't their fault. They were just doing what comes naturally," Grace said. She turned to Sarah. "I've always been partial to those birds."

They continued eating for a few minutes before Sarah spoke again. "What made you decide to move to this area?"

"Oh, we just wanted to leave the past behind. Make a new life for ourselves," Grace said, smiling reminiscently. "We were so young then. Our families were dead set against our leaving, of course. An unmarried young lady and a young widow, just imagine!"

"That was very brave of you, especially after you lost your husband," Sarah said admiringly.

"We both missed George very much, but we had to get on with our lives. And we were determined to have an adventure!" Grace laughed. "We took the train across the country and ended up in Los Angeles."

"Grace wanted to be a movie star," Marie said.

"Well, I got over that idea rather quickly. And it was so hot and dry there, and we wanted to live in a green place with lots of water. We bought a 1946 Packard and kept driving north until we finally ended up in Seattle. We loved the area, but we didn't want to live in a city. Not that Seattle was much of a city back then," she said.

"One day we took a boat across to the Island and we just loved it right away. We knew this was where we wanted to stay," she continued. "There wasn't much we could do to make a living, though. We didn't want to be secretaries and we didn't want to teach. We thought how nice it would be if we could just stay home and cook and garden and be with friends. That's how we got started."

While Grace talked, Marie remembered how the long dining table was often crowded with chattering people eating her good food. In those days, paying guests looking to get away from Seattle for the weekend often filled the bedrooms and cottages. Often writers or artists looking for a secluded place where they could work, explore the island, or just relax and dream in the beautiful gardens would fill one or more of the rooms for the entire week. Some of them stayed in the little cottages by the lake for weeks at a time. Marie especially enjoyed these people, who could always be counted on for lively dinner conversation.

Oh, it was a busy place during those years! During their peak times in the summer, they often had three young girls to clean the house and help with the meals. Grace ran the day-to-day operations of the guesthouse with Marie's help, while Annie cared for the gardens and the acres of strawberries and lavender they tended each year. They were a family.

Then about five years ago, Annie's health began to fail. For a while, she tried to hide it, but she couldn't disguise her thinness and loss of appetite from their sharp eyes for very long. By the time Grace got her to go to the doctor, the cancer had begun to spread.

The rounds of surgeries, medications, and treatments began. They phased out the operations of the guesthouse and the fields as Annie required more and more care. It broke their hearts to see Annie's years of hard work become ragged and overgrown. Grace spent most of her time with Annie, bathing her, reading to her, coaxing her to eat. Marie helped out when she could, but it was exhausting work. Friends dropped by and helped where they could.

Dr. Emily and Annie were great friends and she came to see Annie often. They both loved to plant and putter, and Emily encouraged Annie to be out in the garden as much as possible. "No use lying around in bed when you can be out among the flowers!" she said.

So whenever the weather was good, Annie

would sit outside in a big green Adirondack chair, and when she got weaker they moved her to a hammock. They plied her with Marie's famous chicken soup, ice cream, and her favorite rice pudding, but she didn't have much of an appetite. Hospice nurses, aides, and massage therapists visited frequently and made her as comfortable as they could. Reverend Leah came by often, and together they speculated about the mysteries of the universe.

One day Annie said to Grace, "You know, honey, I'm close to my expiration date, way past my shelf life. But there are some things I want you to promise me before I go."

Grace began to cry. "Oh, love, I'm not ready. I don't want to let you go!"

"I know, and I don't want to leave you, and Marie, and our animals, and our home. And I know you know how precious you are to me, part of my heart and soul. We've been together for so many years." She paused and took a breath. "I loved you from the first time I saw you, when my brother brought you home to meet the family. I didn't know what to do with those feelings."

"I thought you were just shy. You never would look at me," Grace said, fondly.

"I couldn't. It hurt to breathe, you were so beautiful, and you were with George. I could see you loved him by the way you looked at him. I knew you would never look at me that way."

"But I've been looking at you that way for all these years. I loved George dearly, and you know I missed him terribly. I still do. He was a dear, sweet man, so strong and gentle. I knew he would always try to protect me. But it was different with you. You made me feel strong, like I could do anything, but tender too."

"You are the strongest woman I know. You are so delicate and ladylike, but I know there is a lioness inside." Annie smiled.

"And you. I loved seeing you out in the garden, fixing things, building things. You were so sexy; I would get breathless just watching you." She laughed.

"You're making me feel all mushy inside, darn you. I wanted to have a serious conversation, and now you're making me cry." She dabbed at her eyes with her sleeve.

"I'm sorry. I distracted you," she paused. "No, I'm not sorry at all!" she said defiantly. "I'm not ready to have this talk." She blew her nose on her handkerchief. "Now you're making me cry, too!"

"I just want to make sure that you'll be all right. I want to know that you'll keep going, take care of yourself and this place. And when I die, I don't want to be buried in some cemetery. I want to be cremated, and I want you to keep my ashes here. I'm part of this place, and I want to stay here. With you."

"I promise. You'll always be here, on this land. And part of me."

"And I don't want you to be lonely. I don't want you to shut yourself away."

"Don't worry about that. Marie will be here, and our friends will come around."

"You know what I mean, Grace."

"For goodness sake, love, I am an old lady. I'm not about to find someone else. There is nobody else like you, you know."

"Never say never, Grace."

The next day, Annie could not get out of bed.

"I'm so very tired," she said. "I just want to rest."

Grace and Marie gathered up her favorite music and played it for her: Billy Holliday, Nina Simone, Cris Williamson, Meg Christian, Joni Mitchell, Judy Collins. They played Ferron, Holly Near, Heather Bishop, and the Indigo Girls. Sometimes she would smile, and now and then, they could hear her humming softly. But she did not open her eyes.

That evening, several of their old friends came to say their good-byes. They whispered in her ear, held her hand, cried softly at times as they talked about the past. As her breathing became more labored, they began to sing – The Water is Wide, Amazing Grace, Swing Low Sweet Chariot. Reverend Leah came by and joined in the vigil. Grace held her hand through it all.

Her breaths became sighs, slower and slower. Then, at last, there was silence. Grace felt a wave of love as Annie's spirit entered her. And, at last, they were one.

≈≈≈≈≈

Grace fell silent and looked over at Marie and Sarah. All three of them were red-eyed and had little balled up tissues in their hands, and their plates had long grown cold.

"My goodness," she said. "I can't believe we've been talking so long. Poor thing, you come out here and end up watching two old ladies ranting on and crying. You must want to get back on that ferry and get out of here."

"Oh, no, it was wonderful to hear your stories. Thank you for sharing with me," Sarah said. "But you must be exhausted, Grace."

"Yes, it's time we got you upstairs and settled," Marie said, jumping up.

Sarah stood, too, and moved to Grace's side. "Here, Grace, let me help you."

"No!" Marie said. "I'll help her! You don't know her routine or what she needs."

"Well, it would be great if you could show me what needs to be done," Sarah said.

"No, I can take care of it," Marie said, moving Sarah aside. "I know what to do."

Sarah looked at Grace. She shrugged slightly and winked at Sarah. "I think we're okay for tonight, my dear. Why don't you get settled in tonight and we can start tomorrow."

"Okay, I guess," Sarah said. "I'll just clear up down here then."

"No!" Marie said, her tone clipped. "I will take care of it myself. Don't touch anything!"

Shaking her head, she watched Grace and Marie head toward the stairs.

❧❧❧❧

Grace woke slowly, savoring the last few minutes of her dream.

They sat on a blue blanket at the edge of the field, drunk on the scent of strawberries ripening in the hot sun and the soapy clean smell of lavender. The soothing buzz of fat black and yellow bees made her eyes grow heavy. She could barely focus on Annie's hands, brown and square, wrapped around the delicate teacup. Such strong hands, yet so gentle.

Annie raised the cup to her lips and drank off the dregs. She liked her tea light and sweet. Grace had laughed at her over the years for her love of sugar. "Just a little child, that's what you are."

"Don't pick on me, Grace, you know I can't help it," she would say with the smile that made Grace want to run into the kitchen and bake her a thousand cookies.

"I'm so sleepy, A," she said drowsily.

"Come here and lay your head on my lap, Miss Grace," she said. She reached out and drew Grace down. "Now close your eyes and wish for something sweet."

"You. I wish for you, and here you are," she said. She opened her eyes to look at Annie again, but she saw Sarah's face instead.

※※※※

Margret thrust her wet nose against Sarah's eyelid just as the clock started to buzz.

"Mmmph, no, stop," she murmured, both to the cat and the clock. She grabbed Margret, rolled toward the clock, and pounded the snooze button. "Urk. Feh."

Margret crouched down and wiggled her butt as she positioned herself for another attack.

"Can't you give me just five more minutes?" Sarah pleaded. She pulled the comforter over her head. Margret pawed at the covers, meowing.

"All right, all right. What a pest you are!" She swung her feet over the edge of the bed, yawned, and scrubbed at her eyes. The morning light was just starting to filter in through the blinds.

She staggered into the bathroom, turned on the shower, and adjusted it for industrial-strength massage. She needed a major jump-start this morning.

Grace and Marie were early risers. She smelled coffee as she finished brushing her teeth. She could hear the grind of the electric stair climber through the door. Quickly, she threw on her clothes and ran a comb through her damp hair. She picked up the cat and planted a quick kiss between her ears. "I'll be up in a minute with your breakfast," she said. "You behave yourself now."

Marie was just lifting the breakfast tray from the stair climber seat as Sarah opened the door. "What a good idea. Here, let me help you with that," she said.

"No, I've got it," Marie gasped. "Just open the door a little more." Sarah held the door open and Marie carried the loaded tray to the table. Tantalizing smells came from the covered dishes.

"Good morning, Grace," Sarah said. She was surprised to see Grace already sitting in her chair. "My, you've got an early start this morning."

"I never was one to sleep late," Grace said. "Marie usually comes up to give me a hand in the morning before she starts breakfast."

"I'm sorry, I should have gotten up sooner," Sarah said. "It will take me a while to get used to your routine."

"That's all right, dear. Marie and I are used to dealing with each other in the morning. Would you like a cup of coffee?"

"I would love some, but I can go downstairs, unless you need some help with your breakfast?"

"You can stay up here if you want," Marie said. "I brought up extra for you."

"Thank you," she said, and pulled up a chair next to Grace. "This is so decadent, almost like having breakfast in bed. Can I fix you a plate?" she asked.

"I've got it," Marie said. "I know what she wants." She put a cup of coffee and a buttered scone in front of Grace, then handed Sarah a plate. "Help yourself."

"Thank you," she said again. She helped herself to a warm scone, some strawberry jam, and a scoop of scrambled eggs. "Mmm, this is wonderful. I can't believe you get up so early to bake."

"It's like Grace said, we're used to getting up early." She began to make up Grace's bed.

"Why don't you let me do that, Marie?" Sarah said. "I'll get the room squared away after breakfast."

"Don't trouble yourself," Marie said. "I can do it."

Sarah sighed. There were going to be some difficult adjustments. For all of them.

"Did you sleep well, dear?" Grace asked.

"Oh, yes, that bed is very comfortable. I slept like a rock until Margret decided it was time for me to get up," Sarah said with a smile.

"Margret is your cat, yes? What an unusual name!" Grace said.

"She thinks she's a most unusual cat. She's a Siamese, and she has pretty strong ideas about how the world is supposed to be."

"Well, I'd love to meet her. And as far as I'm concerned, you don't have to keep her in your room. She can have the run of the house. Right, Marie?" Grace said.

"Hmmmph," she answered, thumping the pillows.

"I appreciate that. She doesn't like being locked in. She's a good cat. Would you like to meet her now?"

"Yes indeed," Grace said.

Sarah opened the door to her room and Margret

strolled out, looking around curiously. "Come here," she said. "Be sociable."

Margret sniffed at Grace's slippered foot, then bowed and purred. Grace patted her lap. "Come here, pretty girl," she said. Margret jumped lightly onto her lap and pushed her nose into Grace's hand. Slowly she moved her hand over the smooth head. Margret turned up the volume and closed her eyes.

"I guess she likes you," Sarah said. "I'm not surprised."

"Be careful, now, Grace," Marie said. "You two don't know each other."

"Oh, Margret is usually pretty low key," Sarah said, reaching for another scone. "These just melt in your mouth."

"Marie used to wow our guests with her cooking," Grace said proudly. "I'm sure some of the guests came back just for the goodies."

"Well, I can understand why. A beautiful place, great food, what more could you ask for?" She reached for her napkin—cloth, she noticed. "What's on your schedule for today?"

"Well, if it's all right with you, I'd like to get cleaned up after breakfast, then Carol will be here about ten. She's the physical therapist."

"Okay. Do you usually take a shower? And when do you take your meds? I'd like to take a look at your records."

"Marie has been helping me shower. But finish your breakfast and we'll get to all of that stuff in a few minutes. Meanwhile, tell me something about yourself. We were so busy talking about us last night we didn't hear anything about you."

Sarah filled her in briefly about where she

grew up, what her parents did, and how she ended up becoming a nurse. She carefully skirted around why she had decided to leave Seattle and take a home case. She didn't want to get too personal. She wanted to be friendly, but she needed to maintain a bit of professional distance. And besides, she wouldn't—couldn't—talk about some things.

After they finished eating, Marie piled the dishes on the tray and put it aside. Slowly they went through the steps of Grace's morning care and medications. Marie alternated between exhaustive explanations of each detail and crossing her arms with a loud "hmmmph." Sarah was feeling a bit irritable by the time they were done, though she tried not to show it. She could imagine how Grace felt.

They didn't have much time to catch their breath, though. Carol was already ringing the doorbell.

༄༅༄༅

Carol enjoyed the sweet warmth of the morning air. Early flowers were starting to unfurl and disperse their heady scents.

She backed out carefully, avoiding Zoe's car in the driveway. She'd been up late last night, working on a new piece, and was still sacked out, Abby Tabby curled around her head like a stripey red hat.

She checked in at the clinic, picked up her messages, and saw a couple of patients before she headed out to The Meadows. It was always a bright spot in her day. Grace was one of her favorites, and Marie always saved a biscuit or cinnamon roll for her.

She perked up when she saw a purple van with a rainbow hanging from the rear-view mirror parked at the edge of the drive. She pulled up close behind it and noticed a little goddess decal on the rear window. On one side of the rear bumper was a Hate Is Not a Family Value bumper sticker. On the other side was one that said Coexist. Definitely a dykemobile. She thought she knew all the lesbians on the island. She wondered who it could be.

As usual, Ralph raced out to greet her, but it took Marie a couple of minutes to answer the door. When she saw her face, Carol knew she was not having a good day. "What is it, Marie? Is something wrong? Is Grace okay?"

"I guess she's all right," Marie said stiffly. "They're upstairs. Come in." She stepped back so Carol could pass.

She could hear a low murmur of voices as she climbed the stairs, then a sudden silvery laugh. "Hi, Grace! It's me!" she called.

"Come in, dear," Grace answered. "We're just trying to get organized here!" Grace sat in her chair, one foot extended toward a sweet-faced woman who sat on the floor in front of her, a long white sock in her hand. "Carol, this is Sarah Chase, who has come to stay with us. She's a nurse. Sarah, this is Carol Bigelow. She's a physical therapist and comes to see me three times a week."

Carol remembered that Grace had mentioned hiring a nurse to help out. She was glad they would have some help. There was certainly too much for Marie to do alone.

"Nice to meet you," Sarah said, holding out the hand without the sock. "We're just finishing up here."

Carol took her hand and felt a little quiver run up her arm. Uh oh, she thought. "No hurry. I hope

Marie has saved me a goody."

"Of course, dear, she wouldn't forget you," Grace said with a smile.

"And who is this?" Carol asked, pointing to the Siamese peeking out from under Grace's bed.

"That is Margret," Sarah said. "She likes to assist. With everything." She laughed, that same silvery sound. "No, that's not quite true. She likes to supervise."

"Hi, Margret. You're very pretty," Carol said. And so are you, she thought as she looked the woman up and down. She was one of those people who always looked like she'd just stepped out of the shower, clean, flushed, sweet smelling. The morning sun picked up the red highlights in her short chestnut hair. Dangerous. She took a deep breath. "Is that your van?"

"Yes. I'm sorry. Is it in the way?" Sarah asked quickly.

"Oh, no, I was just admiring the color. And your bumper stickers. And your goddess," she said carefully.

"Really." Sarah looked at her closely for a moment, then smiled. "There's not too many people who would notice. Or recognize her," she said.

"What does your bumper sticker say, dear? I haven't seen it yet," Grace said.

"Oh, not much of anything," Sarah said hastily. "There's a little picture of a statue…"

"She speaks for herself," Carol said, and winked.

"True." Sarah laughed, then turned back to Grace's foot. She pulled up the sock, slipped on her shoe, and tied the laces. "There," she said. "Now let's see that other foot."

"Actually, I'd like to take a look at her foot before you put her sock on," Carol said. She sat down next to Sarah on the floor. "I want to see if the swelling is down."

"Well, isn't this nice? Handmaidens at my feet." Grace smiled. "Or I guess you would be footmaidens?"

"I don't know about you, Sarah, but I think I'm a bit past the maiden age." Carol chuckled.

"Never too old," Grace said. "I'm going through my third or fourth maidenhood myself."

"Grace! What a thing to say!" Marie exclaimed, shocked. They hadn't heard her come in.

"Well, it's true!" Grace said wickedly. "You're probably on your fifth or sixth go-around yourself, you old biddy!"

"Well, I never!" Marie exclaimed. "I'm not going to stay here for that kind of talk. I'm going downstairs to make lunch!"

"Better make plenty," Grace called after her. "We're hungry!"

Sarah got to her feet and dusted off her butt. "Do you mind if I watch while you work, Carol? Maybe you can show me some things I can do for Grace between your visits."

"Sure," Carol said. "If Grace doesn't mind, that is."

"Oh, no, put me through my drill. I want Sarah to see how mean you are to an old lady."

Sarah watched as Carol did her manipulations and put Grace through a series of exercises. When she was done, they took Grace downstairs for a stroll around the garden.

"It's so nice to be out here in the fresh air again," Grace said. "How I hate being shut up in the house."

"Well, you're doing so well you should take a short walk or two every day. You don't want to lose your muscle tone!" Carol said. "And now that you've got Sarah with you, you should be back to your old self in no time."

"Well, I doubt that," Grace said with a sigh. "For that you'd have to dip me in the Fountain of Youth!"

"Or the pool!" Carol said. "We're going to make good use of that as soon as your incision heals a bit more." She looked at Sarah. "Maybe Grace can show you around the place. She can walk a little, rest, take her time. She could push the wheelchair like a walker, then she could sit down if she gets tired."

"That's a good idea. I haven't been around the grounds myself since I fell," said Grace.

"C'mon now, everything's ready," Marie called. She'd set a table out on the porch with tea things, plates of sandwiches, fruit, and cookies. "Time to eat!"

"Thank you, Marie. This is lovely," Grace said. "Sit down, ladies. Marie, do you want to pour?"

"Thank you, ladies. What a nice treat," Carol said. She pulled out a chair for Grace, then one for herself. Sarah sat down opposite her. Carol couldn't help but notice how the sun glinted off her hair.

They spent a pleasant hour talking while the food disappeared. Carol and Sarah each sketched out a bit about their backgrounds for each other's benefit. Carol found herself watching Sarah's hands, thinking how graceful they were, and how strong.

"This must be so boring for you, Grace," Sarah said. "You already know this stuff."

"Oh, no, it's lovely to have new people to talk to. Isn't that right, Marie?"

"Hmmmph," she said.

"Besides, it gives me an excuse to tell you some more things about The Meadows. You certainly can collect some stories after forty years of running a hotel!"

Carol looked at her watch. She had another appointment coming up soon. "I wish I could stay, but I have to get going," she said. "Thanks for lunch!"

"Let me walk you out to your car," Sarah said. Ralph led them down the driveway towards Carol's Volvo. Sarah noticed that she also had a rainbow decal on her back window. "Small world," she said with a smile.

"We're everywhere," Carol answered, smiling in turn.

"I'm glad to hear that. I'd hate to think I was the only dyke on Bainbridge Island. Although – when I was coming across on the ferry, I saw a dykey-looking woman working there."

"You must mean Jen. There's a bunch of us here. Some folks commute to Seattle, but a lot of us work here on the Island. How long are you planning to be here?"

"I'm not sure yet. Maybe a couple of months. It depends on how Grace's recovery goes."

"Well, maybe I could introduce you to some people. Do you know the Island at all?"

"Well, I've been out here a couple of times, but I just rode around town and picnicked at Fay Bainbridge Park with my friend. Or rather my ex-friend," she said ruefully.

"Aha," Carol said. "I see. Well, we're having a potluck on Saturday. Why don't you come and join us? It'll give you a chance to get acquainted."

"A potluck! That sounds like fun. And I am off on Saturday," Sarah said, then hesitated. "I feel kind of funny, though. I won't know anybody there."

"You'll know me," Carol said. "I'm looking

forward to getting to know you a bit better. I think we have a lot in common."

※ ※ ※ ※

"I know Marie means well, but she's making my job very difficult," Sarah said. "I don't know what to do." She tossed the green tennis ball to Ralph for the fifty-seventh time. Finally, he got bored and wandered off, and the squirrels reappeared.

Grace pulled some peanuts out of her pocket. "I love to watch squirrels," she said. "I know a lot of people think they're pests, but I've always been partial to them." She smiled reminiscently. "Annie was always trying to find the perfect squirrel-proof bird feeder, and then she would catch me feeding them." She sighed. "I'm sorry; I know this is a difficult situation. But Marie has been with us—with me—for years," Grace said, stirring her tea thoughtfully. "And you've only been here a few days."

"I know she's worried about you, and it's hard to have me doing things that she's used to doing." Sarah said, frowning. "But I feel like I bump into her whenever I turn around. Whenever I want to do something, she's already doing it. I don't feel like I'm earning my money."

"Oh, no, dear, don't feel that way. It's just going to take some time for all of us to adjust to each other. It will work out, you'll see." Grace reached over and patted her on the hand.

"I hope so," Sarah said, glumly.

"I'm sure of it. Would you like me to talk to her?" Grace asked.

"Oh, no," Sarah said hastily. The last thing she

wanted Grace to do was let Marie know that Sarah was complaining. "I'm sure you're right. It will just take time."

"We shouldn't let Marie get too stressed out," Grace said. "She has a bit of angina, but she doesn't like to make a big deal about it. She'd probably be mad that I told you."

"Okay, I'll keep that in mind," Sarah said. "Are you ready to go on? Or have we seen everything?"

"Oh, no. I want to show you the back garden. And there are a couple of cottages back here where guests used to stay, and the caretaker's house. Nobody lives there now, but it's quite charming," Grace said. "And of course, I want to show you the lake."

"Great! I thought I heard water, and lots of frogs."

"Yes, and the salmon come through the creek on their way to spawn, and there's a lovely blue heron who lives back there."

"That's wonderful. I'd love to see that."

Grace pushed the wheelchair slowly down the paths, showing Sarah the creek, the little lake, and the strawberry and lavender fields, now sadly grown over.

"Oh, I love to garden," Sarah said. "Would it be okay if I did some digging around back here?"

"Certainly! We have all kinds of tools, gloves, and such. And we love fresh vegetables, if you feel like planting some. And wait till you see the rhodys!"

They passed the pool house on the way back and stopped in to take a look. It was a low building with white clapboards that matched the house. Cobalt blue tiles lined the pool, and there was a matching hot tub big enough for six acquaintances or eight close friends.

"Oh, it's beautiful!" Sarah exclaimed.

"Thank you. You heard Carol say that we would

be using the pool for my therapy. I want you to feel free to use it whenever you like, too."

"Thanks! I will certainly take you up on that!"

"Good," Grace said. "So how are you planning to spend your day off?"

"Well, I thought I'd ride around the Island and look around a bit," Sarah said. "And Carol invited me to a potluck at her house."

"Really! Well! She invited you to her home," Grace said, surprised. She looked Sarah over carefully. "You two must really have hit it off."

"Carol said she thought we had a lot in common," Sarah said with a smile. "I think she may be right!"

"Very interesting," Grace said. "I wonder what she's thinking. Oh well, I'm sure you'll have a good time there." She sighed. "We had lots of potlucks at The Meadows over the years," Grace said. "During the winter especially, when business was a little slow. They were great fun. In fact, you may run into some of our old friends at Carol's house."

"Maybe," Sarah said doubtfully. She was pretty clear on the types of people who would be coming, and she couldn't envision any of Grace's blue-haired friends there.

"What are you going to bring? Do you like to cook?" Grace asked.

"I thought I'd pick up a cake in town or maybe some kind of salad. Actually, I do love to cook. But I hadn't thought about actually making something," Sarah said.

"Well, you can use the kitchen any time, of course. If you feel like it, that is," Grace said.

"Thanks, Grace. I appreciate the offer. I wonder how Marie would feel about me messing around in her kitchen, though."

"Well, let's ask her. Here she comes," Grace said, shading her eyes against the sun.

Marie strode toward them through the grass. "I brought you a sweater, Grace. It's getting a little nippy out here," she said, with an accusing look at Sarah. "You've two have been out here for a long time."

"Thank you, Marie, that was very thoughtful. I guess I am getting a little chilly."

Marie draped the sweater around Grace's shoulders.

"Sarah and I were just talking about a potluck she's going to at Carol's house tomorrow evening," Grace said casually. "It's her day off, you know."

Marie's eyes narrowed to slits. "You're going to Carol's house?" She looked over at Grace.

"I told her she could use the kitchen if she wanted to cook something to bring," Grace said. "I said I didn't think you'd mind." She folded her arms across her chest.

"She wants to cook? In the kitchen?" Marie said through stiff lips.

"Actually, I could just as easily buy something to take," Sarah said quickly.

"Nonsense," Grace said crisply. "We want you to feel at home here, and that includes cooking up anything you please! Right, Marie?" She paused and looked at her. "Right?"

"Yes, Grace. Of course." Marie spun around and marched off, her back straight as a ramrod. "Dinner will be ready soon. It's time for you to come inside!" she called over her shoulder.

Grace exhaled sharply and dropped her arms. "There. I told you there would be no problem."

"Right," Sarah said. "No problem."

≈≈≈≈

Marie couldn't believe that Grace was actually going to allow that girl to cook in the kitchen. Her kitchen.

"You know that nobody ever cooks in that kitchen but me, Grace," Marie said later that night.

"Now that's not true, Marie," she said. "I used to cook in there sometimes, and Annie would too."

"Hmmmph," she said, crossing her arms over her chest. "Call that cooking."

"All right, so it wasn't the Cordon Bleu. More like the Cordon Blah. But I'm telling you, Marie, you'd better get over yourself. Sarah is going to be with us for a while, and she should feel like this is her home. She should be free to do whatever she wants. And besides, she seems to be a tidy person. I'm sure she won't make a mess."

"She'd better not," Marie muttered darkly. "She'll move things around, and then I'll never be able to find anything!"

When Marie first came to work at the hotel, the kitchen was disorganized and poorly equipped. Over the years, she'd gotten it just the way she wanted it – wide tiled counters, gleaming metal shelves lined with pots and pans, steel utensils standing at attention in bright pottery containers. Magnetic knife racks held a variety of high-quality chef knives of different sizes and shapes, and one old black-bladed carbon steel knife that had been sharpened so many times it was almost as thin as a razor. Tall cupboards with glass doors held stacks of plain white china and a variety of flowered serving pieces. She could easily cook dinner for twenty-five, and she had done that many times. Aside from their normal complement of guests, they often had small weddings in the gardens, and their Sunday dinners were well known even in certain circles in Seattle.

But in the last few years, fewer and fewer people had come to The Meadows. Occasionally a friend or two came by for a visit and a meal, but most of the time it was only Grace and her. She'd had to learn to cook for two. And now there were three.

❧❧❧❧

Most of the Island was hilly and thickly forested with huge firs, pines, and cedars. The tall trees grew so close to the road in some areas that the sky was reduced to a thin strip, receding to a point in the distance. Permanent twilight bathed much of the land, perfect for all kinds of ferns, mushrooms, and plenty of moss. It was not hard to imagine elves and gnomes peeking out from the leaves.

The housing on the Island was quite varied, though. Hippie shanties shared space with berry farms, llama ranches, and homes right out of *Sunset Magazine*. Daffodils and forsythia were bursting out all over, and the deciduous trees were flocked in pink and white.

And of course, the beaches.

The coastline was jagged and the beaches were covered with driftwood deposited by the restless waters of Puget Sound. Children scrambled around tumbled piles of branches and huge silvery logs. Dogs ran along the impossibly cold water, chasing the seagulls and each other. A couple of teenagers made their brightly colored kites bob and twist in the gusty breezes. Sarah drove carefully onto the hard-packed sand and left her shoes behind. The surface was wet and pocked with clam holes. She found a good-sized walking stick and gathered up shells and sand dollars as she strolled along.

After a while, she sat on a smooth log and wiggled her brightly painted toenails until they disappeared beneath the sand. A bit of the Seattle skyline glowed green in the distance, and for a moment she could believe she was in a different land, very far away from the Emerald City.

And her life on the Island was different indeed. She couldn't believe that only a couple of weeks ago she was running the Oncology Unit at Pacific Heights Hospital. She dealt with patients newly diagnosed with a disease that would end or change their lives forever. Patients who had been fighting the battle for years, through rounds of surgeries, chemotherapy, and radiation. Patients who were too tired to fight anymore and grateful to close their eyes one last time. And some patients who may have had their eyes closed for them, perhaps prematurely.

She saw the same people over and over, grew close with them and their families. She also supervised several other staff members, and, of course, there were mountains of paperwork and endless meetings to get through. It was a grueling, fast-paced job, and when she finally fell into bed, she continued to relive the days in her dreams.

For the past couple of years, she'd felt so trapped in her work and her life. She felt guilty even thinking about making a change, but she was tired of the bureaucracy, the paperwork, the schedules. She was tired of the ugliness, the smells, the whole technology geared to prolonging death but not life. At night, she came home to Nancy too wiped out to enjoy herself and their life together. It was no wonder Nancy had decided to look elsewhere for companionship.

Now all she wanted was to kick back, rest, and let herself heal. And she needed to figure who this latest iteration of Sarah Chase really was.

Sailboats cut through the water, leaning in the wind, so clean and free.

※※※※

Marie was waiting when Sarah came back from her ride, laden with green fabric grocery bags. She looked around admiringly at the shining surfaces, everything in order. "This is such a beautiful kitchen," Sarah said. "Thank you for letting me use it."

"What have you got there?" Marie said, trying to peer into the top of one of the bags.

"Oh, a bunch of celery, some onions, eggs, a couple of pounds of shrimp." She took the items from the bags and laid them on spotless counter. "I thought I'd make some shrimp salad."

"We have most of that stuff here already," Marie said. "You should have asked me."

"Well, I didn't want to use your food. After all, I'm taking it with me," Sarah said. "But I did buy some other things that I'd like to leave here—some tea, rice cakes, a couple of other things. If you don't mind."

"Grace says you should feel at home here," she answered. "I guess I could make some space for you."

"Is it okay if I use some of your equipment? A knife to chop up the veggies, a pot to boil the eggs in?"

"I guess so," Marie said. "But don't use my special knife," she said, pointing to an old knife with a thin black blade. "Hmmmph. You'll probably need a dish to carry that stuff in, too."

"Yes, I will. Thanks," she said politely. *Why don't you just get out of here and let me do this*, she thought to herself. *You're in my way and you're making me nervous.*

Marie got out a cutting board and a big pot. "I don't put eggs in my shrimp salad," she said. "Aren't you going to cook the shrimp?"

"I bought some already cleaned and cooked," Sarah said. "I didn't want to smell up the kitchen."

"Hmmmph," she said. "I always cook the shrimp up fresh." She picked up a towel and started to wipe some drops of water off the counter. "Wait, are you putting curry in there?"

Sarah stopped what she was doing and looked at her. "Really, Marie, I'll clean all this stuff up when I'm done. And I'll be out of your way in a few minutes."

Stung, Marie stood back and watched as Sarah put the eggs to boil, washed and cut up the celery and onions. She had strong and capable hands, and worked as if she'd spent some time in a kitchen. Silently, Marie handed her a blue earthenware dish.

"Thank you, Marie," Sarah said. "I've made plenty—would you like me to leave some for you and Grace? Maybe you could have it for dinner."

"I already have dinner planned for the two of us. But if you can't fit it all in that bowl, you can leave some," she said stiffly. She handed Sarah another, smaller bowl.

Sarah carefully washed off the knife, dried it with a cotton towel, and replaced it on the knife rack.

Obviously, she had respect for a good knife, Marie thought. She watched as she loaded the rest of the stuff in the dishwasher, put the shells and trimmings in the trash, and wiped down the counters and the sink, leaving no fingerprint behind. It looked as if she hadn't even been there.

"Thanks for your help, Marie," she said. "Have a good evening."

She grabbed the blue bowl and disappeared through the swinging door.

Marie dipped a spoon into the bowl and tasted a bit of the salad. It was very good. "Hmmmph," she said. She sat down on the high kitchen stool, her eyes filling with tears.

※※※※

Sarah edged the van between two large oaks. It was a tight fit, but there were several other cars, two trucks, and a couple of motorcycles parked in the gravel drive that curved in front of the cozy log house. Large terra cotta planters filled with primroses and daffodils flanked the porch steps. A long bamboo wind chime bonged softly in the breeze. Suddenly she felt self-conscious, a stranger arriving alone.

She looked at herself in the rear view mirror and ran her fingers through her hair. She wondered if the yellow silk blouse and tan slacks she wore were appropriate. She wondered if Carol would like the way she looked. She'd spent quite a bit of time thinking about her in the last couple of days, her strong, slender body and her dark red hair. She took a couple of deep breaths and put her hand to her hot cheek. She hated that she blushed so easily.

She picked up the dish of shrimp salad and slid out of the van door, careful not to hit the tree. A few fat, multi-colored chickens sped by, cackling loudly. The front door opened as she approached, and an enthusiastic black lab spilled out, barking and wagging her whole body. And there was Carol, looking too good in a long batik shirt and billowy purple pants. Sarah felt her pulse pick up a bit.

"Hi! Welcome!" Carol said. "I'm so glad you could make it! Did you have any trouble finding us?" She reached out and gave Sarah a quick hug. Sarah drew her breath in sharply as she felt an electric tingle in her stomach. Oh my, she thought.

"You gave me excellent directions," she answered. "I never would have found this place on my own." She smiled as the dog sniffed at her and looked expectantly at the dish in her hand. She reached down and scratched the sleek black head. "And who is this?"

"This is kd lang," Carol said. "She likes people almost as much as she likes food. Mind your manners, now," she said to the dog, who wiggled in delight.

Sarah took in the length and breadth of the house, the honey-colored logs, the steeply pitched roof. "What a beautiful place," she said admiringly.

"Thanks! We built it ourselves," she said proudly.

"You're kidding!" Sarah said. "Who's we?"

"Oh, you'll meet her. See," she said, pointing in a big arc at the forest all around. "All the trees came from right here on our land. This old guy actually came out here with a portable sawmill and cut up the logs. It took weeks, and then they had to dry." She sighed, reminiscing.

"That's incredible! I would have loved to see that," Sarah exclaimed.

"It was amazing to watch him. I even got to help a little," Carol said proudly.

"You must feel so connected to this place. I grew up in an apartment in the city. I can't even imagine." Sarah shook her head.

"Do you want to look around before we go in? It'll be dark pretty soon."

"Lead on," Sarah said. "I'm ready for the tour!"

"Why don't we leave your dish right here where it's safe," she said, putting it up on the windowsill. "We'll just be a few minutes. Mmmm, it smells wonderful. Is that curry? I love shrimp salad!"

"It had better be wonderful," Sarah said. "Making that salad was a very emotional experience – and not just for me!"

"Here, come around this way," she said. She hooked her arm through Sarah's and guided her down the path that circled the house. kd lang brought up the rear, snuffling loudly. "Let me show you the garden, and you can explain that cryptic statement!"

"My goodness, this is a huge garden! Do you take care of this all yourself?" Sarah asked.

"I do most of the hoeing and the picking. The fun stuff. Zoe likes to do the prep and the planting. It works out pretty well."

"I love to garden," Sarah said. "Who is Zoe?"

"My partner. She's an artist, and a carpenter. We've been together for years and years. You'll meet her in a few minutes."

Sarah felt a twinge of disappointment. "I'm sorry, I didn't realize," she said, pulling away. "I thought you were single. I mean…" She stopped in confusion, feeling herself blush in the twilight. Am I dumb, she thought.

Carol laughed softly and reclaimed Sarah's arm. "Thank you for thinking that. But I'm an old married woman." She smiled mischievously. "But I must admit, you made me wish I was single for a minute when I saw you sitting on the floor in Grace's room!" She laughed again. "Now, tell me about your shrimp salad."

Sarah cleared her throat. "Mmm, yes. Marie is very proprietary about her kitchen. Actually, she's proprietary about everything, Grace included. The whole time I was cutting up the stuff she was breathing down my neck. Every time I moved a dish or a bowl, she was right behind me, wiping the counter and, well, breathing, you know? She didn't say anything to me, just kind of glared. It was creepy!" She feigned a shudder, then laughed.

"You poor thing," Carol said sympathetically. She patted Sarah's hand. "Marie is a presence to be reckoned with, but she's really a lamb. And I could imagine her being a little jealous. After all, it's just been the two of them since Annie died. But don't let her get you down!"

"It's been really hard not to pack up and go back to Seattle," Sarah said, suddenly serious. "Grace is wonderful, of course, but Marie and I definitely have some issues to resolve. Her eyes widened. "You have goats!"

"They're pygmies. This is Xena, and this is Thelma. This is Gabrielle, and that's Louise in the back. And this is Boy George," she said, pointing at the goat with the small, curved horns. "He thinks he's really something." They hung over the fence, reaching down to stroke the tiny heads that butted against their hands. The goats pushed each other out of the way, bleating, vying for attention.

"They're so sweet," Sarah said.

"Yes, and they do a great job of keeping the blackberries from taking us over, too," Carol said. "Would you like to see the workshop?"

"Sure, if – I'm sorry, what was her name? – wouldn't mind," Sarah said.

"Zoe. And no, she loves to have people look at her stuff. And she's too busy watching the Mariners to show you herself right now."

The workshop, practically hidden in the trees, was an octagonal building, also made of logs. Carol pushed on the old-fashioned wooden latch and the door swung inward. The scents of raw wood, paint thinner, and wet clay engulfed Sarah. She could barely make out some swathed shapes through the gloom. Carol flipped a switch and the room was flooded with light.

The space was divided into two areas. A table saw and a router flanked a long workbench backed by a pegboard with a neat array of woodworking tools. Several large clamps held together a child-sized rocker. On the other side of the room stood an easel covered with a cloth, a smaller workbench with a large draped object on a turntable, a potter's wheel, and a silver kiln. A black woodstove crouched in the corner.

"My goodness! This is quite a setup. Zoe must be pretty talented if she can do carpentry, pottery, and painting. I'd be happy to be able to do any one of those things."

"Actually, I'm the painter. Zoe does the wood and clay. Would you like to see some of our work?"

"Sure!" Sarah said.

Carol pointed to a rack of matted watercolors and Sarah looked through them admiringly. "These are just lovely!" she said.

"I use a lot of pen and ink, too, and some acrylics." She showed Sarah a few things from a stack of sketchbooks. She could imagine a couple of them hanging on the walls of her new room.

"Amazing! I'm so jealous. I can't even draw a straight line," Sarah said.

"Well, there aren't many things in nature that are straight lines," Carol said with a laugh. "Here are some of Zoe's things."

Carol reached out and gently pulled the drape from the strong, slim figure. Her arms rested on her folded legs and her face was raised as if to catch the sun. Carol's face. Sarah gulped as she felt the blood rush to her cheeks.

"She's lovely," Sarah said. "I mean, you are. I mean..." She laughed, embarrassed, unable to meet Carol's eyes.

"Why, thank you, ma'am," she said, her eyes gleaming with mischief. She hooked her arm back through Sarah's again. "Let's get out of here. Suddenly I'm starving!"

kd lang raced down the path ahead of them, barking. The twilight had fully settled in now, and the night creatures began to stir. Neither woman said a word as they walked down the path toward the house, lost in their own thoughts.

Carol reached up, took the shrimp salad from the window ledge, and pushed the door open. A mix of talk, music, and good smells greeted them. "I'm back at last, everybody. This is Sarah," she said, pulling her into the room.

Sarah looked around her quickly. Smiling women, all eyes trained on her, filled two large couches and several easy chairs. She felt a bit dizzy for a moment.

"Now, I'm going to go around the room and introduce everybody, but I know you won't remember anyone's name. Now this is Zoe, my honey," she said as a tall woman with skin the color of a four-shot Starbuck's latte uncoiled slowly and stood, her hand extended. "Welcome! Glad you could make it," she said.

Sarah took her hand, feeling the hard calluses against her palm. "So nice to meet you. Carol showed me some of your work. Incredible!" she said.

"Thank you very much. It's nice to be able to do what I enjoy," she said. She moved gracefully around the couch and draped an arm around Carol's shoulders. "Is that shrimp salad? Mmmm," she said, checking out Sarah's dish appreciatively. "Better get on with the intros, sweetie. We're all hungry!"

"Okay, okay," Carol said. "Keep your mitts off this dish!" She moved the bowl out of reach of Zoe's exploring fingers. "Now this is Savannah. She's one of those people who gets to ride to Seattle on the ferry every day," she said, indicating a silver-haired woman with sparkling blue eyes. "Over there on that couch, from left to right, we have Isobel, Luanne, and Ro. And this lovely pair are Rachel and Dr. Emily," she said, pointing to a couple who sat hand in hand on the other couch. One had long, curly, light brown hair, and the other's dark hair was close-cropped and furry. Sarah wondered how it would feel to run her palms over it.

"Now, we're missing someone," Carol said. "Where is she?"

"Here I am," a voice called from the kitchen. "Don't forget me!"

"Of course I didn't forget you, silly," Carol said.

"Sarah Chase, Jen Pelosi, Jen, Sarah."

Sarah looked up to see the deckhand from the ferry. Suddenly she felt as if all of her focus was pulled to the spot where Jen leaned against the doorframe, steaming mug in hand. The rest of the room receded, the conversations melting into the background like the hum of bees.

Jen looked her up and down and greeted her with a slow smile. "Well! I believe we've met. And I think I owe you this," she said, handing the mug to Sarah.

"Oh, thanks! How's your arm?" Sarah asked. She cradled the coffee, warming her suddenly cold hands. She couldn't quite meet her eyes, couldn't quite look away.

"Oh, I'm just fine," she said. "You really didn't hurt me."

"Now where do you two know each other from?" Carol asked.

Sarah blushed. She seemed to be doing a lot of that tonight. "We ran into each other on the ferry. Or I ran into her. I tried to amputate her arm with my van door," she said.

"No, I just wasn't watching where I was going," Jen said. "Do you want to sit down? Let me get another cup of coffee, then you can tell me how you know Carol."

"No, you don't," Carol said. The undercurrents she felt between the two intrigued her. And she was a bit miffed when she saw Sarah's eyes. She felt that she could have fallen through a hole in the floor and neither of them would have noticed. "First things first. Grab a plate. We're hungry!"

A cheer rose from the other women, who got up eagerly and headed toward the laden table. There were mounds of fresh vegetables surrounding dishes of artichoke dip and hummus, some kind of tofu dish with weeds and seeds, bowls of tabouli and pasta salad, chili steaming in a crockpot, deviled eggs cradled in a scoopy platter, Sarah's shrimp salad, and a big bucket of KFC. For dessert, there were big plates of blond and chocolate brownies and red, yellow, and green Jello jigglers shaped like cats, dogs, and stars.

"Obviously you people have done this before," Sarah said appreciatively.

"Well, it's actually a sex-linked trait. Lesbians just love to have potlucks. We can't help ourselves, you know." Carol chuckled.

"Actually we did pretty well this time. One time we all brought salads, and another time we all brought desserts!" Isobel said.

"Yes, that was my kind of potluck," Carol said. "Bring on the sweets!"

"I think you were born with a chocolate spoon in your mouth," Zoe said. She put her arms around Carol and nuzzled her neck.

"But wait, you haven't seen my special dish!" Jen said, and disappeared into the kitchen. A moment later, she reappeared with a plate. The women laughed as Jen proudly displayed her contribution.

It took Sarah a minute to realize what she was looking at...a big stack of McDonald cheeseburgers, cut in fourths and pierced with frilly toothpicks. She laughed. "My favorite recipe!"

The women filled their plates and for a few minutes, there was little conversation. Somehow, Sarah and Jen found themselves sitting together on a couch.

"This food is delicious," Sarah said, but suddenly she wasn't so hungry anymore.

"Yeah, your shrimp salad is pretty terrific."

"Thanks. But I can't compete with you. Your dish is the most popular food on the planet," Sarah said, spearing a burger wedge.

"So what are you doing here on the island, Sarah? Are you on vacation?"

"I have a live-in nursing job. I was on my way there when we met."

"That's right; you told me you were a nurse. Where is your job?" Jen asked.

"It's in this place called The Meadows," she said. "My patient fell and broke her hip, and I'm going to stay until she gets back to herself again."

"Really! You're at The Meadows!" Ro chimed in. "What a great place. You're so lucky!" She turned to Emily and Rachel. "You know that old bed and breakfast that closed down after that woman died? That big white house that looks like a boat? I've never been inside, but I'm sure it's wonderful."

"Oh, it is," said the furry-haired Emily. "I've been there many times."

"I remember; that's where we met. I used to go out there pretty often for dinner when the bed and breakfast was open," Savannah said. "Now I go out there to do some financial stuff for Grace and Marie every so often. It is a lovely place, and Grace and Annie were great. We used to have the best times out there. Sometimes a bunch of women would come over from Seattle and rent the whole house. And then we would party! Musicians, writers, all kinds of women. And they have a great pool, and we would go skinny dipping!" She sighed. "It's much quieter now," her voice sad.

"It is an incredible place," Sarah said. "I haven't gotten to see all the grounds yet, but I'm looking forward to exploring it a little more."

"There's a special little spot there I think you'll enjoy," Carol said, smiling.

"Oh? Where is it? What should I look for?"

"You'll know it when you see it. It's a perfect spot for a picnic."

"Okay, I'll check it out. Now you all have to tell me something about yourselves."

The next couple of hours sped by as Sarah learned that Ro was a lawyer, specializing in women's issues and civil rights, Luanne was a massage therapist, Isobel had a small Montessori school, and Savannah was a financial consultant. Rachel was a weaver and fiber artist, and Emily was a family practice doctor at the Island clinic.

"Oh, I love massage. We go to this wonderful women's spa in Tacoma about once a month and hang out all day and get massages and scrubs," Sarah said. She stopped for a moment. "At least, we used to. I guess I won't be doing much of that now."

"Who is we?" Jen asked. "A friend?"

"Well, yes. She was a friend. An ex, actually." Sarah sighed.

"It's awful when you break up, and have to divide up the furniture, the kitchen stuff, and the massage therapist," Carol said with a grin.

"Is that why you decided to come out here?" Jen asked.

"Well, that was certainly part of it," Sarah said. "But I needed a change from my job as well."

"But you won't have to give up on massage, unless you just want to," Luanne said. "I make house calls! As a matter of fact, I come out to see Grace every week."

"Oh, that's wonderful! I'm glad Grace is doing that. I think it really helps the healing process," Sarah said.

"Yes, and I love to go out there. Marie always plies me with goodies!"

"She's a wonderful cook. I'll have to watch myself out there," Sarah said, patting her trim belly. "Speaking of which, I need to get back. We start the day early out there."

"Oh, don't rush off," Carol said. "It feels like we hardly got to talk at all!"

"I'm sorry; I don't mean to be a party pooper." She stood and looked around. "I certainly have enjoyed meeting all of you." She looked down at Jen with a little smile. "And seeing some familiar faces, too."

"Yes, I have to be going too," Jen said quickly. "I'll walk you out."

Sarah retrieved her dish and headed toward the door. "Good night, everyone," she said.

Carol and Zoe walked them to the door and gave each of them a hug.

"Take care, Zoe. Don't forget we're playing softball tomorrow," Jen said.

"I can't forget. Carol will drag me out of bed," she said, grinning.

The night was clear with just a slight edge of chill. "You have a van, right?" Jen asked.

"You have a good memory," Sarah answered.

"I always remember the vehicles that hit me," Jen joked. "Especially if they're driven by pretty women with interesting bumper stickers."

Sarah felt herself blush again. "Thank you, ma'am. You are pretty cute yourself, you know," she said boldly.

"Cute!" she snorted. "I might be a lot of things, but I'm certainly not cute!" she said indignantly.

"All right, handsome then," she said. She cleared her throat. "Well, good night." She reached for the door handle.

"Umm, what if I dropped by some evening after work," Jen said cautiously. "Maybe we could go for a ride?" She pointed at one of the motorcycles in the driveway.

"Well, I don't know. I've never been on one. I think they're kind of scary," she said.

"We can figure that out when I come by," Jen said. "I'll bring an extra helmet, just in case." She stopped. "The old ladies wouldn't mind, would they?"

"Well, I'm a grown-up, you know. And I'm sure they wouldn't mind," Sarah said. She envisioned Grace and Marie sitting on the porch and Jen riding up to the house in her black leather jacket. The image made her smile.

"Good night, then," Jen said. She bent and brushed Sarah's cheek with her lips. Sarah felt a tingle start there and flow down through her body. "See you soon."

"Okay!" she practically sang the word. She hopped into the van and watched as Jen got on the bike, put on her helmet, and gunned the engine. As she followed her down to the road, she found herself humming a bit of kd lang.

❧ ❧ ❧ ❧

Ralph barked once when she pulled in, then settled down on his bed when he saw it was she. Sarah opened the front door as quietly as she could. A stained glass lamp threw soft colors against the walls of the foyer. The whole house was still as she tiptoed up the stairs.

Grace's door was open slightly, and she heard the sound of light snoring as she went by. The days started early in this house, and ended early too.

Margret wound around her legs, meowing. Sarah petted her and picked her up, kissing the top of her soft head. Sarah was tired, but her body twanged with the excitement of the evening and her mind raced. First seeing Carol, then Jen – and then there was that little kiss at the end. *Screw you, Nancy*, she thought. I'm back.

She washed her face, brushed her teeth, and pulled on her PJs. She started to get into bed when she heard a sound, like a low moan, coming from Grace's room. Quietly she opened the door, but the room was dark. She tiptoed toward the bed and hesitated, waiting for her eyes to adjust, hoping that Grace was not in pain.

But Grace was sleeping soundly in the big bed. And so was Marie.

❦❦❦❦

"What do you think about the new girl?" Zoe asked, as they were getting ready for bed after the party.

"Pretty cute, huh? I told you so," Carol answered.

"Well, you certainly weren't exaggerating," Zoe said. She stood behind Carol as she slid out of her shirt and skirt. "Here, let me help you with those," she said, cupping Carol's breasts.

"Uh, thanks!" she said, laughing. "Very helpful!"

"I try," Zoe said, kissing her neck.

Carol turned and backed Zoe up against the bed, pushing against her till she sat on the edge, her legs spread. She ran her hands gently along the silk of her inner thighs until Zoe purred. "Did you notice how Jen zoomed in on her?" Carol said.

"Or maybe Sarah zoomed in on Jen," Zoe said. "Hard to tell!" She cradled Carol's hips gently with her big rough hands, squeezing, gathering.

"I like her," Carol said. "She seems like a really nice person."

"I sure hope so. We have to watch out for our Jen."

"Yes, because she's such a tender girl." Carol laughed.

"She's been on her own for too long," Zoe said. "She hasn't been with anyone in the longest time."

"Not since Ella," Carol said. "Tell you the truth, I'm a little jealous," she confessed.

"Of who?" Zoe asked.

"Both of them," Carol said with a wicked grin.

Sarah was glad to see Carol on Monday. She was bursting to tell her about what she'd seen.

"You know, the other night when I left your house, I checked on Grace, and Marie was sleeping in her bed. I couldn't believe it!"

"Yeah? So?" Carol asked.

"Well, I shouldn't really talk about my patient, but I was pretty blown away."

"How come?"

"Well." Sarah paused. "I guess I was just surprised, is all."

"I'm surprised you didn't know," Carol said.

"Oh my," Sarah said. She shook her head. "I feel so dumb." Carol patted her shoulder and passed her the cooling cup of coffee. "Now let me see if I've got this right. Annie and Grace were sisters-in-law."

"Yes," Carol said. "And then a while after Grace's husband – that's Annie's brother – was killed in the Second World War, the two of them hooked up. They knew that being together as a couple wouldn't fly back in Massachusetts. They couldn't live the life they wanted around their families, so they moved out here."

"Wow," Sarah said. "So they lived together..."

"Yes, for years and years..."

"And Marie worked for them."

"Well, yes, but not at first. She helped run the bed and breakfast, cooking and supervising the other staff, and then she helped take care of Annie until she died. But of course she'd been madly in love with Grace forever..."

"No," Sarah said. She couldn't believe it.

"And then finally about two years ago they got together," Carol finished.

"*No!*" Sarah said. She put her head in her hands. "Oh my God, no wonder. But who would have thought? How was I supposed to know? Stupid, stupid." Conversations with Grace and Marie echoed through her head. No wonder Marie had been so possessive.

Carol put her arm around Sarah's shoulders and gave her a squeeze. "Don't be so hard on yourself," she said. "And anyway, it doesn't matter."

"But you don't know," Sarah said. "Marie acts like she hates me. Now I know why! I thought I was just trespassing in her kitchen, but it's so much more than that!"

"Sure, how could you tell? After all, they're old,

they don't wear dykey clothes, they don't have Indigo Girls music piped in, or Judy Chicago vaginas on the walls," Carol teased.

"I guess I need to adjust my gaydar," Sarah said with a laugh.

☙☙❧❧

Grace woke from a light sleep when Marie stirred. The gray of early dawn filtered through the curtains as the first birds tuned up.

She loved the early spring, when the world was starting to move back into the light. A dark dome covered the Pacific Northwest for sixteen hours a day from Halloween to St. Patrick's Day. After that, the light increased two minutes a day until the summer solstice, when you could read the newspaper on the lawn at 4:30 in the morning or at ten o'clock at night. It was the up cycle of the year, the time she felt best.

She reached over and draped her arm over Marie, knowing that her snuggling time was limited. In a few minutes, Marie would push herself out of the big bed and hurry downstairs to start breakfast. She had tried to get her to stay in bed a little longer in the mornings when they stopped having guests, but Marie had never gotten used to the quiet of their days, with no guests and no Annie to care for.

Suddenly Marie sat bolt upright and reached for her glasses.

"Good morning, dear," Grace said.

"Good morning, my love," Marie answered. She reached down and raised Grace's hand to her lips. "Are you feeling all right? Did you sleep well?"

"Off and on," she said. "I was just lying here

thinking how suddenly it's spring again."

"Can't come too soon for me," Marie said. "I feel like I never get anything done in the winter. Saps my strength."

"Well, it doesn't show," Grace said. "You're always so busy." She sighed. "Why don't you stay here with me for a few more minutes? You feel so nice."

"Well, all right, but just for a few minutes. I have to get up and start breakfast." She settled back against the pillows.

Grace sighed. She couldn't understand why they still needed to get up so early. It wasn't as if they needed to be any place at a certain time. Marie was such a creature of habit. She rested her head on Marie's shoulder and took her hand, caressing the scar in her palm with her thumb. "I wonder if Sarah had a good time last night."

"I'm sure she did, unless she didn't realize about Carol. That would have been interesting."

"Well, I'm still not sure about Sarah, either."

"Now Grace, I told you I saw that sticker on her car. Carol saw it too. She said something to Sarah about it, and they both laughed. I'm sure she is. She just doesn't look it," Marie said.

"And you and I are so obvious! Just two little old ladies!" Grace laughed. "I wonder if Sarah knows about us."

"I doubt it," Marie said

"Do you think we should tell her?" asked Grace.

"Hmmmph. I don't think so. If she stays around here she'll know soon enough!"

"Well, I hope she does stay around. I like her," Grace said.

"So I noticed. Should I be jealous?"

"You old fool! Don't be silly!" Grace elbowed her, none too gently.

"How could you help it when she looks so much like Annie?"

"Well, that's certainly true enough. She gave me quite a start when she first got here," Grace said. Suddenly her eyes stung and filled. She ducked her head, surprised.

"I don't think she's really like her as a person, though."

"Well, she's a strong person, too, and smart," Grace said, then laughed. "You're right, though. She's much more civilized than our Annie ever was! And she doesn't look like a lesbian."

"I don't even know what that means anymore. Used to be pretty easy for me to tell. Especially when half the women we knew wore suits and ties!" Marie laughed.

"Yes. Remember what we had to go through to get Annie to take off that flannel shirt, and those boots! But you're right. Even a few years ago, it was easier to tell. They had those kind of choppy haircuts, and those ear cuffs. And those clunky Doc Martens. Now everyone dresses like that," she said.

"Except us," Marie said.

"We're out of style, Marie. Again."

"Hmmmph!"

"What is it? Queer on the streets, straight in the sheets? Or is it the other way round?"

"Grace! I'm shocked!"

"Right, I bet you are," she said. She laughed and poked Marie with her elbow. "Personally, I prefer my women queer on the streets, queer in the sheets!"

Grace laughed softly as Marie turned toward her.

"Don't you have to make breakfast?"

"I'm not hungry for breakfast," she said.

❧❧❧

Sunday morning was not really much different from the rest of the mornings at The Meadows. Marie was up early, as usual, banging pots and making the house smell wonderful.

Sarah helped Grace shower, then set the table for breakfast in her room. By mutual agreement, they didn't say much. Marie was the one who was wound up in the mornings – it took Sarah and Grace longer to wake up enough to have a decent conversation.

Finally, they heard the stair climber grinding away, and Sarah went to get the tray of goodies from the hall. She put the teapot, wrapped in its flowered cozy, on the table, and set out three matching teacups. Before coming to The Meadows, Sarah couldn't function without at least a triple-shot latte from Starbucks. Since she started working on the Island, she found that she was developing a taste for tea. There was French toast made with cinnamon bread, accompanied by a silver pot of warm maple syrup for Grace and Marie, a dish of orange marmalade especially for Sarah, and soft-boiled eggs in little china egg cups.

The three women held hands and bowed their heads for a moment.

"Happy happy, joy joy!" they said, and felt to.

Sarah smeared butter on her French toast and followed it with a spoonful of marmalade. Grace reached for the syrup as Marie tapped the top of her egg. They ate quietly for a minute, then Grace cleared her throat.

"So, dear, did you have a good time at the potluck?" she asked.

Sarah looked up. "Why, yes, yes I did. It was very interesting!"

"Oh?" Grace asked innocently. "Interesting how?"

"Well, there were several women there, all very nice. We had some interesting conversation, and the food was really good." She turned to Marie. "Thank you again for letting me use your kitchen to make the salad," she said.

"Hmmmph," Marie said.

"I thought it was really good," Grace said. "I loved the curry in it. Thanks for leaving us some. It was a lovely dinner. So who was there?"

"Let's see. Carol and Zoe, of course, and Savannah, and Ro and Isobel, Luanne, and Rachel and Emily. And this woman, Jen, that I ran into on the ferry when I was on my way over here."

"We know some of those women, Zoe, Luanne, Savannah, and Dr. Emily, of course. And what did you talk about?" Grace asked.

"Oh, just hen talk, you know. There were no men there," Sarah said, looking down at her plate.

"No roosters," Marie said.

"Not a one," Sarah said. "I did notice something kind of interesting, though."

"What is that?" asked Grace.

"Well, I looked around and all of those women were wearing comfortable shoes!" she said, with a mischievous grin.

Grace and Marie looked at each other for a moment.

"And you?" Grace asked, raising an eyebrow.

"Doc Martens!" Sarah said.

"I'm glad that we've cleared all that up!" said Grace. She raised her teacup. "Let's hear it for comfortable shoes!"

※ ※ ※ ※

Sarah noticed an area behind the house that looked like it had been a garden at one time. It was overgrown with blackberries and weeds, but there were some raised beds and a decent fence. She opened the gate and kicked at the dirt – it was loose and black, and smelled good and mulchy. Her fingers itched to dig in.

She remembered how much she had enjoyed each spring, breaking up the ground and getting ready to plant. Her dad, Jordan, and Nathan would be out there with her, pulling weeds, fluffing up the soil in the raised beds, throwing rocks into the wheelbarrow, spreading fertilizer. Her mom would be puttering around in the flowerbeds, planting seeds for the annuals and clearing the way for the bulbs that would be sprouting soon. They would work until they were bone-tired, then pile into the kitchen for the chili that had been cooking on the stove all day. And she thought about how she missed those times.

She'd been at The Meadows for just a short while, and Grace had improved under her care. She was getting more independent, and the two of them were taking short walks in the afternoon without bringing along the wheelchair. Carol was still coming out regularly to help Grace with her physical therapy, and she was pleased with her progress as well. So Sarah would just have a few more weeks at best before she moved on to another job. But she could at least get a garden started for them before she left.

She brought up the subject at lunch.

"I was walking around in the back and went past your garden," she said.

"Oh, yes, we used to have a beautiful garden. We grew all kinds of things – squash and cucumbers and peppers and green beans and peas, and of course, tons of tomatoes. And loads of strawberries and lavender in the back fields. We sold the berries at a little farm stand every summer, and made little lavender wands and wreaths. We used to can quite a few veggies, and fruit too. We always had fresh vegetables for our guest dinners during the summers. We used to keep a few chickens, too, just for eggs." Grace laughed. "We couldn't get ourselves to eat them once we'd looked them in the eye!"

Sarah laughed.

"There's nothing like homegrown food," Marie said.

"Oh, I know," Sarah said. "I always loved gardening. We used to have a pretty good-sized plot when I was growing up. We even grew grapes for jam, and pie pumpkins!"

"We have grapes, too. Used to make a bit of wine," Grace said.

"Um um." Marie smacked her lips. "Good wine, too."

"Oh, we made some jam, but never wine. Our church doesn't allow drinking," Sarah said. "We're not even supposed to drink coffee or tea, but I do that now. Love my Starbucks!" Sarah said.

"What church is that?" Grace asked.

"We were Mormons," she said. "And they still are, I guess. But I don't go to church anymore. I've gotten away from all that stuff." She sighed.

"How come?" Marie said.

"Long story," Sarah said. "I was excommunicated."

"Oh my goodness! Are you a serial killer or a pedophile or something?"

"If only," Sarah said, an edge of bitterness in her voice. "They wouldn't have excommunicated me for that!"

"Well, we didn't mean to pry."

"No, that's okay. I just don't feel like talking about it right now."

"Sorry," Grace said. "Our friend Reverend Leah has a little church in town. We used to go on most Sundays, but not so much the last few years. We were busy taking care of Annie for quite a while. Then after Annie passed, we just still didn't get out much. But they are pretty laid back, different from the churches we grew up in. And Reverend Leah comes to visit out here pretty often, especially since my accident," Grace said. "She's always fun to talk to, has kind of a unique perspective. Maybe you'll meet her some time."

"Ummm," Sarah said doubtfully. "So about the garden…I was thinking…maybe I could do some digging around out there, plant a few things?"

Grace and Marie looked at each other.

"Nobody's done anything with that garden for several years," Grace said.

"I know. And I know I won't be here that long. But I thought I could just get some things started for you…"

"Oh, I don't know. Maybe." Grace looked over at Marie again.

Marie shrugged. "That's up to you, Grace. Whatever you want."

Grace straightened up in her chair. "Yes, why

not! It would be fun to have things growing around here again!" She turned to Sarah. "You do whatever you want, dear. There are tools out there, gloves, everything you might need. We can get plants from the nursery when the time is right, and seeds—"

"Thank you!" Sarah beamed.

"No, thank you," Grace said. She picked up her napkin and dabbed at her eyes while Marie blew her nose loudly.

※※※※

Jen swung a leg over the bike and tightened the strap on her helmet. She had plenty of time before she was supposed to pick Sarah up at The Meadows, but she wanted to ride around and calm down a little before she got there.

She eased the bike out of the drive and rode slowly through the streets of Winslow, past the Streamliner Diner, where she ate too many of her breakfasts, and the Blue Horse Café, where she ate too many of her dinners.

She wasn't much for cooking. She rented a tiny studio carved out of a sprawling old pink house on the edge of town. It had a hot plate and a half-size refrigerator that rarely held more than a couple of Monsters or a six-pack of Henry Weinhard's. And a few candy bars, of course.

She'd been thinking about this evening for days, ever since the potluck. She'd wanted to call Sarah immediately after the party, but she didn't want to seem too eager. After all, they'd just had that one conversation, if you didn't count that business on the boat. She wondered how often Sarah bought lattes for strange women.

They'd spoken on the phone a couple of times since, but there were a lot of awkward pauses. It was difficult for her to do small talk, especially if it was with someone she barely knew. Especially if it was with someone she thought was pretty damned cute.

Jen was surprised and pleased when she saw the house. It reminded her of a Mississippi steamboat. The house had the same kind of feel to it, massive and majestic, with fancy porch railings and trim. A furry black and white dog with orange eyebrows and a curly tail ran alongside her, barking, and it seemed friendly enough, but she was happy when she saw Sarah come down the porch steps to meet her. She was glad she wouldn't have to meet the old ladies. She wasn't quite up for that yet.

"Hush, Ralph!" she said. The dog stopped and waved his tail. "Hi," Sarah said. "Don't mind Ralph. That's a great-looking bike. What is it?"

"Uh, hi," Jen said nervously. She took a deep breath. "It's a Harley." She flicked an imaginary speck of road dust off the immaculate purple seat. "Last motorcycle company in America."

"Really! Well, it's beautiful," Sarah said. She spun around. "Are these clothes all right?"

Jen smiled. "Sure, you look great." She'd told Sarah to wear jeans, boots, and a jacket for her first motorcycle ride, and Sarah more than did them justice. She handed her a purple helmet that matched her own. "Let me just tell you a couple of things about bikes before we go," she said.

"OK. I'm a little nervous," Sarah confessed.

"No need," Jen said confidently. She pointed out some things on the bike, told her about holding on, leaning into the turns, and keeping her legs away from the muffler pipe. "Okay, hop on," she said finally.

Sarah swung her leg over and clutched Jen's jacket. "Okay, I'm on," she said breathlessly.

Jen was very aware of that. She could feel Sarah's chest touching her back lightly, feel her legs against Jen's own. Suddenly it was hard for her to breathe. "Okay, we'll go slow at first," she said.

She cranked up the bike and she felt Sarah gasp as they started to move forward. Slowly, they rode along the circular drive, kicking up gravel. Jen made a couple of circuits around the house, picking up a little speed each time. She turned and looked over her shoulder. "Ready?" she asked.

"I think so," Sarah said, holding on little tighter.

She thought she saw two white faces pressed against an upstairs window as they passed the house for the last time and pulled out into the road.

They rode all the way to Silverdale to the movie, about twenty-five miles. By the time they got there, she could feel that Sarah was relaxed and leaning with the bike.

She sat there through the whole movie, clutching a bag of popcorn, her face growing hot whenever Sarah reached toward the bag and brushed her arm or touched her hand. It was one of those quiet movies where there was a lot of talking. A chick flick. Breathe, breathe, she kept reminding herself.

She wanted so much to put her arm around her. That would go over real big in that theatre, she knew. Blonde teenagers on dates and older Swedish and Norwegian couples, straight as could be, made up most of the audience. Instead, she concentrated on the spot where Sarah's leg touched her own.

After the movie, they stopped for some burgers and fries. Jen didn't do much better with her food than she had with the popcorn. She noticed that Sarah wasn't eating much either. She was glad Sarah didn't want to talk about the movie, because she couldn't remember much of it.

She couldn't understand why she felt so giddy and fumble-footed around Sarah. She'd certainly had her share of girlfriends, though it had been awhile. She liked watching her small, efficient movements, liked looking at the round softness of her. And she was funny, too.

Finally, they started talking, a bit hesitantly in the beginning. It was their first real conversation, and they ended up sitting in the restaurant, talking, for hours. Sarah told Jen about being a nurse, and Jen told Sarah how she'd spent a couple of years in the Navy, then worked on a fishing boat in Alaska before coming back to Seattle and getting a job on the ferry. They talked a little about things they liked and disliked, and Sarah was pleased to know they had so much in common. They both liked Barbara Kingsolver, Anne Tyler, and Jane Austen. Then, of course, there was Rita Mae Brown, Katherine Forrest, and the whole lesbian crew. And they loved Desert Hearts, Go Fish, and Imagine Me and You. The Indigo Girls, Melissa Etheridge, Ferron, and Ani DeFranco. It was a good start.

The light on the big porch was lit when they pulled into the driveway, but Jen stopped the bike in the shadow of the trees. Ralph came out to greet them with a wag, then retreated to his house.

"I had a really nice time tonight," Sarah said, handing her the helmet. "And the ride was very exciting!"

"Um, me too," Jen mumbled. "Maybe we could get together again another time?"

"I'd like that," Sarah said. She leaned over and brushed Jen's cheek with her soft lips. Jen felt a tingling heat pass downward through her body. She swallowed and looked down. Sarah looked so small standing next to her. "So, I'll give you a call, right?"

"Or I'll call you," Sarah said softly. She reached up and put her arms around Jen's neck. Jen could smell the spicy clean scent of her hair and could feel the soft pressure of her breasts against her own. Her hands traced the strong muscles of Sarah's back, and she couldn't catch her breath.

They stood like that for a few moments. "I have to go, it's getting late," Sarah said, finally. She tipped her head up and looked at Jen with a soft smile, her face as delicate and luminous as a moonflower.

Jen bent her head and brushed Sarah's lips with her own, then leaned in a bit more when she felt Sarah's response. "Good night," she whispered. For a moment, she wondered if the two old ladies were watching them through the window.

Quickly, she pulled on her helmet and cranked up the bike. Sarah stood by the porch rail as she pulled out of the driveway. She had to restrain herself from doing a wheelie as she picked up speed, whistling to herself.

"So how was your date?" Grace asked next morning. "Did you have fun?"

"Oh, yes, it was very nice," Sarah said carefully. She didn't want to share the feelings that rose up inside her when she thought about Jen. For now, she just needed to calm down.

"That Jen is quite the looker," Grace said. "Handsome."

"Yes, I know." Sarah said with a smile. She took a breath. "Do you know her at all?"

"No, not really. Carol might have mentioned her. I believe she plays softball." Grace sighed, thinking of all the softball games she'd watched, Annie on the pitcher's mound. "We don't get out very much, you know. But if she's a friend of Carol and Zoe's, she must be a good person," Grace said.

Sarah hoped that was true.

She didn't waste any time getting started in the garden. She was glad she brought some old jeans and her favorite work shirt to the Island with her. For some reason, she felt energized. She laughed to herself when she thought about that kiss, the source of the energy. She felt like she could jog all the way into town—backwards.

Grace couldn't help but smile at the picture she made – plaid shirt rolled up above her elbows, run-down jeans, beat-up sneakers, big grin.

She helped Grace get ready for the day and brought her down to the back patio so she could see what was going on. She got her settled in a big Adirondack chair with a hat, sunglasses, a pitcher of iced tea, and the ubiquitous Ralph, who rolled around before her, begging for a tummy scratch. When Marie was finished cleaning up after breakfast, she joined Grace on the patio.

They told her where to find the garden tools in the shed by the caretaker's house, and Sarah was surprised to see how much equipment was out there.

The usual rakes, hoes, and diggers of every kind were neatly arranged on hooks, and weed eaters of different sizes, a lawn mower, and a small tractor filled the shed. The lawn mower and weed eaters were the only things that looked like they'd been touched for several years. She wouldn't need anything but plants and seeds. Sarah filled a wooden basket with tools and gloves and headed back out to the garden site.

She dug, pulled, and cut and raked happily for a couple of hours while the women called out encouragement from the patio. Finally, she plopped herself down on the steps in front of them and wiped her face with a red bandanna she pulled from her pocket.

"Whew!" she said. "That felt good! I've been sitting around too much. It's good to stretch out."

Marie handed her a glass of iced tea. "I know what you mean. I hate sitting around."

"But Marie, you never sit around! You're always busy with something," Sarah said.

"It's not like the old days," she said. "We were really busy then! Tell her, Grace."

"Oh yes, we were all running in the old days. Never a dull moment. And Annie too...she was always out here in the garden, or the flower beds, or tending the berries, or the lavender..."

"I'm so sorry," Sarah said sympathetically. "I know you must miss her."

"Yes indeed," Grace said.

Marie stood abruptly. "Well, speaking of sitting around, I guess I'd better get lunch a'rollin'," she said, her voice husky. She turned and marched off.

They were just finishing lunch when the doorbell rang. "Oh, that must be Luanne," Grace said. "It's time for my massage."

Marie ushered her into the room. "Hi, Grace, and hi to you, Sarah. It's so nice to see you again."

"Hello, dear," Grace said. "I'm so glad you're here! I'm stiff from watching Sarah working in the garden."

"So she must be stiff too," Luanne said.

"Oh, no, it felt really good. I was telling Grace and Marie that I wasn't used to hanging around."

"And now she's put herself back to work," Grace said. "Not that she doesn't have plenty to do, taking care of me."

"No, Grace, you're so easy to take care of. Sometimes I feel guilty!"

"No need. Are you ready, Luanne?"

Grace took Sarah's arm and they walked to the pool house. The air was warm and humid and smelled of chlorine. Luanne opened the door to the massage room and turned on the light.

"Oh, this is lovely," Sarah said, looking around. The walls were jade green and the light was dim and soothing. In the center of the room was a massage table made up with burgundy sheets. There was even a small bathroom and changing room where Sarah helped Grace undress. Strains of Enya floated from the sound system.

"Sarah, why don't you take a swim or sit in the hot tub while I have my massage?" Grace said.

"Wow, that sounds great! Are you sure you don't mind?"

"No, no. Luanne and I will be busy for the next hour. Or at least Luanne will be busy. I'm just going to lie here and be spoiled!" Grace said.

So while Grace got her massage Sarah did some

laps, then floated in the warm pool and thought about last night. Good thoughts. Very, very good.

When Luanne was done, Sarah helped Grace dress. "How do you feel?" she asked.

"Like a wet noodle," Grace answered. "A very happy, very relaxed wet noodle."

Luanne laughed. "Then my work here is done," she said. "Unless you would like a massage, Sarah? I don't have another appointment until three o'clock."

"Uh, no thanks," Sarah said quickly. It was too much. "Maybe another time."

"For sure," Luanne said.

Sarah walked her to the door. "I'm so glad you could come out here for Grace. I know she enjoys your visits," she said.

"Thanks!" Luanne said. "Don't forget, the offer is good any time."

"No, I won't," Sarah said.

"By the way, how was your date?"

"What?" Sarah was dumbfounded. "Uh, it was very nice. I had a good time." She paused. "How did you know?"

"This is a really small community," Luanne said with a smile. "Everybody knows."

❧❧❧❧

Grace and Sarah sat out on the porch, sorting through a big box of photos. Grace arranged them chronologically, and Sarah placed them in big albums. Periodically Grace would stop and tell Sarah stories about the people and places in the pictures.

Sarah was particularly interested in seeing pictures of Annie, because several people had remarked that there was some resemblance between them. Obviously, Annie was quite a cutup, turning cartwheels and making silly faces at the camera. Then there were pictures of Annie and Grace together, and the depth of feeling between them was obvious. Sarah sighed. So romantic!

Sometimes she would catch Grace or Marie looking at her with sadness in their eyes, and Sarah could see how much they missed her.

Grace showed her one picture that caught Sarah's attention. Annie was perched on a black horse, and Grace stood beside her, leaning against Annie's leg, her arms crossed in front of her. She looked straight into the camera, proud and possessive.

Grace told her about where they were and what they were doing that day. But as Sarah looked at the picture, she realized that it was familiar. She felt a jolt in her stomach. She'd seen the same picture many times in her own family's album.

"Oh my goodness!" she said. "Grace, this is you! Look, right here!"

"Yes, that's me," Grace said, puzzled.

"But that's my great aunt Annie up on that horse! I never met her, but I heard a lot of stories about her, how she moved across the country when she was a young girl after the War, opened a hotel. That was your Annie! I always wondered about the lady with her, but my family never would tell me anything about her." She shook her head in wonder. "How weird!"

Grace was amazed. "I can't believe it!" she exclaimed. "Marie! Marie, come out here!" she called. "You have to hear this!"

Marie was astounded. "So you and Annie are related!" she said. She shook her head. "Didn't I tell you, Grace? She reminded me of Annie the moment I saw her! Didn't I tell you?"

"Yes, yes, you did. I can see it. So I guess we are kind of related in a way." Grace pondered. "I can't believe it!"

Sarah was still in shock. "So what does that make you? My great-aunt-in-law?" She shook her head in disbelief.

"I guess." Grace smiled and held out her arms for a hug. "Welcome to the family!" she said.

※ ※ ※ ※

In the couple of weeks since their first date, Jen and Sarah spent a few evenings together. First, they went to McGill's and played some darts with Carol and Zoe. Another night they had dinner at the Gull and Crossbones and shared a bottle of wine at the marina, then strolled along the docks in the moonlight. On the ride home, Sarah felt like shouting into the wind, but she kept her mouth shut and held on tight as they raced over the road.

It was hard to let go of Jen when they got back to The Meadows. Her body felt so strong in Sarah's arms, and she was breathless when Jen finally let her go. "Good night," she whispered softly.

"Pleasant dreams," Jen answered, then pressed against her, arms, breasts, thighs, and finally, deeply, lips.

"Whew," Sarah said as Jen slowly released her. She felt a hot trickle of liquid start deep inside.

Jen flashed her a crooked smile, then jumped on the bike and quickly disappeared.

"Whew," she said again. Her legs were shaking

and she couldn't catch her breath for a moment. She clung to the porch until she could breathe again, then fluffed up her helmet hair, straightened herself up, and stepped through the big white door.

Grace and Marie were sitting in the living room, having some after-dinner sherry. Quite a lot of after-dinner sherry, from what Sarah could tell.

"Well, hi there, dearie." Grace said, and waved towards a chair. "Come and join us! Tell us about your date!"

Marie was listing slightly toward the left. "Yes, come and have a little drinkie," she said.

Sarah wasn't feeling very sociable. She wanted to go over every word, every touch, every kiss, in her mind. But she didn't want to be rude, so she headed for the chair opposite them.

"Here, let me get you a glass," Marie said, and started to pull herself out of her chair.

"Oh, no, I can get it," Sarah said hastily. She got a crystal glass from the cabinet and poured herself a bit of sherry.

"So where did you go tonight?" Grace asked. "Here, have a cookie."

Sarah bit into the crispest lemon cookie in the world and ummmmd appreciatively. Marie really did make the best goodies, and she kept everyone who happened by well supplied.

"Well, we went to the Gull and Crossbones, and I had some really good shrimp," Sarah said. "Nice and garlicky."

"Oh, I hope you both ate it, then," Grace said.

"Yes, Jen had mussels in garlic and wine, so we were equally stinky by the end of dinner." She laughed. "And we had some nice wine. It was lovely."

"Ah," said Grace.

"Ah," said Marie.

"What?" Sarah said. "You asked me what we did. We had a nice time!"

"Ah," they said again.

"And then what did you do?" Grace asked.

"We just walked around for a while, and we looked at the boats. It sure is pretty out there."

"I'm sure you had a lot of time to admire the scenery," Marie said, wickedly.

Sarah laughed. "Now that you mention it, it was kind of …uh…"

"Romantic?"

"Yes! It was kind of romantic. Now that you mention it."

"Look, Grace, she's blushing!"

Sarah held her hands up to her flaming cheeks. "I am not! It's the sherry!"

"Stop picking on the girl, Marie," Grace said. "So when are we going to meet this Jen of yours?"

"Uh, I don't know. I hardly know her myself—"

"We have to make sure we know who you're gallivanting around with until all hours, and on a motorcycle!"

Sarah laughed. "Okay. I'll introduce you to her soon, I promise. Now come on. Are you two ready for bed?"

"Oh, I guess so," Grace said. She drained the last bit of sherry from her glass. "Okay, I'm ready."

"Me too," Marie said. "Gotta get up early!"

Grace just shook her head and took Sarah's arm. "I just don't understand," she said.

Sarah surfaced slowly from her dream in response to the tapping, light at first, then harder against her cheek. She kept her eyes closed and pulled the covers over her head, still feeling the heat of the images in her dream. "Go 'way," she said.

She started slipping back into sleep and once again, she could see Jen, feel her long body pressing against her, feel her hot breath, her cold nose…

"Mmmph," she said, opening her eyes. Margret's blue eyes blinked an inch from her own, her body stretched the length of her chest, furry paws clutching her neck.

"Raoh," she said, and pressed her nose against Sarah's nose again.

Sarah reached up and stroked her dark, silky mask. "Leave me alone! It's my day off, you bad cat," she said. "You're supposed to let me sleep in." Suddenly she remembered what was happening today, and glanced over at the clock. The black hands showed a little past eight. "My goodness, it's late! Well, it's a good thing you did wake me," she said. They were going to a softball game today, then hanging around with the players and fans. She only had a few hours to get ready. She wanted the food to be something special.

She stretched her legs slowly, luxuriating in the flex and pull of her muscles. Like in the dream…

She sat up on the edge of the bed and listened. She didn't hear any sounds from Grace's room. Marie had probably dragged her out of bed and gotten her downstairs long ago. Sarah couldn't understand why old people liked to get up so early. It wasn't like there was someplace they needed to be.

"Where are you two headed for today"? Marie asked, looking around the kitchen. Every pot and disk was back in its place after a whirlwind of activity that had sent her running upstairs after breakfast. It was still hard for her to see anyone else in her kitchen.

"Softball game. Jen pitches." Sarah tucked the last sandwich into the cooler and topped it off with a foil-wrapped packet of cookies she'd baked that morning. There was enough food in there to feed an army of hungry dykes. "Okay," she said. "That should hold us."

"Do you play softball?"

"No, I'm a charter member of the cheering section," Sarah said.

"You two have been spending a lot of time together," Marie said.

Sarah blushed. "We've been having a good time," she said. "Or at least I have."

"Hmmmph," Marie said. The way that girl hangs around here with those puppy eyes, she thought. She stopped, looked back over her shoulder, cleared her throat. "You just be careful on that bike thing."

She heard the buzz of the bike coming up the drive now. "Of course," she said. "Jen is a very good driver." She paused and looked around. "Do you need me to do anything before we take off?"

"No, thank you. Have fun!" Marie said. Suddenly she reached over and surprised Sarah with a brief hug.

"Wow! Uh, thanks!" Sarah said. "You too!" She grabbed the cooler and trotted out the kitchen door, marveling at Marie's change in attitude. She'd been a lot mellower lately, had even let her fix the picnic lunch without leaning over her. Of course, her attitude toward Marie had changed too, now that she knew the truth of her relationship with Grace. And that Marie was her great-aunt-in-law once removed. Or something like that.

❦ ❦ ❦ ❦

Jen was just pulling off her helmet when Sarah reached her. "Look at you," Sarah said, admiringly. She put down the cooler and stood on her tiptoes to give Jen a peck on the cheek.

"You like it?" she asked. She pulled her shirt down across her chest so Sarah could better see some Xena-style warrior women and the Island Amazon logo against the purple cotton.

"Yes, very much." She grinned and slowly looked her up and down. "Oh, you mean the shirt." She laughed as Jen's face reddened.

"Today we're playing the Tacoma Titilators. They're pretty tough, but we can handle them," she said dismissively.

Sarah laughed. "If the rest of your team is as tough as you are, you've got it made." She slid the van door open. "Let's see. I have chairs, a blanket, sunscreen, a hat, food, drinks, an extra shirt..."

"Hey, you know we're only going to a ball game, not camping," Jen said, shaking her head. "We certainly couldn't fit all this stuff on the bike!"

"That's why you have a motorcycle, and I have a van," Sarah said sweetly. "I like to be prepared for anything."

Jen pulled Sarah to her and laughed deep in her throat. "Anything?"

"Oh, yes," she said, reaching up.

There were about thirty or so women and some kids scattered around the bleachers, all armed with hats, sunglasses, and drinks. The Tacoma Titillators had lavender shirts with a picture of an amply endowed woman holding a ball and a bat. Jen grabbed her glove and bat from the van and trotted off to warm up. Some of the players were already doing stretching exercises or swinging their bats. Zoe and Jen started tossing a ball back and forth. Sarah headed toward the shadiest area with drinks and snacks.

Several women called out to her and gestured for her to join them. Sarah was touched – she'd just been on the Island for a couple of weeks, and she'd already met several people that could be new friends. Ro and Luanne were there, and, of course, Carol. Rachel held onto the first aid kit and Emily joined Jen and Zoe for three-way catch.

"Hey, Sarah, how are you doing?" Ro asked. "Glad you could come out!" She waved at the ball field. "Do you play?"

"I'm doing okay, as long as I don't try to play softball. Last time I played, I tripped over my own bat, sprained my ankle." She laughed ruefully. "How about you?"

"No, one player in the family is enough," Ro said. "Luanne usually plays first base." She looked up at the cloudless sky. "What a beautiful day!"

"I know, and I'm glad it's not too hot. Doesn't take me much to look like an escapee from Red Lobster." Sarah grimaced, holding up a tube of industrial strength sunblock.

"So you are an all-around bleacher babe."

"Yes. I always have to look for the shade. My mother should have named me Fern. But of course I couldn't miss this game."

Ro laughed. "Especially when your sweetie is playing? Right?" She paused for a moment. "She is your sweetie, isn't she?"

"Oh, I don't know if I would call her that." Sarah blushed. "We've been out a few times, that's about it."

"Uh-huh," Ro said with a knowing look. "She's quite the catch!"

Sarah just smiled.

※ ※ ※ ※ ※

After the game, the players and fans spread out their blankets and chairs and pulled enormous quantities of food out of their vehicles. Now that they were done (with the Island Amazons victorious, of course, 3-0) the players relived each hit, run, and error, cheered or reviled the umpire, threatened and insulted each other, and in general had a good time.

"What a nice bunch of people," Sarah said as she packed up their gear. "It's so different from going to guy sports. Like when my brothers played football, my father would get so emotional, and everyone around us jumping and screaming...and the boys would get so bummed out if they lost..."

"Wow, I forgot that you had brothers. You never talk about them...but I guess I don't give you much time to talk, 'cause I'm always shooting my mouth off..."

"No, you're not—I love hearing about your family."

"But what about yours?" Jen set the picnic basket in the van.

"Not a cheerful topic," Sarah said shortly. "I'll tell you about them sometime." She hoisted the lawn chairs into the van. "And guess what! I'm related to Annie, the woman who used to be Grace's partner." She filled Jen in on seeing the photograph in Grace's album.

"Small world!" Jen said.

"Are you ready to meet Grace and Marie?" Sarah asked as they were driving back to The Meadows.

"But I'm a mess, all picnicky and sweaty..."

"I think you smell great," she said, sniffing appreciatively.

Jen blushed.

"Besides, they won't mind. They've been wanting to meet you."

"Are they like your stand-in parents or something?"

"Sometimes I feel like they are!"

Grace and Marie sat on the front porch, rocking and drinking tea. They waved as Sarah pulled the van up to the front of the house. Just like parents, waiting for their little girl to come home, Sarah thought, amused. Somebody's parents, anyway.

They hopped out, and Sarah made the introductions.

"So nice to finally meet you. Sarah has told us almost nothing about you!" Grace said slyly.

Jen laughed. "Nothing much to tell, I guess," she said.

"Hmmmph," Marie said. "I'll bet!"

"Here, pull up a chair!" Grace said. "Have some tea!"

In a moment, they were installed in matching rockers, holding teacups. "Wow, I can't remember the last time I drank tea! Except for Long Island iced tea, that is," Jen said. "I'm usually a coffee girl, double shots." The three women watched in amazement as Jen put in four sugar cubes and filled the cup to the brim with milk. She took a sip. "It's good!"

"Here, Sweet Tooth," Marie said, and handed her a plate of lacy ginger cookies.

"Ummmm!" She said, appreciatively. "Who made these? Was it you?" She looked over at Sarah.

"Oh, no, Marie is the cake and cookie and bread and most everything baker," Sarah said. "I just putter around in the kitchen, but Marie is the chef. She makes the best mushroom soup, and the best roast chicken, and of course the best cookies—I've really gotten spoiled since I've been here!"

"Thanks," Marie said. "It's just plain cooking."

"Speaking of which, I hope you're planning to stay for supper," Grace said.

"Oh, thanks, but I ate plenty after the game," Jen said, patting her stomach. "Those softball girls know how to have a picnic!"

"I'm sure you'll be hungry again, soon as Sarah shows you around the place," Marie said.

"Thanks, ladies," Sarah said. "We'll be back soon."

They walked around the grounds for a bit, and Sarah filled her in about the history of the place. She showed her the lake, the three little cabins, and the caretaker's cottage. They strolled by the overgrown rows of lavender and strawberries, and especially the garden, where new seedlings were starting to poke out of the ground like tiny green stitches.

"What a place!" Jen said. "Amazing!"

"Hey, do you want to check out the pool? That would make you feel better," Sarah said.

"Uh, I brought a change of clothes, but I didn't bring a suit," Jen said hesitantly.

"Don't worry; your modesty is safe with me." Sarah laughed. "There are suits and towels in the pool house."

"What a relief," Jen said.

They took quick showers and jumped into the pool, then glided smoothly through the blue water like a pair of dolphins. They were both strong swimmers, and they raced the length of pool several times before turning on their backs for a float.

"How decadent," Jen said.

"I know, right? This is the best job ever!"

"And the best day," Jen said.

Sarah smiled. She was having a great day, too. "C'mon, we'd better get out of here before the ladies think we got kidnapped or something. And I can't believe I'm getting hungry again."

Every so often, they would stop and kiss with increasing urgency, and by the time they got back to the house, they were both quite flushed and warmer than the weather again.

Sarah showed her around the house too, and they stopped in her room for a moment. "This is Margret," she said, pointing to the curled up ball on the bed. Margret lifted her head for a moment and sniffed Jen's hand, then allowed Jen to pet her soft head while she purred her approval. "Well, I guess you must be okay, if Margret likes you."

"I didn't know I was being tested. Thank you, Miss Margret, I appreciate your vote," Jen said.

"Grace and Marie like you too, or they wouldn't have invited you for supper," Sarah said.

"Well, that's a relief. But you know, I've been on my best behavior…"

"And you have excellent behavior…at least so far," Sarah said, pulling her head down for a kiss.

"I'm very happy that Grace and Marie and Margret all like me," Jen said. "But the big question is, how do you feel? Do you like me, too?"

"Oh, you're okay, I guess."

Jen looked crestfallen

"You silly thing, of course I like you. What do you think?" Sarah said, and leaned in again.

They sat on the bed, exchanging more kisses. Margret jumped off the bed and flounced out.

"We'd better go down before they think we got lost," Sarah said, breathlessly.

"I am lost," Jen said.

They managed to make their way through steaming bowls of beef stew with noodles, kale salad, and freshly baked rolls while the ladies politely grilled Jen.

"So how long have you worked on the ferry?" Grace asked. "Do you like it?

"About six years. I like being around boats, and I like working outside. I could never be an office person. It can be boring sometimes, though. Except, of course, when a beautiful woman hits me with her van door…"

Sarah blushed. "I'll never live that down, will I?"

"Nope," Jen said.

"You never told us about this, Sarah. What happened?" Grace asked.

They told her about how they met on the ferry, and then again at the potluck. "It was fate!" Jen said.

"Yes, I was so taken with your potluck contribution!" Sarah said. They all chuckled at Sarah's description.

"Hey!" Jen said. "At least I took them out of the wrappings and put them on a plate!"

Jen offered to help with the dishes, which endeared her to the ladies, but of course, Marie wouldn't let her do anything. Sarah walked her out and they stood on the far side of the van so they could say good night, safe from curious eyes.

"Whew!" Jen said after a long kiss. "You make me weak in the knees!"

Sarah clung to her and tried to slow her breathing. She didn't want Jen to see how strongly her body reacted to her touch. Her knees were weak, and so was everything else. Her feelings for Nancy had been loving and sweet, until they died a natural death, but she had never felt the fiery energy that she felt with Jen.

"When will I see you again?" Jen whispered.

"I'm off again on Saturday," Sarah said. "But if you happened to come by some evening during the week, I might be able to go for a ride or something..."

"Or something..." Jen said. She finally pulled herself away after one more long kiss, then playfully staggered to the bike, clutching her heart. "See ya!" she said, and drove slowly up the driveway. Sarah could hear her gun the bike when she got to the road.

She stood out there in the dark for a few minutes to regain her composure. On the outside, anyway.

※ ※ ※ ※

The sky was so blue it was almost painful, especially coming after a series of damp, blah days. But it was mid-May, and soon the rains would stop. For now, though, the grass was fresh and fragrant, and a million rhododendrons bloomed. All the excitement that was spring was evident everywhere she looked, and within her as well.

Sarah felt like two different women – one a professional nurse, devoted to her patient, the other totally preoccupied with Jen and the way she made her feel. They'd been hanging out, getting to know each other, riding around, walking on the beach. They had talked about getting together with some of her friends, but Sarah wasn't feeling very sociable today. She wanted Jen all to herself. She'd been putting off acting on her feelings, wanting to get to know Jen a little better, but she'd held out long enough. Today was going to be the day. She knew it. She felt it.

Sarah heard the buzz of Jen's bike approaching as she finished hulling the last of the strawberries. She sprinkled them with a little sugar to make them juicy and popped them into the basket as Jen strode through the door.

"Wa-hey thar, little lady!" Jen did her best John Wayne as she swaggered in. She put her arms around Sarah and lifted her off her feet. She buried her nose in her neck and inhaled. "Mmmm, you smell good."

Sarah laughed and wrapped her arms around Jen's neck. "Must be the cookies. Now put me down, you fool."

Jen held her tighter for a moment before letting her down. "No. I know the smell of cookies, and I know the smell of woman!"

"And which is your favorite dessert?" Sarah asked, slyly.

"Depends on the cookie!" Jen said, and ducked

as Sarah swatted at her. "Now, what have we got here," she said, peering into the basket. "Strawberries, tomato salad, French bread. Cookies, of course. Yum! Look, I brought some salmon." She reached into her backpack and pulled out a couple of bright orange fillets rolled in Chinese five-spice powder, a bottle of wine, and the tiniest propane grill Sarah had ever seen.

"Look how cute!" Sarah said. She closed the top of the basket and picked up the red-and-black checked blanket. "I'm ready if you are!"

"Now, where are we going?" Jen asked.

"I found the prettiest spot on the other side of the lake. There's a picnic table and lots of flowers. It felt really nice there," Sarah said. "It's not very far."

"Lead on!" Jen said, picking up the rest of the goodies. "Hey, where are the ladies?"

"They're lazing around upstairs, reading the paper and watching weird movies," Sarah said. "*Cold Comfort Farm*. Ever see it?"

"No," Jen said.

"I guess they've seen it a bunch of times. We'll have to have a movie day some time. We all had breakfast, got Grace fixed up, then they went back upstairs. They probably won't surface until late afternoon."

The air was thick with the songs of birds and buzz of insects. They passed by the little white gazebo and around the garden. The daffs and tulips were done, but the irises were blooming and the roses were just starting. The tomato plants they had put in a couple of weeks ago were looking perky, and already had some yellow flowers. Countless lavender plants were sending out new shoots. Sarah inhaled deeply. "I love this place," she sighed.

Soon they came to the spot Sarah had described.

Huge rhodys—pink, white, yellow, and purple—formed a long row that separated the woods from the gardens. Several small paths cut through the giant hedge. Sarah led them between a pink and white bush to an open space where an old wooden picnic table stood, shaded by tall firs and cedars.

She plopped her basket on the table and turned to Jen. "Well, what do you think?"

"This is great. These rhodys are incredible!" she said. She put her arms around Sarah and held her close.

Sarah lifted her face, and Jen brushed her lips softly with her own. Sarah felt a charge travel from her lips to her very core, and she clung to Jen tightly. Goddess, that woman could light her right up. She half expected to see little sparkles coming from Jen's fingers as she caressed her arm. She stepped back a little, trying to catch her breath.

But Jen didn't let her go far. She reached out, cupped Sarah's face in her hands, and drew her in. Slowly, she pressed her lips against Sarah's. She felt, rather than heard, the little moan in Sarah's throat as she tasted her. "Oh, I've been waiting for this," Jen said softly, and leaned into her mouth again.

Sarah pulled back again, her pulse racing. Her face felt hot and her legs trembled. "Wait!" she said. "I can't breathe!"

"Wait!" Jen said in a shaky voice. "I've been waiting! This is all I can think about!"

"Me, too," Sarah confessed. "I've been having all these dreams about you." She reached out and cupped Jen's head. "Hot dreams. Wet dreams," she purred softly, and stepped closer. "I just want to take it slow. Or I might faint!" She gave Jen a swift kiss.

"Well, okay," Jen said, pushed Sarah back a little.

"I'm starving anyway. I'd rather eat!"

"Liar!" she snorted. "No cookies for you!"

"I will have your cookies, Miss!" Jen said throatily, stroking an imaginary moustache. "You know you cannot resist my charms! Resistance is futile!"

Sarah put a hand against her brow in her best melodramatic manner. "Oh, no! You'll not have my sweets! Help me! Help me!"

"I'll save you, little lady!" Jen cried, reverting to John Wayne. She swept Sarah up in her arms.

"My hero!" Sarah giggled, and put her arms around Jen's neck. "No – my heroine! No – that makes me sound like I need a fix. I know – Shero! You are my shero!" Her giggles died as she pressed her lips against Jen's again, but inside she was smiling so wide...

Jen sat Sarah on the end of the picnic table, their lips still locked, their breaths coming hard and fast. Jen parted Sarah's trembling legs and leaned in. Sarah reached under Jen's shirt and slid her hand slowly against her silken back. Jen growled softly in her throat and pulled Sarah even closer, their breasts pressed tightly together.

They rubbed against each other, slowly at first, their hips making faster, tighter circles as their bodies focused, flushed with heat. Their flowing wetness did nothing to douse the flames.

Sarah pulled back, gasping. Jen's features had blurred, her parted lips soft and wet, more primal somehow. She reached for Sarah again. "No, wait!" She leaned her forehead against Jen's chest for a moment. "Let me catch my breath!"

"That's okay, we'll breathe later," Jen said, starting to come down a little. "Please, Sarah!"

"What if someone comes along?" Sarah said. She

slithered forward until she was standing. She wound her hand in Jen's hair and planted another kiss on her lips. She laughed throatily. "Besides, this picnic table is pinching my butt!"

Jen looked around for a moment. "I know!" she said, grabbling for the blanket. "Come on!" She grabbed Sarah's hand and pulled her toward a massive pink rhody whose branches swept the ground.

She dropped to her knees, pulled Sarah down, and parted the branches. They crawled under the bush into a dim pink and green cave. Slivers of sunlight filtered through the branches.

Somehow, the blanket got spread, and somehow, the clothing came off, slowly at first, then faster and faster. Somehow, breasts molded to fit fingers and fingers molded to fit breasts, hips, other parts. Somehow, legs wrapped around legs and arms around arms until it was impossible to tell where one person stopped and the other began. And somehow, the soft twitters of the songbirds changed to cries like hawks and eagles.

⚜⚜⚜⚜

"I'm so hungry, I think I'm gonna die," Sarah moaned.

"You thought you were dying a while back, too." Jen laughed. They were still pressed together, and their sticky skin protested wetly as they pulled apart. Jen sat up, took Sarah's hand and kissed it, and inhaled appreciatively. "Mmmmmmm!"

"I had a different kind of hunger," she said.

"Are you still hungry for those kinds of sweets?" Jen asked.

"My brain is, but my body is not. Not until you feed me, anyway." Sarah sat up and started pulling on her jeans. They were still damp. She rolled up her underwear and stuck it in her pocket.

"Better hurry up then or there won't be anything left for you." Jen crawled quickly out of their cave.

Sarah finished dressing, folded the blanket, and crawled out. Jen already had the propane grill lit, and was pulling plates and cups out of the basket. "Hey, what time is it? It looks late," she said.

"A little after five," Jen said, putting the salmon on the rack.

"I guess we fell asleep," Sarah said, running her fingers through her hair.

"That's for sure. You were snoring!" Jen laughed.

"Liar! I don't snore!" She grabbed the basket and unloaded the rest of the food. "Cookie!" She grabbed a huge macadamia nut disk and began stuffing it into her mouth.

"Don't spoil your dinner now," Jen scolded. "This salmon is going to be ready in just a few minutes."

"Don't worry about me," Sarah said. "I could eat all the cookies in the world, and you too!" She stopped chewing and blushed as Jen started to laugh.

They made short work of the picnic. "Yum!" Sarah said. "That salmon was delicious! And I thought you didn't cook!"

"Why, thank you kindly, ma'am," Jen said as she repacked the basket. "I like these two-ingredient recipes!"

"I wonder if Grace and Marie are up and around yet," Sarah said. "I don't think I'm quite ready to see them."

"Yeah, let's go around the long way. I'd like to

see what else is back here," Jen said.

Sarah took Jen's hand and they strolled slowly along the edge of the woods as the sky began to turn pink and orange. They almost missed the glint of sunlight on metal as they rounded the bend. "I wonder what that is," she said.

"Let's take a look."

A bronze figure of a young woman of slight build was seated cross-legged on a rough granite pedestal. A delicate hand brushed the bronze curls that had escaped from the knot on her head. An impish grin lit her face.

A granite bench stood nearby, and Jen and Sarah sat down quietly. It was a peaceful spot, with only bird songs and the buzz of insects to break the silence. Pink and purple flowers grew in a wild tangle, and a couple of butterflies danced across the blossoms.

"Well, this is a surprise. I wonder who she is," Sarah said, looking at the little statue.

"I don't know, but she sure is pretty. She kinda looks like you," Jen said thoughtfully. "In an old fashioned way. Like if you had longer hair."

"You think so? I don't know. I'll have to ask Grace about her." She stood and stretched. "Wow, I'm tired. It's been quite the day, huh?" She grinned at Jen, looking more like the sculpture than ever.

"Yes, this is the best picnic I've ever had!" She bent and kissed Sarah on the lips for a long moment. "I sure could use a shower, though."

"Me too. And I happen to know where there's a nice one. Right next to the hot tub!"

"What are we waiting for?" Jen said, taking Sarah's hand again as they headed back towards the house.

❧❧❦❦

That night, she lay in bed, reliving their thrilling afternoon. Her hands brushed her lips, breasts, thighs, that tingled with the memory of Jen's touch. Finally, she fell sweetly asleep, her head full of lavender dreams.

❧❧❦❦

"You're doing so well. I'm very pleased with you! You're getting a lot of your range of motion back," Carol said, slowly moving Grace's leg up and down.

"Yes, she's been working very hard," Sarah said. "She drags me out for a walk several times a day!"

"Well, I'm tired of sitting around. And I feel bad for Marie, leaving her with all the work. It's too much for her," Grace said.

"Don't let Marie hear you say that," Sarah warned. "You know she'd kick up a fuss!"

"I know. But it's true. It's such a big place for her and Lindy to keep up, and I know you're trying to help her, but that's not really your job. And she is so stubborn!" Grace sighed.

"I enjoy helping out. But you're right, she does try to do too much," Sarah said. "Sometimes I worry about her. She's looking tired. She should go back to see Dr. Emily." Grace had told her about Marie's angina, which flared up when she was tired or stressed.

"You're right. She hasn't been in for a checkup for quite a while. She's been so busy fussing over me!" Grace said.

"I really liked Emily. We didn't get to talk much at the potluck, but she seemed like a nice person,"

Sarah said.

"Oh, yes, she's lovely," Carol said. "And so is her partner."

"She's a weaver, isn't she?" Sarah asked. "I talked to her for a few minutes too."

"Yes, she does all kinds of fiber art. She has a little shop in town, and makes beautiful things," Carol said.

"I don't think I ever met her," Grace said. "We just haven't done much socially for the past few years. Since Annie got sick. We're out of the community loop!"

"You must miss it," Carol said. "This place used to be busy all the time!"

"Yes, I do miss it. And Marie does too. She loves cooking for a lot of people. It's no fun cooking just for two!" Grace said. "It was a big adjustment for her. She would still cook big pots of soups and stews, and we'd have leftovers until we couldn't look at them anymore. She's getting a little better about it now, though. But our freezer is probably still stuffed!"

"Maybe you should invite some people over," Sarah suggested. "I would be glad to help. And I could volunteer Jen as well!"

Carol laughed. "Don't be so quick to volunteer Jen for kitchen duty. Remember her dish at the potluck?"

Grace clapped her hands. "That's a great idea. We could have a little luncheon in the garden. Just a simple meal," she said. "Who should we invite?"

"Well, I think you should definitely invite me!" Carol said. "And Zoe too, of course."

"Of course! And how about Emily and her partner?" Grace said. "And Savannah, too. I haven't seen her in a while."

"How about the other women at the potluck? Luanne and Ro? And Isobel, of course." Sarah chimed in.

"Ten people. That sounds perfect," Carol said.

"Yes, it does. I'm so excited!" Grace said.

"What's so exciting?" Marie asked, putting down her tray of tea things.

"Guess what, Marie!" Grace said. "We're having a party!"

※ ※ ※ ※

"I almost wish I still smoked – I would love a cigarette right about now," Jen said. She traced an imaginary smoke ring in the air.

"Well, I'm glad you don't," Sarah said. She rubbed her head against Jen's brushy hair.

"Me too. Stinky habit. But it sure was nice afterwards." She smiled. "You know, transition to the real world." Jen turned on her side. "I guess I'll have to do something else to transition," she said, lazily tracing circles around Sarah's breasts.

"That's not a way to transition," Sarah said with a grin. "It's a way to start things up again."

"Okay then!" Jen said, and gently began to kiss Sarah's breasts, tonguing her nipples gently, first one, then the other.

"Ummm…" Sarah sighed. "Ummm…"

※ ※ ※ ※

"I almost wish I still smoked – I would love a cigarette right about now," Jen said. She traced an imaginary smoke ring in the air.

Sarah laughed. "Haven't we already had this conversation? Or is that all you can think about, smoking and sex?"

"No, just hot, smoking sex."

"No, no, down! Bad girl!" Sarah said, wagging her finger. She lay back, arms under her head.

She looked around. It was the first time she'd been to Jen's apartment. She could see the whole place from the bed. It was pretty much the way she had imagined it –Ikea furniture, including a couple of overflowing bookcases, a couple of comfortable easy chairs in blues and greens, not a lot of frills or fuss. The kitchen was tidy, with just enough for one person. She was pleased with what she saw. No dark secrets here. She rolled onto her side and draped an arm across Jen's hip. "Tell me a story," she said.

"What kind of story do you want?" she asked.

"Tell me how you came out." Sarah said. "How old were you when you knew you were gay?"

"I guess I always knew; I just didn't know what to call it. Or if those feelings really had a name. I thought I was the only one," Jen said.

"I know what you mean. I thought I was different from everyone else. I was scared to death that someone would know." She sighed. "But tell me about you."

"Well, I have two brothers, Sean and Michael. Sean is the oldest, then Michael, then me. And I have a little sister, Shelly. She's the youngest." Jen laughed. "She's not so little anymore, all grown up, kids of her own."

"So?"

"Well, I was always hanging around with Sean and Michael, whenever they let me. We played all kinds of games, and ran around in the woods playing cowboys and Indians. Not very politically correct, I know, but we were just kids. My brothers always wanted me to be the Indian. All the Indians." She laughed. "And I also had to be the cowgirl, depending on what we were playing. I hated that. I was as good at being a cowboy as they were."

"What about your little sister?"

"Oh, she didn't like playing with us very much. One day Sean and Michael tied her to a tree in the woods and left her there. She was supposed to be the captured Indian princess. Some princess! She was such a crybaby. I guess they went off and forgot about her." Jen laughed. "Well, mom sent me out looking around for her, and there she was, still tied to the tree, bawling her head off. Mom gave us what for, and Dad did too when he got home."

"Bad, bad!" Sarah said. "No wonder she didn't want to play!"

"Yeah. Well, my dad and the boys and I used to play catch after dinner sometimes, and I did pretty well. And I was pretty good at basketball too. Once I could beat the boys, I told them I didn't want to be the cowgirl anymore. So my job description changed."

"What were you then?"

"Wonder Woman, or any other female superhero you can think of."

"What did your parents think about that?"

"Well, Mom tried to get me to wear dresses and shoes, but she gave up after a while. I wanted to wear overalls and go barefoot like my brothers. I liked having a cape, though. My dad thought it was funny. He called me his third son."

"What about Shelly?"

"Oh, she was always girly, you know, liked to

dress up and fix her hair. Sometimes Mom would let us play grown up with her makeup and hats and stuff. My mom liked that. I always felt a little weird. I would look in the mirror, and I looked like somebody I didn't recognize. I liked it better when I could draw on a moustache with Mom's eyeliner and be a pirate."

"What about school?"

"Well, sometimes the boys would poke fun at me, but I was a pretty good fighter. And sometimes the girls would whisper and laugh at me, but I didn't mind that too much. I didn't want to play with dolls when I was younger, or dress up and giggle about boys when I was older. I didn't want to be like them, I just wanted to watch them. Especially Sheila."

"Who is Sheila?"

"Oh, she was my first crush. We were in the fifth grade. She was so beautiful. She had this shiny brown hair, straight, like a curtain that swayed when she turned her head. I sat next to her in class, and she always smelled like clean sheets. She had the sweetest face, and sometimes she would smile at me. It made my heart beat funny. And she could sing!"

"And what happened to her?"

"Oh, we went to different middle schools, and I didn't get to see her anymore. She still makes my heart beat funny."

"You must have missed seeing her."

"Oh, I did. I wonder if she knew how I felt about her. I wonder if she's gay or straight, if she's married or what." She sighed.

"So what about coming out?"

"Well, in middle school I kept having crushes, but they were always on the girls. There was Louisa and Mae and Carol. Then when I was in high school there was Geri and Marcia..."

"Whoa! What a busy girl! That's a lot of crushes!"

Jen grinned. "Yes, I've always had an eye for the ladies."

"Then what?"

"Well, I had this gym teacher, and she fascinated me. I know that's a cliché. Her name was Ms. Fredericks. She was the first Ms. I ever met. She wore her hair very short, and she had such a strong face. She didn't wear makeup like the other teachers, and I never saw her in a dress. She felt so familiar to me, like I was looking at myself in a way. Although I never wanted to be a phys ed teacher. She sort of scared me, to tell the truth."

"Yes? I can't imagine you being scared."

"Well, intimidated, maybe. I was still pretty good at softball, and at basketball too, so she liked me for that," she said proudly. "I tried to show off in front of her. Then when I was in high school, I had this friend. Barbara." She sighed.

"Uh-huh."

"Well, she was my partner in biology. Neither of us was crazy about cutting up critters, but we got through it somehow. Then, wouldn't you know it, I ended up working on a fishing boat and was up to my eyes with fish goop. I never want to do anything that has to do with blood and guts again!"

"Not much of that on the ferry..."

"No. Hopefully not. Unless a passenger hits you with a van door..."

"Hey!" Sarah said, swatting at her.

Jen laughed and ducked. "Well, anyway, I used to go over to her house so we could study. And we talked and talked. She was very pretty, but she didn't fuss about her looks too much. She was natural looking, you know? She didn't have a boyfriend. My brother Sean really liked her, but she wasn't interested. He wanted me to talk to her, to get her to like him, but she just laughed. Said he wasn't her type."

"And what was her type?"

"Well, apparently, me. I did notice that when I was close to her I started feeling funny, like I used to feel around Sheila back in grade school. Sometimes when she touched me, the hair on my arm would stand up and I would get a chill up my arm. Then sometimes I had trouble breathing. I did the best I could to hide it."

"Okay, this is getting good."

"Then one day we were at her house, and we had Fleetwood Mac playing. I love Fleetwood Mac. Especially Stevie Nicks. Do you like her?"

"Yes, I do. But the suspense is killing me. What happened?"

"We were sitting on her bed, looking at our lab book, then all of a sudden she leaned over and kissed me. On the lips!"

"What did you do?"

"I was so blown away, I just jumped up. Some kind of sounds came out of my mouth, but I don't think they were real words. I know I was as red as a beet."

"What did she say?"

"Oh, well, I looked at her, and she looked so upset. 'I'm sorry, I'm sorry,' she said, over and over. 'I made a mistake. I thought you liked me.' 'I do like you, Sheila,' I said. 'I like you very much. Maybe more than that.' And then I kissed her back, right on the mouth. I'm telling you, it was magic! Electric!"

"Wow!" Sarah said. "So what did she do?"

"Well, she kissed me and then I kissed her and then she kissed me and then I kissed her, and then I lost track of who was kissing who. We didn't get our biology homework done that night. When I got home I couldn't eat dinner, and I couldn't sleep that night. My lips were sore! I kept seeing her face, and then I would start to breathe funny again."

"So did you keep the relationship going?"

"Yes. But our biology grades went down that quarter, and our parents weren't too happy about that." She chuckled. "We were studying some different kind of biology."

"Did your parents ever find out what was going on?" Sarah asked.

"I guess we weren't very good about hiding how we felt," Jen said. "I couldn't take my eyes off her. I couldn't keep from touching her. It was like we were sleepwalking," Jen said ruefully. "We were so pathetic!"

"Yes?"

"Then one day we were in her room, supposedly studying. We both had our shirts off. Her mom got off early from work, and we didn't hear her come in."

"Oh, no! That must have been terrible! What did she say?"

"She totally freaked out, started yelling and screaming, crying like anything. She grabbed Barbara's arm and pulled her away from me. Told me to get out, and never come back. I was already running for the door, trying to get my shirt back on."

"Oh, no! So what happened then?"

"Well, I rode around on my bike for a while and tried to think. All I could see was Barbara's face, crying, and her mother's voice, telling me to get out. By the time I got home, Barbara's mother had already called my house. My parents were both waiting for me when I got in."

"And?"

"My mom sat me down and we had 'the talk.' My dad tried to talk to me too. Of course, by that time, all I could hear was love songs, breaking up songs. We were both pretty dopey, I admit. We should have been more careful. But we were so in love..."

"Yeah. So then what?"

"Well, my folks were actually pretty cool about it. Once they realized what was going on, they just told me they loved me, even if they couldn't really understand."

"That's lucky. What about Sheila's parents?"

"They weren't quite so understanding. They screamed and yelled at her, threatened her. They told her we couldn't see each other anymore."

"That must have been really hard for both of you."

"Yes, it was. Sheila's parents sent her to a shrink, who tried to talk her into being straight. Seemed like she was crying all the time. She promised that she wouldn't see me anymore, and at first, we tried. But we would see each other at school. Then we started sneaking around, under the bleachers, in the locker room, wherever we could be alone."

"Poor things! That must have been awful for you."

"It was, but it was pretty exciting to be sneaking around, too."

"So then what?"

"One day, we got caught. The teacher saw us kissing in the locker room. I was so blown away. I didn't know what she'd do. Sheila was petrified, and so was I!"

"So what did she do?"

"She just stared at us for a minute, then she turned around real slow and walked out. We beat it out of there."

"I can imagine. You must have been freaked out."

"Really, I was. Fortunately, she didn't report us. But after that, we weren't close anymore. Sheila would just walk away when she saw me. I tried to talk to her, call her, but she would just clam up. She told me not to call her anymore. After all we meant to each other! I couldn't believe it! We'd made plans, how we were going to go to college together, share a place…we'd be happy, and free. She broke my heart."

"So sad…I'm sure she didn't want it to end that way."

"Yeah. I don't know. I looked her up on Facebook a couple of years ago, just out of curiosity, you know,"

"Yeah, right. I'm sure. So what did you find out?"

"Well, she got married to Bobby Benton, from our English class. He played football. They had a couple of kids, and a dog. I saw a picture of her…she was smiling, still beautiful. Her little girl looked a lot like her. Bobby had a potbelly, and was losing his hair. She was working in a real estate office. The All-American life for the All-American wife." She sighed and shook her head. "But enough about me. What about you?"

"I'm so sorry. It must have been so painful for you. I don't know why it always has to be so hard."

"I don't know, but someday things will be different. I'm just lucky that my parents and my sibs are supportive. I don't know what I would do if I didn't have my family."

"You are lucky. My parents weren't so cool."

"How so?"

"Well, they were always very Mormon-fundamentalist-churchy, you know, talking about sin, and how homosexuals were so bad, and were going to hell – or h-e-double hockey sticks." Sarah laughed bitterly. "No bad words around them!"

"Did you ever come out to them?"

"Yes, later. I also had crushes when I was a kid. I would have been all over you if you sat next to me in class! But I knew it was wrong, and I ignored my feelings, as much as I could. I felt like such a sinner, having those thoughts! I dated a few guys in high school, but I never had much in common with them, and I felt so out of sync—and I went to a pretty fundamentalist-churchy school, you know? Not much action there, everybody so straight and righteous. And I never really felt anything if they tried to kiss me. Then I met Justin."

"Yes? What was his story?"

"Well, I tried out for the school play—it was *Oklahoma* that year. I got the part of Ado Annie. I thought she was so funny. She was completely different from me! She loved to flirt with the boys, and I didn't really want anything to do with them."

"I wish I could have seen that! I bet you were the cutest Ado Annie ever."

"You bet!" Sarah said, twirling her hair around her finger and batting her eyes at Jen. "I'm just a girl who can't say no…" she sang.

"So then what happened?"

"Well, this guy Justin had a part in the play too. He played that peddler who was trying to get next to any woman, Ado Annie included, so we had a few scenes together. He was so funny. He really played it up. He was a great bad guy. He made me laugh. And we started hanging out."

"What was he like?"

"Well, he was really into the whole theatrical thing. Loved to act, dance, dress up...he was really pretty fabulous, you know? I knew he was gay as soon as he opened his mouth."

"Ah," Jen said.

"Right. We went to the movies, went shopping together...we could talk about almost anything. He really got me, you know? And of course, he was raised like me, homophobia city. He couldn't hide who he was."

"Was he seeing anyone?"

"He didn't have much luck with the fellas. Everybody in the school acted so straight, whether they really were or not. He definitely stood out, and the guys called him fairy and faggot, you know. They even beat him up a couple of times, bullied him, you know. He took his share of crap. That was the only thing he didn't want to talk about."

"I don't blame him. That's terrible." Jen shook her head. "So what happened then?"

"Well, as far the girls were concerned, we were a couple. We ran around together, even went to the prom. Boys asked me out, but stopped bugging me when I told them I was with Justin. And my parents were happy that I was seeing a boy who was such a gentleman. Hah!" She sighed. "People thought we were just like everybody else."

"So you never came out to your parents?"

"No, not then. Justin and I went to the same college, so we kept the myth going for a while. We were both living in dorms, and we still hung out."

"Didn't you meet anyone in college? "

"One day, I was walking through the Student Union building, and I saw a notice up for a gay-lesbian event. I couldn't believe it! It had tear-off phone numbers on the bottom of the sheet, but I walked by it a bunch of times before I stopped and tore one off and stuck it in my pocket. I'd never imagined that I would actually see something like that up in a public place. The next day, two or three other phone number slips were torn off. I called Justin, and I told him about it. He was really excited. 'Let's go! Let's go!' he said."

"So?"

"Well, I was really nervous. I didn't know what to expect. I still thought lesbians were all dykey and butch with a lot of leather and tattoos, mean and bristly-looking. I thought all lesbians wanted to be men. But I wasn't like that, and they scared me. I knew I wanted to be with a woman, but I didn't know how to go about it, or be open about it, and be myself."

"So what did you do?"

"Justin and I went to the meeting. It was like a get-acquainted group. There we were in this 'in your face' meeting on this very straight, conservative campus. We felt very brave. We were certainly not like the Act Up folks at other schools."

"What was it like?"

"It was kind of like middle school, in a way. The girls on one side and the boys on the other. But it was different in one way...in school, the girls were talking and whispering about the boys, and the boys were standing around in groups, talking about the girls in hushed voices. Here, the girls were looking at the girls, and the boys were checking out the boys. "

"So what happened?"

"Then Justin saw this guy from one of his classes. 'Hah!' he said. 'I knew he was gay the minute I saw him! Isn't he gorgeous? I'm gonna go over there and talk to him!' And he left me standing there, alone."

"Yeah?"

"Well, I thought I'd just leave. I was so embarrassed, and I didn't know what to do. I looked around, and there were about a dozen women. Some were leathery types, and some of them had real swoopy James Dean kind of haircuts. The others wore their hair long, and had makeup on. There were all kinds of women! I didn't look like I belonged with either group."

"So, did you leave?"

"No, I decided to sit down for a bit and watch those women. Someone put some music on, and a couple of the guys started dancing. I was so blown away. I'd never seen men dancing together before."

"Yeah?"

"Well, this woman came over and sat next to me. She was one of the James Dean types. She told me her name was Con, and she asked me to dance. My heart was beating so hard, and I could feel myself getting red. Con asked me if I was okay. I said yes, but I'd never been to a event like that, and I'd never danced with a woman before. Not really, just my cousins, they don't count.'

"'Well good, I wouldn't want you to mistake me for one of your cousins. Although I know they're cute if they look like you,' Con said. She was smiling.

"She held out her arms and I stood up. She put her arms around me and I could smell her shampoo. Herbal Essence, my favorite. I felt so awkward! 'Don't worry, I won't bite,' she said. 'Yet.' She put her arms around me and I felt like I couldn't breathe. 'Just relax, honey,' she said. 'I'll be gentle.'

"We danced a couple of times, some slow and some fast. She was a really good dancer, and very sweet when I stepped on her foot. And we talked a little. She asked me if I had a girlfriend, and I just shook my head. I couldn't even imagine that. I looked around, and I didn't see Justin anywhere. 'Well, I came here with a friend…'

"'I saw your friend when you came in,' Con said. 'I think he's occupied.'"

She smiled, and I couldn't help noticing how strong she looked. She was so hot!

"'I hope he's okay,' I said. I was worried – I didn't see him anywhere. 'Don't worry; I'm sure he's fine. And I don't think he wants you to look for him!' she said. I knew she was laughing at me."

"Then she said she would walk me back to my dorm, even though she lived off campus. We walked back slowly, and I was so tongue-tied I couldn't say a thing. While we were walking, she took my hand. And it felt so good, warm and strong. Every bit of my brain was focused on my fingers. I felt pulses of electricity all the way up my arm.

"We stopped outside the dorm, and she asked if she could call me. I just nodded like a dummy. I couldn't speak. She handed me a little note pad and I wrote down my number.

"'Is this a real number?'" she asked. 'Of course it is,' I said. 'Okay then,' she said. She gave me a sweet hug and kissed me on the cheek. I watched her walk away, and I still felt the energy running through me. I felt so alive!"

"So then what happened?"

"Well, she did call me and we got together. I was so nervous at first. Being with her was like being out in a rushing wind...I felt like we were flying...she was carrying me with her. I would close my eyes and my body felt tingly, weightless. I learned so much from her. I learned things about my own body that I'd never known before. Huh!" She paused. "She was a great teacher."

Jen grinned. "She must have been. And now I am reaping the benefit. So what happened to her?"

"Oh, we saw each other for a while, through most of my junior year. We didn't really have all that much in common. Once we got out of bed, we didn't have much to talk about." Sarah laughed, remembering. "Then she met someone else, and so did I. We just kind of drifted away from each other, but I know we really enjoyed the time we had together. We loved each other, but we were not in love. We were just different, and we wanted different things."

"I want different things, too," Jen said. "Lots and lots of different kinds of things..." She buried her face in Sarah's neck. "Starting right here..."

※ ※ ※ ※

Breakfast was over, and the day promised to be beautiful. Grace and Marie sat on the side porch in white wicker chairs with fat, flowered cushions that matched the pink and magenta fuchsias that cascaded from the woven hanging baskets. Ralph was flopped out, belly up, at Grace's feet.

Marie peeled potatoes, the long curls dropping onto the newspaper spread out on the wooden table, then popped each potato into a large pot of water.

Grace shelled sweet peas into a white ironstone bowl. She popped one into her mouth and savored the green flavor.

"Ummm, these are delicious," she said. "So crisp."

"Yes, Sarah picked them early this morning," Marie said. "That girl is a bundle of energy."

"Yes, she's always doing something, just like you! She's done wonders with that garden. Annie would be so proud!" Grace said. "Well, she's used to running around in the hospital, I guess. And I think she missed having a yard in the city, too. And we are so quiet here. She's probably getting bored."

"Not with that new girlfriend of hers hanging around. All those moony-eyed looks. The two of them are floating about two inches off the ground!"

"Ah, young love!" Grace sighed and patted her heart.

"Old love isn't so bad either," Marie said, reaching out for her hand.

"You've got that right," Grace said, and raised Marie's hand to her lips. "They are very cute together, aren't they? I like that Jen. Even though she worries me with that motorcycle."

"Yes, me too. I hope she's careful." Marie rolled up her peel-filled newspaper. "They really seem to care about each other."

Grace smiled. "I'm glad she found someone. And it certainly picks up the atmosphere in the house. All those hormones!"

"I think those feelings are contagious. I've noticed that you're a bit friskier yourself lately, missy!"

"No, it's definitely you, fresh thing!"

Margret strolled out, touched noses with Ralph,

then stretched out on the porch next to him. Lazily, she inspected a neat brown paw. Grace reached out a small bare foot and stroked her soft belly. "What a lovely girl you are!"

Marie pouted. "Hey! You're only supposed to say things like that to me!"

"I can't believe you are jealous of this poor cat!" Grace laughed.

"I can't help it, I love you so," she said. "I don't want to share you with anyone!". She leaned over and gave Grace a peck on the cheek.

"You silly." Grace chuckled. "You know I'm all yours."

"Now."

"Yes, now. And forever."

They sat quietly for a few moments, Margret's purring the only sound.

"Well, I'm glad those women are coming over today. It will be nice to have company again," said Marie.

"Me, too. I'm glad we decided to have this little luncheon. We haven't seen some of these people in ages!"

"Yes, it's been too long. I miss the cooking and the bustle. I miss having people around the table!" Marie said. "Speaking of which – it's going to be awfully quiet again when Sarah leaves."

"I know. I don't like to think about it. I've enjoyed having her here so much." Grace smiled. "*You* didn't in the beginning, though."

"No. We spent all that time taking care of Annie, and just the thought of a stranger taking care of you made me nervous. And I didn't want to have some closed-minded judgmental sort of person who would have been upset about us being together," Marie said forcefully.

"No, of course not! But this is our home, after all," Grace said.

"It would have been terrible," Marie said. "She'd have been gone so fast…"

Grace laughed. "I don't think I could sleep without you anymore." She paused. "We haven't had a single night apart. Even when I was in the hospital, you were right there."

"Well, I'm glad it wasn't an issue. We were just lucky!" Marie said.

"No, I called the agency and told them they had to send us a dyke nurse!" Grace said. "A relative!"

"Yeah, right! As if." They laughed, then fell back into companionable silence.

"I wonder what will happen to Sarah and Jen when she finishes up here," Grace said thoughtfully.

"Well, if they really love each other, they'll figure something out."

"I hope so. I probably won't need her much longer. I'm feeling so much better now, and I can do a lot more for myself. And I know Sarah likes to be busy, but she wants me to be independent, and of course, Carol does too. And I hate to say it, but my insurance won't cover her salary anymore, or the agency fees." Grace frowned.

"Let's not think about that now. I think Sarah should stay here as long as you need her."

❧❧❧❧

Ralph barked and ran back and forth as the cars started to arrive, tail waving madly. Sarah hurried to answer the doorbell. "Come in! Come in! Welcome!" she said, and stood back to let the women step into the foyer.

They all spoke at once while exchanging handshakes and hugs. "Thanks! It's great to see you again!"

"Wow! What a place!"

"Gosh, I haven't been here in so many years. It's still gorgeous!"

"Thanks for inviting us!"

"Grace is waiting for us out in the garden. Let's go out and have some lemonade," Sarah said, guiding them along. She opened the white French doors that led to the garden. They stopped for a moment, admiring the scene before them.

Masses of climbing roses bright as a starlet's toes ran up arched white trellises surrounding the flagstone patio, while the more sedate rose bushes lined up along one side and displayed yellow, pink, and white blooms of every shape and shade. On the other side of the patio, the garden overflowed with vegetable plants, herbs and several kinds of flowers. And overall, the scent of lavender. The air was warm and heady, and the bees dived and circled, furry and yellow with pollen. Two Anna's hummingbirds circled the red feeder, stopping just briefly to dip their tongues into the sweet liquid.

Grace presided over the long table that took up the center of the patio, looking fresh and cool in a pink silk blouse and white slacks. A straw hat with pink roses perched on her white curls at a rakish angle. She grasped her cane and rose slowly to greet her guests. "Hello, ladies! How nice to see you all!"

A chorus of greetings answered her.

"Have a seat and make yourself comfortable.

Let's have some lemonade, then I'll see if I can figure out who all of you are."

Everyone found chairs and settled in while Sarah poured pink lemonade into tall ice-filled glasses and passed them around. "Okay, Grace, we're ready for introductions," she said.

"You already met Ralph, our watchdog. If anybody tried to break in here, Ralph would lick him to death." She chuckled. "And this is Margret, Sarah's kitty." She pointed as Margret strode regally onto the patio. Immediately, a bunch of hands reached out to let Margret have a sniff, and she moved from one to the other, considering. Finally, she jumped up on Zoe's lap and settled in for a petting session.

"And now for the humans." Grace greeted the woman in the chair beside her with a warm smile. "Now of course, I know Carol, and Zoe, too," she said, nodding at her companion. "Carol keeps me busy moving around. And the two of you do such beautiful work. And dear Savannah. So glad you could make it."

"You know nothing could keep me away from one of your gatherings, Grace," Savannah said with a smile. "Or from Marie's cooking!"

"Yes, and she has some excellent helpers today. Grace answered. "Now let me see. I know you, Dr. Emily, but I don't know whose hand you're holding."

"I'm Rachel. Rachel Carmichael."

"Well, Emily and Rachel. I'm getting a little forgetful, so forgive me if I don't remember your name the first time around," Grace said.

"I've heard so much about you!"

"Nothing too alarming, I hope. Emily has been taking good care of us for such a long time."

"I know. It looks like you're making a good

recovery!" Rachel said. She fished around in her bag. "Here, I brought you a little present." She handed Grace a small basket made of brightly colored fabric coils.

"Oh, it's just lovely!" Grace exclaimed, turning it around in her hands. "I've never seen anything like it!" She examined the small tag on the bottom. "Rachel Carmichael, Fiber Artist. Why, Rachel, did you make this?"

"Yes. I have a little workshop in town."

"You are very talented. I'd love to come out and see your work sometime. I adore baskets."

"Any time! I'll give you the grand tour."

"And Grace, I think you know Ro, and her partner, Isobel."

"Yes, Ro, it's been quite a while since we saw you," Grace said. "Sarah, Ro has done some legal work for us in the past."

"Yes, but I mostly do civil rights and discrimination work now. But I still have some clients I've worked with over the years."

"Well, hello Isobel, it's lovely to meet you. And what do you do?"

"I have a little Montessori school in town. It's called Journeys, and we take children up to age six."

"My goodness, to have the energy! I envy you, though; it's such a gift to spend time with little ones. We hardly see any children out here," Grace said, sadly, Sarah thought. "And of course, here is Luanne. Thank you for coming out here on your day off!"

"Oh, no, this is such a treat, spending time with my friends in this beautiful place."

"I'm lucky to know so many talented women," Grace said.

"Thanks, Grace." Carol said. She looked around. "Anybody hear from Jen? I thought she was coming out here today."

At that moment, Jen came out of the kitchen door, wrapped in a big flowered apron. She carried two big bowls of salad. "Hey, folks!"

"Oh my stars!" Zoe gasped. "Are you wearing an apron? Oh, Goddess! Carol, are you seeing this?" She shook her head in disbelief.

Carol laughed. "Have they got you cooking?"

Jen blushed to the roots of her hair, then laughed and shook her head. "No, no, don't panic. I'm just helping out. I'm not cooking!"

"Yeah, yeah. I think we've seen the last of the cut-up potluck cheeseburgers! Maybe next time we have a potluck you'd like to make some quiche?" Zoe said.

"That'll be the day," Jen growled.

"Wow, Sarah, she must really love you," Carol said.

Sarah just smiled.

"Don't tell the rest of the team, Zoe," Jen pleaded. "They'll never let me live it down. Promise!"

"What team is that?" Grace asked.

"Softball. We bowl too."

"Really! We used to have lawn bowling out here. We even had tournaments! I must say, Annie and Marie and I whipped quite a few unsuspecting guests!"

Marie came up to the table, carrying a tray of fresh rolls and butter. "Hello, everyone," she said. "I heard you talking about lawn bowling. Goodness, I haven't thought about that in years!"

"Maybe we could set up a game again sometime, teach everyone how to play," Grace said. "Have some people out!"

"That would be so nice," Sarah said. "You've been talking about how you miss having people around the place."

"It's true! It gets mighty quiet around here sometimes." Marie said. "Help yourself, ladies!"

Grace took Marie's hand. "Happy happy, joy joy, everybody!" she said, and smiled at the group.

They smiled back. "Happy happy, joy joy," they responded, then fell to. They loaded their plates with smoked salmon, cold green beans with dill, potato salad, and baby greens with cherry tomatoes and balsamic and basil dressing. For several minutes, the chink of cutlery and appreciative hums replaced the conversation.

Finally, they began to slow down.

"What an incredible feast!" Carol said, pushing her chair back. "Everything is so good!"

"Really! That salmon was amazing! And those green peas! Excellent!" Emily said.

"Yes, I love peas. I planted tons!" Sarah said. "Everything grows so well out here!"

"It's so nice to have a garden again," Grace said. "Those store-bought vegetables can't hold a candle to home-grown."

"Yes, we used to have a huge garden, but it's been several years." Marie sighed. "We used to grow all sorts of things, and lots of berries of course. And tons of lavender. We used to sell bouquets, potpourri, and sachets at a little stand at the farmer's market."

"I remember that," Carol said. "I love making wands with it, and putting those little sachets in my linen closet and my dresser."

"Me, too," Sarah said. "I'm enjoying puttering around, especially now that Grace is feeling so much better."

"She's quite the gardener," Marie said.

"She's been keeping me busy out there, too. I never realized that gardening was so much work," Jen grumbled, then grinned.

"Poor you," Sarah said, and ran her hand over Jen's spiky head.

"Well, I hope you all left room for dessert," Marie said. "We have strawberry trifle."

"Oh, no, I'm too stuffed right now. I need to walk around a little!" Carol said, leaping to her feet. Ralph immediately jumped up, tail waving.

Jen stood. "Me too!" She picked up a green tennis ball and threw it down the hill, and Ralph immediately dashed after it.

"Yes, let's go for a walk!" said Rachel.

"Sarah, dear, why don't you and Jen show the girls around? We'll have coffee and dessert when you come back."

"Great idea! I'm so stuffed, I can't even think about taking another bite," Zoe said, patting her slender belly.

"Yes, we can make some room, then we can pay full attention to Marie's strawberry trifle!" Jen said.

A chorus of yums! and lipsmacking greeted her comment.

"Grace, do you need anything before we go?" Sarah asked.

"No, dear, I don't need anything, and Marie is close by," she said, waving them off.

Slowly the little group moseyed down the rolling lawn with Ralph dancing attendance, ball clenched tightly in his teeth. They chatted and stopped here and there to admire the flowers and the view of the water that shone through the trees.

They passed numerous unkempt lavender beds, and the scent engulfed them.

"Oh my goodness," said Rachel. "This is incredible! Look! There must be four or five different varieties!"

"Yes, they come back every year, but nobody has taken care of these beds for a long time," Sarah said. "It's sad."

"Yes, Annie was in charge of the grounds. She had an amazing green thumb," Savannah said.

"I'd love to take some home," Emily said. "Do you think they would mind?"

"No, I'm sure they would be happy that someone was enjoying it," Sarah said. Everyone filled their hands with lavender, and they continued their walk past the little lake.

Finally, they ended up on the path that led to the little spot where Sarah and Jen had had their picnic just a few weeks ago. Sarah's whole world had changed on that day.

The rhododendrons had finished blooming, but the buds for the coming year were already forming, and the place was shady and cool. The statue of the young girl was dappled with stripes of sunlight that moved as the trees moved with the breeze.

Jen reached out for Sarah's hand and gave it a squeeze, and Sarah smiled. Jen winked at her. "We haven't been down here in a while," she said quietly.

"No. That was a wonderful...picnic," Sarah said.

"A wonderful everything," Jen answered. She put her arm around Sarah and kissed her. For a moment, they forgot the other women.

"Hey, you two, get a room!" Carol said. "All this

mushy stuff! I can't stand it!"

"You have something against mushy stuff?" Zoe demanded, coming up behind her. She circled Carol's waist with her arms and planted a kiss on the side of her neck.

Carol giggled. "Maybe this place is enchanted," she said.

"I always thought so," Zoe said. "When we were setting up the statue, I felt her spirit. I think she likes having visitors. Especially people in love!"

They heard a soft laugh, and Emily and Rachel strolled from behind a great rhody, hand in hand, smiling.

"See what I mean?" Zoe said.

Savannah let out a big sigh. "I'm so jealous!" she said.

"Sorry, dear," Carol said, sympathetically. "We didn't mean to make you feel bad."

"Oh, no, that's okay. I'm used to it," she said.

Emily put an arm around Savannah and rubbed her back. Savannah smiled a little, then sighed again.

"What did you mean about setting up the statue?" Sarah asked.

"Well, when I finished it, we brought it down here. She doesn't look it, but she's pretty heavy, and it took a bunch of us to get her up on her pedestal," Zoe said.

"You made this statue?" Sarah said, dumbfounded. "Why, Zoe, it's beautiful!"

"Thank you," she said. "I'm glad I was able to do it. She was a very cool woman. We all loved her." She stopped and studied Sarah for a moment. "Come to think of it, you kind of look like her."

Savannah stood back and studied Sarah for a

moment. "Now that you mention it..."

"Well, believe it or not, Grace and I were looking through some old photos, and found that Annie and I have some relatives in common," Sarah said. "She was actually my great aunt or something!"

"No kidding!" Zoe said. "That's so weird! What are the odds?" She paused. "Of course, she didn't really look like that when I knew her. She was already sick. I worked from old photographs. Probably the same ones you looked at!" She shook her head, amazed. "It was a real challenge."

"I'm curious about it. She's a little treasure, hidden here in this wonderful spot, so graceful."

"Talk about romance! What about Annie and Grace? Now that was a romantic story."

"What do you mean? I know Annie was her sister-in-law, and they came out here together and bought this place after Grace's husband died," Sarah said.

"Well, more than that, you know," Jen said. "They were together for all those years."

"What do you mean, together?" Sarah asked, confused.

"What do you think she means?" Carol said. "They were lovers, silly!"

Sarah's mouth dropped open. "No way!"

"Yes! I thought you knew that!" Jen said.

"But what about Grace and Marie? They're together! I saw them!"

"Well, yes, but just for the past couple of years. Not until after Annie died."

Sarah swayed for a moment, and Jen tightened her arm around her. "Hey!" she said, and sat Sarah down on the bench.

She heard a roaring in her ears and tried to fight off a wave of dizziness. She bent over and put her head between her knees. "Oh, my goodness," she said weakly.

Jen sat beside her and held her shoulders. "Honey, what's the matter? Are you all right? Emily, can you help her?"

Emily knelt beside her. She raised Sarah's chin and looked into her eyes. "What happened? Do you feel faint?"

Slowly Sarah straightened. "I'm sorry, that was so silly of me. I don't know what happened." She shook her head. Grace and Annie. Grace and her aunt. "I just thought – I don't really know what I thought. I guess I'm just surprised, that's all." She rubbed her face and ran her fingers through her hair. "Really, I'm okay now. I'm sorry."

Emily stood up and brushed at her knees. "I think you need a good dose of strawberry trifle, young lady."

"I think you're right, Doctor," she said. "That's a prescription I'll be glad to take."

She stood and took a deep breath. Jen's arm still circled her protectively. "See, I'm fine now."

She went to look at the statue once again, its lustrous patina gleaming. Gently, she ran her hand over the curve of her cheek, her smiling lips. "Hi, Aunt Annie," she said. For the first time, she felt like she was part of this place. "Out of curiosity, Zoe, why did you put her here? Why not someplace where everyone could see her?"

Zoe smiled gently. She took a handful of lavender and placed it in front of the statue. "This is where half of her ashes are. It's her resting place."

"Half of her ashes?" Sarah asked. "Where are the

rest of them?"

"Why, in the garden, of course."

※※※※

They started back to the house, each woman lost in her own thoughts.

Finally, they ended up back at the patio, where the table was now set with fine flowered cups and saucers. A big crystal trifle dish and a stack of matching bowls took up the center of the table. White carafes of coffee and hot water stood on a small serving table next to Grace's chair, along with a basket of teas, a pitcher of cream and one of honey, some sliced lemons, and a dish of raw brown sugar cubes with tiny silver tongs.

"Hello, hello!" she called. "Oh, good, I see you found the lavender! Did you have a nice walk?"

"Oh, it was beautiful, Grace," Emily said. "This is a magical place."

"I've always thought so," she answered. "Please sit down! I hope you made room for trifle!"

"Not that I'm one to be trifled with..." Jen said.

There was a chorus of boos from the women.

"Oh, yes, I've heard about Marie's wonderful desserts. That's all Carol could talk about this morning," Zoe said, pinching Carol playfully on the arm. "She has a bit of a sweet tooth, you know."

"Me, too, I'm afraid," said Savannah. "I've been looking forward to this myself."

Marie bustled out of the house, waving a big serving spoon. "Sorry! Bet you thought you were going to have to dish this up with your hands!"

The women laughed.

"Marie, this looks incredible," said Emily. "I've

never had trifle before. What's in it?"

"Oh, it's just some pound cake and mascarpone cheese with some black currant liqueur. And fresh strawberries, of course, from our field."

"Did you make the pound cake yourself?" Carol asked.

"Of course. And the liqueur too!"

"No wonder you have such a wonderful reputation," Emily said.

"And of course the strawberries cancel out all the rest of the calories!" said Zoe.

"Of course," Marie said. "Not that you have anything to worry about." She eyed Zoe's buff form. "Now hand me those bowls!"

Again, silence descended as they lapped up the creamy goodness, but Sarah couldn't help thinking about what she'd heard down in the little grove. She looked at Grace, and then Marie. Everything she'd thought about them had changed in an instant.

She'd imagined them meeting out here on the Island, or maybe in Seattle. She'd thought they'd been together for years and years. Now suddenly she realized that they were practically newlyweds. She blushed at the thought. And she thought about the garden, too, and why everything was growing with such enthusiasm…

"Oh, Grace, did you hear what happened to Edna?" Savannah asked.

"Edna Rogers? No, what happened to her?"

"It was awful. She had a stroke while she was taking a bath. Ginny was visiting her daughter, and didn't find her until later that night. She couldn't get out, and the poor thing sat there in the tub all day."

"Oh, no, I hadn't heard. That's terrible! Is she all right?" Grace cried.

"Well, she's doing a little better now, but her skin is all peely and she still has pneumonia, on top of her stroke. She's starting to do a bit of rehab now, though, and they think she'll recover some use of her arm and leg. And maybe some of her speech."

"She must have been so scared!"

"I'm sure! She can't really talk about it yet. And what words she can say are pretty garbled. But when Ginny is there, she doesn't want to let go of her hand. She doesn't want to let her out of her sight!"

Marie shook her head. "It must be even worse for her, being a schoolteacher and all. She loved to talk, and she loved to read poetry aloud. Do you remember how she would come out for our literary weekends and read to the guests?"

"Yes, she was a wonderful reader, so expressive," Grace said. "Is she still in the hospital?"

"Yes, but she won't be in there for long. Once she's stable, she'll probably have to go to a nursing home. Ginny can't take care of her by herself," said Emily. "But Edna's a tough woman."

"That will be very hard on her," Zoe said. "I know she'll just hate that."

"We'll have to go and see her. Sarah, maybe you could drive us over," Grace said.

"Sure, I'd be glad to," she said. "Have you known her for a long time?"

"Sure, we go way back," Grace said. "Probably forty-five or fifty years. I could tell you some stories…" She smiled reminiscently.

"She was something, all right. A hellion!" Marie said.

"I wish there was something we could do for her," Grace said sadly.

Sarah looked over at her. "You look tired, Grace. Are you all right?"

"I guess I am, a little. It's been so nice having company again," she answered. She looked around the table. "Such lovely women."

"I guess we should go and let you get some rest, Grace," Savannah said. "Marie, let me help you clean up."

"Yes, we'll all help," Carol said, jumping to her feet. "We'll get this place picked up in a heartbeat."

"No, no, I won't hear of it!" Marie said briskly.

Sarah noticed that Marie's face looked a bit drawn and gray. "Now, Marie, I know you're tired too," she said. "Why don't you both go and get a little rest. Come on, I'll go up with you."

Marie shook her head, then shrugged in resignation. Grace cast a worried glance in her direction.

"Before you go, Grace, I want to set some time to get together with you. There are some things we need to talk about," Savannah said.

"Certainly. Why don't you call me tomorrow," Grace said.

"And Marie, why don't you give me a call too. It's been a while since we had a visit," Dr. Emily said.

"Sure, Doc, I'll call you," Marie said.

"I'll make sure she does," Grace said.

"Hmmmph," Marie said.

The women said their goodbyes and gave hugs all around, then began clearing the table as Sarah walked slowly toward the house, a gray-haired lady on one arm and a white-haired one on the other.

"So you never finished telling me about how you came out," Jen said.

"Well, I told you about Sheila and Con and my experiences in college," Sarah said carefully.

"No, I mean how you came out to your family."

"I don't really like to talk about it," Sarah said. She slapped Jen's butt. "Come on, lazy. We've been in bed all day. Let's get up and do something."

"We have been doing something. A few somethings," she chuckled.

"Another time. I'll tell you another time."

"Okay. But I love you, Sarah. I want to know everything about you."

"I promise. I'll tell you. Some other time."

☙☙❧❧

Jen rubbed her face slowly between Sarah's shoulder blades, then outlined each delicate vertebrae with her tongue. "Mmmmmmmm," she purred. She knew it was getting late, but was in no hurry to open her eyes.

"Mmmmmmmm yourself. That tickles," Sarah said. She wiggled her butt backwards, tightening up the spoons, then arched her back as Jen's hand cupped her breast.

"Does this tickle too?"

"Yes, inside my belly."

"How about this? And this?"

"Yes, oh yes."

"So how come you're not laughing?"

"Move your hand down a little. See? I'm smiling! All of me is smiling."

"That feels more like a grin," Jen said, her fingers tracing a delicate pattern.

"Grins, giggles, guffaws," Sarah said, her voice husky. "I might get hysterical if you keep doing that!"

"I like a cheerful woman," Jen said, moving faster.

※ ※ ※ ※

"Whew!" Sarah said.

"I'll second that."

"What time is it?"

Jen opened one eye and peered at the clock. "6:30."

"Oh, no! We have to get up!"

"Okay."

"You have to move first. I'm stuck to the wall!"

"Uh-uh," Jen said, burrowing deeper in the covers.

"No, really, I have to get back to the house. Grace is probably up already."

"So? Marie will take care of her."

"But that's my job!" she said. "I wasn't expecting to fall asleep again. I thought I'd be back by now! It's all your fault!"

"I didn't mean to distract you, ma'am," Jen said, reaching for her again.

"You are very distracting, you fool." Sarah smacked her lightly on the hip. "Now get up!"

"It's not right, I tell you. We should be able to stay in bed all day if we want." Jen pushed herself up and dangled her long legs over the side of the bed.

Sarah swung her legs over and stood up. "That would be sweet. Maybe I'll take a couple of days off when I'm done and we can do that." She started towards the bathroom.

"Done with what?" Jen grabbed her hand.

"With the job, of course."

"What do you mean, done with the job?"

"Well, honey, you know Grace isn't going to need me for much longer, probably just a couple more weeks."

"I don't understand. What happens then?"

"Well, I'll have to take another assignment from the agency. You know, another job."

Jen sprung to her feet, wringing her hands. "You mean you'll be leaving?"

"Well, yes. I have to work," Sarah said.

Jen's voice rose. "But what about us? We're just starting. How can you think about leaving?"

"There's probably no work for me here on the Island right now. But maybe I can find something close by here, or in Seattle. We'll still see each other."

"But we hardly get to spend time together now! Between your work schedule and mine, we're lucky if we get a few hours a week! And how could we be together like this?" She waved her hand at the bed.

"You know I want to be with you, but I have to earn a living," Sarah said, running her hands through Jen's brushy hair.

"Why don't you just get a regular job? You know, with a regular schedule."

"I don't want a regular job right now. I'm tired of working in a hospital, and there isn't one on the Island anyway. And where would I live?"

"We could work something out, Sarah." Jen gulped. "You could live here," she said, looking around the tiny apartment.

Sarah shook her head. "But we hardly know each other! I'm not a two-date U-Haul kind of girl. And I'm just barely out of my situation with Nancy. I just need to do my own thing for a while." She turned and moved into the bathroom, stepped into the shower stall, and turned on the spray.

Jen stepped in after her. "I can't believe this. I can't believe you could just walk away," she said over the pounding of the water.

"I'm not walking away," she said. She picked up the soap and began to lather herself.

Jen took the soap out of her hand, ran it across Sarah's back, and scrubbed her briskly with the washcloth. It was not the leisurely, exploratory wash they'd come to enjoy over the last couple of weeks. "You know I want to be with you."

"I want to be with you too. You know I have feelings for you," she said over the sound of the water. "But I'm not ready to make a commitment."

"So when are you leaving?" Jen was glad the water hid her welling eyes. She cupped her hands and splashed her face.

"I don't know anything yet. But right now, I have to get back. We can talk about this later," Sarah said, stepping out of the shower.

Silently, they dressed and left the apartment. Motorcycles don't allow for much conversation.

❧ ❧ ❧ ❧

Savannah pushed back her dish and sat back. It was still piled high with cherry cobbler, the rivulets of vanilla ice cream marbled with pink. "I give up! Honestly, ladies, I cannot fit in one more bite. But it's so good, I just want to keep eating! It's even better than your strawberry trifle!"

"Hummmph," Marie said, obviously pleased. "There were no leftovers that night, I can tell you that!"

"That's for sure." Grace chuckled.

Marie started picking up the plates. "There's nothing like cobbler and pie from a pie-cherry tree. Montmorency, I think they're called. People don't grow them so much anymore because they don't bake as much, I guess. But I love them. But if you try to eat them out of hand they will make you pucker up!"

"That's for sure," Grace said. "Pretty soon we'll have peach cobbler, and blackberry as well. Marie keeps the blackberry vines from taking over this place by making cobbler. Pick and chop, pick and chop. And then there's the jam, and syrup, and of course, the wine."

"Now we get a couple of the neighbors' kids to do it for us, but in the old days Annie and I would get out there with a picnic, our buckets and machetes, and come home covered with scratches at the end of the day, our hands and mouths blue…" Grace smiled, a far-off look in her eyes.

"And your clothes, just a mess!" Marie said.

"We'd be picking thorny little twigs and tiny spiders out of each other's hair for hours… It seems so long ago." Grace sighed. "And no, I don't miss those spiders!"

"I used to make those blackberry pancakes for the guests. Everybody seemed to like them," Marie said.

"We sure did. I remember them well. Carrie and I used to come out here for breakfast, especially when you'd have those literary weekends. We sure did enjoy them," Savannah said. "The pancakes, and the writers too! I loved listening to them talking about their work, and reading bits and pieces to everyone in the garden." She sighed.

"When you were out here last week we hardly got to talk, there was so much going on. I didn't even get to ask about Carrie," Grace said. "When did you see her last?"

"Saturday. I try to get out there pretty often, even though it's a waste of time," she said sadly. "Her family doesn't want me to see her, and her sister got a restraining order so I can't get close to her. It's been five years since the accident, and I go out there whenever I can…" She paused to dab at her eyes with her napkin. "She must think I abandoned her!" She sniffled. "Sorry! It just sneaks up on me sometimes." She blew her nose and dried her eyes again. "When we walked down to Annie's place the other day, I felt so lonely. Everyone else had someone but me. It's just not right. I miss her so much."

"Of course you do. I can't believe it happened so long ago. Such a sweet woman!" Grace said.

"It's a terrible thing," Marie said angrily. "After all the years you two spent together."

"I know. Twenty-one years!" Savannah said. "And now, when she really needs me, I can't be there for her." She reached for the plate of cobbler, took another bite, and sighed again.

"Every now and then, her brother sends me a note to tell me how she is, and he's even sent me a couple of pictures. I can imagine what her sister would say if she ever got wind of it! Carrie's in a wheelchair, of course, and she can't say much. I don't know how much sense she can make of things. But she's smiling in the pictures," Savannah said. "She looks different, though, like a child."

"We miss her too," Grace said. "She was a bright spirit."

"Yes indeed," Marie said.

"And she still is!"

"Of course, dear. I didn't mean to talk about her in the past tense," Grace said, apologetically.

"I do that, too. She's been gone for so long..." Savannah took a deep breath. "I want so much to be part of her life."

"As well you should be! You've been married in spirit for all these years, even if you couldn't legally say the words."

"I know. We did have that little ceremony years ago, and I've always felt married, even if it wasn't legal. And of course, we made out those domestic partnership papers, but they don't really mean much. But maybe someday..." Savannah said, dabbing at her eyes again.

"Well, you let us know if we can help you in any way. I would be happy to go up there and knock that bitch's block off!" Marie puffed up like a little banty hen.

Grace laughed. "Now that would be helpful!"

"Well, it would make me feel better!" Marie retorted.

"Me too!" Savannah said. "I wouldn't mind getting in a few punches myself." She glanced at her watch. "But it's getting late, ladies, and we need to talk business."

"Must we? It's such a lovely day," Grace said. "Just keep things the way they are. I think you're doing a fine job."

"Well, thanks, but things are changing, Grace," Savannah said, pulling a file folder out of her briefcase.

"We need to go over some things, make some plans."

"What kind of things? What plans?" Grace asked. She gathered her sweater tightly around herself.

"Well, we have your money invested in a number of different places to minimize your risk, and so far you've been able to manage pretty well," Savannah said. She handed Grace and Marie several pages of facts and figures. "But your expenses have gone up considerably in the last few months, especially with your medical bills and the changes you had to make to the house, like that stair climber. And of course, your insurance won't continue to pay for Sarah much longer. The taxes on the property are up, too. And you know you haven't had any real income since the bed and breakfast closed."

"Well, we have our Social Security, of course," Grace said.

"Yes, but you still have to pay for maintenance, and the gardeners, and the girl who comes in to clean, and the utilities are so high now. Your Social Security just won't cover everything."

"So what does that mean?" Marie asked. She shook the papers in her hand. "You know I don't understand any of this number stuff."

"Well, you're going to have to figure out some ways to cut your expenses," Savannah said. "And Grace may have to cash in some things."

"I see," Grace said quietly.

"But she can't do that! That's her security!"

"Our security," Grace said firmly.

"I know, and I would hate to see that happen. Have you ever thought of reopening the bed and breakfast? They're so popular now."

Grace paused for a moment. "You know, I've

thought about it many times. I miss having people around, and all the bustle. And I miss the dinners, too. So many good times…" She sighed. "But with Annie gone, and all the staff moved on – and you know, we're not young people anymore. It's hard for me to get around. And it would be very hard for Marie to get things started up again. It's so much work!"

"We could do it, Grace!" Marie said, excited. "We could start off slow. Maybe just a couple of rooms at first. We could serve dinners again, too! It would be fun!"

"Calm down, Marie," Grace said. "I hate to say this, but you're just remembering the good parts. Remember how much time you spent on your feet, cooking and cleaning? And watching out for the staff? And shopping, and keeping up with the guests? And the laundry! Whew! Just thinking about it makes me tired. We haven't got Annie to help us, either. And I know I couldn't keep up with all the other things," she said sadly. "No, I'm afraid our time for running this place as a bed and breakfast is long gone."

They all sat for a moment, lost in their own thoughts.

"I guess you're right, Grace. I miss it, but just thinking about it makes me ache," Marie said. "It could never be the way it was."

"And you have your work cut out for you just taking care of me!" Grace said.

"And you are quite a handful," Marie joked. She reached over and squeezed Grace's hand.

Savannah cleared her throat. "Of course, you could consider selling this place. Land values are up on the Island, and you could get a good price. It's such a big house for the two of you. And so much land!"

"No!" Grace said fiercely. "I could never sell this place! I lived here most of my life, and I'll die here too!" She slammed the papers down on the table. "And what about Marie? And Annie! No! We will never leave here!"

"Now, Grace, calm down. It was just a thought."

"Never, never," Marie said in a hoarse whisper.

Grace looked over at her. Marie's face was pale and contorted with pain, and her hand clutched her chest. "Marie, are you all right? Marie!" She tried to reach Marie, but couldn't get out of her chair. She grabbed for her hand. "Savannah, call Sarah, now!"

"Sarah! Sarah! Help!" Savannah yelled.

Sarah poked her head out of her room up the stairs. "What is it? What's the matter?"

"Sarah, it's Marie! Her heart!" Grace cried. "She needs her pills!"

Sarah disappeared, and a moment later came thundering down the stairs, a tiny brown bottle in one hand, a blood pressure cuff and stethoscope in the other. Quickly, she unscrewed the top, popped out a pill, and stuck it under Marie's tongue. "Take some deep breaths, Marie," she said. She reached for Marie's wrist and glanced at her watch. Her pulse felt weak and thready. She wrapped the cuff around her thin arm and pumped it up. "Hmmm," she said. She listened to her chest, then knelt beside her chair and rubbed her back gently. "Is the pain letting up?"

"A little," Marie gasped. Her face streamed with sweat.

Sarah took a napkin, dipped it in Marie's water glass, and gently dabbed her cheeks and forehead. She looked at her watch again. "It's been five minutes, Marie. Here's another pill." She popped it under

Marie's tongue. "Take slow, deep breaths. Easy does it."

Marie's face began to relax. "I'm feeling better now. The pain is going away."

Sarah checked her pulse again. It was stronger now, and more regular. Her face began to pink up. She checked her blood pressure again. "Do you want to go to the hospital, Marie?"

"No, no, I'm okay now. I don't need to go," she said. "This has happened before, and I've always been okay."

"Thank you, Sarah," Grace said. "I don't know what I'd have done if you hadn't been here. I certainly couldn't have gotten to her medicine."

"You should keep a couple of extra bottles around the house," Sarah said. "Upstairs and down. And it wouldn't hurt to have you carry a bottle in your pocket, Marie, or they make these little containers that you could wear around your neck."

"Hmmmph," she said. "I know I should, but I always forget. Hey, how did you know about those pills, anyway?" Marie asked. She looked almost back to normal now.

"Well, Grace mentioned that you had angina, and I figured that you probably kept nitroglycerin pills next to your bed," Sarah said. "I'm just glad it was there."

"Me too. Thank you, Sarah."

"You're welcome. Now, why don't you go upstairs and see if you can take a little rest, Marie. I'll give you a hand, then I'll clear off the table and put the things away."

"I'll help too," Savannah said.

"Thanks, you two," Marie said. "Sorry to spoil

the party. So long, Savannah. See you later, Grace."

"I'll be up in a few minutes, dear," she answered. "I just want to talk with Savannah for a little while longer."

"We'll never leave here, Savannah," Marie said. Sarah helped her up and they walked slowly away, Sarah's arm around her thin shoulders.

A moment later, they heard the grinding of the stair climber.

"Gosh, Grace, I'm so sorry. I didn't mean to upset the two of you!" Savannah said.

Grace shook her head. "No need to be sorry, dear. It wasn't your fault."

"I had no idea Marie was having problems," she said.

"It's angina. Most of the time she does pretty well, but she has to be careful about getting too tired, or too emotional. Usually the medicine takes care of it," Grace said.

"If I would have known, I never would have brought up this stuff in front of her," Savannah said.

"Well, this is her home too. But as you can see, we both feel strongly about staying here. Neither of us has any family left. All we have is each other. And we could never pack up our lives and move to another place."

"Okay. I'll look over the figures again, and see what I can come up with," Savannah said. "Thanks for the coffee and the wonderful cobbler."

"It was so nice to see you again," Grace said. "Come back soon!"

"I will. Meanwhile, let me know if there's anything I can do." Savannah stood. "Don't get up, now, Grace. I can find my way out."

"Nonsense. I'm just fine." She pushed herself out of her chair with the help of her cane. She smiled and took Savannah's arm and they walked slowly toward the door. She opened the door and reached up for a hug. The top of her head was barely even with Savannah's chin. She felt very fragile in Savannah's arms.

"You take care, now, dear." She lifted her hand to wave.

"I will, Grace. Thanks."

Savannah walked down the steps to the driveway. When she got to her car, she turned around to see Grace, still waving.

༄༄༄༄

Marie mopped her face with a damp cotton towel. That kitchen sure could hold some heat in the summer, especially when she had a lot of people to cook for, not that she liked to complain. Of course, she could have asked Grace to get an air conditioner in there, but she felt like she needed to keep a stiff – if sweaty – upper lip.

She cleaned the cornbread crumbs out of her favorite iron skillet carefully, and put it on the gas burner to dry off. She knew better than to wash it and scrub it like other pots and pans, or Goddess forbid, put it in the dishwasher. She and that skillet had been together for many years. They were old friends. They had history.

She began to feel a tightening in her chest, and tried to keep going. She wanted to finish the dishes quickly so she could lie down for a short while before she started the next round of peeling and chopping. Grace didn't know about these little 'rests', as Marie thought of them, and she wasn't about to tell her about them. Grace had enough to worry about.

She had to give in, though, and sat down in a kitchen chair to catch her breath. She hated any sign of weakness in herself. She looked on it as a sign of failure. If only she'd been stronger, her whole life might have been different. But then again, she never would have ended up here at The Meadows, which had given her both home and family for all these years.

After a few minutes, she pulled herself up and walked the few steps to her room. Slowly she lowered herself to the thick cotton bedspread, kicked off her shoes, and lay back. "Ahhhh," she sighed. The pain in her chest started easing up, and in spite of herself, she drifted off. Once again, she found herself in the kitchen where she'd grown up – at least partly grown, at fifteen.

Her parents were at work in their little general store, and it was Marie's job to start dinner when she got home from school. She didn't mind, though, because she loved to cook.

She set some chicken pieces into a dish of buttermilk, peeled some potatoes and cut them into chunks for frying, and snapped some green beans. Then she mixed up some cornbread as her mother had shown her, and put the cast iron frying pan into the oven to heat. It always tasted better and had a crisper crust if the pan was hot before she put the batter in.

She peeled some apples and put them into a baking dish for a crisp, then mixed up the oats, butter, and brown sugar for the crust. Finally, she put the chicken into the grease to fry, and poured herself a big glass of lemonade. It was hot in the kitchen.

She could hear tapping at the door, and went to

see who it was. A tall man stood outside the door. He pulled off his hat when her saw her, and she recognized him from the store. He worked at a farm a couple of miles down the road.

"Hi, there, Marie. How are you today?" he said, and smiled.

"Hi to you, James, is it?"

"That's right," he said, and smiled again. He was on the younger side of forty, and had crooked yellow teeth and dusty overalls. He caught sight of the lemonade in her hand. "Sure is hot today. Mind if I trouble you for some of that?" He nodded at the glass.

"Uh, sure," she said. She felt a little uneasy. It was unusual for people to come around while she was cooking dinner. "What can I do for you? Do you want to talk to my folks? They're down at the store."

"Oh, I just thought I'd come around and pay you a little visit," he said, stepping into the kitchen. "I seen you around the store, just thought I'd see how you were doing."

Her uneasiness increased, but her parents had taught her never to be rude.

She grabbed a towel, pulled the frying pan out of the oven, and poured the batter in. It sizzled as it hit the hot pan. "I'm doing fine, but I'm real busy with dinner right now," she said, then handed him a glass of lemonade. "If you could just drink up, I have to finish here. My parents will be home soon."

"Aren't you gonna ask me for dinner?" he asked. He came toward her, ran his hand down her arm. She flinched. "I bet you could cook me up something real good, couldn't you?"

She could smell liquor on his breath, and backed away. "Don't come any closer," she warned.

"Or what? What are you gonna do, little thing like you?"

He reached out and grabbed her, tried to kiss her. She twisted around, seized the hot pan, and flung it at him. They both screamed in pain, and he turned and ran out. "You bitch, I'll kill you!" he yelled as he ran.

She sank to the kitchen floor, clutching her hand. She could smell burned flesh – she did not know if it was his or hers. She had never known such pain.

Marie gasped as she struggled to surface from the dream as she had a thousand times before, her heart racing, aching.

※ ※ ※ ※

"Say, what do you think about moving Sarah into your old room so Jen can stay over sometime? Sarah goes to Jen's apartment house on her night off, but they only get to stay together once a week."

Marie got quiet for a moment. That room used to be her refuge, the only place she could go when things were hopping at the bed and breakfast. And now she could duck in there when she needed a little snooze, or when her heart started getting jumpy, like today. But she didn't want to tell Grace that.

"That's a good idea," she said finally. "It will give me an excuse to pack up my things. I haven't stayed overnight in that room for a long time." She paused. "Three years."

"Three wonderful years." Grace squeezed her hand. "I'll talk to Sarah about it."

※ ※ ※ ※

Sarah was reluctant to move downstairs. "What if you need me? I might not be able to hear you if you call! It's my job to be nearby, to help you, and keep you safe!" she said. "Both of you!"

"But Jen never stays over here," Marie said. "This way she could stay when she wanted to, and you two would have some privacy."

"And Marie and I could have some privacy, too," Grace said, and winked. "That's why we have modern technology, my dear. We can have an intercom, you know. And cell phones! So we could call you if we need you."

Sarah thought for a moment. "That would be great...I don't know. I don't even know if Jen would be comfortable here...I'll talk to her."

"If you just move downstairs, it will be a done deal. But there's one condition," Grace said.

"What's that?" Sarah asked.

"You don't listen in on us – and we won't listen in on you," Grace said.

"But I'm probably not going to be around here much longer," Sarah said. "I'll be looking for a new job soon."

"Let's just see what happens," Grace said.

Sarah called Jen that evening. "Guess what! Grace wants me to move downstairs so you can stay over when you want to!"

"Hey, that's terrific!" She paused. "Uh, how do you feel about it?"

"Well, I think it would be wonderful! We would be able to spend some more time together. Umm...do you think it would be a good idea?"

"Yes! You know how hard it is for me to let you go after you've been over to my place." She laughed.

"Then I wouldn't have to get up at the crack of dawn to get you home before I have to go to work!" she said.

"Or me to drive home in the van," she said. "Tell you the truth, I'm a little nervous about being so far away from them."

"That's what they make intercoms for, silly. You could hear them just fine if they needed you."

"Yes, that's what Grace said. But still..."

"And cell phones! No eavesdropping, though," Jen said.

"Who knows, maybe we could learn something!" Sarah said, with a wicked laugh.

※ ※ ※ ※

Sarah, Jen, and Carol helped move Marie's stuff up and Sarah's stuff down. They moved Marie's little bed to Sarah's old room too, and the big four-poster bed down. It was quite the challenge, but they finally got things squared away.

"Have a blast, you two," Carol said, and winked.

"We will. Thanks for your help!" Jen said.

Finally, they were alone, and tried out the bed in its new position. "This is a nice room, but I'm going to miss the balcony," Sarah said. "And that big bathroom!"

"So you would rather have a big bathroom than spend nights with me?"

"Of course not, you dope. I'm just saying..."

"And you have a good view of the lake from here, honey." Jen said. "Let's try it out tonight and see how you feel."

"Fine, I hope. I don't want to drag that bed around again!"

"No," Jen said. "I do want to drag you around on the bed, though."

Sarah was glad that Grace and Marie decided to go upstairs early that night, sherry in hand. Sarah and Jen were eager to try out their new space. They had tried out the new intercom system, and it seemed simple and foolproof, and they had their phones on the bedside table.

They inaugurated the new room very sweetly and lovingly, with maybe a few more moans and giggles than they'd made upstairs, and all was well. Afterwards, they lay in bed, talking.

"So you never finished telling me about how you came out," Jen said.

"Well, I told you about Sheila and Con and my experiences in college," Sarah said carefully. "And you know about Nancy, of course…"

"No, I mean how did you come out to your family?"

"Oh, let's not talk about them," Sarah said.

"Well, you have to tell me sometime. Just spit it out, get it over with!"

Sarah heaved a heavy sigh. "Oh, all right," she said. "But you know I don't like talking about this…"

"I know, I know!"

"Okay. By the time I finished college, I was tired of hiding who I was. Justin and I didn't hang out much anymore, and I dated a couple of women, but of course I never brought any of them home."

"Yes?" Jen said. "Go on."

"So finally I decided to get it out in the open and get it over with. I waited until I was back at the house on spring break, just about ready to go back to school, and we were having dinner, just me and my parents," she said. "I'll never forget it. My mom made my favorite dinner, lasagna, and she made these fresh rolls that I just loved. My mom is a really good cook."

"Yes," Jen said.

"After we finished eating, my mom brought out dessert, spumoni ice cream, my favorite. I was feeling really spoiled that night."

"So?"

"So I said, 'Mom and Dad, I have something to tell you.'" She paused, gathering her thoughts. "'You know Justin?'"

"'Of course, dear. You two have been dating forever.' Then my mom got all excited. 'Oh my God, are you two engaged? Finally! You're getting married!'

"'Hurray!' my dad said. 'Congratulations!'

"'Uh, no, no, Mom and Dad. That's not it. We're not getting married.'

"Instantly the joy left her face. 'Oh, no, did you two break up, dear? I'm so sorry!' my mom said.

"'No.' My ice cream was melting. 'Justin was never my boyfriend. He's gay. And I'm gay, too, Mom. A lesbian.'

"They were quiet for a few moments. 'What do you mean, honey? I don't understand!'

"'You know what gay means, Mom,' I said. 'I like women. I don't feel attracted to men. That's what a lesbian is.'

"'So...you've been lying to us all these years?' Mom started to cry. 'A lesbian? A pervert? A homosexual?'

"'A dyke? A manhater?' my dad said.

"'No, I don't hate men, Dad,' I said. 'I just like women. I love women. That's who I am.'

"My parents looked at each other. We were all

crying by then."

"Yes, so what happened?" Jen asked urgently.

"My mom started to yell. Told me to get out. Called me dirty, filthy! Told me I wasn't fit to be in the family. I can hear her words as if it was yesterday. She said, 'After all we've done for you, all these years, loved you, prayed with you, prayed for you – and you turn out like this? You throw yourself in the face of God! Sinner!'"

"Oh, no," Jen said.

"Yes! It was awful! I thought the truth was supposed to set you free! Hah!" She paused to collect herself, tears running down her face. "Then I looked over at my dad. He was crying, had his eyes covered with a handkerchief. I used to iron those handkerchiefs for him when I was growing up!"

"Oh, honey, I'm so sorry," she said. She tried to put her arms around Sarah, but she was as stiff as a board.

Gradually her tears dried and she was able to catch her breath.

"So what happened then? Did you ever make up?"

"No," Sarah said shakily. "That was the last time I was home. I packed up my car and went back to school. I guess they called my brothers and sister and told them the news." She took a deep breath. "I never saw any of them again."

❧❧❧❧

Grace, Marie, Sarah, and Carol sat around the table in the garden, having their usual cup of tea after Grace's physical therapy session. The garden was still beautiful, but the pinks and reds were starting to give way to oranges and golds.

Marie dished up slices of the plum tart she'd just made, spooned some freshly-whipped cream on top, and began to hand them around.

"I'm so bored, I could just scream!" The air was electrified around them as Grace shoved her teacup aside, sloshing the light green liquid onto the saucer and tablecloth. "I'm tired of sitting around till my backside is stiff and I'm tired of having everyone ask me if I'm hungry or if I moved my bowels today. And I'm tired of talking to all of you!" A single sob burst from her, and she dabbed angrily at her eyes with her lace-edged hanky.

The three women looked at her, startled. This was certainly not their usual Grace.

"Why, honey, what is it?" Marie reached out for her hand.

She pulled her hand out of Marie's reach. "I don't know. I'm just sick of this, I tell you! I want to go someplace, do something!" She beat her clenched fist against her thigh for emphasis.

"All right, all right!" Marie said. "Would you like to go to town? We could go to a movie."

"More sitting? No! And I see too much shoot-'em-up on the TV."

"How about a trip to Poulsbo? We could go down to the Central Market and pick out something nice to have for supper. Or maybe we could go down to the marina and have some coffee at the Pegasus," Marie said, ticking off ideas on her fingers. "Oh, I know! We could go visit Rachel the weaver. You said you wanted to see her shop."

"That sounds like a good idea. What do you

think? We could take your wheelchair in the van in case you get tired," Sarah said.

Grace sniffled, then blew her nose. "Oh, I don't know. Maybe. Let's just get out of here!"

"How about going to see your friend in the hospital," Sarah said. "The one you were talking about at the luncheon. What was her name?"

"Edna. Edna Rogers," Marie said.

"That would be wonderful!" Carol said. "I know she would be happy to see you!"

"Well, I don't know. Maybe," said Grace, doubtfully.

"She's not in the hospital anymore, though," Carol said. "She's at the Manor. In fact, she's one of my patients. I'm scheduled to see her this afternoon."

"Edna in a nursing home! Well, I can't imagine," Marie said.

"Well, come on, time's a'wastin'," Grace said briskly. "I'm not getting any younger, you know. Marie! Wrap up some of that plum tart! Carol! Cut some flowers! Sarah! Bring the van around! We're going on a road trip!"

❧❧❧❧

Sarah drove carefully around the hills and curves of Lavender Lane as they headed toward the Agate Pass Bridge, the tiny span that connected Bainbridge Island to Poulsbo and the rest of the Kitsap Peninsula. Grace rode shotgun, clutching her cane in her knobby fingers. Carol followed close behind in her little car, Marie sitting beside her. Sarah could see Marie's mouth moving and her arms waving in the rear view mirror. Carol was shaking her head. Apparently, Grace was not the only one who had things on her mind.

Grace rolled down the window and stuck her face out in the breeze. "Ah, it's good to get out in the fresh air," she sighed.

"Grace, you are outside for hours every day when the weather is nice. It's not like you are a prisoner in the house," Sarah said, casting her a sideways glance. "What's really bothering you?"

"I don't know. Cabin fever, maybe. I'm just tired of all this. Sitting around is making me feel old." She laughed. "Well, of course, I *am* old. But I guess I'm just noticing it more now."

Sarah frowned. "Why do you think that is? Physically you're doing very well."

"I just don't have any reason to do anything. It doesn't matter if I sit in my chair all day, or nap all afternoon. I'm used to being busy, doing things for myself!" She thumped her cane of the floor of the van.

"This is a big adjustment, I know," Sarah said.

"You're not kidding! If I need something, you are there to help me, and of course, Marie would be right beside me every minute of the day if she could. That woman would chew my food for me if I'd let her."

Sarah laughed. "She loves you very much. You two are so sweet together." For a moment, she flashed on what she and Jen would be like at that age after years together. She could see Jen as a feisty old lady.

"I know she loves me, and of course I love her too. But I feel like I've lived past my purpose."

Sarah looked over at her, concerned. In her experience, when people felt they had no reason to live, they often died shortly after. She couldn't bear the thought of that happening to someone as vital and alive as Grace. "Well, what kinds of things do you miss doing?"

"Well, I used to enjoy running the house, making sure everything was going smoothly. There was so much to do! I worked on keeping the reservations straight, and I checked the rooms, saw about the linens, ordered the supplies, helped Marie with the menus, all kinds of things. And I kept the books, too. Of course, Annie needed help with the gardens and the buildings – a million details. And just having her around, being with her every day..." She stopped talking abruptly as her breath caught in her throat. Tears welled in her eyes again. She fished around for a handkerchief in her purse. "Damn it, damn it," she said, softly.

"You've had a busy life," Sarah said.

"Yes. Then of course, when Annie got sick, we took care of her. That took every ounce of strength I had. It was a long, slow process, and she was in so much pain. It was so hard to watch her slip away. And of course, Marie worked like a dog until we decided we had to close the place. It was awful."

"I'm so sorry," Sarah said. "You've had so many things happen, had to make so many changes."

"Yes," said Grace. "I suppose so. Of course, it's been wonderful being with Marie now. I don't know what I'd do without her. But I think she also feels pretty useless now. She can't even take care of me the way she'd like. We're just two old ladies sitting in that great big house." She blew her nose and tucked her handkerchief back in her purse. "Take this road to the left and you'll see it up there," she said.

Sarah smiled when she saw the Viking Manor sign at the end of the driveway. There were plenty of Scandinavians in the little town.

The long brick building sported bright green

shutters and window boxes filled with the last of the begonias and geraniums. Several people in wheelchairs were sitting around on the flagstone patio area in the shade of a huge cedar tree. She pulled into the visitor's parking area, and Carol pulled in right behind her. Sarah was surprised for a moment. She'd been so intent on her conversation with Grace she'd forgotten that Carol and Marie were following them.

"Well, this looks like a nice place," she remarked.

"It's a nursing home!" Grace sniffed, then shrugged. "I guess it's not bad for what it is. You know I was in here for a couple of weeks when I first got out of the hospital. It was noisy all the time, and the food was terrible, of course. I couldn't wait to get out of there and get back to my home."

"I bet," Sarah said. "Of course, you've been spoiled by Marie's cooking." She walked around the van and opened the door. "Here, let me give you a hand."

Grace grabbed Sarah's hand, hoisted herself out, and took a moment to steady herself with her cane.

Carol and Marie joined them. "I saw you two gabbing away in the rearview mirror," Grace said. "What were you two talking about?"

"You, of course," Marie retorted. "How bratty you are."

Grace's face crumpled. "I'm sorry, dear," she said. "I don't mean to be ill-tempered."

Marie put her arm around her. "Oh, Grace, I didn't mean it. I know you're just feeling out of sorts, and I don't blame you. Come on, now, let's go in."

"I hate going back in there," Grace said. "But I do want to see poor Edna."

Sarah opened the glass door for Marie and Grace.

The lobby was pleasant enough, with flowered couches and pale pink carpeting. Pictures of flowers, puppies, and kittens covered the walls. A couple of residents watched a quiz show on a big, flat-screen TV. There was a faint tang of disinfectant in the air.

The receptionist smiled when she saw them. "Well, hello, Mrs. Meadows. How nice to see you! How are you doing?"

"Very well, Sharon, thank you. We're here to see Edna Rogers today."

"Well, I know she'll be happy to have some company. She's in room 108."

Grace held on to Marie's arm as they walked down the hall, carefully avoiding the residents sitting in wheelchairs or moving slowly along, holding the handrail. Sarah dropped back to walk beside Carol. "Wow, it looked like Marie was giving you an earful," she said.

Carol nodded. "Yeah, Grace is not the only one having a hard time. Poor Marie is feeling pretty frustrated herself."

"I guess I can't really blame them," Sarah answered. "I know I'd be feeling down myself if I was in their situation."

"Yes, poor Marie is so worried about Grace," Carol said. "She wants to help her, but she feels like there's nothing much she can do."

"Yeah, Grace said she feels there is no purpose to her life."

"Oh, that's not good," Carol said.

"No. And I'm kind of worried about Marie. She hasn't been feeling too hot either," Sarah said, thinking about the day of Savannah's visit. She hadn't heard anything more from Marie about chest pain, but Sarah noticed her leaning against the wall a couple of times, catching her breath. Once she'd even caught her using the stair lift, which embarrassed her tremendously.

Carol sighed. "I hate to hear that. I love those ladies."

"Me, too," Sarah said. Suddenly, she realized it was true.

Carol looked at her watch. "I think I'll see one or two patients before I go to Edna's. Give you folks some time to visit." She turned and walked off.

Edna sat propped up in bed, pillows under her swollen left arm. Her stiff white hair stood up like a rooster comb, and the neck of her blue nightgown was askew. The skin on her arms was pale, but peeling as if from a sunburn. Sarah reached out her right hand. Sarah noticed how the left side of her face drooped, as if caught up by a different kind of gravity. But the right side of her face was smiling, and her dark eyes sparkled when she caught sight of Grace and Marie.

Sarah got some chairs and placed them on the side of the bed for the ladies.

"Edna, I'd like you to meet Sarah, my nurse," Grace said. "She's been taking care of me since I broke my hip."

"Hello, Edna," Sarah said. "Nice to meet you."

"Aaaaahhh," Edna answered. She bobbed her head a little, then turned back to her friends. "Aaaaaaaaahh," she said again. She reached out her left hand toward them. Marie took it in her own and gave it a little squeeze.

"I'm sorry it's been so long since we've seen you, dear." Grace leaned over and straightened Edna's nightgown. "I've been laid up at home for a couple of months since I broke my hip. And I just heard about your stroke a few days ago."

"Mmmmmmmmmmmm." Edna screwed up her face in concentration. "Grace," she said clearly then, and gave her a crooked smile.

"That's right! How wonderful. My dear, you'll be back to your old self in no time."

Suddenly, Edna's mouth turned downward and a couple of big tears tracked down the furrows in her cheeks. She shook her head. "No," she said.

Grace and Marie looked at each other, uncomfortable. They didn't want their friend to be upset, but it was hard to know what to say.

"Well, hello, ladies! What a nice surprise!" They all turned toward the doorway to see a short pillowy woman with lacquered blond curls

Edna bounced up and down in excitement. "Gin! Gin!" she cried.

Ginny rolled into the room and gave Edna a resounding kiss on the forehead. Gently she smoothed back her hair. "Hello, love."

"Ginny! So nice to see you," Grace said. "We just heard about what happened with Edna the other day."

"We appreciate you coming out. Edna loves to have visitors," she said. "I heard you were laid up yourself, Grace."

"Yes, I slipped in a pile of goose poop out by the lake. Disgusting! But I'm on the mend now, thanks to Marie, and to Sarah, my nurse. Sarah, this is Ginny, Edna's partner."

Sarah nodded at her. "Nice to meet you."

"We brought you some plum tart, girls. I made it myself just this morning," Marie said. She unwrapped a slice of tart and took a couple of forks and paper plates out of her bag.

"Why thank you, Marie. It looks delicious," Ginny said. She sighed and patted her ample stomach. "I always did have a weakness for your pastries."

Marie passed her a plate and started cutting a second slice.

"Just one plate is enough, thanks. We can share." She prodded off a corner and popped it into her mouth. "Yum!" she said. "Look, sweetheart, Marie made us a special treat!"

Edna gurgled with pleasure. Ginny spread a towel across Edna's shoulders and chest and raised the head of her bed. She loaded a small chunk onto the fork and moved it toward Edna's mouth. "Take your time, dear. Be careful now." She deposited the bit of tart in Edna's mouth. "Chew now, honey," she said.

"Mmmmmmmmmm!" Edna said. She grinned crookedly and began to chew. Plum juice and crumbs leaked from the corner of her mouth. Ginny dabbed at it with a corner of the towel.

"Take your time, dear," she said, and delivered another morsel.

Suddenly Edna began to choke. She grabbed at her throat with her good hand as her face became dusky. Her eyes bulged as she attempted to cough, but no air came through. Tears streamed down her face as she fought for breath.

"Help!" Ginny yelled.

Sarah pushed her way to the side of the bed and grabbed Edna. She pulled her around sideways so Edna's back was against her chest and gave her a couple of quick abdominal thrusts beneath her rib cage.

"Huh!" Edna gasped as the bit of tart shot out of her mouth and hit the wall. She took a deep shuddering breath and coughed. Her face began to pink up.

Ginny threw her arms around her. "Oh, darling, are you all right?" She mopped at Edna's face with the towel, then dabbed at her own tears. "You scared me half to death!"

She turned to Sarah. "Thank you so much. I'm so glad you were here!"

"Me, too. I know a lot of people have trouble swallowing after a stroke."

"Yes, she's working on that with a speech therapist. She hasn't been eating much solid food yet." She shuddered. "I hate to think what could have happened if you hadn't been here." She looked back at Edna, whose color was almost back to normal.

Carol appeared in the doorway. "What's going on in here? What are you doing to my patient?"

"Oh, nothing much," Grace said. "We were just trying to kill Edna with a piece of tart."

Carol looked at them askance. "Well, I'm glad you didn't succeed."

"No, Sarah jumped in and saved the day," Ginny said. "She put the squeeze on her. She's a hero."

"A shero," Carol said, grinning.

"I was channeling Florence Nightingale," Sarah said. "And Dr. Heimlich!"

Edna smiled as best she could.

"Enough slacking off now, Edna." Carol shook her finger with mock sternness. "Time for you to do some work. How else are you going to get well?"

"Well, we should get out of the way, Grace, and let these women do their thing," Marie said.

"Yes, of course. Edna, you take care of yourself. We'll come back to see you again soon." She pushed herself up with cane and bent to give Edna a quick kiss.

Marie kissed her too and they turned toward the

door.

"Wait a second, I'll walk out with you so Carol and Edna can do their work," Ginny said. "I'll be right back, sweetheart." She smiled and waved at Edna.

The four women walked back slowly toward the lobby, Grace and Marie arm-in-arm.

"You poor thing. This must be terrible for you, for both of you," Marie said.

"Oh, it is, it's awful," Ginny said. Her breezy manner had disappeared. "You know what a ball of fire she is, and now she is stuck like this. It breaks my heart." She sighed. "Here, why don't you sit down with me for a few minutes? It's so long since I've seen you." She steered them toward a group of pink wing chairs.

"Were you with her when she had the stroke?" Sarah asked.

"No, I was visiting my son and his family for a couple of days. They live up in Bellingham. I tried to call Edna on the phone, but I couldn't get her and I started to worry. Thank goodness, I decided to come back a little early. She was in the bathtub when the stroke hit her. I don't know how long she was in the water, but it must have been at least a full day and night. It's a miracle she didn't just die from the stroke, or drown."

"Or have hypothermia," Sarah said.

"No, apparently she was able to turn on the hot water with her foot when she got cold. The doctors were amazed that she was able to do that. She did get pneumonia, though, but she seems to be recovering from that now. She's a tough old gal. But you probably noticed her skin. She was so waterlogged." Ginny sighed. "Do you remember how beautiful her skin was? Thick and white as a magnolia petal, not a pore on her."

Grace and Marie nodded. "She was lovely," Marie said.

"Yes, and she always took good care of herself," Grace added

"Well, she's doing better now. When this first happened, she couldn't talk at all. Of course, now she's starting to realize that her life – both our lives – are changed forever," Ginny said bitterly.

Sarah sighed as she thought about the conversation she'd had with Grace earlier. At least Grace's mind was still sound. She knew how depressed people with strokes tended to be, and how quickly their moods changed. Many of those who lived had at least partial recoveries, especially if they received treatment and physical therapy immediately, but others progressed to a certain point and no further.

"So what will happen now? Will she just be staying here?" Grace asked.

"I don't know what else to do," Ginny said. Her face crumpled. "I hate to keep her in here, but she's not stable yet. And she still needs therapy. I just don't know what's going to happen. She doesn't want to be here. She cries every day when I have to leave. She wants to go home."

"I understand," Grace said. "I was in here myself for a couple of weeks after I broke my hip. It's not a bad place, but it's certainly not home. And I was able to talk and ask for what I needed. I wasn't really sick. Just broken."

"Could you care for her at home?" Sarah asked.

Ginny shook her head. "I'd like to, but I don't think I'll be able to do it."

"It's not easy to care for a stroke patient. You

would need a lot of help."

"I'm a teacher, too, and I'm still working. I can't retire for another three years. And our funny little house. We've been living there forever, but it's not really a good place for someone who's sick. The bedrooms are upstairs and the bathroom is downstairs. The stairs are narrow and so are the doorways. There's no way to use a wheelchair in there. I just don't know what we're going to do." She wiped angrily at her eyes. "Oh, hell. I hate to cry, and it seems like all I do lately."

Marie shook her head. "What about your families? Can they help you at all?"

"Why, there's hardly anyone left, you know. And those that are don't want to have much to do with two crazy old dykes."

"Dear me," Grace said. "I wish there was something we could do."

"You have your own troubles," Ginny said.

They were quiet after they left Viking Manor, each lost in her own thoughts. Finally, Sarah broke the silence. "Are you okay, Grace? Are you tired?" she asked. "And how about you, Marie?"

"No, not tired, just a little sad," Grace said. "But I'm not ready to go back home yet."

"I know! Let's go see Rachel in her shop!" Marie said. "We haven't been anywhere in a long time."

"Oh, that sounds like fun!" Sarah said. "Where is it?"

"Oh, it's in Poulsbo, not too far from here. Just take that road to the left."

They followed the road through the little town, checking out the art galleries, Scandinavian shops, and bakeries. Finally, they pulled up in front of a little red house with blue shutters and a picture of a spinning wheel on a hanging sign. "Oh, it's so cute," Sarah said.

Silvery bells rang out when they opened the door, and Rachel stepped out of the back and greeted them with a welcoming smile. Her strawberry blond curls, bedecked with several blue and green fluffs, were caught up in a chopstick, and her glasses hung from a twisty purple cord. "What a nice surprise! I'm so glad to see you!" she said, giving hugs all around. "How nice to see you up and around, Grace!"

"Yes, we had to stop and see your beautiful things!" Grace said, admiring the counters and walls filled with shawls, scarves, sweaters, and bags in muted earthy colors.

"And we brought you some plum tart," Marie said, handing her a dish.

"Oh, thank you! Do look around, please! And there's more stuff in the back room. I'll make some tea!"

Slowly they made their rounds, touching everything and exclaiming over the beautiful textures and hues. "Oh, I love these things!" Sarah said. She was picturing Jen in the knitted burgundy ski sweater and made a mental note for her Christmas list. "What an artist she is!"

They sipped chai tea out of thick earthenware mugs while they told Rachel of their visit to Edna.

"What a bummer!" Rachel said. "It's awful when you have to be separated from someone you love." She paused. "I don't even know if I could fall asleep without Emily in the bed!"

"What about those calls she gets in the middle of the night, people having babies and such like?" Marie said.

"Well, that's different. I know she's going out to

help somebody. I don't mind that!"

Sarah bought the sweater and a beautiful basket just the right size for Margret. "Now, don't say anything to Jen about this sweater," she said. "I'm going to give it to her for Christmas.

"Christmas is a long way off," Grace teased. "You must be planning to keep seeing her."

"Oh, yes," Sarah said, smiling. "She's a keeper!"

❧❧❧❧

The women lay tightly entwined, foreheads touching, as their breathing slowed. Sarah could still feel a few tiny sparkles jumping from nerve to nerve as her body gradually solidified.

"Hey," she said experimentally, surprised that she was still capable of making a sound.

"Hey yourself," Jen said. She took a deep, trembling breath. "Your eyelashes feel like little butterflies. Tickly."

Sarah laughed softly, then touched her tongue to Jen's glistening cheek. "Salty," she said. "And so sweet."

"I can't move. You melted my bones!"

"A marrowing experience," Sarah said.

Jen groaned. "How can you do that? My brain is not even working yet."

Sarah moved her head back far enough to see that Jen now had two eyes. "What brain?"

Jen smacked her smartly on the rear. "Smartass."

"Ow!" Sarah cried.

"Oh, I'm sorry. Did that hurt? Here, let me rub it for you."

Sarah giggled as Jen's hand began to move, then she reached back and grabbed her wrist. "I think you've rubbed me quite enough for today, young lady."

"But not the wrong way, I hope."

"No, definitely the right way." She grinned and began to untangle herself from the jumble of arms, legs, and sheets. Their sweaty bodies parted reluctantly. "Whew!" she said, sat up, and crossed her legs, yoga style. She laughed. "Uh, so how was your day, dear?"

"Well, this clown in a Hummer almost ran me over today," Jen said. "He was in such a hurry to get off the boat he wasn't looking where he was going."

"Wow, that's scary. I worry about you getting hit by crazy men with crazy cars…"

"And crazy women's car doors…"

Sarah laughed, thinking back on how she and Jen had met on the ferry. "Maybe I was just trying to get your attention."

"Now wait just a minute. There's a big difference between hitting and hitting on," Jen said. "You did get my attention, though, that's for sure."

"It's a good thing that Carol invited me to that party. Otherwise we never would have gotten together," Sarah said.

"Kismet," Jen said. "We were meant to be."

"Do you believe that? Do you think people are really meant to find each other?"

"I don't know. I'd like to think so." She picked up Sarah's hand and pressed it to her lips. "Being with you seems so right. I feel like I've known you forever."

She ruffled Jen's spiky hair. "I feel that way too." She sighed. "I wonder if we'd feel the same if we'd been together for a long time."

"What do you mean?"

"Well, Grace decided she wanted to go see her friend Edna in the nursing home today, so we went over for a while. It was heartbreaking. She seems like a sweet old lady. Edna's paralyzed on one side, and sometimes she's able to talk and sometimes she's not. It's hard to know how much she understands about what's going on."

"Poor thing!"

"Really. You know how in wedding ceremonies they say that thing about 'in sickness or in health'? If people could see how things were going to be years down the road, maybe nobody would get married."

"That might be true of some people, but not everyone," Jen protested. "I think most people who get married really commit to be in it for the long haul."

"That's a pretty optimistic view, considering the divorce rate," Sarah said. "But maybe dykes are different. I don't know. While we were there, Edna's partner Ginny came in to see her. I guess they've been together for years. You should have seen how Edna perked up when she saw her. They still seemed to love each other."

"Sweet," Jen said. She scooted across the bed and put her head in Sarah's lap.

"Yes, it was. But now everything is changed for them. Ginny was talking about how hard it was going to be to take care of Edna if she leaves the nursing home. She's still working, and she can't retire yet. It's a very tough situation."

"Hmmm," Jen said. "That is tough."

Sarah traced the delicate line of Jen's vertebrae with a fingertip. "I would take care of you," she said seriously, then laughed. "Although you'd probably be a terrible patient!"

"I bet you'd be happy to boss me around," Jen said.

"I would. But you probably wouldn't listen to me."

"I would certainly listen if it meant we could stay in bed all the time." She rubbed her head against Sarah's belly while she hummed to herself.

"Hey!" she said suddenly. "Maybe you could get a job taking care of Edna when you finish up here! You could stay with them, and you would still be on the Island," Jen said, excited. "We could still hang out."

Sarah shook her head. "That would be great. But Ginny was saying that their house wasn't set up for that. It's a little place, the bedrooms are upstairs and the bathroom is downstairs. It just wouldn't work. I don't think Ginny will ever be able to bring her home."

"Too bad. That would have been really fine." Jen said.

"Yes. Now Grace's house would be perfect. It's set up really well. The rooms are big and there are several bathrooms upstairs and down. And there's the stair master. I bet you could have five or six patients in the house at a time."

"Yes. It's probably not really that different from having a bed and breakfast, only the people would actually be living there. And you could take care of them, Ms. Nursy Nurse."

Sarah laughed. "Now wait a minute. It's not that easy. I couldn't take care of a house full of people by myself."

"No, of course not. Wouldn't it be cool, though?"

"Yes," Sarah said. "Maybe. I don't know. But you know Grace and Marie would never go for it. It's their home."

Grace sat in her wing chair, her feet propped up on her ottoman. Margret lay across her lap, purring contentedly, as the theme from "Law and Order" filled the room. "Hurry, Marie, our show is starting."

"I'm coming, I'm coming," Marie said. She set the red Chinese tray with its customary glasses of milk and plate of cookies on the table between them. She also took two little crystal glasses from the lacquered cabinet and poured out some sherry.

"Cheers!" they said as they clinked glasses.

"What kind of cookies do we have tonight?" Grace asked.

"Oatmeal raisin. I made them this morning." She handed one to Grace.

"Delicious," she said with a smile. "I'm surprised Sarah left any. You know how hungry she gets when she spends the night over at Jen's." She broke off a piece of cookie and held it under Margret's inquisitive nose. In a split second, the morsel was gone.

Marie snorted. "Sugar babies. If those two lived together they'd probably be huge by the end of the first year."

"Not if they keep burning off the calories the way they've been doing," Grace said with a wicked grin.

"Well, they don't get to spend that much time together. Just a couple of nights a week."

"I know. I feel kind of bad about that, like we're keeping them apart." Grace reached for her sherry and took another sip. "A bit more tipple, I think, dear."

Marie pulled a silver flask out of the pocket of her fuzzy blue bathrobe and poured a healthy dollop into each of their glasses. "Why not!" she said.

"We must keep up our strength!" Grace raised

her glass. "I know. Let's drink to Edna. May she recover soon."

"Hear, hear! And to Ginny. They have a hard road ahead of them." Silently they drank.

"I wish there was something we could do to help them. I hate to think of Edna stuck in that place. You know how she is. I hated it, and I was just there for a couple of weeks."

"I know, and I hated to leave you there with strangers. And come back to this empty house." Marie shuddered.

"We were lucky we could work out having Sarah come to stay with us. I've really come to think of her as a friend."

"Me too," Marie said. "She's a dear. And to find that she is family, too!"

"And you gave her such a hard time in the beginning, you old bat."

"Here's to old bats," Marie said, raising her glass again. You, me, Edna, and Ginny."

"Hear, hear," said Grace, and tossed back a swallow. "You know, I'm really going to miss her."

"Mish who?"

"Sarah, of course. When she leaves."

"Oh. Yes. Well, maybe she could get another job around here, so we could still she her." She frowned. "See her," she corrected herself, then lifted her glass again. "Hey! I know. She could go work for Edna and Ginny. When Edna gets out of the Old Bat Home."

"Honey, you remember what that house is like. We could barely fit our poker game in the dining room. And they have all those stairs. It would never work." She broke off another bit of cookie for the cat, then poured a tiny bit of milk into the plate and held it out for her. She sniffed at it delicately, then lapped it up quickly with her pink tongue.

"We're all gonna sleep good tonight, Gracie," Marie said with a chuckle. Suddenly she sat up straight. "Why, hey! Say! Let's bring her here!"

"Bring who? What are you talking about?"

"Edna! Sarah could take care of her here!"

The two women looked at each other as a million scenarios raced through their head. Of course. Suddenly everything seemed so obvious.

"Hear, hear!" they said, and drained their glasses.

❧❧❧❧

"There's something we'd like to discuss with you, dears," Grace said. She looked across the wide table at Sarah and Jen. Her spoon clinked softly against the flowery porcelain teacup.

"Sounds serious," Sarah said.

"Well, yes, I guess it is." She cleared her throat and looked over at Marie, who nodded encouragingly.

"You've helped me so much, Sarah. Of course, you made me work very hard, and you didn't let me sit around and feel sorry for myself."

"Well, you are a great patient. And it wasn't just me. Marie and Carol were great helps, too."

"Yes. And Jen, I've appreciated your help as well. The four of you got me back on my feet again, and now I'm almost as good as new," Grace said.

Sarah and Jen exchanged glances. They knew the time had come. Jen felt a sudden wrenching in her gut, and her eyes stung for a moment. She ducked her head, embarrassed.

Sarah took a deep breath to calm herself. The

thought of leaving these women was very hard. "I know you don't really need me anymore, and I'll be moving on soon," she said softly. She looked at all three of them in turn, her eyes lingering on Jen for an extra moment. "I just want to tell you how much I've enjoyed working with you and getting to know you. You are my friends."

"Well, that's just it," Marie said loudly. She banged her hand down on the table, making the cups jump. "We don't want you to leave either!"

"Oh, thank you so much. I appreciate your saying that." Sarah said. "Maybe I can find another job close by, and I'll still be able to come and visit you."

Jen made a sound halfway between a snort and a sob.

"No, really. We don't want you to leave." Grace took a deep breath, then they both started talking in a rush. "Marie and I...you know we have this big house..."

"Empty, with just us here..." Marie added.

"And we thought, maybe we could do something..."

"Bring some life to this old place!"

"Maybe you could help us..." Grace appealed to them.

"We thought that if we could get a few people like Edna..."

"You are such a good nurse; you could take care of them..."

"And then you wouldn't have to go!" Marie finished triumphantly.

"Whew!" The two old ladies stopped and looked at each other, then looked at Sarah expectantly. "Well, what do you think?"

"I, uh, well, hmmm. Well. I don't know. You want to open the house to other people, like, an adult family home, or something? Hmmm," Sarah said.

Jen started laughing, softly at first, then louder and louder, thinking back on the conversation they'd just had. Then Grace started, then Marie. Sarah looked from one to the other, frowning at first, then slowly her face relaxed into a big grin.

"So then I could stay here," she said.

"Yes, yes, you and Ms. Margret too." Grace chuckled. She dabbed at her eyes with a napkin.

"I could keep working here," she said.

"Yes," Marie said.

She shook her head slowly in disbelief. "It's a lot to think about," Sarah said.

"Yes, but we could do it! Savannah could help us, and Carol, and Dr. Emily…"

"And you wouldn't have to leave," Jen chimed in. "We could still be together."

"Yes," Sarah, Grace, and Marie said together.

Jen closed her eyes for a moment. "Thank you, Goddess!" she said. "Thank you, ladies." She nodded at Grace and Marie. She got to her feet, pulled Sarah up, and gave her a resounding kiss. "Thank you, my love." The she turned, pulled Grace and Marie out of their chairs, and swept them all into a slow and stately dance.

༄༄༄༄

Savannah reached across the bed, her hand patting the empty pillow beside her. She sighed. After all this time she knew she should be used to waking alone, but part of her brain, or her heart, would not accept the truth.

"Old fool," she muttered, opening her eyes.

At the sound of her voice, Isis jumped on her chest, purring loudly, and began to knead away with her multicolor paws. "Ow!" she said. "That hurts!" She rolled the cat off her chest as she did every morning and began to massage her back and belly. "I swear, I'm going to have you declawed. I mean it!" she said. The cat purred louder. "Just kidding, really."

Finally, she swung her legs over the side of the bed and rubbed the sleep out of her eyes. She was so glad it was Saturday, that she wouldn't have to jump out of bed and stuff herself into her business persona, a task her feet vigorously objected to. She could just take her time today.

She padded to the bathroom and peered out the window. It was still early, but it had the makings of another beautiful day. She began to feel hopeful, optimistic. Maybe today would be the day. Maybe today it would be different.

She took a quick shower and put on some weekend clothes, jeans that had seen many washings and a soft cotton shirt with dancers in long patterned robes. She brushed back her graying hair, marveling at the changes in her face. She had looked the same to herself for so many years. Now she thought she looked different, older somehow, every day. She shook her head.

She fed Isis and put a bagel in the toaster. She couldn't stand the bagels at the Safeway – rolls with holes, she called them – preferring to go to Bagel Oasis or one of the other bagel shops in Seattle. Sometimes she was lucky enough to score a bialy or two, but it was hit and miss. There weren't enough people who were familiar with them to make them popular yet, but she had hopes.

She walked out into the garden where the hollyhocks were blooming and inhaled their fresh scent. She had white ones, pink ones, and dark purple ones, her favorites. She clipped off several stalks heavy with blooms and put their stems in a plastic bag with a bit of water and closed it with a rubber band. She grabbed her keys, her purse, and the flowers and headed out to the garage, noticing that the Subaru had a light coating of pollen. Time for a wash, she thought. She backed out slowly, waving at Fred, who was starting his mowing early today. She drove down the familiar street, feeling that her car could find its way to the place they'd driven so many times before. Her mind raced as she parked the car – maybe today would be the day. Maybe today it would be different. She pulled her shoulders back, put a smile on her face, and marched through the entrance. The woman at the reception desk smiled and nodded at her, and Savannah nodded back. They didn't need to speak to each other anymore.

She walked down the long corridor to the nurse's station. Judy was on duty today. The nurses rotated weekends, and she knew all of them in the rotation.

"How are you doing today, Savannah?" she asked politely.

"I'm fine, Judy, how are you? How's it going?" She nodded toward the door to the left of the nurse's desk.

"Just about the same, sorry," Judy answered.

"Did you hear from anyone this week? Did anyone come in?"

"No, nobody came. No word from anyone. Sorry. My, those are lovely hollyhocks. And they smell so good!"

"Yes, they are from our yard. I love this time of year, and Carrie does too."

"I know she'll be glad to see them," Judy said. She stood up and reached for the flowers.

Savannah handed her the bouquet and a tiny candy bar from her purse. She followed Judy to the hall opposite the closed door and stood while she swung back the door. "Good morning, Sunshine," she said to the pretty white-haired woman in the bed. "See what's come for you today!"

Savannah could hear a loud laugh coming from the room. She edged over until she could see the figure in the bed try to reach for the flowers.

"Pitty! Pitty!" she said, and laughed again.

Judy took the vase from the window ledge and dumped last week's flowers into the trash. She rinsed the vase, put the hollyhocks in, and set it back in its place. "There now," she said. "Now you can see them."

"Pitty! Pitty! Ummmm!" Carrie said.

Savannah felt her eyes well up, and the tears traveled down the well-worn tracks in her face as she turned and slowly walked away.

≈≈≈≈

Savannah drove slowly back toward her house, but somehow she didn't feel like being alone today. On impulse, she decided to drop in and see how Grace was doing.

Marie was glad to see her, as always. Savannah gave her a quick hug, marveling at her delicate, bony frame. The years had diminished her once stocky figure. She remembered how her face had looked in the mirror that morning, and smiled grimly to herself. Nobody was immune. Better to die young, maybe. Maybe not.

"You're just in time for lunch," Marie said. "Why don't you go upstairs and visit with Grace for a few minutes?"

"Okay," she said, and headed up the stairs. She shook her head at the stair climber that hugged the inner wall. Hard to believe that Grace would need such a contraption. But she was glad that she was able to be back in her home.

"Hello, Grace," she said. Her eyes took in the flowery room, which looked like spring even in the gray days of winter.

"Savannah! What a nice surprise! It's so good to see you!" Grace said.

"I was just out and about, and I thought I'd drop in to see how you were doing."

"Yes, I know. It's Saturday," she said, sympathetically. "How are things?"

"The same, you know. Just the same," she sighed. Suddenly she noticed Sarah coming toward her, smiling. "Wow," she said, doing a quick double take.

"Hello," Sarah said.

"I'm sorry, it's just when I saw you now, you reminded me of someone else. Sorry, I didn't mean to stare..."

"I know, I know," Grace said. "Uncanny, isn't it?"

"Really." Savannah shook her head.

"She doesn't really look all that much like her when you look carefully, but now and then I catch sight of her and it just gets me, you know?"

"Yes, I understand," Savannah said.

"Oh, you must be talking about Annie," Sarah said. "We just discovered that Annie was my great aunt. Amazing, isn't it?"

"Hard to believe. It's like you coming here was meant to be!" Savannah said.

Grace nodded in agreement. "I think so too!" she said. "Well, I think Marie is probably ready. Let's go down." She reached for her cane and stood slowly. She took Sarah's arm and they walked to the stairs. Sarah got her settled in the seat and Grace began her descent. Savannah walked beside her.

Marie appeared like magic when the stair climber began to hum. "Wait! I'll help you! I'm coming!" she said, moving quickly toward the stairs.

"No, Marie, we're fine here. I have lots of help!" Grace said.

Marie stopped. "Oh, yes, I see. Well, okay then." She turned and went back to the dining room.

The table was set with pretty china plates, and a bowl of day lilies nodded in a crystal vase. Marie quickly slipped in another place setting and went back to the kitchen.

Sarah pulled back Grace's chair and helped her slide in. Marie appeared with a steaming soup tureen and placed it within reach.

"Ummm, that smells so good," Savannah said, sniffing appreciatively. "What is it?"

"Wild rice soup with shitake mushrooms," she said. "I just got those yesterday. And we have grilled cheese sandwiches."

"I assume you know about mushrooms," Savannah said playfully. "I don't want to eat any of those poisonous ones!"

"Don't worry, I don't want to kill you, Savannah."

She looked over at Sarah briefly. "Or Grace, either."

Grace filled the soup bowls while Marie passed the platter of crispy golden triangles to each woman.

Sarah took a bite and moaned. "This is the best grilled cheese sandwich I've ever had!" She dipped a corner of the sandwich into the soup. "Delicious!"

"Marie does make the best grilled cheese ever, I must say."

"And the best soup too!" Savannah said.

"Hmmmph!" Marie said.

For a few minutes, there were no sounds except the tapping of spoons, some low hums, and a request for seconds from Savannah.

Finally, Grace pushed her plate back. "Wonderful, Marie! Thank you!"

Marie stood and began to gather up the plates.

"Let me help you with that, Marie," Sarah said, jumping to her feet.

"No thanks, I don't need any help." She set a large bowl of fruit near the center of the table and disappeared into the kitchen.

"Well, some things never change," Savannah said, looking at Sarah sympathetically. "Marie is a bit on the persnickety side, you know."

"I know!" Sarah said. She reached out for the bowl and chose a perfect orange. "I love fruit!"

"I know. And that includes strawberries, and blueberries too," Grace said. "We'll be up to our eyes with them very soon."

"Mmmmmmmm," Savannah hummed.

"Yes, and Marie makes the best jam...and strawberry shortcake...and blueberry cobbler...and that trifle!" Savannah closed her eyes and smiled reminiscently.

Grace chuckled, then became serious. "So, dear, how are you?" she asked Savannah.

"Well, you know, same same. Carrie seems to be in good shape. I heard her laughing."

"I'm glad." Grace shook her head. "I could just kick that bitch of a sister right where the sun don't shine!"

"Grace!" Marie said, shocked, standing in the doorway.

Sarah laughed. It was funny hearing Grace talk that way.

"Oh, Marie, I was just talking about Carrie's sister," Grace said.

Marie sniffed. "You're right, she is a bitch."

Savannah laughed, then paused for a moment as tears welled up again. "I do miss her so – and knowing that she's right there, and I can't talk to her or touch her..." She pulled a tissue from her pocket. "Oh damn, and I didn't want to cry again today. I just can't help it! It's so stupid!"

"No, honey, it's not stupid. I wish there was something we could do. It's so unfair!" She turned to Sarah. "Savannah's partner Carrie was in a car accident years ago and has a brain injury. She was in a coma for a long time, but she's more alert now and can talk a little bit. And Savannah goes to the nursing home very often, but she's not allowed to see her."

"Why on earth not?" Sarah asked.

"Her family has a restraining order against me. I'm not allowed to come closer than a hundred feet of her. And we were together for twenty-one years!" Savannah said. She blew her nose.

"Why would they do that?" Sarah asked.

"Because we are lesbians. Dykes. Can you

believe it?" she said bitterly. "And they call themselves Christians!"

"No, surely not!"

"Yes, and there was some big lawsuit, and there was an insurance settlement, and they went to court and got custody of her while she was in the coma. They've siphoned off as much money as they could. They even bought a fancy van with her money, and now they don't even come to see her. They don't care about her!" she said angrily. "They just want to make sure I don't see her. God, they are so hateful!"

"Incredible. I can't believe it!" Sarah said. "And how long has this been going on?"

"Five years," Savannah said. "Five glorious, wonderful years."

"Disgusting," Sarah said.

They all sat silently for a moment.

"Um, Savannah, dear, we want to run something by you. If you don't mind talking business on a Saturday," Grace said.

"Oh, no, go ahead. I'm always ready to talk business." Savannah settled back in her chair.

"Remember we were talking about how we needed to make some adjustments financially?" Grace said.

"Yes, bring in money or cut your expenses."

"Excuse me, I'll just get out of your way and let you talk," Sarah said.

"Oh, no, Sarah, this has to do with you too. And can you get Marie and ask her to come in?"

Savannah looked at Grace, mystified. "What's going on?" she asked.

Sarah and Marie came in and sat at the table.

Briefly, they told Savannah their idea for an adult

family home, and she thought it was a wonderful idea. "Just don't be in too much of a hurry," she warned. "There are a lot of things to consider."

"Yes, and we're going to need your help. That is, if you want to help us," Grace said.

"Of course I do. I'll help you put together a business plan, and then we can see if it's a feasible idea. If it is, this could really turn things around for you and Marie," she said.

"And for this place," Grace said.

Once they put the adult family home idea into words, it took on a life of its own.

Sarah called Jen to come over, and the five of them sat around the table and brainstormed. Sarah got a yellow legal pad and tried to jot down their thoughts as fast as she could. There was so much to think about, so much to do before they could even get started. They alternated between furious rushes of words and stunned silence. Sarah filled page after page until her head spun and her hand ached. They tossed around plans, implications and contingencies for hours until finally Grace held up her hand. "Enough!" she said. "We don't have to figure out everything today!"

Sarah laughed. "You're right. I'm sorry, ladies. Look, the day is almost gone and we haven't even done Grace's exercises…"

"Or much of anything else," Marie added.

"Well, I don't know about you, but I'm exhausted. And hungry." Grace grimaced at the cold dregs in the bottom of her cup.

"And my butt hurts from sitting here!" Marie

said. She stood up stiffly, holding the table. "I'll make us something to eat."

Jen, who'd also been sitting for hours, practically sprang out of her chair. "No, no! Why don't you and Grace just go sit in the living room and relax for a while. I'm sure Sarah and I can find something to fix for dinner." She bounced up and down on the balls of her feet.

Sarah looked at her in surprise. "Who are you, and what have you done with my girlfriend?"

"Ha ha," Jen said.

They rummaged around in the kitchen and found a chicken-and-rice casserole in the freezer. Jen started heating it up and sliced some tomatoes while Sarah steamed green beans, threw in some butter and toasted walnuts and cut up lettuce, cucumbers, and bell peppers from the garden. In no time, they had some dinner and a new pot of tea.

Grace and Marie were already drowsing on the sofa when they brought in the trays of food. It was all they could do to get down a few bites. Sarah took her sleepy new partners upstairs and helped them get ready for bed while Jen and Savannah cleared up the dishes.

"Wow! Can you believe this?" Savannah said when Sarah reappeared. "I'm so blown away! This is all so sudden!"

"I know," Sarah said. "But maybe it could work. Wouldn't that be wonderful?"

"Yes indeed. It would be great for all of you!" Savannah said. "Just remember, take your time – and stay in touch!"

"We will, don't worry! I'm sure you'll be sick of hearing from us!" Sarah said, walking her to the door. "Good night!"

Sarah came down the stairs and collapsed against Jen, who grabbed her around the waist and spun her briskly around the hallway. "I'm so excited!"

Sarah laughed, then rested her head against Jen's chest as they slowed. "Me too. I don't know what to think. My brain is on overload." Sarah rubbed her eyes. "Ow. And I think my hand is broken."

Jen took her hand, kissed it, and massaged it gently. "Poor little paw," she crooned.

"I just can't believe it," Sarah said. "It's so amazing! I never thought I would get to stay around here. I love this place! And I thought I was going to lose you."

Jen shook her head. "You never told me that. You acted like it was no big deal to you."

"Of course it's a big deal. I love you. But I thought we were just a short-time thing. Then, you know, you'd promise to keep in touch, we'd say nothing will change, we'd see each other a few times, then the phone calls would slow down, and then eventually we'd just drift off, and another woman would hit you on the ferry, and..."

"Whoa! How much of this script do you have written? This could be the first dyke mini-series." She put her arms around Sarah and gave her a long, sweet kiss.

"To take place at the first dyke adult family home!"

"I like the sound of that," she said.

Sarah clung to her tightly. "Mmmm" she said. "My girl."

Jen released her reluctantly and stepped back. "I'm tired too. It's been a big day." She ran her hand through her hair. "I guess I'd better be going."

"No! I don't want you to go," Sarah said, stepping back into her arms. "I want you to stay here."

※ ※ ※ ※

Sarah was exhausted. Her yellow pad bulged with sticky notes, issues to research, to-do lists, pros and cons, people to contact. She and Grace made a million phone calls. So far, the reactions they received were mostly positive.

Sarah called Carol, who practically jumped through the phone. "That's an incredible idea! It's perfect! Count me in! I'll be your physical therapist. We can put some equipment in the pool house, and we can use the hot tub…"

"Wait! Wait!" Sarah laughed. "You're getting as bad as me. One step at a time!"

She called Dr. Emily, who was cautiously optimistic. "It would be wonderful to have a place like that on the island. There are so few options for people who can't live alone anymore, but aren't sick enough to be in a hospital or nursing home."

"I know. Most families aren't able to take on full-time care of a relative," Sarah said.

"True," Emily said. "I would love to help you make this happen. It would be great to know there was a place to send my people where they could get good care and I could keep an eye on them."

"You know, we're going to need a good doctor," Sarah said, smiling into the phone.

"Count me in!" she said promptly.

Ro, the lawyer, was full of questions about how the state certified adult family homes, the legal requirements, the physical changes that would have to be done to the old house, the responsibilities that would fall on everyone, and what paperwork would be required.

Sarah spent days in Olympia, the state capitol, making her way through one bureaucratic mess after another. Licenses. Regulations. Insurance. Credentials. It seemed endless. But she picked up lots of tips and information, which she fed back to Grace and Savannah for their business plan. When Jen wasn't working, she collected information on building codes and safety requirements. Even Margret helped, purring on Sarah and Jen in turn when they collapsed into their bed at night.

Sarah went to visit a few adult family homes in Seattle and Tacoma. She saw things she liked and things she didn't, and got some valuable input from a few of the owners.

"When you meet with prospective residents, don't just look at their physical problems. Try to envision how each resident will fit in. Remember, you're building a family," one said.

She spoke with one couple who were putting their home up for sale. "Make sure you build in time for yourself," the wife said.

"It's easy to get sucked in to working day and night if you're not careful," her husband chimed in. "You have to have a life apart, or you'll get burned out, like we did."

"I'll be careful," Sarah promised.

"Seriously," she said. "We haven't been to a movie together in seven years."

※※※※

The newly formed committee, consisting of Grace and Marie, Sarah and Jen, Carol, Savannah, Emily, and Ro, sat around the table in the dining room, snacking out once again.

"Honestly, Marie, if we keep having meetings like this, I won't be getting out of my chair," Carol said, licking the brownie crumbs from her fingers.

"You're right," Marie said. "From now on, healthy food only. Carrot sticks and seaweed all around!"

"Wait, now, don't be hasty," Carol said quickly. "I just wish you weren't such a good baker."

Marie smiled. "Thank you, my dear."

"She's got a point, you know," said Emily, blowing a bit of powdered sugar off her sleeve. "Women will want to come here to live just so they can eat your food."

A chuckle went around the table.

"I've been getting some estimates for changes in the house," Sarah said. "You know, redo the bathrooms, install handrails, put in a wheelchair ramp, lots of things. And there's equipment to get too – and none of this stuff is cheap. I don't know about your finances, Grace, but I know the main reason you want to start up this home is to bring in some money. But do you have the money to get this place going?'

All eyes turned to Grace. "Well, I think I could raise some money somehow. Maybe take out another mortgage? Sell off some of the woods? I don't know…" she trailed off.

"Don't worry," Marie said. "We have the money."

"What do you mean? Where do you have money?" Savannah asked.

Marie looked at Grace. "Well, honey, you've been paying me all these years, and gave me a place to live and bought the food – and I've been squirreling that money away!"

"Oh my!" Grace cried. "Oh my girl!" She pulled Marie out of her chair and they stood for moment, hugging. "Thank you, thank you!" she said, and gave Marie a big kiss on the lips.

"Anything for you, my love," she said. "Anything for you, and for our home."

There were cheers all around, and the women started pushing their chairs back to stand.

Savannah cleared her throat. "We still have one more important issue to discuss," she said.

"Oh, no, that's not possible!" moaned Jen. "I think we've discussed everything into the ground! I don't want to talk anymore!"

"You know, it's a sex-linked trait," Emily said. "Political correctness and endless discussion, and consensus—part of the lesbian genome."

Everyone groaned.

"Seriously now," Savannah said. "We've talked about everything but a name. What are you going to call this place?"

Sarah laughed. "Now wait a minute," she said. "Let's talk about this."

Marie made a rude noise. "No more talking! I'm tired of talking!"

"I know we're all tired, but the thing is, we haven't really thought about what you want this place to be," she said. "Sure, an adult family home, but what does that mean? An adult family home is for people who need help with activities of daily living, which means bathing, dressing, eating, that kind of stuff. But it's not for people who are completely bedridden or need complicated care that they could only get in a hospital or nursing home."

"Oh, I didn't really think about that," Savannah said. "So what's the criteria?"

"Well, they would have to be ambulatory – you know, able to get around. And that includes people who need to use canes, walkers, or wheelchairs, as long as they were able to get around with minimal assistance. The physical care could be given by certified nursing assistants or other kinds of health care people, but it needs to be overseen by an RN."

"That's you," Grace said.

"Yes, but I can't be here every minute. I would have to teach the staff members how to do certain things, like helping residents to take their medicine."

"Well, you could do that, couldn't you?"

"I guess I could, but we'll have to work all this out in advance. We don't want ugly surprises!" Sarah said.

"Yes, I guess we'd all have to be careful that we do everything by the book," Marie said.

"Ah yes – the Book of Sarah!" Jen said with a laugh.

"Argh," Sarah said.

"So what kind of residents do you want? I think we need to know that before we settle on a name."

"Women," Jen said.

Everyone nodded.

Sarah turned to yet another blank yellow page and started a new list.

"Okay," she said. "Women."

"Old women."

"Sick women."

"Handicapped women."

"Nice women."

"Feisty women."

"Wrinkly women with big hairy moles."

"Eeeuw!"

"That would be quite the selling point!"

"Younger women with chronic health problems."

"Dying women."

Sarah wrote down all the suggestions, then looked around the table. "All these ideas sound good. And I think it's important to find women who can get along together. Maybe with some things in common."

"Lesbians."

"I agree," Grace said. "So many of us have lived in the closet for most of our lives. It would be so nice to have a place where lesbians could just be who they really are, let their hair down, so to speak."

"Or their crewcuts!" Carol said.

"Hear, hear!" Marie said loudly. "Where they wouldn't have to de-dyke the house when they were expecting visitors."

Everyone nodded in agreement.

"Of course, we couldn't discriminate," Emily said.

"Are you kidding?" Carol said, shocked. "People discriminate against us all the time! They would go out of their way not to be around a bunch of lesbians!"

"True," Savannah said.

They all laughed.

"Old Ladies' Rest Home," Marie said.

"And Used Car Lot," Carol added.

"ET Crone Home," Jen suggested.

Sarah pinched her arm. "Terrible!"

"Dykes 'R Us," Grace said.

"Grace! Honestly!" Marie cried, scandalized.

"Amazon Manor," chirped Ro.

"How about the Crones' Nest? Or Ye Olde Crones' Home?" Savannah said, wickedly.

"Stop! Please!" Sarah turned to Grace, pen poised. "What did you call it when it was a bed and breakfast?"

"Lavender Meadows," Grace said. "After all, we had all that lavender. And we were the Meadows girls, Annie and I..." She stopped suddenly and took a deep breath. For a moment, they felt her presence in the room.

"Why, that's a lovely name," Sarah said.

"Yes, keep the name!"

"I like that."

"It sounds so peaceful..."

"Lavender Meadows Adult Family Home. Sounds good to me."

"I don't know. I like the Lavender Meadows part, but Adult Family Home sounds so stuffy," Zoe said. "And it doesn't say what we really are."

The discussion went on for a few more minutes before everyone was satisfied.

"Finally!" Emily said. "A group of lesbians who have reached consensus. Incredible!"

Sarah smiled, and on the top of the first page in her yellow pad she wrote in big block letters –

LAVENDER MEADOWS

A FAMILY OF WOMEN

"Hear, hear!" Grace said, thumping her hand on the table. "Okay, Marie, let's break out the bubbly!"

"And the goodies!" Carol said. "After all this work, we deserve it!"

❧❧❧❧

The team somehow managed to survive putting

together a business plan and a marketing strategy. Sarah visited the Aging and Adult Services, Department of Health, and nursing agencies for guidance and encouragement. She also went to some other adult family homes in the area and talked to the owners. They were able to give her a lot of insight to help them get started.

For weeks, the sound of hammers and drills and the smell of new paint filled the place. Jen turned out to be handy with tools, much to Sarah's delight, and installed new wooden handrails along the walls, grab bars in the bathrooms, and an intercom system to all the rooms. They bought some new reclining chairs for the living room, a flat screen TV, and several sets of headphones. They had the state people out to do inspections.

At last, their preparations were done. Now all they needed were some residents.

Zoe and Carol designed a web site, Facebook page, brochure, and some business cards. Marie organized a tea-and-work party to send the information out to lesbian organizations, publications, and healthcare providers in three counties. Five women showed up and made short work of the task, promising to return if Marie would keep bribing them with cookies.

Sarah was only moderately crazed, switching back and forth between cockeyed optimism and gloom and doom, sometimes within the same minute. "What if we can't find any women? What if we get too busy?" And of course, "What if I can't handle this?"

Jen did the best she could to help her stay calm. "Of course women will want to come here. This is a great house, on a beautiful island. There's no other women's place like this anywhere around." She grinned and squeezed Sarah's shoulder. "And I hear the Director of Nursing is some hot chick! The lezzies will be beating down the door!"

Sarah stuck out her chest and fluffed her hair. "Come on out and see us sometime, girls," she said huskily. "We're waiting to take care of all your needs!"

Jen laughed and punched at her playfully. "You could be a bikini barista!" Then she reached out and took Sarah's hand. "Seriously, honey, I mean it," she said. "You're a great nurse, and you have a big heart. The old girls will love you. Everything will work out, you'll see."

❧❧❧❧

The phone rang, startling Grace from her nap. "Hello! Hello? Wait a minute, please." She groped for her glasses. "Yes. Okay now. I can't hear you without my glasses, you know. Are you still there?"

"Hi, Grace. This is Emily. How are you?"

"Doctor?"

"Yes. I'm sorry, did I wake you up?"

"I was just resting my eyes for a few minutes."

"Sorry to disturb you. I know you've been working hard."

"Yes, so many details to take care of. But I think we're about done now."

"I'm glad to hear that. Are you ready for your first resident?"

"Oh, my goodness. Who is it? When is she coming?" Grace said, excited.

"Not so fast. We have to work out some details. You've all been so concerned about Edna. How would you like having her there? She's improved quite a bit, but she still needs some help, and her speech is still difficult. Her Medicare benefit has run out, and they can't afford to have nurses in the house. And their place is not really set up for care. Besides, Ginny will need to go back to work."

"That would be wonderful! We love Edna! I can't wait to tell Sarah."

"Great. I'll have Ginny give you a call."

"Thanks, Emily. This is so exciting!"

She put down the phone, smiling, and punched the button on the new intercom. "Sarah! Sarah!" she cried. "Come quick! I have good news!"

She looked around the room that had been her refuge for so many years and a little sigh escaped her. She knew things were about to change – for the good, she hoped.

Edna was so pleased to get out of Viking Manor, she crowed. Ginny was there to help her into the wheelchair and walk beside her as the aide pushed her out to Sarah's van. She had told Edna about their plans, but at first, she wasn't sure that Edna knew that she wasn't going back to the house they had lived in for so many years. But it was clear to her that Edna was happy going anywhere.

She smiled her way to the porch and up the long ramp that had just been built to accommodate wheelchairs. (Jen thought it would also work pretty well for skateboards, but decided not to share that with Sarah.)

She was happy to see Grace and Marie waiting by the stairs. After a round of hugs, Sarah positioned her by the stair climber and helped her stand. Ginny and Sarah got her settled in the seat, then they walked beside her as it ground its way up the stairs. At the top, they transferred her to a different wheelchair and brought her to her room.

Edna looked around the room with its big bed, recliner, and bright pink and green curtains and her crooked smile got even bigger. "Home," she said.

Part II

Clarisse Cooper had worked hard all her life. Her parents had narrowly escaped Hitler's concentration camps in Poland and had immigrated to the US. Eventually, the family settled in Seattle in a modest house in the Ballard area. Her father worked in a shoe factory for many years, while her mother cooked in a busy diner. As a child, she would go there after school every day and do her homework until her mother finished up. Most of the regulars knew her name and said hello. Some asked her about school. At fourteen, she started waiting tables there. It was what she was meant to do. When she finished high school, she started working at the diner full time.

Almost every day at lunchtime, a young woman came into the restaurant and sat at one of Clarisse's tables. She usually wore a trench coat, belted at the waist, and had her hair caught up in a brown, shiny ponytail that bobbed when she walked. Usually she had her nose in a book, often writing notes in the margins in a quick, precise hand. Clarisse got to know her order by heart – soup of the day and a grilled cheese sandwich. Clarisse was curious about her, but though the woman always smiled, she never made eye contact, or said anything but please and thank you.

One day Clarisse could not contain her curiosity any longer. "What are you reading?" she asked.

The woman looked up at her, and suddenly Clarisse found herself looking into a pair of bright green eyes that made her knees weak. "*David Copperfield*," she said.

"Oh, I read that in my English class last year," Clarisse said. "I read *Oliver Twist*, too, over the summer. I love Dickens!"

"Me too. He can make sad things so funny." She smiled and disappeared back into her book.

Clarisse could hardly breathe. She wasn't sure what was more exciting – the fact that she'd spoken to the woman, or the fact that she'd answered back.

It took two more weeks for Clarisse to find out her name – Andrea, Andie for short. By that time, she was totally, hopelessly, irrevocably in love.

Clarisse's mom took a dim view of their growing friendship. "Remember you're a waitress, and she's your customer," she said. "You're just someone who brings her coffee, someone to pass the time of day with."

But Clarisse knew better. She knew that she and Andie were destined to be together, even if she wasn't quite sure what that meant. She just knew she wanted to be close to her, to touch her – to kiss her. As the days got longer and warmer, she waited breathlessly for Andie to show up at the diner.

She did not usually work on Sundays, but one of the other girls called in sick, and Clarisse had to cover for her. She certainly did not expect to see Andie that day, but she looked up and suddenly there she was, in a beautiful yellow dress, bright as sunshine, her usual ponytail tucked into braids wrapped around her head. She had a man and woman with her, and two kids in their early teens, a boy and a girl. They were also dressed up, and the older couple was beaming.

"Hi, Clarisse!" she said. "See, Mom and Dad, this is the waitress I told you about. She makes sure I eat a good lunch every day!"

"Thank you for taking such good care of our girl." The woman smiled. "You know, a mother has to worry."

Clarisse could see the resemblance, could see what Andie would look like in twenty years. The planes and angles of her face would be softened, with smile lines beside her mouth and the same jade-green eyes. She knew that in twenty years she would feel the same way she felt today, quivery and excited.

Her dad puffed up his chest. "We're so proud of our little girl."

"How come?" Clarisse asked. She pulled out a chair for Andie's mom and handed them some menus.

"Well, because she's graduating, that's why!" her brother said. "She's finished with school!" He sighed loudly. "Wish it was me!"

"You'll have your turn soon enough," her mom said. "You'll be grown up and gone before you know it!"

"Gone? Are you going somewhere?" Clarisse asked. She began to feel cold fingers of dread clutching her stomach.

"We're all going to Europe for the summer, then I start college in September – in California! I'm so excited!" She clapped her hands like a little girl.

Clarisse felt the bottom drop out of her world. Woodenly she took their orders and walked back to the kitchen. Her mother took one look at her and gasped. "Clarisse! What is it? What happened?"

"It's Andie. She's leaving! She's going away!" Clarisse said, trying to stifle a sob.

Her mother clucked sympathetically. "I'm sorry your friend is leaving. But remember what I told you – you are a waitress and she is your customer." She looked more closely at Clarisse's tortured face. "Oh, my poor girl!" she said. She caught her up in a brief hug.

Somehow, she got through it. Somehow, she managed to get platters of roast turkey, meatloaf, and macaroni and cheese out to their table, her eyes downcast. Meanwhile, the stream of chatter went on around her as they talked on about their plans.

Finally, they were done, and Clarisse brought their bill to the table. She saw Andie bend over and whisper in her father's ear, and he smiled and nodded.

"Bye bye, Clarisse," her parents said in chorus as they filed out. "Thanks again!"

Andie sent her a dazzling smile as she walked past. "Bye! Take care! Keep reading!"

Clarisse's knees felt weak and she grasped the edge of the table near the brand new twenty-dollar bill.

Clarisse didn't think she could get past it. How could she when every day at the diner she would look at the clock, expecting Andie to walk through the door?

But of course, after a while, the pain dulled, and life went on as usual. Clarisse went out with a customer she'd met at the diner a few times, and he was very nice, clean cut, he smelled good, and her parents liked him. Joe had a job at the shoe factory where her father worked, and it looked like he would step up to management soon. So after a while, he got her an engagement ring, and four months later they got married in the church she'd grown up in. It was meant to be.

In due time they had two little boys, Mark and Shawn, and they had the life they expected to have, until Joe clutched his chest and keeled over in the shoe factory office at the age of forty-two. That was not how things were supposed to go.

Clarisse worked through the sadness and loneliness she felt, and devoted herself to her boys. She continued to work at the diner, and her customers liked her and usually gave her decent tips. She put the boys through high school, and they both worked at the diner to help out and to save money for their future. First, her mom died, then her dad, and Clarisse missed them terribly, but she understood pain and loneliness by this time and just went on.

Finally, the boys were grown and gone, and she looked around her and saw that she was alone. She took some evening classes and found she could turn out some decent watercolors and a mean stir-fry. She'd never had to use a computer, but now even the diner was computerized, so she decided to take a class in that too.

And the internet opened the world for her. She could travel to places she'd only imagined, follow the people she'd seen on the movies and on TV, learn about a million different things. She was surprised at all the people who wanted to chat, get information – communicate. She opened up Craig's List one evening, and saw the relationship area. Just out of curiosity she looked at some different sites, sent a few notes, chuckled at the answers. Then one day she looked in the Women Wanting Women and Lesbian sections, and she was transfixed. There were other women like her, women who had the kind of feelings she'd had for Andie, but never got to act upon.

She started correspondences, even went to a few meetings and potlucks. She was too shy to talk to anyone there, but gradually, over time, the general friendliness of the women helped her to connect. On her own, she took some field trips to Capitol Hill, looked in the shops, started listening to women's music. She even had some relationships with women, and though none of them lasted very long, she'd reached depths of physical and emotional experience that she'd never had with Joe. But she never talked about it with her boys.

Finally, after years of standing on her feet at the diner, her legs gave out, and she had to retire. She developed diabetes and had to take insulin. Mark talked to her about living with him and his family, and Clarisse reluctantly agreed that she could not live on her own anymore. She loved being with Mark's kids, Shari and Louise, and they loved her too. Things would not be any easier with Shawn and his wife and their kids. So Mark started looking for a place big enough for all of them, but in her heart, she felt it would not work. She didn't want to give away her women pictures, her music, and her lesbian novels. She liked being around her family, but she knew she would not be able to have her friends over. And she wanted her privacy, too. Yet, she knew she was having trouble keeping her medications straight and was unsteady on her feet. She worried about falling in the bathroom and breaking her hip.

She agonized about what to do. She was afraid that her family would draw away from her if they knew the truth about her, about who and what she really was.

Finally, Mark and Shawn sat down with Clarisse and talked to her about finding a different living situation where she could get the help she needed.

She took a deep breath. "I know this is really hard for you boys, and it's hard for me too. You've done so much for me, helping me all these years, and you know that I love all of you so very, very much." Clarisse dabbed at her eyes. "I know I can't stay here alone anymore. I found a place where I can go and get the help I need. Let me show you." Clarisse went to the computer and pulled up a web page – Lavender Meadows: A Family of Women.

Mark and Shawn looked at the web page, at the pictures of the house and the lake, at the smiling women sitting around the dining room table, surrounded by food to rival a fine restaurant. They read it over again, looked at each other, and read it again. "Mom," Mark said delicately, "I think this is a place for a certain kind of woman." Shawn nodded.

"Sons," she said, "I have something to tell you."

※ ※ ※ ※

Sarah pulled the van into the Costco parking lot and began circling, looking for a spot near the door. It was a Saturday, and obviously, everyone had the same idea. Cars shadowed shoppers with carts piled high, hoping to score their spots, waiting impatiently as they unloaded mountains of toilet paper, cases of Coke, huge packages of muffins and croissants, potted plants, fertilizer, and motor oil into their pickups and SUVs. No Smart cars in sight.

Well, I guess I could use the exercise, she thought as she pulled into a place so far into the lot the she could barely see the entrance in the distance. She sighed as she clambered out.

It amazed her how fast they went through food and supplies for Lavender Meadows, now that they were up and running at almost full capacity. Tuna and hand wipes and shampoo and disposable briefs.

Oatmeal and eggs, vitamins, mayo, and laundry detergent. Noodles and beans. Cucumbers and bagels. Rubber gloves and Fixodent and paper towels. She was glad that Marie was so good at putting together the shopping list, divided neatly into categories. Her own lists were more jumbled, stream-of-consciousness.

She flashed her membership card, grabbed one of the few remaining carts, and leapt into the fray. It was getting close to lunchtime, so she headed immediately toward the food area, knowing that there were many smiling (or not) folks waiting to give out samples of everything imaginable. She knew she could stave off her hunger on those bits of cheese and little cups of macaroni salad until she could hit the hot dogs on the way out, one of the high points of her weekly shopping trips. Kosher Polish dogs, loaded with sauerkraut and onions. Everyone in the house could tell where she'd been just by her breath.

She was reaching for the last sample of ravioli on the tray when another hand swooped in and grabbed it. Sarah looked up, annoyed, in time to see a tall figure disappearing into the crowd. The demonstrator shrugged and smiled at her. "Gotta be fast here on Saturdays," she said.

"I guess," Sarah said, backing her cart out. "I'll be back!"

She scored a chunk of brownie, a bit of Dave's Killer Bread (her favorite), and a tiny cup of soup before she was beaten out again for the last tiny shrimp. "Hey!" she said, as the grubby hand wearing several menacing looking rings and leather bracelets scooped up her prize. Sarah recognized the same tall figure who had snatched her snack earlier. "That is so rude!"

"Sorry 'bout that," the figure said with a grin,

showing white, widely spaced teeth and several lip rings and studs. Her black, spiky hair pointed every which way.

"Get out of here, you," said the sample lady, waving her hand at the food sample thief. "This is the fourth time you've come through here today!"

"Just to see you, my love." She winked at the woman and backed away.

"Whew! Some nerve!" said the sample lady. "I swear, some people just spend all day in here, grabbing samples, crowding out the other shoppers and taking all our food! Here," she said, handing Sarah another morsel.

"Thanks, that's really good." Sarah took her cart and headed off to the pet section.

By the time she finished loading up cat and dog food, toilet paper, and vitamins, she was ready for a break. She stood in the checkout line for eternity, spent a fortune, and headed gratefully to the snack bar. She loaded up her hot dog with sauerkraut, onions, and mustard, as she wasn't expecting to see Jen that night, then headed for the only empty spot in the sea of red-and-white picnic tables.

She inhaled a couple of juicy bites and looked around. She was sitting near the tall woman with the piercings, who was hunched over a little plastic bag stuffed with what appeared to be samples from a bunch of different demo stations. She also had part of a slice of pizza and a couple of hot dog fragments. She ate quickly, making little sounds of satisfaction as she chewed.

Sarah watched her for a moment, and felt her hunger melt away. She took a big sip of her drink, then slid off the bench, leaving the rest of her food on the table. By the time she turned around and got her cart, the partially eaten hot dog and her soda had joined the remnants of others' meals in front of the woman. She did not look up as Sarah passed by her. Ugh... she said to herself. She felt very lucky.

❀❀❀❀

Emily made her way around the kitchen with quick, precise movements – filling the kettle, scraping the plates, loading the dishwasher. She sniffed appreciatively. The kitchen was still fragrant with ginger and spices.

She got out two mugs and deposited a tea bag in each – lemon ginger for her, green tea for Rachel. When the kettle whistled, she poured in the hot water and put a dollop of honey in each mug. She walked back into the living room and handed off the green tea, then plopped herself into her recliner. "Whew!" she said. She fanned herself with the crossword puzzle book and pushed back her short dark hair. "Warm tonight, isn't it?"

"Thank you, honey," she said. "You feel warm because you've been working hard in the kitchen," Rachel said.

"It's you who were working hard," said Emily. "That was an amazing dinner."

"I love curry," she said. "And I love the way the house smells."

"I think that is your best dish."

"Thanks," Rachel said. "And thanks for cleaning up."

"It's only fair," she said. "Besides, you're a much better cook than I am."

"I'd rather cook than clean up any day," she said.

"So that works out well, then." Emily sat back with a sigh and put her head back.

"Long day?"

"Oh, you know. The usual. It's summer. Lots of kids coming in for allergy shots, people putting their backs out doing yard work, folks cutting off their toes with their lawn mowers…"

"Eeeew. TMI! How awful!"

"Ha ha, not really. Just trying to gross you out."

"Yuck. It worked too," she said, and pulled her needlework basket towards her.

"How about your day? Have many customers?"

"Oh, a few. A couple of women signed up for the weaving class next week, and Marie and Grace and Sarah came in."

"She is such a nice woman. I'm glad Grace found her. Marie was really tiring herself out."

"I know. And she's so stubborn. She doesn't want to take help from anyone."

"Yes, but she needs to slow down some. She has some heart issues, and she needs to take care of herself," Emily said. "If they can manage to run Lavender Meadows as an adult family home it will be a tremendous boon to women in this area." She paused. "But enough about them. Let's talk about us."

"What is it, honey? What's the matter?" Rachel asked anxiously. "Are you angry with me? Did I do something wrong?"

"No, no, nothing like that," Emily reassured her.

"Oh no. Do you still love me? Have you met someone else?" Rachel's face crumpled.

"No, of course not. It's just, well, we've been together for a long time…"

"I know, five years. In July." Rachel took a deep breath. "Are you tired of me? Do you want to split up? Should I move out? I can move into the back room of the shop…"

"No, no, honey. Really. Of course I don't want you to leave. Of course I still love you," Emily said.

"Maybe we could go to counseling. I would never stand in your way, whatever you want to do."

"Goodness, Rachel. Please. I've just been thinking…"

"What! What! Tell me! What is it?"

"I um, wanted to ask you, um," Emily stuttered.

"Yes? Yes!"

"Let's have a baby."

Rachel looked at her, thunderstruck. The she started to laugh, and cry, and she stood up and whirled around. "A baby! A baby! You want to have a baby!"

"I want us to have a baby. You and me. If you want. Now don't say anything yet. I know it's a lot to think about…"

"Of course! Of course I want us to have a baby. Oh, love. Of course. Of course," Rachel cried, circling the room, faster and faster. "A baby! A baby!"

Emily reached out, grabbed her as she went by, and pulled her into her lap. She hugged her hard and kissed her lips, her neck. "Our baby. Our baby!"

⁂

Sarah forgot about the woman until she went back to Costco the next time. They were planning to have a cookout for the residents and their families, and she needed to get a new barbeque grill. The old one hadn't been used for several years and had rusted through. She finally settled on one with all the bells and whistles, sleek and chromey as a new car. She remembered feeding her dad's hamburgers, cremated and smelling like lighter fluid, to the grateful dogs beneath the table. She remembered joking with her brothers that if someone lit a match near the dogs, they would explode. She knew she could do a much better job on the grill, and she was a sucker for cooking equipment. And she loved putting things together.

She was trying to get the grill onto a flatbed cart, but it was heavy and clumsy and the cart kept rolling away from her. She growled softly in frustration, pushed her hair back, and tried to grab it again.

"Need some help with that?" Sarah looked up and saw the woman lounging against a picnic table. She had the same black jacket on.

"Thanks," Sarah said. "I appreciate it. This thing is so big!"

"No problem," she said. She grabbed one end and Sarah the other, and they jockeyed it into position on the cart.

"Wow, this is a beauty," the woman said, inspecting the box. "You could cook a whole bear on this thing. Hmm, complicated, though. Lots of parts."

"I know. It could probably kill the bear and make the biscuits too. But I just can't resist," Sarah said. She thought for a moment. The memory of the woman scarfing up the remains of Sarah's hotdog crossed her mind. "Hmm, I tell you what. If you help me get this beast into my van, I'll buy you some lunch."

The woman hesitated for a moment. "Uh, sure, okay, thanks," she said.

"I tell you what, let me pick up the rest of the stuff I need and meet you at the snack bar," Sarah said.

"Okay," she said.

Sarah got the rest of her supplies and headed to the front of the store. When she got there, she saw a Costco employee talking to the woman. He reached out and grabbed her arm. "You cannot stay in here all day. You never buy anything. You just eat samples and pick at other people's food. It's disgusting! Now get out of here!" She pulled away from him and fixed him with a death-ray stare.

"Excuse me, is there a problem?" Sarah said, looking at the man's ID badge. "Tony."

"No problem, just a little discussion. Nothing to worry about."

"Why are you talking to my friend like that?" Sarah asked. "We were just about to have lunch, but I guess we'll just have to go somewhere else." She turned and pointed her cart toward the door. "Let's go."

The woman fell in behind her, turning briefly to shoot Tony the finger. He scowled and shook his fist.

They jammed the groceries and the grill into the van. "Get in," Sarah said, opening the passenger door.

"Why?" she asked.

"Well, I owe you some lunch," Sarah said.

"Oh, no, you don't have to do that. I was glad to help," she said.

"No, no. Let's go! I'm hungry!" Sarah said. She clambered into the driver's seat, thoughts of the hotdog fading away.

The woman didn't say anything on the drive, and soon they were sitting in a booth at a little café near the water. "Get whatever you want," Sarah said, noting her pinched face and the clothes hanging loosely on her long frame.

"Thanks," she said, and buried her head in the

menu.

After they ordered, they did not say another word until their food arrived – grilled cheese and beef barley soup for Sarah, a chicken salad sandwich, fries, and a big glass of orange juice for the woman.

"Umm!" Sarah said, breaking open a pack of crackers. "I love soup." She looked across at the woman and smiled, trying not to stare at her pierced nose and lip and her hacked-up hair. Several tattoos peeked below the sleeves of her jacket and from the neck of her tee shirt. Now that she could see her up close, she was more girl than woman. "I guess we should introduce ourselves since we're eating together. My name is Sarah."

"Lee," she said.

"Nice to meet you. And thanks for your help. Are you from around here?"

"Seattle."

"Me too. I just came here to work, and now I live here, over on Bainbridge Island."

"Oh."

"Yes, it's so beautiful here. I love watching the ferry go across, and we have so many flowers and trees. And everything smells so good. I don't even mind the rain so much over here. I had a little apartment on Capitol Hill, but I'm glad I moved on." She stopped for a minute, thinking to herself how true that was.

"Oh."

"But here I am, rattling on and not letting you talk. Where did you say you lived?"

"Out on the edge of town. Not too far."

"I'm going to get a piece of pie. Would you like some?"

"Sure. Apple."

Sarah flagged down the waitress and ordered two apple pies with vanilla ice cream. "This is one of the first places I discovered when I came to work here. They make great pies," she said. She watched as Lee tucked into her pie, head held low, making it disappear before Sarah got two bites in. "Good, huh?"

"Umf," she replied, finally raising her head. "Yes. Thanks." She pushed herself back and wiped her mouth. "I'll be going. Thanks for lunch."

"Wait, I'll drop you off," Sarah said.

"No need," Lee said.

"At least let me take you back to the store," Sarah said.

"No, I don't need to go back there now," she said.

They walked back toward the van. Sarah saw her staring at her rainbow and Goddess stickers, then back at her. "Good-bye," she said.

Sarah was loath to let her go. "Let me ask you—are you any good at putting things together? I'm terrible. I don't even think I could get it out of the van by myself. I know it will take me forever to get this grill together, and I'll probably have a ton of parts left over. Do you think you could help me?"

"What, here? I don't have tools."

"No, I didn't mean here. Maybe you could come back to the house and you can do it there. I have all the tools. I sure would appreciate it. And then I'll bring you back."

The woman eyed her warily. "You want to take me to your house?"

"Yes, that would be great, but it's getting late, so if you want to go, let's go now."

Lee looked at her again, considering. "Sure," she said. "Whatever you want." She got into the van and closed the door.

Sarah tried to make conversation as she drove back, but she only got one-syllable answers in return. It was obvious that she did not want to talk. She brought up several topics, but stony silence met her. Instead, the girl gazed out the window, her head pressed against the glass. "Not much of a talker, huh?" she said finally.

"No," the girl said.

At last, they got to Lavender Meadows, and the girl whistled softly when she caught sight of the house. Sarah opened the garage door with the remote. Ralph raced out to greet them, barking enthusiastically. The girl jumped out and stuck out her hand and Ralph licked it, tail wagging. The girl squatted and rubbed Ralph's head. "Hi, boy," she said, stroking his soft ears.

"That's Ralph," Sarah said.

"Good boy, Ralph," she said. He stuck his face out and touched her nose.

Between the two of them, they wrestled the grill out of the van and onto the driveway. "There's all kinds of tools in here," she said, pointing out pegboards with tools neatly hung on silver hooks, and boxes filled with enough stuff to stock a small hardware store. "Let me know if you need anything."

"Okay," she said, and began prying the staples out of the big cardboard box.

Sarah entered the kitchen through the garage and heady smells of vegetables sautéing for stew and baking bread assailed her. Marie was busy peeling carrots and cutting up red and yellow peppers for salad. "How are you doing? Everything Okay?" she asked. "It sure smells good in here."

"Sure, everything is fine," Marie answered. "Did you get the grill?"

"Yes, a nice big one. We can cook enough for the whole town," Sarah said. "I even brought someone home to put it together."

Marie frowned in surprise. "What! You told me you were good at that kind of stuff, and Jen is handy too. What made you get someone else?"

"I don't know. She looked hungry, kind of lost."

Grace came into the kitchen then, pushing her walker. She stopped to give Marie a peck on the cheek. "Who is lost?"

"Oh, Sarah brought home a lost puppy. I bet she has big brown eyes," Marie teased.

"A puppy? Oh my. That's a surprise," Grace said, frowning. "What kind of dog? Where is it?"

"In the garage," Marie said. "You'll see later."

The sun was starting to go down when there was a light tap at the door that connected the kitchen to the garage. "Now who could that be?" she said.

"It's the puppy," Marie said. "Go on, Sarah, let her in."

She opened the door. "All done," Lee said. "Wanna take a look?"

"Sure," she said, and stepped out past Lee and into the garage. The grill was all done, gleaming in the sunset. "Wow, that was fast," she said. She looked at the grill, ran her hands over it. "It's a beauty, huh? I can't wait to fire it up! Thank you so much!"

"No problem," she said proudly, arms akimbo. "Are you ready to take me back? Or I can try to catch a ride."

"No, no. I'll take you home. But I was just thinking – dinner is ready. Would you like to stay? It's stew." The garlicky scent wafted from the kitchen door.

Lee ducked her head and mumbled. "Yeah, I can

smell it. Sure smells good. But I don't want to keep you from your dinner. You don't have to feed me, I can just wait out here..." she trailed off.

"No, really. We're having a barbeque tomorrow. You saved me a lot of time, and probably a lot of swearing," she said with a grin. "And we have plenty of stew!"

"Okay, thanks," she said, and followed Sarah into the kitchen.

The ladies were all in the dining room. She had a feeling that Lee would not want to be confronted by an inquisitive crowd, so she sat her at the kitchen table and dished up two bowls of fragrant stew and a couple of hunks of warm bread.

Lee ducked her head and quickly shoveled stew into her mouth, making little sounds of satisfaction. As she got near the bottom of the bowl, she finally slowed down. "Wow, that was great," she said, mopping up the remaining gravy with her bread. She sat back and patted her stomach.

"Marie does most of the cooking," she said. "I hope you left room for dessert." She cut two wedges of coconut custard pie, one big and one small, and put the larger one in front of Lee. It disappeared almost as quickly as the stew.

"Wow, two kinds of pie in one day! I'm so lucky!" She moistened her finger and picked up the crumbs. "Who is Marie? Is she your roommate?"

Sarah picked up the dishes and set them in the sink. "No, she's one of the women who owns this place. Maybe you could meet her sometime." She paused for a moment. "You know, if you want, you can stay here tonight. I could bring you back in the morning."

Lee hesitated for a moment, then got up and

stood behind her. "I'd like that," she said, her voice husky. "A lot." She slid her arm around Sarah's waist and kissed the side of her neck.

Sarah jumped as if she'd been shot. "Hey!" she said, "What are you doing?"

Lee stepped back, alarmed. "Oh my God! I'm so sorry! I thought…"

Sarah pressed her hand to her chest, breathing quickly. "Oh, no, I'm sorry! I didn't mean for you… I'm flattered, but I didn't mean for you to think…I just wanted some help with the grill, honest!"

"I saw the stickers on your van. I thought you were gay. You bring me up here, give me dinner, ask me to stay over…"

"Not *with* me," she said. She took a deep breath. "I am gay. But I'm with someone…I just thought you'd like to stay here. You know, get some rest. I'd bring you back in the morning…you looked hungry!"

"I'd like to go back now," Lee said, eyes down.

Neither of them said a word until they were almost back to town. Lee directed her down a quiet road. The only thing down there was a public storage place with rows and rows of lockers. As the van approached, a raucous chorus of barks greeted them. "Quiet!" Lee yelled out the window. Instantly they stopped. She opened the door.

"Wait," Sarah said. She reached over and pressed some bills and a Lavender Meadows business card into Lee's hand. "Thanks for your help," she said.

She wouldn't meet Sarah's eyes. "Thanks for the food," she said. "And this." She held up the money. She looked at the card. "Lavender Meadows, Sarah Chase, RN, Director," she read. She looked up. "What's this?"

"It's an adult family home for gay women. We

help people who need a place to live, get some care, help with their meds, stuff like that. Right now we're looking for a few more women."

Lee laughed. "An old-age home for dykes, huh? I never heard of such a thing! That's really cool!"

"You'll have to come back sometime and see for yourself. We have a good time."

Lee slid out of the seat. "Yeah, right," she said. "Thanks again for the grub. And I'm sorry. I didn't mean to freak you out."

"You're welcome. And I'm sorry too." She paused for a moment. "Good night, Lee."

"Good-bye, Sarah." She stood on the road until the van turned around, shading her eyes against the glare.

❦❦❦❦

The sun shone warm and bright on the day of the barbeque. Every kind of flower vied for attention, showing off their red, white, yellow, and purple blooms, and sweet scents and the buzzing of the fat, pollen-covered bees filled the air. Jeweled hummingbirds paused at the red feeder for an instant and vanished.

A long green-and-white striped tent covered tables of salads, dips, chips, and big platters of hamburger patties and veggie burgers with tons of toppings, all ready to be cooked on the new grill by Sarah and Jen. And of course, there were a million desserts – everything from cream puffs and cheesecake to chocolate pots de crème in tiny white ramekins.

Marie presided over the goodies, making sure everyone had plenty of everything. She'd made sure there were things that anyone could eat, no matter their diet, allergies, or preferences.

Sarah had laughed at her, but Marie was adamant that no one feel left out, deprived, or (Goddess forbid!) hungry. "I bet someone who was diabetic, vegetarian, lactose intolerant, and allergic to tomatoes and gluten could come to this party and still have a full plate," she teased.

"And it would taste good, too!" Marie said proudly.

Sarah gave her a quick hug, then turned to the Guests of Honor sitting at the head of the table. Grace sat next to her, dressed in a lacy white top and white linen slacks. Beside her sat Edna, in a sparkly silver top and a red-and-silver tiara, then Ginny in flowery polyester.

Sarah tapped on her glass of bubbly cider until the hubbub died down. "Ladies, I would like to propose a toast to our number one resident, Queen Edna the First!"

Edna crowed happily and waved her fork, knocking her crown slightly askew and dislodging Margret, who had been collecting crumbs on her lap.

"Hear, hear!" said Ginny, raising her glass. "And to the success of Lavender Meadows, where the dear old crones are gay!"

※ ※ ※ ※

Over the next couple of weeks, the phone rang incessantly as people called for information on their services. Several people came by for tours, and two more women were thinking about moving in.

Clarisse was trying to help her family come to terms with her after she'd spent her whole life in the closet, and Paula had arthritis and needed help with her every-day care. She'd moved in with her daughter and her family after her partner of thirty years died, and they had two boys and a new baby on the way. She spent most of her time in a wheelchair, and her family couldn't give her as much help as she needed.

"Tell you the truth, I'm looking forward to some peace and quiet," Paula said. "Too much ruckus for me!" She leaned forward and whispered, "I do want them to feel a little guilty, though, so they'll be sure to come and visit me!"

Edna was thriving, and Ginny came by the house to hang out with her every day. "Hell, I'm so used to being around her all the time, I might as well be here. Our house seems so empty now. Besides, school is almost out and I'll have all this time! It feels kind of weird!"

※※※※

Sarah was just helping Grace out of the shower when her pocket started to vibrate and play Jen's ringtone. Surprised, she picked up the call. "Hi, honey, I'm right in the middle of something. Can I call you a little later?" It was unusual for Jen to call when she was out on the boat.

"No, I'm sorry. This is Jim Johnson – I work with Jen on the ferry. Is this Sarah?"

"Yes, what is it? What's wrong?" she asked fearfully.

"I'm sorry—there's been an accident."

Sarah's heart plummeted. "Oh no! What happened? Is Jen all right?"

"Well, she slipped on the stairs and took a nasty

fall. They're just putting her in the ambulance now. She asked me to call you."

"Oh God, oh God," she said. For a moment, she couldn't catch her breath. "Where are you? Which side are you on?"

"We're on the Seattle side. They're taking her to Harborview."

"Hang on just for a second!" Sarah said. She tucked the phone under her chin, sat Grace in a chair, and threw a big towel around her. Grace waved her hand. "Go ahead and talk, dear, I'm all right!"

She took a deep, shaky breath. "What kind of injury does she have?"

"It's her leg. Her ankle, actually. I think she's probably going to have to have surgery. I could see the bone," Jim said.

"Oh, no," she said. "Okay, I'll be there as soon as I can. Can you tell her that? And please tell her I love her. And thanks for calling me!"

"Don't worry. I'm going to the hospital with her and I'll wait for you there," he said. "Drive carefully!"

Sarah hung up and squatted down, tears streaming down her face. "I'm sorry, Grace, I'm going to have to go. The guy said she fell down the stairs, broke her ankle. They're taking her to Harborview."

"Poor thing! Both of you. Of course you have to go," Grace said. She reached out and gave Sarah a big hug. "Harborview is a great hospital, you know. They'll take good care of her."

"I know. Thanks. I'll send Marie up," she said.

She told Marie what had happened and dashed out to the van. She grabbed the ferry schedule from the glove box and struggled to read it through her tears. There wouldn't be a boat for a couple of hours and it would take forever to get there. But she couldn't just sit calmly by waiting for the boat.

On impulse, she called Carol and filled her in.

"I'm at the clinic. I'm almost done for the day," Carol said. "I'll get someone to cover for me. I'll come and get you!" she said.

"Oh, thank you, thank you," Sarah said. She paced up and down for what seemed like forever until Carol showed up.

"Get in!" she said.

"Oh, thank you so much! I'm such a wreck, I don't think I could drive," Sarah said gratefully.

Carol drove as quickly as she could to the bridge on the other side of the island, and an hour later Sarah went running into the Emergency Room. Staff in scrubs, patients waiting to be seen, people on stretchers and in wheelchairs, small knots of friends and family speaking in hushed tones filled the area. She stopped at the nurses' station and smiled when she saw a familiar face.

"Hi, Amy! How are you?" she asked

The nurse looked up and a smile spread across her dark features. "Sarah! How are you? I haven't seen you in a dog's age!"

"I'm doing okay, a little freaked out right now," Sarah admitted.

"Well, what are you doing here?" she asked.

"I'm here to see Jen Pelosi. She had a fall on the ferry boat," Sarah said.

"Oh yes. There's a young man with her now. Are you a family member?" Amy asked.

"Well, I'm her girlfriend," Sarah said. "Why?"

"Oh yeah? What happened to Nancy?"

"Yesterday's news."

"Good for you!" she said with a smile. "I think she's much hotter than Nancy, even with all the blood and the moaning."

Sarah gasped.

"Just kidding!" she said, as Sarah swatted at her. "No, really, I thought she had something going on with the guy. He looked so worried. Well, I believe she is going to have surgery soon, and she needs some papers signed," she said, flipping through Jen's chart.

"Can't she sign her own paperwork?" Sarah asked.

"Normally she would be able to, but she's had some pain medication. Legally, she can't do it if she's sedated, you know, and it would be awful if she had to let the pain meds wear off—it would be better if she had a family member around to sign, just in case there's any problem."

Carol came in and put her arm around Sarah. "How's she doing?" she asked.

"Well, I guess they need a family member to sign her consent, because she's sedated," Sarah said. "This is Amy, ER nurse extraordinaire. This is my friend, Carol. She's a physical therapist."

"Nice to meet you. How do you two know each other?" Carol asked.

"I used to work here," Sarah said. "Do you know anything about Jen's family? I've never met her folks, and I don't even know their names."

"Let's call them," Carol said. "They don't live too far from here, and I'm sure they'd want to know what was going on. Do you have Jen's phone?"

"No, I don't," Sarah said. She turned to the Amy. "Can we see her?"

"Sure, she's in room three." She pointed down

the hall. "Nice to see you again. You'll have to come back and tell me what you've been up to."

"I will," Sarah promised.

Jen lay on her back, asleep, her right leg elevated on pillows and surrounded with ice packs. A big dressing that was starting to bleed through covered her ankle. An IV dripped into her arm. A young man in a ferry uniform leaned back in a chair by the bedside, his eyes closed. "She looks so pale," Carol whispered.

"I know," Sarah said, dabbing at her eyes. Tentatively, she touched Jen's arm. "Hi, love. We're here."

Jen opened her eyes and smiled weakly. "Hi, honey. Thanks for coming," she said to them. "I guess I really messed up, huh?"

"A sneaky way to get some time off from work, I think," Carol said. "Do your folks know what happened?"

Jen shook her head.

The young man opened his eyes and straightened up. "Hi, I'm Jim," he said. "I'm the one who called you."

"Hi, I'm Sarah. And this is Carol. Thank you so much for calling and for coming in with her."

"Sure, no problem. I couldn't let Jen hang out here alone. We're buds!"

"That's right!" Jen said. "We've been working together since I started with the ferry." She looked at him and grinned. "How are you gonna manage without me?"

"I know it won't be for long. You'll be back before you know it," Jim said. "I gotta get back to work now, though. I see you're in good hands. And Sarah – you're as pretty as Jen says you are."

Sarah blushed. "Well, thank you – thank both of

you!"

"I'm going to take your phone and call your folks. They should come in," Carol said.

"Don't scare them, now. I'm all right," Jen said.

"Yeah, I see how all right you are," Sarah said. She took Jen's hand. "Are you hurting?"

Jen nodded. "They gave me a shot in the ambulance, and then another one right before you got here. I think. Anyway, I feel the pain, but it seems far away."

"How did this happen?" Sarah asked.

"I don't know. I was going down the stairs, and they were wet. I guess somebody spilled something. Next thing I know, I was flying through the air…" Jen sighed and closed her eyes. "I'm so glad you're here, love," she said.

"Of course I'm here," Sarah said. She put her head down on Jen's chest. "I'll always be here."

"So you're Sarah. Jen has told us so much about you," Jen's mom said. "I'm Catherine," she said, holding out her hand. "And this is David, Jen's dad," she said, indicating the slender white-haired man beside her. "I know you're a nurse – maybe you can tell us what's happening."

"I don't know too much. The doctor hasn't been in yet. I think he wanted to speak with all of us at the same time," Sarah said. "I think it's a pretty bad break, though. She'll probably be pretty bruised for a while, too. It was quite a fall." She paused. "Did you sign all the papers?"

"Yes, we took care of all of that at the front desk,"

she said.

Sarah was so glad that Jen's family was able to come in to sign the consents and other papers. She wondered what would have happened if she'd been the one who fell. Nobody would have come in to sign for her. The thought made her ache.

"Knock knock," said a voice behind the curtain. "I'm Dr. Reyes. I'm the orthopedic surgeon on call. Can I come in?"

"Yes, doctor, of course," Catherine said. He was a short, blocky man with bushy black eyebrows and powerful hands and arms. "Somebody move so the doctor can sit down."

"Hi, Jennifer," he said. "How are you feeling?" He looked down at her leg, gently touched her toes.

"Crummy," she said. "I'm starting to hurt pretty bad again."

"I'm sorry, but we're going to take you to the OR in just a few minutes and you'll be asleep. There are two bones in the lower leg, and it looks like you've broken both of them, and a couple of the ankle bones as well."

Catherine moaned softly and took David's hand.

"It's a pretty bad break, and the bones pierced your skin. That's what we call a compound fracture. We'll stabilize it with pins, and you're going to have to take it easy for a while. You're also going to need a lot of physical therapy. But we'll get you fixed up, maybe not quite as good as new, but almost." He smiled and patted her hand.

"Will I be able to go back to work anytime soon?" Jen asked.

"We'll just have to take it one step at a time," he said. "I'll be in to talk with you after the surgery."

"Time to go," Amy said, pushing the gurney into the cubicle. "If all of you could wait outside." Jen's mom and dad kissed her and backed out of the room.

"Let me help," said Sarah. She gathered up Jen's things and put them into a plastic bag, then slid her arm under Jen's shoulders to help her scoot over. She moaned a little as Amy lifted her leg and moved it onto the gurney. Sarah felt as if she'd been stabbed when she heard that sound and saw Jen's lips, tight and bloodless. She leaned over and gave her a quick kiss. "I'll be waiting for you, babe," she said. She walked with them and held Jen's hand until Amy pushed the gurney into the elevator. Tears filled her eyes again as the door slid closed.

※ ※ ※ ※

Jen's mom sat in the cafeteria, idly stirring a cup of cooling coffee. "This is awful. Just awful. What is she going to do now?"

"She's probably going to need quite a while to recover," Sarah said. "Her bones were broken in several places, and they're going to take time to heal, even with the surgery. And she probably won't be able to bear weight on her leg for a while." She tried her best to keep her voice calm and professional. Just the facts, ma'am.

"She's probably gonna lose her job. She won't be able to do it anymore," David said gruffly. "I always worried about her working on the boats. No place for a woman, I think."

"It's a good thing Jen didn't hear you say that," Catherine said, smiling wanly. "You know she would have given you what for."

"I know, I know. I'm just saying."

"Well, we could fix up her old room. She'd like to be home, I think, and I could take care of her, help her with things," she said.

"Now Cathy, you know that's not gonna work," David said, counting on his fingers. "One—her bedroom is upstairs. Two—there are bunk beds in there now and the grandkids wouldn't have a place to sleep if they stayed over. We'd have to change the whole room. Three—she probably wouldn't be able to use the bathroom up there. A wheelchair just wouldn't fit. Four—you'd have to quit your job," he said.

"But I'm her mother! It's my job to take care of her," she said, shaking her head. "And she can't be alone in that little apartment."

"I know. You know how she hates to sit around. And she doesn't like anyone to do for her. This will drive her crazy!" he said.

Sarah's mind raced. "Let's wait and see what we find out after the surgery. We'll have a better idea of what she's going to need then."

"Yes, we'll figure it out," her dad said. "I just hope she'll be all right."

Me too, Sarah said silently. Oh please, let her be all right.

It was a long week in the hospital before Jen was transferred to the rehab wing at Viking Manor. She was so down in the dumps she could barely talk. She worried about her job and whether she'd be able to go back to the boats. She worried about her apartment and about money. And she worried about Sarah and their relationship.

"Stop worrying," Catherine said. "Everything will be all right."

"You can't know that. Nobody can!" Jen said.

She worked as hard as she could in physical therapy, but she was in a lot of pain. She couldn't bear weight on her leg, and she spent her time either in a wheelchair or on crutches.

"Jen, you need to ask for pain medicine when you need it. You can't accomplish as much in physical therapy if you're hurting," Carol said.

"That's right. Listen to her!" Sarah said, looking down. The leg was purple and green and swollen, and the stitches made it look like the work of Frankenstein.

"You know I don't like to take that stuff. It makes me feel weird."

"You *are* weird. It's not the meds, it's you." Sarah laughed.

"Ha ha. I'm gonna tell my mom you're picking on me."

"What is she gonna do? Beat me up? She knows it's true," Sarah said.

"I'm not looking forward to being with them. I love my mom and dad, but you know I'll be in the looney bin before you know it. And my room is upstairs. I'll never make it up there." She covered her face with her hands for a moment and took a deep, trembling breath. "And I hate being so far away from you. I know you can't hang with me. Grace and the other ladies need you."

"Ummm, about that," Sarah said in her most diplomatic voice. "I talked to Grace and Marie, and we think you should come home with us. Now that I have the room downstairs, it would be easy for you to stay there. You could go out to the porch or the garden, and we could keep you in line. Or try to, anyway!" She grinned as Jen reached out to pinch her. "And Carol could see you as often as necessary."

"No, I can't do that. It's asking too much. I'd be in the way. You have a lot of stuff going on with the other ladies."

"You'd be doing us a favor. Remember, we are looking for other residents. And now you can be one." She grinned. "And it would give me a chance to spoil you a little."

"But I'm not an old lady."

"Well, we could make you an honorary crone, and you'd fit right in. And then I could take care of you, and wash you, and kiss your neck, and rub your back...and maybe your front..."

"Sold!" Jen said happily. "But maybe I wouldn't want to get better too fast..."

※ ※ ※ ※

A bright full moon hung in the summer sky. The Lavender women had put together a potluck of major proportions to celebrate the season and invited a bunch of other lesbians from the island and as far away as Seattle and Port Townsend. Long strings of Japanese lanterns illuminated the scene as songs were sung, instruments played, dances danced – circles and couples and lines and women dancing alone to their own private music. Every now and then Sarah leaned forward and tossed another piece of wood on the fire and they watched it spark and snap.

"Could you make me another marshmallow, please, dahling," Jen said.

"Certainly, my love." She stuck a couple of marshmallows on the end of her stick and held it over the fire until they were toasty brown.

Jen shifted restlessly in her wheelchair. "Why don't you go and dance?" she said. "I know you love it."

"I do, but I'd rather dance with you," she said. She lit a joint and inhaled deeply. "Ummm," she hummed, and passed it to Jen.

"Thanks," she said, and took a hit. "You'll have to wait a while for that!" She sighed. "I feel funny smoking out here in public. I can't believe it's legal now."

"Well, we're not really out in public – nobody here but us chickens!" Sarah said. "But I know what you mean – it makes me feel a bit wicked." She chuckled.

"Wicca? Wicca? Did somebody say Wicca?" said a woman with a long flowery skirt and ombre hair as she danced by them. She stopped and sniffed the air. "Oh, what is that I smell?"

Jen laughed and passed her the joint. "Just a bit of wicked wacky weed for a magical night!" she said.

"Don't mind if I do," she said, and breathed in deeply. "Nice! And legal, too! Can you believe it?"

"We have a lot to celebrate this year," Sarah said. "Legal marijuana and gay marriage in one year! We are truly blessed!"

"I never thought I'd see these things in my lifetime," the woman said.

"Really, really." Jen stuck out her hand. "I don't think we've met. My name is Jen, and this is Sarah," she said.

The woman flopped down on the ground in front of them. "Nice to meet you. My name is Willow. What happened to you?" she asked, pointing at Jen's leg.

"I tried to do somersaults on the ferry stairs," she said wryly.

"Nice!" said Willow. She looked around. "Wow, this is some place, huh?"

"It is, isn't it? We love it!" Sarah said.

"Do you know who lives here? I just heard about this party, but I don't really know many people around here. I live in Port Orchard."

"Well, we live here – sort of. See Grace and Marie over there?" She pointed at the two of them sitting on the other side of the fire, toasting their toes and marshmallows too. She waved at them and they waved back happily, sherry glasses in hand. "They own this place. It's an adult family home and rehab place for lesbians. And critters!" she said as Margret jumped into her lap. She smiled.

"Wow! I didn't know there was such a place. Amazing!"

"I'm a nurse, and the director. And assistant to the queens." Sarah said with a smile.

"Very cool. Not about you falling down the stairs, of course. I mean being able to recuperate here."

"I'm playing the pity card for all it's worth," Jen said, taking another hit.

"Are you a Wiccan?" Sarah asked.

"No, I'm a nurse. Too." She laughed. "Of course, I could be a Wiccan, and a nurse, but I'm not. Wait, I am a nurse, but not a Wiccan. Not that there's anything wrong with that," she said, laughing. "Some of my best friends are Wiccan." She laughed again and held out her hand. "Maybe I need another hit, if you don't mind." She took a deep drag and handed it back to Jen.

"What kind of nursing do you do?" Sarah asked.

"I do home health around the peninsula."

"I bet that's a fun job," Jen said. "You ride around and see bunches of people in their homes, right? So if I didn't have this beautiful woman taking care of me, you could come out to see me!" She patted Sarah's leg.

"That's right, but I see you're well taken care of," Willow said with a smile. "Parts of the job are fun, but I'm getting a little tired of it. I feel like I spend my whole life in my car! And there's so much paperwork!" She sighed. "I spend more time writing than I do with my patients!"

"I know what you mean. I don't miss all the writing. Of course, we have to document things here too, but it's certainly not the same. Are you an LPN or an RN?" Sarah asked.

"I'm an LPN, but hopefully not for too much longer. I want to go back and finish school. How about you?"

"I'm an RN, but I was an LPN, too. And an aide and a candy striper. I guess it was meant to be," Sarah said. "I can't really imagine doing anything else."

"Me either. There's certainly a lot you can do with it. Like, I wouldn't mind working on a cruise ship or being a traveling nurse. I'd like to see some new places. After I finish school, I guess." She jumped up. "Well, I'd better get to dancing. The night is young!" she said, and spun away.

"She's fun," Jen said. "If you ever get tired of taking care of me…"

"Fagetaboutit," Sarah said, and pinched her.

The pace of the music and dancing picked up as it got later and later. Friends stopped to say hi and make sympathetic sounds over Jen's leg. The softball players gave her a rough time about abandoning them in the middle of the season. Sarah met so many women her head began to spin. "I'll never remember all of your names," she said. "Don't tell me anymore!"

Suddenly a familiar face caught her eye. It was Lee, the woman she'd met at Costco. She still wore the black leather jacket Sarah had noticed that day. "Well hi!" she said. "I know you!"

"I know you too," Lee said.

"Lee, this is Jen, my girlfriend," she said. "Jen, this is Lee, the woman I met at Costco. She's the one who put our barbeque together."

"I see you're putting it to good use tonight," Lee said. She checked Jen out and nodded to herself.

"You bet!" Jen said. She stuck out her hand. "Nice to meet you."

"Same. Quite the party," Lee said.

"Yes, Grace and Marie are quite the party girls," Sarah said. "How are you doing?"

"Okay, staying busy, trying to stay out of trouble," Lee said.

"I was hoping I'd run into you again," Sarah said. "We have some things that need to be done around here, and as you can see, Jen had to go and break her ankle so she could get out of helping out."

"Bummer. What did you do?"

"I work on the ferry, and I fell down the stairs. Embarrassing!"

"Really." Lee shook her head. "That's a tough way to get out of work."

"Yup, it gave me the opportunity to feel both useless and stupid."

"Or neither!" Sarah said. "So, can I call you? If you feel like picking up some work?"

"I don't have a phone," Lee said. "And I do have a job. I don't think I would be available."

"Okay," Sarah said. She thought about Lee picking through the leftovers at the food court. "I'm glad things are going well for you."

"Thanks," she said. She stared off in the distance. "Oh, there's some people I know," Lee said. "I'd better go say hi. Nice seeing you again. And nice meeting you." She stuffed her hands in her pockets and walked away, heading toward the food tables and the enticing smell of the barbeque.

"Wow," Jen said. "She really likes you."

"What do you mean?" Sarah said.

"She couldn't even make eye contact with you. I could've been on fire and she wouldn't have noticed."

"Don't be silly. She's just a kid."

"She looks like more than a kid to me. Kind of reminds me of that *Girl with the Dragon Tattoo* chick."

"Yeah, now that you mention it," Sarah said. "Another marshmallow?"

"You bet."

The sun was coming up when the last of the partiers headed out. Sarah helped Grace, Edna, and Jen to bed while Marie and a couple of sleepy women packed up the rest of the food. When she was done, Sarah went out again to turn off the lights and make sure the fire was out. She was checking out the barbeque when something caught her eye on one of the chairs – a black leather jacket. She picked it up – it smelled like smoke.

≈≈≈≈

The scent of ripe fruit sweetened the air in the kitchen. Rows of sparkling glass jars lined up on the newspaper-covered counter, big canning pots billowed steam, women of all ages gathered around the table cutting up tomatoes and peaches and tossing the pieces into big bowls. It looked like a Norman Rockwell painting.

"Whew!" Sarah said, wiping the sweat from her face with a big bandanna. "Sure is warm in here!"

"Open the doors!" Marie said. "Let some of the steam out!"

"No, then the flies will come in!" Savannah said, fanning away imaginary critters.

"Stop being such babies," Grace said briskly. "Here, I need some more berries!" She held out her empty basket for a refill.

"You are just a hulling machine, Grace," said Sarah, passing over another load of the blackberries she had just picked that morning.

"You young girls just can't keep up!" Grace said smugly.

"I'm working on it," Jen muttered, bent over her basket.

"Slow down! You girls are so competitive!" Ro said.

"We are not working by the hour, like some people we know," Grace said sweetly.

"No, this is more like pro bono work," Ro said, smiling. "I'm used to that!"

"Because you like to get people out of a jam!" Sarah said.

"Boo!" Jen said, and tossed a berry at her.

"Food fight!" Jen yelled, raising a handful of blackberries. Sarah raised a purple-stained hand to defend herself and growled threateningly.

"You are no better than a pack of wolves," Marie said. "You better behave, or there will be no lunch for you!"

"Yes ma'am," Jen said meekly, returning her ammunition to the bowl.

"I've got my eye on you, young lady. We know how to keep your kind in line," Ro said sternly. She turned to Marie. "What's on the menu at the Lavender Wolf Lodge today?"

"Let's see." Marie counted off on her fingers. "Chicken salad with almonds, scones with plum jam, and peach pie," she said. "Oh, and peach daiquiris, of course."

"Can we have some of those now?" Grace said hopefully.

"Belly up to the bar," she said.

Finally, the jars were filled and taking their turns in the water baths. The women adjourned to the garden to eat their lunch, which actually did contain a few items other than fruit. The daiquiris flowed freely to everyone but Rachel. "No thanks, I'm not drinking," she said. She smiled and held her hand over her glass.

"But you love daiquiris," Carol said.

"Yes, but I guess I'll have to wait for a few months," Rachel said with a big grin. "We're having a baby!"

It only took an instant for the good news to sink in.

"Congratulations!"

"Wow!"

"Cool!"

"Awesome"

"Incredible!"

They gathered around the two of them with hugs and kisses, and Jen waved at them from her wheelchair.

"Who's the donor?" she asked.

"We decided to go the anonymous route," Emily said. "No political agendas that way."

"When are you due?" Grace asked.

"About thirty-six weeks from today!" Rachel laughed. "Beginner's luck!"

"And skill!" Emily said proudly. "And strong swimmers!"

"So, are you going to get married?" Ro asked.

"We'd like to," Emily said. "Make this kiddo legal! But we're not in a hurry. We already had a ceremony, you know. And we made out domestic partnership papers when Reverend Leah did the commitment, and that was a couple of years ago. So we are married, as far as we're concerned."

"And you are also married, as far as the state is concerned," Ro said. "Domestic partnerships now become legal marriages after two years, you know."

"Yes, but isn't it cool that you can actually be official now," Grace said. "I never thought I'd see this in my lifetime." She looked over at Marie.

"Wait a minute, now," Savannah said. "You mean that if you have domestic partnership papers that are more than two years old, you are automatically married?"

"Yes, unless the partnership is revoked. This is a new thing that happened recently. It's not just for gays, though." Ro laughed. "I think there were some straight couples in this state who were surprised to find out that they were married, too. They filled out the papers, then broke up later, and never thought about undoing their agreements. It's a legal nightmare!"

Savannah took a deep, shaky breath. "So does that mean Carrie and I are married?"

"I guess, I don't know," Ro said. "Who is Carrie?"

"Carrie is my partner," she said. "Has been for many years. You've never met her."

"What do you mean? Are you holding out on us?" Ro asked.

"Well. Carrie and I were together practically forever, and then she got into a car accident. She was hit by a drunk driver and was in a coma for a long time." Savannah drew a ragged breath. Grace patted her on the shoulder.

"So what happened then?" Ro asked.

"Carrie was not out to her family, and after the accident I had to explain that we weren't just roommates. They totally freaked out. They're very homophobic, and they took out a restraining order against me. I haven't been allowed to see her or speak to her for all these years. She's not in a coma anymore, but she has some brain damage and she's in a nursing home. I guess her sister is her legal guardian."

The women all spoke at once.

"Oh my!"

"That's horrible!" "

"I can't believe it!"

"Isn't that something!"

Grace and Marie looked on grimly, shaking their heads. "Poor Savannah," Grace said. "We thought she was going to die. Her heart was just broken."

"So they took out a restraining order," Ro said. "Did you ever see a lawyer or go to court?"

"No," Savannah said. "It seemed pointless. The family wouldn't even talk to me. They wouldn't budge."

"So you haven't seen her for how many years?" Ro asked.

"Well, I guess it's five years, so I haven't seen her officially. But I go to see her every week, and I can see her through the door. I always bring her flowers, she loves them so."

Ro shook her head. "Does the family come to visit?"

"I don't think so. They don't really care about her. I think they feel like she's dead. But she's not!" Savannah said fiercely.

"So what would you want to happen?" Ro asked carefully.

"I would want to be back in her life! Of course! I want her with me! She's my love!"

"But you know, there's a lot of responsibility that goes along with this," Ro said. "I don't know what all is involved, but I could check it out if you want."

"Oh my goodness! Of course! Of course!" And Savannah wept, tears of relief, tears of joy.

✥✥✥✥

Sarah got her list together for another assault on Costco. She couldn't believe how much they needed – paper towels, toilet paper, denture paste, shampoo, cat and dog food, tuna, plastic bags of every size. And of course, she had to pick up a few Costco rotisserie chickens – the best in the Northwest. She was glad she had a van. Which now had a bright new Lavender Meadows logo on the door.

"Wanna go for a ride, honey?" she asked Jen. "You haven't been anywhere for a while. You must be getting cabin fever."

"No, not really. Yes, I do. No. Wait. I don't know." Jen said. "No, it's such a pain to get in and out of the van, get out the wheelchair, yatta yatta. "

"Okay. Hopefully it won't be too much longer

until you're up on your feet," Sarah said sympathetically.

"It better not be – or I'll go mad! Mad! Mad, I tell you!" She ran her hands through her hair and made it stand straight up, bugged her eyes out and cackled.

"Oh, uh-oh, she's losing it," she said to Marie. "I'd better get out of here. Don't frighten the ladies, dear. Anything else?" she asked the air. "The bus is leaving! Sarah has left the building!"

"How about a nice box of wine?" Marie said. "A good vintage, fruity but not pretentious. And some sherry, too, please."

Sarah laughed and headed out to the van. Then on second thought she went back in, picked up the black leather jacket that had been there since the party, and threw it into the back of the van.

She was glad to get away for a couple of hours and took her time getting to the store, stopping along the way to take in the water views from the cliffs around the island. She finally got hungry, and headed to Costco with visions of a great hotdog with lots of mustard and onions.

The parking lot was crowded, as usual, but she found a space fairly close to the door. She snagged a cart and began walking, looking up each aisle as she went. Suddenly she realized that she was looking for a glimpse of a goth person with lots of piercings and plenty of ink. Silly, she thought. But she still looked by the sample tables and the snack bar too, remembering how the woman rummaged for leftovers scattered around on the picnic tables. No Lee.

She finished her shopping, had her hotdog, and headed back to the van. She unloaded her cart and caught sight of the black leather jacket on the back seat. Too bad, she thought. She would have liked to return it, even though it was July and pretty warm.

She drove back toward The Meadows, then turned off the highway on a sudden impulse. She made a left onto the road by the storage place where she had dropped Lee off that night and into a space in the front. Silly, she thought. But she got out of the van and went into the office.

"Hi, how can I help you?" said the pleasant-looking woman behind the desk.

"Hi. I know this is kind of weird – I'm looking for someone, and I wonder if you could tell me if you'd seen her."

"Are you with the police?" the woman asked doubtfully, looking at Sarah's jeans and roughed-up shoes.

"No, she's a friend, but I lost her phone number and I don't know where she lives. I dropped her off here a few weeks ago, but I don't see any houses on this road."

"Your friend – what does she look like?"

"She's young, maybe in her late teens or early twenties, with spiky hair and lots of tattoos," Sarah said.

"Oh, you mean Lee. I don't know if she's around. You can look over by her unit, number fifty-four. It's around back – you can drive if you want."

"Thanks!" Sarah said. She knew that the odds of running into her there were very slim. She got back in the van, ready to give up and drive to the highway, but somehow she ended driving around the back to the unit.

The door of the unit was rolled partway up, and Sarah could hear Brandi Carlyle singing. She pulled over and got out of the van. "Hello? Hello? Lee, are you here? It's Sarah, from Lavender Meadows."

She heard the sound of footsteps and the door clattered upward. Sarah peered into the dimly lit space until her eyes adjusted to the gloom. Lee stood there wearing cut-off shorts and a blue tank top with crescents of sweat under the arms. A sheen of sweat covered her face. She looked Sarah up and down. "Uh, what are you doing here?" she said, amazed.

"Uh, well, you left your jacket – I was hoping to run into you at the store," Sarah said, embarrassed. She looked past Lee and saw that the light was coming from a tiny lamp on an upended milk crate. A small pile of books and magazines and single mattress covered with an old blanket took up half of the cement floor. A cardboard box held a couple of shirts and pairs of pants, neatly folded. A guitar case leaned against the wall. Sarah could feel the waves of heat coming from inside the small space. "Gee – do you live here?"

"Yeah, so?" Lee said, scowling.

"Oh, I'm sorry – that was so rude. I was just surprised, that's all. I didn't know people stayed in places like this," Sarah said hastily. "I'm sorry – I'm just making it worse, aren't I?"

"Not everyone gets to live in a fancy house and drive a nice van," Lee said sarcastically.

"That's true," Sarah said. "I guess I just never thought about it."

"Well, I'm not the only person who lives here. There's a family with two little kids in number ninety-nine, and there's a guy who stays in 104."

"Does the manager know there are people staying here?" Sarah asked.

"We help them out and they kind of look the other way. I sweep up the place, clean the bathrooms, and take out the trash. Jeff cuts the grass and stays around at night, like a watchman. The family – I don't speak Spanish. The mom's got a big belly again. I don't know what the man does, some yard work or something, I think. They have an old beat up car, and I guess they lived in it for a while. They just don't have any place else to go. It's better to be inside someplace, I think. At least in here I can stretch out. Sure is hot in the summer, though. And cold in the winter!"

Sarah paused for a moment. "I'm starving. How about you? Want to grab some lunch?"

"Uh, no thanks. I just ate," Lee said, patting her concave stomach.

"Okay – are you sure?" Sarah said.

"Yes, thanks," she said.

"Okay, another time then," Sarah said, opening the van door. A cloud of warm roast chicken scent wafted out. Lee swallowed hard and looked away. "Would you like a chicken? I just bought a whole bunch. Maybe you could share it with the other people."

"Uh, ok. I'll do that. Thank you." She sniffed appreciatively as Sarah handed it over. She cradled it like a precious baby.

"Oh, I almost forgot. Would you be free to do some work for us? It's a big place and we sure could use some help. Especially since Jen is laid up with her ankle. I asked you during the party, but maybe you might have time now."

"What kind of work?" Lee asked suspiciously.

"Oh, I don't know. There's a bunch of stuff. I can't do it all myself. I play around in the garden a little, but mostly I take care of the ladies, and Jen too. I could use the help."

"Er...I'll think about it."

"Okay. Why don't you call me when you have some free time? Here's my number." She handed her another Lavender Meadows card with her cell phone number. "And let me get your jacket." She grabbed the jacket, sneaked a twenty-dollar bill into the pocket, and handed it over. "Here you go."

"Thanks for bringing it back. I couldn't believe I left without it. Stupid."

"No problem. You be safe." She climbed into the van and waved as she drove away.

Later, she brought up the subject of Lee at the dinner table. "You remember that woman who put our barbecue together? I ran into her today on my way home from Costco."

"Yeah, I remember. Lots of ink. She did a good job on the barbeque. Those things are a pain in the ass to put together," Jen said.

"I'm glad I found her. I wanted to give her back her jacket. I'm sure it's important to her," Sarah said.

"That was nice of you," Grace said.

"I felt bad about leaving her there. Living in a storage unit, sleeping on the floor. Awful! And who knows what kind of trouble she could get into?" She thought of Lee trying to kiss her, and imagined what kinds of things she might have had to do to feed herself. It gave her the chills. She took a deep breath. "Do you think we could give her some stuff to do? It would help me out a lot, and probably her too."

"That's a fine idea," Grace said. "Is she a lesbian?"

"Yes, I'm pretty sure," Sarah said. "If my gaydar is right." She thought back to that almost-kiss again. "We didn't really talk about it."

"Do you think she's trustworthy?"

"I don't know – I only met her a couple of times.

I can't vouch for her, but I have a good feeling," Sarah said.

"Not too good of a feeling, I hope," said Jen.

"Oh, you," Sarah said, and pinched her arm.

༄༅༄༅

Savannah anxiously awaited a call from Ro after the conversation they'd had on canning day. She could hardly restrain herself from calling and pestering her, even though she knew it would probably take a few days for her to get the information about Carrie. She rehearsed what seemed like a hundred scenarios in her head – Carrie's family would take her to court. The new law about same sex partners would not apply to them. The police would arrest her if Carrie's family found out that she'd violated the restraining order. She would be accused of kidnapping. Ro wouldn't be able to help them. Or, the worst scenario of all, Carrie wouldn't want to see her.

At last, her phone rang, and when Ro's name showed up on her phone, Savannah could barely catch her breath enough to answer. "Hi, Ro, this is Savannah," she gasped.

"Hi, Savannah. You must have had the phone in your hand."

She laughed shakily. "I've been afraid to put it down. I'm so wound up. Did you find out anything?"

"Yes indeed. Sit down and catch your breath," Ro said.

"Is it bad news? It is, isn't it? I knew it!" Savannah said. She felt the tears welling up for the hundredth time in the past few days. "It's hopeless, isn't it?"

"Now, don't jump the gun. Let me explain what I

found out. Are you okay?"

"Yes, yes, please! Just tell me!" Savannah grabbed a pillow from the couch and held it tightly in her arms.

"Okay. Back in 2012, the Washington state voters passed a law that said that on July 1, 2014, any same-sex couple who were registered domestic partners and below the age of sixty-two were officially married. "

"That's incredible!" Savannah said excitedly. "Of course, I'd heard some things about it, but I didn't really pay attention because I didn't think it pertained to us – what with the restraining order, and Carrie's injuries, and that harpy of a sister getting guardianship."

"So her sister got control of her finances, is that right?" Ro asked.

"Yes. The insurance company made a settlement that was supposed to take care of Carrie's medical bills, therapy, and other expenses. I don't know what happened to that money."

"Well, apparently Carrie's sister got a pretty hefty chunk of change for keeping track of her finances. That money is gone. There is still some left for her future care, though, so I guess her sister couldn't access that," Ro explained. "I'll have to look into the financials a little more. But I was more interested in finding out what kind of shape Carrie is in, and whether or not you would qualify to be her guardian."

"Well, I hope so. Carrie's sister shouldn't be able to get her mitts on any more of that money. That's not really a big point with me, though – I just want to see Carrie and be with her again. I've missed her terribly these past five years, and I felt so helpless."

"Well, if you're officially married, that relationship should supersede her sister's guardianship claims. This is not really my area of expertise, but we'll check it out."

"So what happens now?" Savannah asked. She tried to keep her voice calm.

"First, let's contact the court and see if we're on the right track here. Then let's see about getting the restraining order lifted. You're not going to go crazy and threaten Carrie or beat her up or try to take advantage of her, are you?" Ro chuckled. "No? Then we need to meet with her sister and get all the bits and pieces straightened out."

"So what happens then? Does she have to stay in that nursing home? Or can I take her home?" Savannah said. "I don't even know what kind of care she needs. I know she's not in a coma anymore. But she may not even recognize me. She may not know who I am!"

"We'll get all that information from her doctor and the facility, and then we'll know what she needs."

"Okay, okay! So how long do you think this will take? When can I see her?" Savannah asked anxiously.

"We should probably be able to get some things worked out in the next few days. I'll let you know as soon as I hear something," Ro said. "Oh, and Savannah? Let me be the first to congratulate you on your marriage!"

Ro laughed as she heard Savannah's whoops on the phone.

⁂

A week later, Savannah and Ro went to the nursing home where Carrie had been living for almost five years. Carrie's sister Joyce came in with her husband and her lawyer. Savannah noticed that she looked a lot like Carrie, but she had a hard and bitter edge. She wouldn't make eye contact with Savannah.

Joyce's husband looked at Savannah, shrugged, and smiled apologetically.

They took turns signing paper after paper. In addition to financial details, they also had to sign over the handicap-accessible van they had bought from the settlement. Carrie had never gotten to ride in it, but maybe now it could be used for its intended purpose.

Finally, Savannah and Ro saw Judy, Carrie's nurse. Savannah hugged her, and she handed out tissues all around. "I never thought this would come about," Judy said. "It's like a miracle! What a happy day!"

Savannah knocked on Carrie's door. Slowly, she pushed it open and stood in the doorway, a big bouquet in her arms. Carrie looked up and saw her standing there, and she waved her arms and smiled a smile bright as the sun. "Sa! Sa! Sanna! Ah!" she cried. Savannah ran in and took her legal wife in her arms for the first time, sobbing with love and joy.

Sarah had just finished getting Edna up in a wheelchair so she could go downstairs for lunch when her phone buzzed. She looked at it quickly and saw an unfamiliar number. She was used to letting calls go to voicemail but since they started Lavender Meadows up again, she had to be better about taking her calls. After all, they were still looking for a couple of new residents, and there were also lots of business calls she had to take as well.

"Damn," she said. "Hold on, Edna, I'll be with you in a minute. Hello," she said. "This is Sarah Chase at Lavender Meadows. How can I help you?"

"Hi, Sarah. This is Lee."

"Oh, hi, Lee, how are you?"

"I'm doing okay." She paused. "I was wondering if you were serious about needing some help up there."

She tucked the phone under her chin and started pushing Edna's chair toward the stairs. "Sure, I was serious. Am serious. But right now, I'm in the middle of something. Can I call you back in a few minutes?"

"Uh, no, that's okay. I don't want to interrupt you." She took a deep breath. "I'll call you another time, I guess."

Duh, Sarah, she thought. If Lee was living in a storage unit, she probably didn't have a phone. "No, wait, don't hang up," Sarah said. "Why don't you come up here and let's talk about it?"

"Okay, if you're sure. I'll catch a ride up there sometime."

Sarah thought quickly. She had the feeling that if she didn't see Lee soon that she wouldn't call back. "Where are you? I can come and get you," she said.

"I'm at the unit. But I know you're busy," Lee said.

"Give me a little while to get down there," Sarah said. "I'll be there as soon as I can."

She helped Edna onto the stair lift and called down the stairs. "Incoming!"

"Be right there," Carol called back.

Sarah waited until Carol came to the bottom of the stairs with a wheelchair before she clicked the button to start the stair climber. She walked beside Edna, making sure she was sitting securely. As they moved downwards, Sarah thought back to her first days at the house, when Marie was so worried about getting Grace up the stairs safely. She was certainly familiar with it now.

"Hey, Edna," Carol said with a smile. "Your limo awaits!"

Edna giggled. "Ride!" she said.

Sarah and Carol got her settled in her chair and wheeled her into the dining room. Grace was already there, and so was Jen. Marie ran in and out of the kitchen, carrying serving dishes and pitchers of iced tea. Sarah tucked a napkin under Edna's neck, dished up her food, and started to cut it up into manageable chunks. Savannah did the same for Carrie, smiling and watching her as if she could never get enough of the sight of her.

"Come on, Marie, stop running and sit down!" She looked around at the faces around the table and took Sarah's hand. "Okay, everybody, let's do it!" Grace said.

"Happy happy, joy joy!" they said in chorus.

Finally, Sarah and Carol got to bolt down some lunch before they moved everyone on to their next activities – physical therapy for Jen and Edna, hanging out in the garden for Carrie and Grace, back to the kitchen for Marie.

"Honestly, Carol, I don't know what I'd do if you weren't here to help out," Sarah said later. "I don't think I could manage this by myself. I'd never be able to set foot out of here."

"I'm glad to help," she said. "I'm glad you were able to take me on part-time. You know I love the clinic, and visiting my other patients, but I love being here too. This is such a cool place!"

"Well, maybe I can get us a little more help," Sarah said. Briefly, she filled Carol in on her conversation with Lee. "So I'm going to ride down there to Silverdale and talk with her, see what she has in mind."

"To do what?" Carol asked.

"Marie could use some help for sure," Sarah said. "And she's good with tools and working outside. And with Jen laid up for how long…" She sighed. "Maybe if she's interested we could train her to do some physical care, showers and such."

"You trust her? You don't really know her," Carol said cautiously.

"We wouldn't really know anyone we hired, not at first," Sarah said. "We could do a background check, but it wouldn't mean anything unless the person had been arrested. We'd have to keep an eye on everyone, see how they work out, see how they treat the ladies." She paused. "Maybe she's a little rough around the edges, but I have a really good feeling about her. I think she has a good heart."

"I hope so!" Carol said. "We sure could use the help!"

❧❧❧❧

She told Grace about Lee's phone call and asked how she felt about hiring Lee to work at Lavender Meadows. She told her what little she knew about the girl.

Grace shook her head sadly. "Nobody should have to live like that!"

"I agree," Sarah said. "I think she would do well here, help us out and give her a chance to get settled in a safe place. It's a win-win." She paused. "How do you think Marie would feel about having some help?"

"I don't know," Grace said. "She'd probably resent her at first. You know how she is about other people in her kitchen!" She shook her head.

Sarah groaned. She remembered all too well.

"But you know I worry about Marie. She works so hard and she gets tired out. She doesn't tell me much about how she's feeling, but sometimes I look at her and I know she's hurting, and just exhausted. She really does need help! And so do you!"

"Thanks so much, Grace."

"And I'll talk to Marie about it, don't you worry."

She found Jen rocking by herself on the porch, and pulled up another chair. "Hiya, honey," she said. She told her about Lee's phone call. "What do you think?"

"Well, you certainly need the help. I just sit around like a big lunk, watching you buzz back and forth like a little hummingbird, and I can't do anything. I feel so bad for you!"

"Oh, no, don't feel bad, please. You are becoming a champion potato peeler, tomato slicer, and bean snapper!" They laughed together. "You won't be tied up here much longer, and then you'll look back on your sitting-around days with longing!"

"Ha ha. I don't think so! You know I hate sitting around!"

"I know. Poor thing. Do you want to ride down to Silverdale with me to pick her up tomorrow? I know you must be going stir crazy here," she said.

"Well, I am, a little," Jen said. "But you probably need to talk to Lee on your own. I'd just be in the way."

Sarah was relieved. "Thanks, honey. I'll make it up to you, I promise." Sarah gave her a quick kiss.

"You'd better!" Jen said. "And bring me home a treat!"

Lee was sitting cross-legged on her mattress, door rolled up to let in some air. She got to her feet as Sarah pulled up in the van. "Hi," she said. "Sorry, I have no place for you to sit."

"Don't worry about it, just hop in," Sarah said. "I'm so glad you called. I'm feeling a little overwhelmed."

"How so?" Lee asked.

"We have a couple of new ladies, and there's Grace, she doesn't need much help anymore, but you know Jen needs help too. She can't do much with that bunged-up ankle. She probably won't be able to get around on her own for quite a while yet," Sarah said. "Besides, she works for the ferry system, and when she gets better, she'll be going back to work. Maybe. I don't know. Marie is trying to do everything in the kitchen by herself, but she can't manage on her own. She has a bad heart, too."

"Sounds like a lot going on," Lee said.

"It is. And it's a twenty-four/seven place, you know. It's not as if everybody goes home at the end of the day. Except for Carol, our physical therapist. But there are three meals to make and serve every day, and snacks, and cleaning up after that, and of course taking care of the ladies... we're pretty busy, and we're not even in full swing yet. And I planted a garden, and it needs tending..."

"So what do you have in mind for me?" Lee asked.

"I don't know. What do you want to do?"

"Well, I don't know. Don't know much about cooking...but I'm pretty handy with things."

"I know. I remember how you put that barbeque together."

"And I like to garden. I can do just about anything, I guess, if you show me what you want."

"Better and better," Sarah said. She paused. "You know it's about twenty-five miles to Lavender Meadows from here."

"I know. I could hitchhike, though." She stuck out her thumb to demonstrate. "But it depends on how the rides go. I don't have a bike or anything."

Sarah shook her head. "No, I don't like the idea of you hitching around. It's not safe!" She took a breath. She felt she was on delicate ground. "How would you feel about coming up to stay? We have a place for you. If you want, that is."

Lee laughed. "And leave all this?" She waved her hand at the mattress, the milk crate, the small pile of possessions. "But really, I don't want to impose. And I'm not a charity case!"

"I don't think you'll have time to impose. We'll keep you busy, I promise you."

"And Jen won't mind? Not the jealous type?" She grinned, embarrassed, remembering how she thought Sarah was coming on to her.

"Oh no, I'm sure she'll be fine with it. You'll like her, I know."

"Sounds like a deal," Lee said, and stuck out her hand. "I'd like to tell the office person that I'm leaving, though. She's been real nice to me. And they'll need someone else to do my chores."

"No problem," Sarah said.

Lee loaded her little pile of possessions into the van and Sarah drove her around to the front. "Take your time," she said.

Lee ran around to see the other people who stayed there and to say good-bye. She nodded and smiled at the Mexican family and pointed at the mom's big belly. "I'll come back to see the baby," she said. They all smiled and nodded as if they understood each other.

When she left the office, she was wiping her eyes surreptitiously. She would not meet Sarah's eyes. She just slumped over in her seat.

"Let's go home," Sarah said.

※※※※

Sarah took Lee to one of the little cottages behind the main house, just a stone's throw from the door that opened onto the garden. It was small but neat, with a living room containing a loveseat, rocking chair, and small TV, galley kitchen with a mini fridge and microwave, bedroom with a full-sized bed covered with a hand-stitched quilt, and a bathroom with tub and shower, and a pile of clean towels. A tiny porch with a rocker and an Adirondack chair overlooked the lake.

Lee spun around, taking it all in, and dropped her bundle of stuff and her guitar on the small coffee table. "This is all for me? It's like a regular house!"

"Only smaller," Sarah said with a smile. She was glad to see that Lee was pleased. She'd spent a couple of hours last night getting the place together and aired out in hopes that Lee would be coming back with her. She'd thought about finding some space in the house for her, but had the feeling that Lee was a very private person and wouldn't feel comfortable there. "Why don't you get settled," she said. "You can meet everyone later."

"Ummm, okay, I guess," Lee said nervously. "I feel kind of funny, you know, with a lot of strangers."

"We'll take it a little at a time, then," Sarah said.

"There is just one thing, though," she said. "I'd like to take you into town, pick up a few things for you."

"Things? Like what?" Lee asked.

"You know, clothes and stuff. To work in."

Lee looked down at herself, her ragged jeans and skull tee shirt, tattoos up and down her arms. "Something wrong with the way I look?" she said, defensively.

"Uh, I don't think the ladies are much into goth," she said.

"Okay, I get it," Lee said reluctantly. "Is there a Goodwill near here?"

On her insistence, Sarah took Lee to the Goodwill and a couple of other thrift stores. They came home with a few changes of gently-worn jeans and shirts, a new pair of shoes, some soap, shampoo, and odds and ends to make her feel at home. She dropped Lee off to get cleaned up and changed, then went back to the organized chaos that was Lavender Meadows.

※ ※ ※ ※

Marie was busy stirring a fragrant, steaming pot when Sarah came into the kitchen. "Mmmmm, that smells great!" she said, sniffing appreciatively.

"Thanks!" Marie said, bustling around. "I hope everything will be ready at the same time!"

"What are you making?" she asked.

"Mushroom barley soup, salad, grilled cheese sandwiches. And berries and cream, and some gingersnaps," she said.

"Sounds great! And I know you're busy, but I just wanted to talk with you about something. I guess Grace probably talked to you already."

Marie stopped mid-stir. "Yes," she said. "You know how I hate having other people in my kitchen, moving stuff around, getting in the way, making a mess..."

"I certainly do know, Marie," Sarah said, laughing. "When I first came here, I thought you were going to bite my head off!"

"Hmmmph," Marie said.

"But Marie, you know things are much busier now, and you've been doing way more than you should. And we're just getting used to having the ladies here, and I can't manage by myself either. And besides..." she paused, "you have to take care of yourself too. Grace would never forgive me if anything happened to you."

Marie started stirring so vigorously a few barley grains escaped from the pot. "So who is this person?" she asked truculently.

"Do you remember the woman who put the barbeque grill together? Her name is Lee."

"What? That girl with the spiky hair and pointy things sticking out of her face? No thanks!"

"She's really a nice person. You'll just have to get to know her," Sarah said, hoping it was true.

"Hmmmph," Marie said.

"Let's just give her a try. I know she's kind of shy, and I have a feeling she's been through a rough time. So let's be easy with her, okay?"

"Hmmmph," she said again. Her scowl said a thousand words.

※※※※※

Lee peered through the kitchen door screen and

knocked hesitantly.

"Might as well come in!" Marie said, back to the door.

She stepped inside and closed the door quietly behind her.

"Who is it?"

"Are you Marie? It's me, Lee. Sarah told me to come up and see you. Said you might need some help."

"Hmmmph!" Marie shaded her eyes with her hand. "Step over here so I can see you, please – I can't see you with the sunlight behind you."

Lee took a few steps toward her. She remembered the tiny bird-like woman from her last visit to the house, darting around the kitchen, giving orders. Marie looked her up and down, at the blue polo shirt and black jeans. "Well, you look a little different. I remember when you were here before – scary!"

Lee grinned shyly. "Sarah told me you weren't into goth."

"I don't know what that means, but if it means running around looking like you died, or were ready to kill someone, or both, then no, I'm not into it. Here, sit down and have a cup of tea. You do drink tea?" Marie grabbed the kettle and poured the water into the teapot. "And cookies? You do eat cookies?"

"Yes to both. Thanks!" Lee said.

She put down two teacups and a big plate of gingersnaps. "Now tell me about yourself, dearie. What was your name again?"

"Lee," she said.

"So, Lee, where are you from?"

"Well, lately I've been living in Silverdale, but I lived in Seattle, before that Fremont," she said.

"Hmmmph," said Marie. "Family still live there?"

"Yeah. They've lived in the same place for three generations."

"Got brothers and sisters?"

"Yeah, two brothers, four sisters. I'm right in the middle."

"Are you close?"

Lee hesitated. "No, I don't see them."

Marie grabbed a bag of green beans and started snapping them into a colander. "That's too bad. It's good to stay in touch with your family. Before you know it, you're an old lady and they're all dead!" She took a deep breath. "So how did you end up in Silverdale, for gosh sakes? Middle of nowhere."

Lee laughed, grabbed some beans, and started snapping. "Any place with a Costco is not in the middle of nowhere." She found herself enjoying the directness of the old lady's questions.

"That place is too much for me. I went down there myself once, felt like I was gonna get run over by people with a hundred rolls of paper towels and a thousand pounds of potato chips!"

Lee laughed again. "They sure do give good samples, though, and plenty. I got to eat things there I never tried before!" she said. "But I know they don't cook as good as you!"

"Now don't try to butter me up, young lady," Marie said, pleased. "Isn't that where you met Sarah?"

"Yeah. She took one look at me and decided she should drag me back to her house and put me to work."

"Here, have another cookie. You're too skinny. But don't spoil your dinner!" Marie fussed. She got up, grabbed a bowl of potatoes, and brought it back to the table. "Can you peel potatoes?"

"You bet," Lee said.

Marie handed her a peeler and some newspaper. "Put the peels on there and don't make a mess."

"I know, I know. People with seven kids in the family learn how to skin potatoes early!" She set to, peeling like mad. "I don't know much about actual cooking, but I know how to peel! And skin, and hull, and mash, and chop..."

"Plenty of that here," Marie said.

"What are you making?" Lee asked.

"Meatloaf, green beans, mashed potatoes, salad, chocolate pudding."

"I know how to eat, too," she said.

༄༅༄༅

The ladies were crowded around the table when Lee came out of the kitchen, carrying a steaming platter of meatloaf.

"Halt, stranger," Jen said. "Who goes there?"

"I come bearing meat," she said.

"Carry on, then," Sarah said. "Lee, this is everyone. Everyone, this is Lee. Have a seat!" she said, indicating the chair next to her.

Marie bustled in with the mashed potatoes and gravy and took her seat next to Grace. "Well, Sarah, are you gonna do the introductions, or do I have to do everything?"

Sarah laughed. "Okay, I guess I can't get away with it. So let's do it by the clock. At twelve o'clock, we have Grace, our matriarch. She and Marie started this place many, many, many, many, years ago."

"Mind your manners, you," Grace said. "Welcome!"

"Then next to her we have Edna."

The ladies all smiled and nodded as Sarah said their names.

"Then Ginny, Edna's other half. Then there's Carrie and Savannah, and Jen, my spooky girlfriend, you've already met her."

"Hey!" Jen said, and nudged her.

"And I know you've already met Marie. A scary bunch, but they don't bite."

"You do," Jen said slyly.

Lee felt herself blush. She thought back on her own family's dinner table and how different this one was, everybody talking and laughing.

After dinner, Lee and Sarah cleared the table while Marie started the dishes. "Hey, I'll do those," Lee protested.

"No, no, you'll just make a mess of things. You don't know where anything is yet. You don't know how to load the dishwasher. But you'll do plenty of dishes, believe me!"

Back in the dining room, Sarah touched Lee's arm. "What do you think? Can you deal with her?"

"She's kind of a fussbudget, but I like her. If we don't get along, will you return me to Silverdale?"

"I promise," Sarah said.

Later that night, Lee walked to her little cottage, pausing for a moment to admire the lake. It had been a big day, and she was beat. She put the key Sarah had given her in the lock and enjoyed the sound of the tumblers. Her house. She took off her clothes and rolled into the bed. "Ahhh," she said, closing her eyes. It had been quite a while since she'd slept in a real bed. She gulped as her eyes filled. She thought she'd left those tears behind her, but she'd brought them with her after all.

❦❦❦❦

Clarisse's son Mark called Sarah, and asked if they had room for her at Lavender Meadows. "I'm worried about my mom. I don't think it's safe for her to be by herself anymore."

"What's happened?" Sarah asked. She'd been out to see Clarisse a few weeks before, but the family had been trying to adjust to Clarisse's news, and they all decided to put off the decision for a while longer.

"Well, she is having more trouble remembering if she took her meds or not. She's on insulin, and the other day I tried to call her, and when she didn't answer the phone, I went right over. She was sitting at the kitchen table, but she was acting real funny, didn't know who I was. I checked her blood sugar, and it was only sixty-seven. I got her to eat something, and after a few minutes, she started coming around. I don't know if she forgot to have breakfast, or she took too much insulin. It's just too risky."

"I agree. I know it's hard to realize that your mom is having issues...but we could make sure that she was eating and getting her meds at the right time."

"I wish we could take care of her. She's always taken such good care of us. But our families live in small places, and nobody's home during the day." He paused. "It's been weird having the mother you thought you knew better than anyone else in the world come out." He stopped for a moment, cleared his throat. "No offense, I mean, I don't know if you're like that too..."

"None taken," Sarah said.

"It's been hard getting our heads around this, but we love her so much. We just want her to be happy."

He sighed. "I know she's lonely. And we really liked what we saw when we came out there to visit."

"I'm so glad. I look forward to having her with us."

Three days later Clarisse moved into the room next to Edna, and was absorbed into the life of Lavender Meadows.

❧❧❦❦

Marie was running Lee ragged as usual, getting ready for the meeting. "There's so much to do!" she complained, fanning herself with her big apron.

"Now, Marie, I think we're pretty much caught up. The pasta salad is done, the salad dressing is made, and the cupcakes are cooling off right now. The rolls are rising, and they'll be ready to bake in about half an hour. We need to make the green salad happen, but we don't want to do that until the last minute, right?"

"Yes, but, but," Marie sputtered.

"So the only things that needs to be done are raspberry lemonade and to cut up some other fruit. Lunch for the residents is taken care of, and they'll be coming down to eat in a few minutes. So why don't you pour yourself a cold drink and sit down, Marie," Lee said soothingly. "If there's anything else I can't do, or don't have time for, I can ask Jen."

"Yeah, fat lot of good Jen will do you. She can't tell a spoon from a spatula. Everything she makes is either raw or charred."

"Don't let her hear you say that," Lee said. "You know she's trying."

"Hmmmph," Marie said and flounced off. "You know I'm not far. Call me if you need me!"

Lee shook her head. In the few months she'd been working at Lavender Meadows, she'd learned a lot. Cooking and baking, presentation, table settings, food safety. Her family's idea of a meal was opening boxes and cans and throwing the stuff into bowls—maybe—after that everything was up for grabs—the fastest and strongest got the fullest bellies. And she'd learned a lot about taking care of people, listening to them and respecting them, letting them do things at their own pace. It was a whole new world.

She'd also learned a lot about friendship and trust. Hanging out with Sarah, Jen, Marie, and the other ladies gave her a different spin about how people could be with each other, without screaming and arguing. And hitting. The knots in her stomach were starting to release. She hadn't known that the knots were made of anxiety and fear. She could finally take some deep breaths, stretch out her shoulders.

Then one day when Sarah was busy and Carol was at her office, she asked Lee to take Clarisse to town for a doctor's appointment. Lee hemmed and hawed for a while, then finally refused.

"Why won't you take her?" Sarah said impatiently. "You see I'm up to my elbows here!"

"Well, because I don't drive," Lee said reluctantly.

"Why not? The van is an automatic."

"Because I don't have a license," she said, her eyes down.

"Did you lose it for speeding? Or DUI?" Sarah asked.

"No. I don't know how. I'm only fifteen, you know."

Sarah gulped. She knew Lee was young, but she had no idea. She was blown away. She'd just walked away from her home and went out on her own.

※ ※ ※ ※

"I had no idea!" she said that night to Jen. "She's just a child!"

"Some child!" Jen said.

"Maybe we need to call the police, or Child Protective Services or something," she said.

"Now Sarah, you know they'll just take her away and put her in a foster home, or some kind of skeevy group home. You know she's better off with us!"

"Well, that's true, I guess. But what if we get in trouble? They could close us down!"

They decided to talk to Ro and get some advice about what to do. Within days, Sarah became Lee's foster mother and interim guardian,

Jen had to give Sarah a hard time. "Hey, mom," she said. "Your baby is taller than you are!"

Sarah took her new responsibilities as a parent seriously – more seriously than Lee wanted. She talked with her about the importance of an education, but Lee was reluctant to go to high school 'with a bunch of kids.' "I've been out on my own for a couple of years, Sarah. I have nothing in common with those folks. Can you see me trying out for cheerleader or joining the French club? No way." And finally, Sarah agreed to let her finish up her schooling online. Sarah and everyone in the house were very supportive and gave her a hand when she was stuck on something.

"What do you want to be when you grow up?" Grace asked her.

"I am grown up," Lee said. "And I'm happy here."

But the thing she was proudest of was the nice

shiny learner's permit in her wallet. Now that she actually had a wallet. And a bed, and clean clothes too.

Sarah wondered what had brought her to scavenging for food and living in a storage unit, but she didn't want to push Lee into talking if she wasn't ready. She hoped that someday she would find out about how their paths had crossed. She just knew she was grateful that Lee was with them, bringing a breath of fresh air into their family home.

≈≈≈≈

Ralph went crazy when the big hog pulled into the driveway, scattering gravel everywhere. Two people sat astride the cycle. The fierce look of the driver intimidated Sarah a bit. She had short iron-gray hair, skin dark from the sun, eyes covered with mirrored sunglasses. She had lots of tattoos on her arms and neck, and Sarah guessed her black Harley tee shirt, leather vest, and chaps covered up a lot more. The other was a woman with skin the color of a caramel latte. She had a Harley t-shirt too, and her hair was done up in tiny braids that wound around her head. Both of them had plenty of chains and enough piercings to set off the metal detectors at the airport.

"Hi, can I help you?" Sarah asked.

"Yeah," the driver said. "I heard this is a place where women can come and stay, and have somebody see about them."

"That's right. I'm Sarah Chase, the director of Lavender Meadows. What can I do for you?"

"I'm Vick." She indicated her passenger. "And this is Gayle," she said.

Sarah shook hands with both women. She

wondered what they wanted. "Would you like to come in and look around? I can give you some information."

"Okay. Is the bike good here?" Vick said.

"Sure, no problem, it's fine," Sarah said.

She waited while they dismounted and led them up to the porch. "Would you like some tea, or maybe something cold?"

"Sure, iced tea, if you have some," Gayle said.

"Sounds good to me," Vick said.

Sarah showed them into the living room and went to the kitchen to ask for the drinks. Marie wasn't around, but Lee was sitting by the sink, peeling potatoes for tonight's dinner. "Hi. Would you mind getting a couple of iced teas and some cookies, if we have any?"

"Have you ever known that cookie jar to be empty? Marie feels it's her civic duty to bake every day," Lee said.

"I know." She patted her slender belly. "I have to watch myself."

"Me too. No more than twelve a day, unless Marie's trying out something new. It's my civic duty to try out everything she makes." Lee laughed. "Hey, who just came in on that bike? It's a beaut."

"Come out and meet them when you bring out the drinks," Sarah said and went out to find her guests.

Vick was checking out the bookshelves, and Gayle was gazing out at the water. "This sure is a pretty place," she said.

"Thanks! We love it here." She sat down and Vick wandered back and sat down close to Gayle. She handed them a packet of information on Lavender Meadows and gave them a minute to look it over. "So what can I do for you? Do you have a relative that needs some care?"

"No," Vick said. "It's for me. I have Alzheimer's Disease."

"Oh!" she said, surprised. It was unusual for people who needed an assisted living facility to ride up to the door on a Harley. "When were you diagnosed?"

Vick shrugged.

"About three years ago," Gayle said. "She started to get some memory loss, and it seems to be getting worse. And it's hard for her to sleep at night. Sometimes she wanders off and forgets where she's going. And I work in our shop, so I'm not always around."

"All right, all right," said Vick. "Enough!"

"Are you on any medication?" Sarah asked.

"Yeah," Vick said. "Ask Gayle about that stuff. She knows it better than me."

Gayle filled Sarah in on the details on her meds and her medical history. "Basically she's pretty healthy, all things considered. She likes to be active, and she's really into sports. She used to be a gym teacher."

"Really!" She looked closely at Vick for a moment, then suddenly something clicked. "What is your last name?"

"Williams," Vick said.

Sarah laughed. She couldn't believe it. "Actually, you were my gym teacher," she said.

"No kidding! Well, I'm sorry, but I don't recognize you," Vick said. "Over the years, I had hundreds of kids. Thousands, maybe."

Sarah was stung for a moment. She wanted Ms. Williams to remember her. "You were a real role model for me," she said. "I never saw anyone like you before!"

"Uh, thanks, I guess," Vick said. She looked Sarah over. "Looks like you turned out all right."

Lee came in with glasses of iced tea and a plate of

cookies and set them on the table.

"Lee, this is Vick Williams, and this is Gayle. Sorry, I didn't get your last name."

"Corcoran," Gayle said.

"Can you believe that Ms. Williams was my gym teacher when I was a kid?"

"Just call me Vick," she said. "I haven't been Ms. Williams in a long time."

"No kidding! Is that your bike?" Lee asked. "It's amazing!"

"Yeah, I know. I love that bike." She shook her head. "We love that bike," Vick said, looking over at Gayle. Stealthily she wiped her eyes. "I don't ride it too much anymore, though." Her voice trailed off.

Sarah interrupted hastily. "Would you like to look around? Meet some of the women? Maybe have some lunch with us?"

"Sure, I guess," Vick said.

Sarah took them around the place. They seemed impressed with the house and the rooms that were available.

The ladies were already gathered in the dining room when they got through with their tour. Sarah introduced everyone. Grace looked at her, her eyebrows raised. She could tell that Vick and Gayle made them a little nervous. Vick and Gayle were obviously a little nervous too. Lee looked like a big-eyed puppy hoping for a bone.

Marie started to dish out chicken enchiladas and Mexican rice. Sarah introduced her to Vick and Gayle, and Lee brought out some apple cider and a big bowl of salad.

"This is great! I love Mexican food," Gayle said enthusiastically.

"Yes, Marie is a great cook," Ginny said. "Nobody starves here, believe me!"

Vick pushed back her chair and got up. She looked very tense.

"Honey? Are you all right?" Gayle asked.

Vick frowned and walked out of the house.

"Is she going to be okay? Should I go bring her back?" Sarah asked.

"There's just too many people. She gets overwhelmed," Gayle said. "She probably went out for a smoke." She sighed. "This is a difficult thing for her."

"I'm know; I'm sorry. We can't allow smoking in the building. State law, you know," Sarah said. She hoped it would not be a deal breaker. They needed a couple more residents, and besides, Sarah wanted to get to know her old teacher a little better. "Lee, why don't you show her where she can go to smoke?"

"I'm sure she'll be okay," Gayle said. "She doesn't smoke too much anymore, but maybe you could keep an eye on her, and maybe hold on to her cigarettes and lighter."

"Sure. We can give her the meds, too."

"That'll be great. I have to work, and I'm not around most of the day. She put something on the stove the other day and forgot about it. Boiled the pot dry. The whole place was full of smoke, and it set off the smoke alarm."

"Oh no!"

"Yes. I'm glad that our neighbor went in to see what was going on. She could have burned down the house, hurt herself, the dogs…and there were some other things that happened too. She mixes up her meds, gets confused at times, forgets to eat. She's pretty good today, but it's not safe for her to be alone while I'm gone."

"I understand. It's a tough decision. How does she feel about it?" Sarah asked.

"I know she's not happy about it, but I think she understands. Then sometimes she gets pretty angry... thinks I'm trying to get rid of her. And I love her so much!"

"Poor thing. Well, if she decides to come here, we'll take really good care of her, I promise," Sarah said. "My partner Jen is a motorcycle person, and they'll have something to talk about. Lee likes bikes too."

"Oh, that's great. I'll go and talk it over with her."

Gayle went out and sat next to Vick.

Lee came in and shook her head. "That's so sad," she said.

Sarah could see the two women talking out there on the bench. A few minutes later, they both came back in, eyes red.

"So what did you decide? Do you want to think about it?"

"No, I think we've come to a decision," Gayle said. "Do you have an opening now?"

"Yes, we do. She can come any time."

"How about today? Can she just stay here now?"

"Oh! Sure! I guess so," Sarah said, surprised.

"That would be great. She has some clothes with her. I'll just go get her stuff."

"Boy, that was fast," Lee said. "I'll go check the room, make sure everything is set up."

Vick had a little satchel and a couple of plastic bags. "Here's her meds, and her cigarettes," Gayle said. "I'll bring more stuff in a couple of days."

"Okay," Sarah said. She stepped back as Gayle

put on her helmet, swung onto the bike, and gunned the engine. Vick bent to kiss her and they hugged each other hard.

Finally, she took off, and Vick stood there for a long time, looking down the empty road.

❧❧❧❧

Vick looked at the ladies sitting around the table that evening as Sarah introduced them, trying to fix something about each of them in her memory. Edna had a lopsided grin, and was wrapped in a fuzzy pink sweater. Plump Ginny had her hair pulled back and a hoarse laugh. Angelic blue-eyed Carrie leaned against Savannah, who was still dressed in her corporate duds. Jen, in a blue plaid shirt, had her leg propped up on a chair, crutches leaning against its back. Clarisse sported a Seahawk cap on her frizzy gray hair. Grace had wavy white hair and a frilly pink blouse. Marie dashed in and out of the kitchen, apron flying, and Lee followed one step behind her, towel tied around her waist. She nodded at each one in turn, but she knew they probably wouldn't stay in her memory for long. "Don't worry about remembering everybody's name," Sarah said.

"I won't," Vick said bitterly. "By tomorrow, I probably won't remember any of you." She looked around again. "So let me see if I understand this," she said. "All of you are gay? Dykes? Lesbos?"

Sarah smiled. "Yes. This is a place where lesbians can come and get whatever care they need. Families and friends can come and visit, of course, and we do the best we can to make sure that everyone is comfortable."

"I never heard of such a thing," Vick said.

"Unbelievable! I saw a blurb about this place in *The Seattle Gay News*, and I saw your web page too. We had to come and check it out."

"Yes, as far as we know, we are the only place like it," Grace said. "We are like family."

"Okay, let's say our words," Sarah said, and held out one hand to Jen and one hand to Vick who looked at Sarah suspiciously. "If you're okay with this, you're free to join in. If not, that's okay too. Happy happy, joy joy!" She smiled and released their hands.

Vick laughed. "Unbelievable!" she said again.

They made quick work of supper, Savannah and Ginny helping Carrie and Edna to eat, Clarisse managing on her own. After the frozen yogurt, Vick pushed back her chair and patted her stomach. "Good chow, folks," she said. "Think I'll go and have a smoke."

"There's a bench out in front on the lawn where you can sit while you smoke," Sarah said. "And there's a bucket of sand where you can put your butts. Lee can show you where it is."

"Sure, I remember. I was out there earlier."

"Okay. We just ask that you don't smoke in the house or near the doors and windows, and we would like to keep your cigarettes and lighter for you."

"Sure, I got it," Vick said. "You don't want me to burn the place down." She nodded at the folks around the table. "Evening, ladies."

After Lee and Vick went out, the ladies twittered like little birds. "Did you see all those tats?" Savannah said.

"I wonder where else she has them," Grace said.

"Grace!" Marie said, shocked.

"Oh, I know the rest of you are thinking the same thing. She looks pretty tough, doesn't she? And did you see that big motorcycle she came in on? A monster!" Savannah said.

"And her nose is pierced. It must be awful when she has a cold!"

"And her lip is pierced too!"

"What happens if she swallows that little ring?"

"Did you see her boots?"

"Well, guess what?" Sarah said. "She was my gym teacher back in the day. I never thought I'd see her again. She was kind of scary, you know? I never saw anyone like her. She didn't look or act like any of the women I knew. I was intimidated! And she didn't have all those tattoos and piercings back then!" She laughed. "I think she was my first crush!"

A laugh went around the table.

"Part of you must have recognized her for who she is and who you are," Jen said.

"Maybe so. I don't know," Sarah said doubtfully.

"But remember, I'm keeping an eye on you! I don't want you to rekindle any crushes!" Jen puffed up like a banty rooster. "If it wasn't for my bum leg, I could take her on."

Sarah batted her eyes, leaned over, and planted a big kiss on Jen's cheek. "My shero!" she said.

❧❧❧❧

Lee and Vick strolled to the teak bench overlooking the lake, Ralph barking and running circles around them.

"Settle down, Ralph," Lee ordered. He sniffed at Vick and flopped over on the grass. She pulled out a pack of cigarettes and offered one to Vick.

"Thanks," she said. "You could have one too, if

you like."

"Thanks! I don't get to smoke very often here. They keep me busy. And they don't like that I smoke. Sarah especially wants me to quit."

"I'm gonna quit someday too," Vick said. "Not!" She leaned back and blew a couple of smoke rings.

"Hey! How do you do that?" Lee said, excited. "Show me!"

After a few minutes, Lee mastered the smoke rings and they sat quietly for a while in the cool breeze.

"Are you warm enough?" Lee asked.

"I'm fine, kid. I just want to hang out for a while."

They sat in contemplative silence for a few minutes.

"I heard Sarah say that you were her gym teacher," Lee said.

"Yeah, but that was a long time ago. I always liked sports when I was a kid. Still do, but now I have to watch from the sidelines. Old age, creaky bones." She shook her head.

"You're not that old," Lee protested.

"Old enough to know that I need to be a little more careful or I'll be sorry the next day."

"I bet Sarah was good at sports, too. She keeps herself in good shape. She's always walking or jogging, or swimming in the pool."

"I do remember her," Vick said. "Wiry little thing, not very competitive. Always hanging around me. I think she might have had a bit of a crush." She looked over at Lee. "Maybe you have a little crush yourself!"

"Oh, no. I don't!" Lee said decisively. She took a breath. "I thought she was coming on to me when I first met her, but we got that straightened out real fast."

"Is that her partner there, the one with the leg?"

"That's Jen. She busted up her leg working on the ferry."

"Too bad. She's pretty hot," Vick said.

"I saw that woman you rode in with," Lee said. "She's hot too. She your girlfriend?"

"Yes indeed. Gayle. We've been together about eight years. I met her at a bike rally," Vick said. "She's something, huh?"

"Yeah. And she looks like a good rider, too. That's some bike you have."

"I know," Vick said sadly. "I wonder if I'll ever get to ride it again."

❧❧❧❧

After breakfast, the ladies wandered off to take naps, watch TV, or hang out in the garden. Around eleven o'clock, the other women started to arrive for their meeting. Sarah wanted to keep channels of communication open between Lavender Meadows, their residents, and the community that had helped them put the place together. Grace and Marie, Sarah and Jen, Ro, Savannah, Ginny, Carol, Dr. Emily, and some other women from town gathered to share ideas every month.

"I love these meetings," Carol confided to Grace and Sarah. "I get to plop my butt down, put me feet up, eat plenty of goodies, and bask in the dykey glow."

Sarah laughed. "I know what you mean," she said. "The hardest part about being around this is saying no to this cookie or that pudding."

"Like you have to worry," Carol said, eying

Sarah's trim figure. "Actually, I thought the toughest thing would be getting a bunch of lesbians to come to any kind of consensus!"

Everyone assembled, and Grace started things off. "So lovely to see you all here today! I'm glad you could come. Now I know the real reason you are so happy to come and see us here – the food – so without further delay," she reached over and took Sarah's and Carol's hands, "Happy happy, joy joy!"

Marie came out of the kitchen and started passing around the bowls of green salad and a bunch of toppings, followed by cloverleaf rolls, still warm from the oven.

"Mmmmhs," and "yummms!" greeted their arrival.

"Lesbians in consensus! And in less than three hours!" Sarah exclaimed.

The women laughed. "If you keep feeding us like this, we'll be in consensus all the time!" Savannah said. "Fat and happy!"

After the last of the cupcakes disappeared, the women got down to business.

"How are things going?" Dr. Emily asked.

"Pretty well," Sarah said. "Everyone seems to be pretty stable. Edna is just fun, always smiling. She's so happy when Ginny is here, and I think she knows that her being here has helped Ginny a lot. At least she gets to rest, knowing that Edna is well cared for. And Carrie – it's so sweet to see you two together, Savannah. She is just glowing!" She looked at Savannah. "And so are you!"

"My whole life has changed," Savannah said. "I feel like I'm in love for the first time – again. After all the years of sneaking around just to get a glimpse of her! And now I can see her whenever I want!" She paused. "If she wants to see me, of course."

"Are you kidding?" Carol said. "As soon as you leave, she starts waiting for your next visit. If it was up to her, I think you'd never get to go home!"

Savannah smiled.

"And Vick? How is she doing?"

"She's pretty sad. She misses Gayle and her friends. And her bike, of course. She's such a free spirit, and she would just love to get on her Harley and go for a ride."

"Does Gayle come to see her much?" Savannah asked.

"Probably not as much as Vick would like. But, you know, Gayle is probably pretty burned out. She had to make sure she was safe, keep her from walking out of the house and getting lost, or hurt," Sarah said. "And she works in the shop full time, because Vick couldn't handle it anymore. But Lee loves hanging out with her. Vick is kind of a super hero – no, super shero – to her. I just worry about her mood swings – you know how difficult that can be with Alzheimer's folks."

"Yes. I'm just glad that Lee can be around for her. They sit out on that bench in the evenings, smoking cigarettes," Jen said.

"Well, you know how I feel about that," Emily said.

"Sure, but I think that's one battle we're not going to win, at least right now. And I'd rather have them out there smoking together than Vick off by herself," Sarah said.

"That's true," Emily said. "Maybe someday they'll be willing to go the vape route. Or better yet, cold turkey!"

"Maybe," Sarah said doubtfully.

"And how about Clarisse? Is she settling in here too?" Dr. Emily asked.

"I think so," Sarah said. "She likes having regular meals, and not having to worry about her meds, and she likes the company. She's having some pain in her feet, neuropathy, you know – we check her feet all the time, don't see anything wrong, though, no open wounds."

"I'll check her out," Emily said. "Maybe there's something we can try, some different meds. That diabetes – scary!"

"Yes," Carol said. "Her family comes to visit, but I don't think they are too comfortable here yet – pretty often they take her out for lunch on the weekends, but they don't hang around here much."

"Well, as long as Clarisse is happy," Sarah said. "I always try to make a point to talk with them when they come. You know, Clarisse didn't come out as a lesbian until just recently, and I think the family is still getting used to the idea."

"It must have been quite a shock!" Savannah said. "Speaking of residents and families, are there any more prospects? I know you could use a couple more people."

"There's a woman named Paula who has arthritis. I talked to her a while back, but she wasn't ready to come here until now. She's in a wheelchair, needs some extra help. I think she and Clarisse would be good roommates. We'll see how it goes. I think that's about all we can do right now until we get some extra help. I'm keeping my eye out," Sarah said. "Any other ideas, Emily?"

"No, but I'll let you know. Why don't you give

me a few brochures to put in my office?"

"So now for the big status question – How's Rachel doing?" Grace asked.

"She's pretty tired and needs to keep her feet up as much as possible. I think she's doing okay, though. The morning sickness has let up quite a bit, and you know that was knocking her out. At least she's not doing pickles and ice cream – but Hawaiian pizzas are not safe around her."

"Well, you send her our love, and tell her to come and visit," Grace said.

"I will," Emily promised. "You know, I wanted to talk with you about something else. Years ago, Rachel and I had a wedding ceremony here. I think some of you might have been there."

"Yes, it was lovely," Carol said. The other women nodded.

"But now that gay marriage is legal here, we thought maybe we'd like to get hitched for real, get actual papers before the baby is born," Emily said.

"What a cool idea!" Savannah said. "A genuine, honest-to-goodness dyke wedding! A legal one! Amazing!" She chuckled, then got serious. "I know I'm old fashioned, but I could never understand why people who have a committed relationship wait to get married until after the baby is born."

"Straight people could take their rights for granted," Jen said.

"And now that it's possible for us, too, we want to do it for a whole lot of reasons," Emily said. "So many gay people have lost their children over the years just because they were gay. It automatically made those parents unsuitable in the eyes of the law. I want our baby to be protected!"

"Yes, all those families torn apart. So much tragedy." Sarah shook her head.

"And what about couples who were kept apart because their families had a problem with it?"

"Like us," Savannah said softly.

"Yes. And all those people who lost their homes because they couldn't inherit their partners' property? People who were institutionalized because homosexuality was considered a mental illness? People who were kept from making medical decisions for their partners? People who couldn't go to their partners' funerals?" Carol said.

"All those people with AIDS," Marie said.

"And on and on," Grace said.

"Preaching to the choir," Jen said.

"I'm with you," said Marie. "So what do you have in mind? Are you going to have a party? Or just a quiet ceremony?"

"Actually, we were wondering if we could have our wedding here again, at Lavender Meadows. We love this place, and I can't think of a nicer spot!" Emily said.

"Or better friends!" Savannah said.

"Oh, that would be so much fun!" Marie said.

"The weather is so beautiful this time of the year. And the garden is lovely! The leaves are just starting to turn," Grace said. "Do you know how many people you would want to invite? When would it be? Afternoon? Evening? Brunch? Buffet? Sit-down dinner? Music? Dancing?"

Emily laughed. "We haven't gotten all this stuff worked out yet. We've barely had a chance to talk about it. But we'll think about it, and let you know."

"Don't wait too long!" Marie said. "We've got to

get busy!"

※ ※ ※ ※

"What do you think about Emily and Rachel getting married?" Marie asked Grace later that night.

Marie poured a glass of sherry for Grace and one for herself. "Cheers!" they said together, then each took a sip.

"I sure look forward to this part of the day," Grace said. "I love sitting here with you, enjoying our bit of tipple, and now that there's so much going on in the house, we actually have things to gossip about!"

"I know. It's so exciting!"

"I think it's a splendid idea," Grace said. "We had their commitment/wedding ceremony here, of course, years ago, and a bunch of others, but this would be the first legal gay wedding here. Ever!"

"And about time, I say," Marie said. "I keep saying this, but I have to say it again. I never thought we would see this in our lifetime! Never!" She paused. "I know you would have married Annie if you could."

"Of course. Well, we felt like we were married. It was our little secret, you know? But we did have our little make-believe ceremony, you know? Just the two of us."

"That was before I came to work here," Marie said. "I know it didn't feel like make believe to you!"

"No, it was as real to us as my marriage to George. Could you imagine what my parents would have thought? And if they were alive now, to see it legal! They would be totally flummoxed if I'd even considered such a thing! Horrified!" Grace said. "And Annie's parents! Her dad was a minister, you know."

"And what about George? What do you think he would have said?"

Grace thought for a moment. "I think he just would have been happy for us. He loved both of us, you know, and we both loved him. Annie was always following him around, and he was always so sweet with her. And me, of course, but the first time I saw George, I heard a roaring in my ears, and it was like everything else in my life receded. I couldn't catch my breath and I couldn't move. I just knew that I wanted to be with him forever, always! I never thought that love at first sight was possible!"

"Oh, it is," Marie said softly. "It surely is."

"And I never dreamed that people could be in love more than once in a lifetime." Grace smiled.

"Yes, but for some of us it's only once," Marie said. She reached out and took Grace's hand, gave it a little squeeze. They smiled at each other.

"Isn't it exciting?" Grace said. "Emily and Rachel have been together for so long – and now they have a sweet little baby on the way! I can't wait! It's a long time since I had a baby fix – or a wedding fix, for that matter!" Grace said.

"We haven't had a wedding here in over five years!" Marie said. "I wonder what kind of wedding they'll want. Big crowd, small crowd, fancy, formal, casual? Music, dancing? What kind of food will they want?"

"Hold on, love. We probably won't know anything for a few days. And we have to remember that our ladies come first. After all, this is their home, and we can't do anything that would make them uncomfortable or disturb their routines."

"But weddings are such a fun disturbance!" said

Marie.

"Yes indeed. I'm so looking forward to it!" Grace paused. "Tell me, do you ever feel bad that we weren't able to get married? Big party, the works?"

"What - ceremonial deprivation?" Marie laughed. "No, not really. I remember that night down by the lake when we made our commitment as if it was yesterday. The moon was so huge, and I cried and cried. You were so sweet, and I was so nervous, I could hardly talk!"

"And we know that's so unusual for you," Grace said with a smile. She looked down at the thin gold band on her left hand.

"Hmmmph," said Marie.

"And really, it wasn't that long ago. What? Three years?"

"Yes. I wanted it so much, but I felt sad, too. I'd been in love with you for so long, and watching you and Annie, and seeing how happy you were – sometimes it was very hard for me." Marie took another sip of her sherry and reached for a tissue.

"I know, I know, love. And I'll tell you right now, I have been lucky in love my whole life. First George, the sweetest man, then Annie, then you. I have been well and truly blessed," Grace said.

"And I never loved anyone but you. I was so lonely before I came here to Lavender Meadows, and then when I met you and Annie, I felt like I had a family again."

"Yes, we always felt like you were family. My people and Annie's people were so far away, we hardly ever saw them after we moved here, and now they're all gone." Grace sighed. "And you lost your parents when you were so young."

"Yes, I was sixteen when they had that accident.

Suddenly, my whole world was gone." She topped off the sherry glasses and took a sip. "Mmmmm. So good."

"Do we have any cookies up here today? Talking about sad things makes my sweet tooth act up," Grace said.

"Talking about happy things makes your sweet tooth act up, too." She reached into her pocket and pulled out a sandwich bag of oatmeal raisin cookies.

"Oh, thank you, honey. I should have known you wouldn't forget."

"Never. I have to keep my girl happy," Marie said. "Speaking of being happy – you know, we're not getting any younger."

"Speak for yourself, old woman!" Grace said. "I'm just entering my prime."

"You certainly are prime," Marie said, smiling wickedly. She paused. "But seriously. We are both going to die someday. "

"Boo!" Grace said.

"And we've never even applied for domestic partnership."

"That's right. There was no reason to."

"Yes, but now we have a business going again, and we should make sure that we are protected in case something happens to us. And Sarah needs to be protected too, since she's in charge."

"You're right," Grace said slowly. "Let's call Ro and make an appointment to do up some papers for us. Medical stuff, wills, whatever."

"Yes, that's a great idea. But while we're doing that, why don't we just get married too?" Marie said.

"How romantic!" Grace said. "Wills and papers and agreements and such, and by the way, let's throw in a marriage license for good measure!"

"No, seriously. Let's do it! Let's finish up our lives together as married people. Proud, gay, married people!"

"You'd better not try going down on one knee, you fool. I'll never be able to get you off the floor!" Grace laughed. "Of course I'll marry you. Of course I will."

"Thank goodness. Who ever thought that I would end up being married to the most beautiful girl in the world?" She got up and gave Grace a big hug and a kiss. "Hey! We're getting married! We're getting married!"

"So, what should we call ourselves? Fitch-Meadows? Meadows-Fitch?"

"Too stuffy. I don't like hyphens. Why don't we just stay with Meadows? Then there will still be the Meadows girls at Lavender Meadows!"

"That sounds good. Marie Meadows. I like that!"

"Better than Itchy-Fitchy. That was my nickname growing up. I hated it!"

"You poor thing!" Grace chuckled and put her arms around Marie. "At last, I'm making an honest woman of you!"

"Yes indeed. And me you. High time, too!" They raised their glasses and made the crystal ring out. "To us!"

"Hey – are there any more cookies?"

🙦🙦🙦🙦

It was a quiet night except for the muted buzz of snoring coming from Grace and Marie's room. Suddenly, a piercing scream, then another, rent the air. Sarah and Jen were out of bed like a shot, bumping into each other in their haste to get through the bedroom door. Lee, who was on call, ran through the hallway, frantically pulling a tee shirt over her head.

"What is it? What happened?" she cried.

"I don't know," Sarah gasped, running up the stairs. "Let's check all the rooms."

Everyone was stirring now, awakened by the screams. Ginny and Edna were awake, and Ginny was pulling on her robe. "What happened? Who's screaming?" she shouted, joining in the search. Grace and Marie were safely in bed, as were Carrie and Savannah. Savannah sat up quickly, but Sarah gestured for them to stay where they were. They dashed to Vick's room, but it was empty, then lastly to Clarisse's room, where they found the source of the trouble.

Clarisse was sitting up in the bed, covers pulled up to her chin. Sarah ran to the bed and gathered Clarisse into her arms. "What is it, Clarisse? What's happening?"

Tearfully, she pointed at Vick, who was huddled against the wall, legs pulled up. "Sorry...sorry...sorry," she muttered.

"What is it?" Sarah said again.

"That man was trying to get into bed with me!" she sobbed.

"What man?" Jen said, looking around the room.

"That man right there!" she said, pointing to Vick, who was also crying by now.

Sarah realized what had happened and breathed a sigh of relief. "There's no man, Clarisse," she said gently. "That's Vick, you know her. She just made a mistake." She helped Clarisse put her glasses on. "See? It's just Vick." She dabbed at Clarisse's face with a tissue.

"Oh, hi, Vick," Clarisse gulped. "Sorry I yelled

at you."

Meanwhile, Lee was helping Vick get to her feet. "Are you okay, Vick?" she said. "Are you awake?"

Vick nodded tearfully. "I'm sorry. I didn't mean to scare you. I'm sorry, Clarisse. I just got lost."

Sarah got Clarisse settled while Jen and Lee led Vick back to her room.

"Honest, I didn't mean to scare her," Vick said. "I had to go to the bathroom, and I thought I was back in my room. I thought I was getting back into bed with Gayle."

"That's okay, Vick. Why don't you get back in your own bed," Jen said.

"I want a cigarette," she said.

"Okay, I'll join you," Lee said. "Put on your slippers. I'll meet you downstairs." She went down and grabbed her jeans and some shoes from the laundry room, then got cigarettes and a lighter from the locked drawer where the medications were kept. "Let's go out back," she said, holding the door open.

"Okay," she said. She sat heavily on the bench by the kitchen door. "Oof!"

Lee handed her a cigarette and snapped the lighter. They smoked in silence for a moment.

"I'm so sorry," Vick said. "Sometimes I just forget where I am."

"That must be pretty scary," Lee said.

"It is. And sometimes I think I know where I am, but I'm not. I miss Gayle, too," she said. "She keeps me straightened out."

"Is she coming to see you this weekend? I know you'll be happy to see her," Lee said.

"Yes," Vick said. "She's a good girl." She paused. "Clarisse thought I was a man," she said. "I get that a lot, 'cause I'm so big, I guess. But it makes me feel bad sometimes."

"Yeah, I know what you mean. I get that a lot too. But I like the way I look, and I like the way you look too! My mom tried to make me look more like a girl, but I never was much for dresses and such. Or panty hose!"

They laughed.

"Let's go back to bed, what do you say?"

"Sure, I'm sleepy now," Vick said.

They walked up the stairs together and into Vick's room. She helped Vick into bed and pulled her covers up. "I'm gonna stay here in the chair till you fall asleep, okay?"

"Okay, Gayle. I love you."

"Good night," Lee said, putting her feet up.

※ ※ ※ ※

"Hi, honey," Ginny said, walking toward the bed. "Did you have a good nap?"

"Hi, honey," Edna answered, her words just slightly slurred. "I just woke up."

Ginny joined her in the bed, tucking Edna's head beneath her chin. "We had a good meeting," she said. "Guess what! Emily and Rachel are getting married!"

"Yay!" Edna said, wiggling with delight. "A wedding! A wedding! Where?"

"They're going to have it right here, at Lavender Meadows. Won't that be fun?"

Edna laughed and moved her arm as if she was clapping – her other arm could not quite make the movement yet, but Carol was working hard to help her recover as much control as possible. "Fun!" she said.

Then suddenly she burst into tears.

"Edna, what is it? What's the matter?" Ginny sat up, concerned, and reached for a tissue. She dabbed gently at the big drops cascading down Edna's cheeks. It was hard to keep up with her mood swings sometimes – she could change from sunny to stormy in a moment. Part of the stroke, Emily had said, but it was still disconcerting at times.

"I love weddings," she sniffled. "I love brides."

"Yes, weddings are fun," Ginny said.

"When I got married, I had a pretty dress," she said. "It had a nice big skirt and I could make it twirl. We were dancing, and we spun around and around."

"I know you were a beautiful bride," Ginny said. "You showed me the picture, remember?"

"Yes. I was pretty that day."

"You're still pretty, my love. Pretty and beautiful and gorgeous too!" Ginny said tenderly.

"Not a bride," she said.

"No, you're not a bride anymore. That was a long time ago." She paused for a moment, thinking. "But – if you wanted to, we could get married too. Goodness, we've been together long enough! Thirty-four years! And we could get married too, just like everyone else does. You could be a bride again!"

"A bride! And I could have a pretty dress." Edna frowned. "But you should be a bride too! Then we could both be pretty!"

"Is that really what you want, love? To be married to me?"

"Yes, yes, of course! Because I love you!"

"And I love you too," she said, choked up. She felt her own eyes fill with tears. Abruptly, she stood. "Well, I guess I'd better head out. See what's happening at the house." She knew very well what was happening – quiet, empty rooms, her footsteps loud on the wooden floors.

"No, Gin," Edna said, reaching for her. "Stay with me!"

"Okay," she said, sitting down again. "I'm not going anywhere."

☙☙❧❧

After many discussions with her daughter, Paula decided that she was ready to move into Lavender Meadows. She looked forward to living in a place where she and her wheelchair could fit into the bathroom, where she could get help with a shower in an accessible stall large enough for a shower chair. She looked forward to feeling safe and cared for. She looked forward to meeting new people that she had some common history with, but mostly she looked forward to being able to do what she wanted and needed without feeling apologetic for interfering or crowding her family and their lives.

She remembered how difficult it was to adjust to living with them after Barb died. Barb had been around to help her, didn't need to have things explained. She didn't feel so helpless when Barb was around.

Paula remembered back when she first went to live with her daughter. She'd left food for Paula's lunch in the kitchen, but Paula couldn't open the mayonnaise or the pickles, spread mustard on the bread, or even turn on the faucet. She cried for Barb and for the fingers that used to be so adept with knitting needles and counted cross-stitch and now were so twisted and gnarled.

She met Clarisse, and they hit it off. They both wanted to keep their expenses down and stretch their Social Security checks as much as possible, and they agreed to be roommates on a trial basis. They had plenty of stories to share about the restaurant where Clarisse had worked, and the school where Paula had taught home economics, cooking, and sewing for so long. Clarisse was relieved that Paula would be there in case anyone got confused in the night and wandered into her room again, and Paula was relieved that she could turn on her IPod and listen to her music without hurting Clarisse's feelings. It was meant to be.

Vick and Lee strolled around the lake, stopping occasionally to throw bread for the geese. "I love these birds," she said. "They're so pretty, but they all look alike to me. I wonder if they can tell each other apart."

"I don't know," Lee said. "Maybe they're just part of the crowd."

"I would hate that," Vick said. "I never wanted to be just part of the crowd."

Lee laughed, looking at Vick and then at herself, tats, piercings, and all. "Neither of us looks exactly mainstream," she said.

"That's true. I had to keep a lower profile when I was teaching, but I think everyone expects gym teachers to be weird and dykey."

"And aren't they?" Lee asked slyly.

"Pretty much," Vick said, and laughed. "But I got out after a few years. It was pretty boring."

"I could see that," Lee said. "So what else did you do?"

"Well, my dad owned a garage, and my four brothers and I grew up around engines and stuff. At first, my mom tried to make me be girlier, you know, dresses and stuff? But it just wasn't me, and finally she just gave up. Sometimes she told people she had five sons."

They laughed and continued their stroll.

"So how did you become a teacher?" Lee asked.

"I worked my way through school at my dad's place, fixing cars and motorcycles and pumping gas. He taught me everything. I can fix just about anything with a motor," she said proudly. "My brothers were also grease monkeys, and we pretty much hung out together. But they were all older than me, and when they started dating they didn't want me around that much."

"I can understand that!" Lee said.

"Then my brother Pete brought home this girl. Her name was Maura, and she was perfect. She knew a lot about cars and stuff, and she had a motorcycle. She and my brother went riding around all over the place. But she was pretty femme, long red hair and this great body. I was a wreck. I couldn't tell anyone how I felt, least of all Pete."

"Yeah, so then what happened?" Lee asked, excited.

"One day, she came by when Pete was not home, and I was working in the garage, and we got to talking. I didn't hear half of what she was saying. I just wanted to touch her." Vick laughed.

"So?"

"So one thing led to another, and she kissed me, and then she kissed me again. I was so blown away! It was crazy! And I said, 'Stop! Hey! What about my brother?'"

"Yeah?"

"So she said, 'You know I like your brother. He's a really good friend. But we're not like girlfriend and boyfriend, you know? I really came here to see you.' Oh my God, I didn't know what to say! I didn't know what to think!" She stopped and shook her head. "That Maura, she was something. She taught me a lot about women, about how to be a woman who loves women. She helped me find myself, know who I am."

Lee asked, "What did your brother say?"

"He knew that Maura considered him a friend, and that hurt his feelings a little. But he got over it. He's married now, and has three kids, so I guess he really is over it!"

"What about your parents? Did they know? What did they say?"

"Of course, they weren't crazy about it, but they were cool enough. They knew I had to be my own person. And my dad was glad that I was still working for him!"

"So then what? Did you stay with Maura?"

"No, we hung around until I went to college. She was older than me, had her own friends. We called each other for a while, got together when I was home from school, but then we called less and less. I run into her every now and then. She has a girlfriend she's been with for years. She's happy, and I'm happy for her."

"I can't believe your parents were okay about it. My parents never could be, not in a million years."

They came to a bench and sat down, looking at the lake. "So how did you end up here?" Vick asked.

Lee filled her in about how she met Sarah and came to work at Lavender Meadows.

Vick shook her head. "But how did you end up in that storage place?"

"I knew I was different. I tried to fight it, but finally I told my parents how I felt about girls. We were brought up knowing that being gay is a sin, and I figured I was damned, so I knew I was taking a big chance trying to talk to them. But I loved them, you know? Even though they were pretty dysfunctional."

"Yeah, I know what you mean. So then what?"

"My mom was crying, and she wouldn't look at me. My dad wouldn't look at me either. He just took me by the arm and walked me out to the car. We drove to the other side of town. He handed me fifty dollars and dropped me off." Tears started rolling down her face and she wiped them angrily on her sleeve. "I didn't get to say good-bye to my brothers or anything." She tried to hold back her tears, but the dam had come down. Vick put her arm around Lee's shoulder and let her cry, not saying a word.

After a time, her crying slowed, then stopped. "Sorry about that," she said. She took a deep shuddering breath.

"No problem. So how long ago was that?"

"About a year."

"You're just a kid. What a load of crap!" She paused for a moment, unsure about whether she should continue the conversation. "So how did you get by?"

Lee shrugged. "Any way I could. I had to do some things I'm not proud of."

Vick shook her head. "You're alive and you're here. That's what counts."

They sat there and smoked another cigarette. Then Lee spoke. "So what did you do after you stopped teaching? Did you go back and work with your father?"

"No, my dad died and two of my brothers own the garage now. We're all good friends – family, you know? I still go by there and hang out when I need a grease fix. But there's something else I love."

"What is that?" Lee asked.

"Flowers. So I bought a little shop, and I've been doing that for years now. Gayle works there with me now. You might have seen it up in Seattle. Butch's Flowers."

Lee shot her a sideways glance – she thought Vick was joking. But no, she was dead serious. She coughed to stifle her laugh.

༄༄༄༄

After the weekly meeting, Savannah went out to see Carrie in her usual spot on the porch overlooking the lake. She was so grateful to the women who helped them reunite and loved being part of the Lavender Meadows meetings. She was also excited about Emily and Rachel's wedding plans, and maybe a little jealous too.

Carrie's face lit up when she saw Savannah coming. "Hi! Hi!" she called.

"Hello, love," she answered as she hugged her and planted a kiss on top of her head. "It is so sweet to see you sitting here with the sun on your hair. Like a dream!" She moved a rocker next to Carrie's wheelchair and sat with her feet against the rail.

Carrie pointed at the hummingbird feeder hanging from the corner of the porch and laughed. Tiny bodies flitted around like jewels with wings. "Look, look!"

"Yes, hummingbirds. Aren't they beautiful! Look

how fast their wings move. Like magic," Savannah said. She reached over and rubbed Carrie's shoulder. "Like you."

Carrie rested her cheek against Savannah's hand. "Yes, magic," she sighed. "Oh, Sannah, I'm so happy!"

She felt the sudden sting of tears and blinked rapidly. "Me too, love." She reached into her pocket for a tissue and dabbed at her eyes.

"Why are you crying?" Carrie asked, her eyes round with concern.

"I'm just so glad you're with me again. We've lost so much time..."

"No. Not lost. We have now."

"Yes. You're so right," Savannah said. She gave her eyes a final dab and put the tissue away. "Oh, good news! We're going to have a wedding here. Emily and Rachel are getting married!"

"Married? How can they?"

"Goodness. I forgot that you missed so much. It's legal for lesbians to get married now."

"Really? I can't believe it." She shook her head. "Do I know them?"

"Well, you know Emily – she's your doctor now. Rachel is a weaver. She's going to have a baby! They've been together for years and years."

"Like us. Years and years." She sighed.

"Yes, I remember when we signed our domestic partnership papers. We had a party! All our friends were there. Do you remember?"

"You said we were married then. We were so happy!" She shook her head, troubled. "But we weren't really married then, were we?"

"No, it wasn't legal then. But we were married in our hearts, weren't we?"

"Oh yes."

"And it's a good thing we did sign those papers, or we would never have been able to get you out of the nursing home. We wouldn't ever have been together," Savannah said.

"So we're not really married. Not really really," Carrie said.

"Well, I guess the law says we are, but we never had a ceremony, so I don't know. It doesn't feel official."

"Well, then, why don't we get married!" Carrie said. "Do you want to? Do you still love me?"

"Of course I do!" Savannah began to cry again, but they were tears of joy. "Of course I do!"

※ ※ ※ ※

Suddenly wedding fever spread through the house, burning quick and hot. Even Jen came down with a mild case, which Sarah quickly cured.

"No, honey, we've only been together for a few months! We're too new!" she said, aghast.

"I know, but I love you and you love me. And we're living together…"

"Because you broke your ankle!" Sarah said.

"Well, gee, thanks a lot!" Jen said, offended.

"Now, I didn't say that to hurt your feelings. But you know we wouldn't have been living together yet if it wasn't for that!"

"Yet. We wouldn't have been living together yet," Jen said.

"Yes. I wouldn't want to be like the lesbian who brings the U-Haul on the second date – especially with me working here."

"So you think we would have been living together

at some point?"

"I guess so. Probably. Sure. If you didn't pick up some floozy on the ferry..." Sarah laughed.

"So you do love me. You didn't just take me in because of my foot."

"Of course I love you, you fool. Now c'mere, let me show you."

※ ※ ※ ※

And thus was launched the Lavender Meadows wedding extravaganza, complete with guest lists, wedding clothes, food planning, music arrangements, and many anxious brides. It seemed that every dyke in the county was included on someone's list, and they all needed to have some input into the arrangements. Even Carol and Zoe, who'd gotten married in New York as soon as it became legal, wanted to be in on the celebration.

Reverend Leah was thrilled to be officiating for so many friends, but bemused by all the activity. She'd agreed to perform ceremonies that would include as many traditions as possible, while creating new ones to pay special homage to the first generation of same-sex marriages in Washington. "Oh my," she said. "I think we're going to need a three-hour ceremony to make sure we don't leave anything or anyone out."

"Oh, Leah, don't worry. You always do such lovely ceremonies. You'll come up with something," Grace said.

Lee was pressed into service on so many projects, her head was spinning. Marie needed lots of help in the kitchen, and Jen called on her to help spruce up the grounds, especially the area by the lake where the ceremony would take place. A big white tent was going to house the food, and a platform was planned for the musicians. Lindy, Kristin, and Bree scrubbed and polished everything to within an inch of their lives. Rachel worked on wedding clothes, and Savannah arranged for the music, calling on musicians from around western Washington. Carol and Zoe created the wedding invitations and programs, and Vick and Gayle planned the flowers. Sarah flitted around, filling in a gap here, helping out there while ensuring that the normal activities of Lavender Meadows ran smoothly. Every available hand was put to some use in the preparations.

Jen checked the weather reports obsessively, worrying about storm systems that were developing hundreds of miles away. It was the only variable they had no control over, they thought. "Do meteorologists take bribes? If it rains, everything will be ruined! Ruined, I tell you!" She clapped her hand to her forehead dramatically.

"Give it up, Sarah Bernhardt, it's out of your control. Let's just hope the goddesses are smiling."

Jen relented. "How could they not be?"

❀❀❀❀

"Emily? Emily, wake up," Rachel said, shaking her shoulder.

"Mmmmf? Wha?" she answered, burrowing deeper into the pillow.

"Emily? Wake up! Something's wrong," Rachel said.

Instantly she was awake. "What is it?"

"I'm not sure. I'm having cramps." Rachel said,

starting to cry. "And I think I might be bleeding."

Emily ran her hand over the small mound that was their baby. "Ok, honey, don't panic. Let's see what's going on." She flipped the covers back and looked between Rachel's legs, where a small pink wet spot was starting to spread on the green striped sheet. "Huh," she said.

"I'm having another cramp, Emily," she said.

Emily kept her hand on Rachel's belly, feeling how it tightened and released. "You're having some contractions, I think. Let's go to the hospital so I can put you on a monitor. Don't get up, okay? Let me just call over there and tell them we're coming."

Rachel nodded, tears streaming down her face. "Oh, honey, are we losing our baby?" she asked brokenly.

"I hope not. Maybe we can stop it. But you know, love, lots of pregnancies end in miscarriages, and nobody knows why," Emily said, trying to keep her voice steady. She wiped her eyes on the quilt Rachel had made for them years ago, Canada geese flying against a dusky sky.

She jumped out of bed and grabbed her phone, calling the hospital on speed dial. "This is Dr. Rothman. I have a patient in premature labor. About five months," Rachel heard her say. "No, I'm not going to call for an ambulance. We're on Bainbridge Island, and we can get there faster on our own. Thanks. We'll be there soon." She grabbed her jeans and a shirt, then helped Rachel get into a long blue cotton dress. "Okay, ready? Let's go." Rachel started to get up, but Emily scooped her up in her arms and headed for the door, narrowly avoiding stepping on PeeWee and Bowser, their tabbies.

She flung open the door of the Nissan and settled Rachel in the back seat. "Are you comfortable, honey?"

"I'm okay," she said, turning her tear-stained face up to Emily.

Emily took a few deep breaths as she started the car. She knew she needed to keep a handle on her feelings to keep Rachel calm, but in her heart, she wanted to scream and weep and drive 100 miles an hour to get to the hospital and save their baby. If she could. If the goddesses smiled.

She pulled into the ER entrance and honked her horn, and two nurses came out to meet them with a gurney. Emily helped lift Rachel gently and place her on it as another contraction started. "Oh, no," she gasped.

"Breathe, honey, breathe," Emily said, pushing the gurney through the door. "Just breathe."

They headed up to the OB floor and the nurses took Rachel's vital signs and hooked her up to a monitor to check the baby's heartbeat and contractions. They could see the contractions on the monitor, but the baby's heart rate was strong, dropping slightly with each contraction, then picking up again when it was done.

Emily pulled on some gloves and gently examined Rachel, noticing that the pink discharged was streaked with red now. She was relieved to feel that Rachel's cervix was tightly closed.

"Who's on call tonight for OB?" she asked the nurse.

"Dr. Martin is on call, and he's sleeping here in the hospital. I'll go get him," she said. Drs. Martin and Lemaire were obstetricians, and the hospital had a couple of midwives as well. Between them, they delivered all the babies in town. Emily was confident about her skills, but she knew that she couldn't be impartial about their baby. Not when his or her life hung in the balance.

"Hi, Emily, what's going on?" Dr. Martin said a few minutes later. He had a bad case of bed head, but his eyes were awake. "Hi Rachel. You're not supposed to be here for a while!"

"I know," she said and blew her nose.

Emily filled him in quickly, and he looked at the monitor tracing. "Well, let's get an ultrasound and see what's going on, and we'll give you some meds to try to stop your contractions, if we can. I don't want you to get up, not even to go to the bathroom. Bedrest, period."

"Okay, I promise. I do hate bedpans, though." She gave him a pinched smile. "Do you think you can save it?" She looked at him, then at Emily, her eyes pleading.

"Well, the baby's heartbeat is strong," he said. "That's a good sign. You know we'll do everything we can."

The ultrasound showed that the baby was moving and looked normal. They had wanted to be surprised about the baby's sex, but everything changed now that it was in trouble. Now that he was in trouble. It did show that a small part of the placenta had started to separate from the wall of the uterus. That was where the blood was coming from.

They started an IV and gave Rachel drugs that made her loopy and weird, but the after a while the contractions slowed, then stopped. At last, she fell asleep, and Emily put her head down on the bed and closed her eyes as the sun was coming up.

※ ※ ※ ※

Dr. Martin continued to follow Rachel closely. "I don't know what to tell you, Emily," he said. "Her contractions have stopped for now, but they may start up again if we take her off the meds. Her bleeding has stopped, too, and the baby's heartbeat is still strong. All we can do now is keep her on bedrest, monitor the baby, and hope that the pregnancy continues to a successful conclusion."

"She's barely five months. I know that if her labor starts up again, the baby probably won't make it. We want to do anything we can to save him."

"Sure. You know we'll do whatever we can. We can keep her in the hospital, keep her sedated, and monitor her periodically throughout the day. The baby is still really small, though, as you know."

"I hate the thought of her being in the hospital for three or four months. I know she'll hate it too. This will be really hard for her."

"Well, I guess you could take her home, but she would need someone who could be there for her all the time. I don't think you would want to take that much time away from your practice, Emily."

She sighed. "I know. I'll have to think about it and talk to Rachel when she's more awake."

"Let me know what you decide," he said and patted her shoulder.

※ ※ ※ ※

"Hello, Sarah? This is Emily. Do you have a minute to talk?"

"Oh, hi there. How are you and Rachel doing?"

"I'm fine, but Rachel is having some problems. The placenta is starting to separate from the uterus, and she started having some contractions."

"Oh, no," Sarah said. "I'm so sorry!"

"Well, the baby is still hanging in there. He is hanging in there." She took a breath. "We were able to stop the contractions, but she needs to be on bedrest and monitoring. We don't want her to have to be in the hospital for months, and I can't be with her all the time. I was wondering if you could help us out."

"Sure, whatever I can do," Sarah said.

"Well, I was wondering if she could come and stay at Lavender Meadows until she has the baby. You could keep an eye on her, and she would be among friends."

"You know I'm not an OB nurse. I can keep an eye on her and make sure she stays on bedrest, though."

"Well, we could bring a monitor out there, and I could show you how to set it up for each session, and what to watch out for."

Sarah didn't hesitate. "Of course! What a great idea! It would be fun to have her, and we'll spoil her like crazy."

And so a couple of days later, Rachel was ensconced next door to Clarisse's and Paula's room at Lavender Meadows, waiting for the arrival of the new generation.

They didn't want her to feel isolated, so they made sure she was included in the activities of the house. They set up a big TV in her room so she could watch movies either on her own or with some of the other ladies. Luanne came in every few days and gave her a massage, and Sarah and Emily checked her contractions on the monitor several times a day.

Emily ran back and forth between her office, their home, and Lavender Meadows. She was tired and worried about Rachel and the baby, of course, and she had to take call at the hospital as well, so she was pretty stressed out. Sarah talked to Grace and Marie about it, then got together with Emily.

"You know, Emily, you're running yourself ragged. You have to take care of yourself, too."

"I know, but I don't have the time. You know I want to spend time with Rachel, and I'm so busy with all my other stuff. And I know you're taking good care of her, but it's hard to leave her here when I go home at night."

"Well, why don't you just stay here?" Sarah asked. "There's no reason why you can't sleep here. The bed is certainly big enough, and I know Rachel would feel better if you were around. Then maybe you could get some rest!"

"But I have to take care of the cats, too. I need to spend some time with them also! They would get so lonely. I can't just leave them there."

Sarah laughed. "It's hard to be indispensable, isn't it?"

"Yes, really. But I'll catch up with myself one of these days," she said, ruefully.

"Yes, when the baby is five years old!" She laughed again and shook her head. "I tell you what. Pack up Pee Wee and Bowser, and let's introduce Margret and Ralph to their new step-sisters."

"Oh, thank you, Sarah! Thank you!"

It took a couple of days, but the cats divided up the bed, leaving as little room as possible for Rachel and Emily, and took turns driving Ralph crazy as well.

Rachel was happy that she got to spend more time with Emily, and she also felt safer knowing that she was around. But she had other things on her mind, too. She tried to stay busy with her needlework, but the wedding day was getting closer, and she didn't know how they would handle that, or whether it would even be possible. She was falling behind on the outfits for the wedding, and it was hard doing a lot of the work while she was in bed. Plus, she was worried about the shop. "I don't want to close up the shop, but by the time I have this baby, my business will be gone," she said fretfully. "Even the group of women who come to the shop to quilt and do crafts together might stop coming! I don't know what to do!"

Grace listened to her concerns, thought it over, and talked to Marie. She didn't need Sarah to care for her anymore – her hip had healed, and she was independent now, though she still had to be careful. Marie was busy most of the time now, cooking and supervising everything she could, and frankly, Grace was bored. She wanted to do something useful, something she could have fun with.

"I love your shop!" she said. "Why don't you let me open it for a couple of days a week?" she asked Rachel. "Just till you get back on your feet. I'm not an artist like you, of course, but I could certainly wait on customers!"

So several days a week, Grace picked up the lunch Marie had packed for her and went off happily to work. And while she was there, she told some of Rachel's craft groups about the situation with the baby and the upcoming wedding, and they offered to come to Lavender Meadows and pitch in with the sewing. Paula could not sew, but she could help direct activities and offer opinions.

So while Rachel rested and the baby grew, a cacophony of purring cats, whirring sewing machines, bursts of laughter, and the ever-present clink of teacups surrounded them.

❧❧❦❦

Marie woke early, as usual, then spent a couple of extra minutes lying in bed while she reviewed her plans for the day. Cranberry orange scones, grilled Canadian bacon, eggs, orange and apple juices, coffee and tea for breakfast, tuna melts and fruit for lunch, and shepherd's pie for dinner, with a crumble from the plums Sarah had picked last night. She liked having her day organized in advance: no surprises.

So it was a shock to see kitchen drawers and cabinet doors open, with knives, forks and spoons scattered around on the counter tops, napkins in a heap on the sideboard, and boxes of half-eaten crackers and cold cereal open on the table. "Hmmmph!" she cried. "What on earth!"

Lee appeared at that moment to help her get breakfast and the mess took her aback as well. "What the hell," she said. "Is it raccoons?" She looked over at the window.

"I don't think any self-respecting raccoon would lay the crackers on the table or move the spoons around," Marie said dryly. "I think it was a two-footed raccoon."

"Do you think someone broke in?" Lee said, looking around. The windows were intact, and the kitchen door was locked from the inside, as usual.

"I don't know. But help me clean up so we can

get breakfast started. I'm all in a tizzy."

Breakfast was only a few minutes late, and everybody arrived in the dining room as usual. The scent of the scones and bacon filled the air, and Marie bustled in with a pot of coffee and began to fill the cups. When she was done, she sat down and started filling the plates. "Happy happy, joy joy," she said, and the women answered. She passed the plates around to each resident or to Jen and Sarah who helped folks eat as needed. As usual, she put together a big plate for Vick, with two scones, a pile of scrambled eggs, and several slices of bacon.

"Not too much," Vick said, stifling a yawn. "I'm not that hungry this morning."

Lee and Marie looked at each other, but neither said a word.

After breakfast, Marie cornered Sarah and told her about the mess in the kitchen.

"I wonder if it was Vick coming down for a late-night snack," Marie said. "She said she wasn't very hungry this morning, and you know that's not like her."

"That's true," Sarah said thoughtfully. "I wonder if she remembers."

"I don't know," Marie said. "Should we ask her?"

"I'm not sure. Maybe I'll give Dr. Emily a ring and see what she thinks."

Sarah called her to discuss the situation. "I don't want to make a big deal of this," she said. "I just want to know whether or not I should talk to her about it and see what she says."

"She may have been sundowning," Emily said. "You know how people with Alzheimer's may get up during the night and walk around. They get their sleeping patterns mixed up and sometimes the changes in the light later in the day can confuse them."

"I know, and I don't want to upset her," Sarah said. "I don't even know if it was her that made the mess. What do you think we should do?"

"Why don't you try giving her an extra little snack before bedtime? Maybe she was just hungry," Emily said. "Let's see what happens."

"Okay, good idea," Sarah said. "I just want her and the other ladies to be safe."

Next day, Sarah and Carol put together a couple of boxes with a bunch of washcloths, some old pillowcases and various objects that were too big to swallow – a toy car, a motorcycle, a Rubik cube, some washable crayons, some paper, a couple of books, and some old costume jewelry – just the thing for a person who liked to rummage. Every night they put the boxes out in the dining room along with a plate of cookies and a bottle of water. And the last thing Marie did every night was to lock the door to the kitchen.

✥✥✥✥

Sarah's pocket vibrated as she climbed the stairs to bring Rachel her lunch. She put the tray down quickly and grabbed her phone just as it was about to go to voice mail. "Hello, this is Sarah Chase at Lavender Meadows. How can I help you?"

"Oh, hi, Sarah. My name is Willow. We met at your party. I'm a nurse. You probably don't remember me."

Sarah's mind flashed back to that warm summer evening, people dancing around the fire, and a young woman with bright red hair sitting on the ground in front of her. "Oh, yes, I do remember. How are you?"

"I'm fine," Willow answered. "I think you said that the house where you had the party was an adult family home for elderly lesbians. Is that right?"

"Yes, but not all the residents are seniors, though – we have kind of a mix of ages right now. Are you looking to place someone here?"

"Er, yes. Me." She laughed. "Not as a resident, of course. I'm looking for a new job and I was wondering if you had any openings."

Sarah had been feeling a bit overwhelmed lately and had thought about getting some more help. She couldn't be everywhere every minute. "Well, we are getting busier and we have a lot of stuff going on here right now. We definitely could use some help. In fact, I was just about to put an ad on Craig's List. What did you have in mind?"

"I'm working at a home health agency, but I'm going to school too, trying to finish up my RN classes. There's so much paperwork in home health that I don't have enough time to do my schoolwork. And my classes are always during the day, so I need to work the evening or night shift. What do you think?"

Sarah's pulse quickened. She could practically smell the popcorn in the movie theater. "Great! Why don't you come up and talk to us, and look the place over?"

"Sure, that would be great," Willow said.

"Can you come up tomorrow and have lunch with us? You can look around and meet the ladies."

She hung up and went in search of Jen, and found her sitting on the front porch, chopping up vegetables for salad. She flopped into the rocker next to her and grabbed a slice of cucumber. "Guess what? Remember that nurse we talked to at the summer party? Red hair, good dancer?"

Jen nodded. "Hard to forget!"

"Well, she just called me, and she's looking for a job."

"Wow, how cool! I was wondering if we were ever going to get to spend time together. Ever since this place got started you've been so busy."

"But we're together here all the time. We get to spend lots more time together than we had when you were working…"

"I know, I know, but it's not the same. I would love to have a little undivided attention…" she said, waggling her eyebrows wickedly.

Sarah thought about their nights, and how she always had one ear open to the sounds of the house, listening for thumps and bangs and yells and tears and who knew what, especially with their recent situation with Vick. It would be so nice to shut that down, to relax in the dark, to hold her honey tight, the sounds of their love being the only ones that mattered. "Yes, me too," she purred.

༺༻

The next day Willow parked her little purple hybrid next to Sarah's van. She smiled when she saw that they had matching goddess stickers in their windows. It was a good omen.

Ralph ran out to greet her, barking, then apparently satisfied, he stuck his nose into her hand and pranced alongside her to the porch.

Sarah opened the door to greet her. "Hi, Willow!" she said, giving her a quick hug. "So glad you could come!"

"I've been thinking about this place ever since I was here," she said. She looked around at the house, the rolling lawn, the lake sparkling in the sun. "I didn't really get a good look at it that night."

"I know!" Sarah said. "It still blows me away!"

Willow stopped to read the sign, painted with pretty sprays of lavender and other flowers. "Lavender Meadows, A Family of Women," she said. "I like that name."

Sarah opened the big white door and stepped back so Willow could pass. "Come in, come in."

The front room was redolent of fresh basil and spaghetti sauce. Willow sniffed appreciatively, suddenly hungry. It was unusual to eat during a job interview, but nothing about the situation was ordinary.

Several women sat around the dining table and a young girl and an older woman carried plates of pasta, bowls of salad, and garlic bread from the kitchen.

"Hi, everybody, this is Willow. She's a nurse, and she's going to check us out and see if she wants to work here with us. Here, Willow, sit down," Sarah said, pulling out a chair next to her. She ran through the introductions quickly.

Willow smiled at everyone and nodded at Jen. "I remember you," she said. "How's your leg?"

"Much better," she said. "Not perfect, but at least I'm off those damn crutches!"

Marie passed her a plate. "Eat up, now," she said.

"Is there meat in here?" Willow asked.

"The red sauce has meat, the pesto does not," Marie said.

"Oh, thanks. I should have said something to Sarah about being vegetarian when I spoke to her on the phone."

"Don't worry, there's always something for anyone to eat, no matter how weird they are," Marie said matter-of-factly.

"Uh, thanks!" Willow said.

After lunch, Sarah took Willow on a tour of the grounds, and they talked about the ladies and how things were done. "I was able to manage pretty well at first, and Carol the physical therapist has been helping us out, but I need to have some time to myself, too. I know you mentioned that you are going to school, and you want to work evenings and nights. That would be perfect for us!" Sarah said.

"Exactly what I need!" Willow said.

"And Rachel needs some extra attention because she's on bedrest until she has her baby. She needs to be monitored every few hours. Are you okay with that?" Willow nodded. "Emily, her partner, is a doctor, and stays here most of the time, but she has her practice and her hospital rounds."

"Okay. You just show me what to do. I love preggies."

"And one more thing. We are going to have a huge wedding here soon, and this place is going to be buzzing. We're probably gonna need some extra help, if you're up to it."

"A wedding? That's very cool. Who's getting married?"

"Almost everyone." Sarah laughed.

They walked around to the little cottages. "People used to stay in these little guest houses when the bed and breakfast was up and running," Sarah said. "Lee has this house, and she also stays up at the main house sometimes so Jen and I can have some space. But she's just a young kid and needs some privacy so she can do her schoolwork. And whatever." Willow nodded. "If you want, you can stay in one of these, but we'll need you up at the house when you're on duty."

"Looks perfect!" Willow said. "There's just one thing – or two actually—I have a dog and a parrot."

"What kind of parrot?" Sarah asked.

"She's a blue-and-gold Macaw, about the size of a small chicken with a long tail. She's very sociable, likes to be in the center of things. I feel kind of bad for her sometimes—she hasn't had much company since April and I broke up, and I'm gone a lot during the day with classes and work."

"What about the dog?"

"She is part Peke, part who-knows-what. She's very friendly and likes other critters – even the bird, who drives her crazy. She calls the dog, and she sounds just like me, and of course the poor thing comes running, and I'm not there, and nothing is happening. It's very frustrating for her."

Sarah laughed at the image. "What are their names?"

"The parrot is Bad Lily, for obvious reasons, and the dog is Won Ton. I'm a sucker for a little dumpling," she said, smiling.

"Me too," Sarah said. "Bring them along."

※※※※

The time dragged on slowly toward the wedding, and suddenly it was upon them. The buzz increased from sedate to feverish in just a matter of days. There were still a million details to be taken care of, but somehow things were getting done.

Marie was in a frenzy, doing the last minute food stuff and dealing with the bakery and the catering staff. "Hmmmphs" filled the air as she flitted around like a hummingbird, sticking her little birdie beak in everything.

Rachel was upstairs, sewing like crazy, her league of minions about her. Emily did her best to stay out of everyone's way while keeping a careful, worried eye on Rachel. She knew that every day the baby stayed safely in the womb improved his chances. She was relieved that there was no further bleeding and no contractions. Every few hours, Rachel stopped her work for monitoring, and every indication showed that the baby was doing fine.

Grace opened the shop several days a week and enjoyed hanging out with the customers. Women from around town stopped in to check on Rachel's condition, and Grace was glad to give good news about the baby's progress to anyone who asked. Several ultrasounds were pinned up on the wall near the cash register.

Because there were so many ceremonies taking place at the same time, Carol and Zoe designed a little book to hand out to the guests, with pictures of the couples and a bit of their histories. They also planned the wedding pictures and videos.

Edna went from cheerful to tearful in a matter of moments in the course of each day, and Ginny did her best to keep her from melting down in all the excitement. She also worked on putting together the music, making sure that all the musicians were lined up for the big day.

Savannah was the main organizer and made sure that everything was on schedule and done according to plan. She inspected, touched, and tasted everything.

Carrie watched Savannah march back and forth with her clipboard and smiled at her serenely from her chair on the porch. "I love seeing you sitting there," Savannah said. "Seeing your smiling face makes me calm down."

"I'm getting married! I'm a bride!" Carrie reminded everyone several times a day. "We're both brides," Savannah reminded her. "I'm getting married too, you know!" Carrie just giggled.

The slightest imperfection caught Savannah's eye and she dealt with it at once. Two days before the big event, she noticed that the grounds near the lake were looking a little rough, and after some discussion, Lee drove happily to Silverdale to get Mr. Sanchez and his family, including the new baby, from the storage unit and bring them back to Lavender Meadows to help out. He exclaimed with pleasure as he looked around at the garden and the flowers and trees around the house and the lake, shook his head sadly at the overgrown lavender. Savannah, Sarah, Mr. Sanchez, and Lee nodded, smiled, and pointed, and soon the area was manicured and tidy again.

Lee was everywhere, now a cook, now an errand girl, now a furniture mover, now a landscaper. She could barely catch her breath. She grumbled, but kept working relentlessly. "Damn, Savannah, you're worse than Marie! If it was up to you, we'd paint the gravel, polish all the squirrels, and paint Ralph's toenails!"

Rosa Sanchez gravitated to the kitchen, propped up her baby in a big basket, and rolled up her sleeves. Her other little ones raced around the porch and in and out of the kitchen, laughing and singing to each other. She joined Marie in putting together tray after tray of goodies, but she was worried about her, because she was obviously running out of steam. Every now and then, she stopped for a moment and put her hand to her chest. At last, Rosa went looking for Sarah, pantomimed Marie holding her chest, then pointed toward the kitchen. Sarah tried to thank her in her rusty high school Spanish and ran up the stairs to get Marie's medicine. Between the two of them, they got Marie into a chair for some nitroglycerin with a tea chaser. Sarah was particularly concerned because Marie did not protest, but after a few minutes, her color started to improve.

Gayle brought a truck full of flowers from the shop, and did whatever she could to keep Vick focused on the bouquets and arrangements. "Oh, honey," she said. "You are a real artist. Nobody can do flowers as good as you." Vick just grunted, but Gayle could tell that she was pleased.

The morning of the wedding dawned clear and beautiful, the sky the hot blue that sometimes manifested in the autumn and provided such contrast to the reds and golds of the foliage. All the women who'd been working so hard let out a collective sigh of relief, including Reverend Leah, who'd been sending sunny vibes to the universe for days. She was grateful that the autumnal grays seemed to be holding off a little longer, but she kept an eye on the sky, knowing how quickly the weather could change in the Pacific Northwest.

Flurries of activity and excited laughter filled most every room as wedding clothes were adjusted and hair was fluffed and patted. The wedding outfits were as different as the individual couples, but all expressed the joy of a festivity long awaited. Edna and Ginny wore soft, drapey black pants and long white jackets with sparkly spirals. Savannah wore a long gold-and-orange dress with a sweeping skirt and fluttery sleeves, and Carrie wore a pearl-gray suit with a scalloped neckline and lots of buttons down the front. Rachel wore a long gauzy shirt that she'd embroidered with whole seasons of flowers, and Emily wore a white tuxedo with a frilly purple shirt and cummerbund. Grace had a lacy lavender skirt and top, and Marie wore a darker purple pantsuit. On their heads, they both wore tiny matching red hats. Sarah and Jen wore matching tuxedos with lavender bowties, and Lee wore a skull tee shirt and rainbow tie-dyed pants, hair spiked to the max. Even Leah was resplendent in a white-and-gold outfit with a martial arts cut and a long gold sash. Around her neck, she wore a narrow purple stole embroidered with the symbols of all the major religions.

Gravel crunched in the driveway as guests started to arrive. Lee and Mr. Sanchez waved cars into rows, and people piled out and headed toward the white tent at the lake. Ralph ran circles around everyone, barking excitedly.

Wheelchairs lined up at the stair climber, and the ladies took their turns heading down, assisted by Willow, Carol, Zoe, and Luanne.

Since Rachel hadn't been out of bed for a while, Emily was especially careful to scoop her up and settle her gently in the chair. Rachel looked up at her, her eyes glistening, and squeezed her hand. "I'm so excited," she said softly.

"Me too," she answered. She bent down and placed a kiss beneath her ear. "You look so beautiful!"

"Thank you, my love. You make me feel beautiful."

A string quartet played softly as the guests took

their places in front of the white platform. Baskets of flowers and trailing ivy hanging from latticework arches and tall pillars swung gently in the breeze from the lake.

All the women lined up on the platform, each couple separated by an arrangement of flowers and bittersweet branches. Vick and Gayle had done themselves proud.

Reverend Leah took the microphone, smiled at the line of brides, then out at the smiling spectators. "Welcome! Isn't this a glorious day!" she said. "And a glorious occasion! One that so many of us have been waiting for our whole lives! And at last, the time is here! A time when we can express and celebrate our love with our friends, our families, and the world.

"We have before us eight women who have decided to share their commitment to each other. Each couple has reached this ceremony through a different path, but somehow have all ended up here, in this place, at this time. Not by accident, but by divine appointment.

"First, we have Grace Meadows and Marie Fitch, the reason we are all here at this beautiful place today. Grace moved here from the East Coast with her sister-in-law, Annie, whom I'm sure many of you are old enough to remember."

The crowd laughed and murmured.

"For years they ran Lavender Meadows, a bed and breakfast catering primarily to lesbians, when such things were unheard of. It provided a place where women could come together to rest and relax, to create, to dream. Unfortunately, they were never able to be open with their families about their relationship, and when they did get the occasional visitor, they had to close down the bed and breakfast for the duration of the visit and 'de-dyke' the house. How many of us have had to take down our books and pictures and make it look like we were sleeping in separate bedrooms? How many of us have had to keep the truth from our own children?"

The audience nodded, murmuring quietly.

"When Annie passed away several years ago, the bed and breakfast stopped operating, and Grace retired. Marie had been working at Lavender Meadows for years, and after the place closed down, they continued to live there and developed a relationship that's been going strong ever since. When Grace took a fall and broke her hip a while back, Sarah Chase came out to Lavender Meadows as her nurse, and has helped her get back on her feet – literally. Together, they decided to reopen Lavender Meadows as an assisted living place for lesbians who needed some assistance with health care, and Lavender Meadows, a Family of Women, including partners, birth families, friends, and whoever they define as family, was born."

A ripple of applause answered her.

"Edna Knowles was born in Dublin, Ireland, and immigrated to the US when she was fourteen years old – young enough to look like a wild Irish rose but old enough to keep her accent." The guests chuckled. "Same-sex love was, of course, forbidden by the church she was raised in. She had to keep the desires of her heart a secret from her family and her church. Ginny Parsons moved here from Yakima, where she always stood out as the odd girl. Her classmates ostracized her and she had to deal with spiteful behavior and bullying until she was accepted at the University of Washington – School of Education and got away.

That's where they met, and Ginny's never looked back except for her annual tomato- and peach-buying orgy at the end of each summer. In fact, they will be driving there tomorrow for a little honeymoon. And for the first time they will register at the Best Western in one room, with one bed and one name!"

The crowd responded with whistles and cheers as Ginny waved, smiling.

"Rachel studied art and design in Portland, and her fiber art works have been shown all over the Pacific Northwest. In fact, she worked really hard to put together some of these beautiful outfits you see here today," she said, waving her hand at the line of women on the stage. "And she did it all without getting out of bed!"

Rachel held up her hands and nodded. "I had a lot of help!"

"Doctor Emily Rothman joined the Army right after medical school to defray some of her enormous medical school bills. She and Rachel met at a craft fair, where Rachel had some of her weavings and beadwork displayed. Emily was stationed at Madigan Army Hospital. They had to be very careful about concealing their relationship, or as we know, Emily could have been brought up on charges, thrown out of the Army, and disgraced professionally. They had to be especially careful to fly below the radar when Emily was transferred to Panama for a couple of years. Emily has a practice in town now, and Rachel has a beautiful little shop, but their main project right now is the little baby that's growing inside of Rachel every day. He's had some problems, but we are sending him love and healing vibes and he is hanging in there. And when that baby is born, his parents will be married. They won't have to lie, or hide their relationship, or worry that their child won't have the legal and financial protections of children born in conventional relationships! Nobody will ever be able to take him away because his moms are lesbians. And he'll have every advantage that love, creativity, and a strong community can bring to him."

The audience broke out into spontaneous applause.

"And then, of course, we have Savannah and Carrie, two star-crossed lovers who have beaten the odds. These two women were together for many years when tragedy struck them, in the form of a drunken scumbag with a suspended license. They were both injured, but Savannah recovered pretty quickly. Carrie had a serious head injury and spent months in a coma. When Savannah tried to see her, she found that Carrie's family had barred her from Carrie's life with a restraining order. Since she was not considered family she was not permitted to see her or speak with her, and when Carrie started to regain consciousness, Savannah could not be by her side. This is a type of hate crime that is not so easy to recognize. But we've all seen or heard about such things during the beginnings of the AIDS epidemic, when partners were separated, were even forbidden to attend the funerals. Carrie and Savannah had signed domestic partnership papers years before, but it wasn't until same-sex marriage became legal in our state that these domestic partnerships were considered legal and binding, and Carrie and Savannah could be together again."

The guests burst out in applause, standing, whistling, shouting, weeping. Savannah and Carrie hugged and kissed, laughing and crying at the same time.

"And so now we are here to celebrate the joining of these four couples, who have suffered in one form or another so that we could all be free to love who we want. Now let's give them a chance to exchange the vows that each of them wrote before we seal these covenants."

Each couple spoke their vows into the mic or whispered to each other as they saw fit.

At the end, Reverend Leah said, "Do you take these women to be your lawful wedded wives?"

"We do!" they said in chorus.

"Loved ones and friends, I give you the brides!"

Lively Irish music replaced the string quartet as the wedding guests lined up to congratulate the brides before heading over to the food tent. After that, the musicians took turns and played music for every kind of dancing and singing.

The white tent was filled to overflowing with hors d'oeuvres, salads, platters of cold meats and cheeses, baskets of bread and rolls, and large, steaming, fragrant pots and pans of curries, chilies, and pastas. The towering lavender wedding cake presided over the dessert table, but there were also lots of sugar- and gluten-free things. Something for everyone.

Marie, Lee, Sarah, Jen, and Rosa plopped themselves down out of the way of the crowd and admired their handiwork.

"I can't believe we got all this done," Marie said, fanning herself.

"Yes, and it's gorgeous. And delicious, I know – I tasted everything!" Lee laughed. "And you even made time to slip away and get married yourself."

"Hmmmph," Marie said, then smiled happily and looked around at her crew. "We couldn't have pulled this together without you and all your help. Thank you, thank you! And gracias! Now go get something to eat before it's all gone!"

Sarah stayed back with Marie for a moment. "How are you feeling, Marie?"

"I'm all right now, thanks. Just a little tired."

"Why don't you go sit with Grace and I'll fix you some plates," she said.

"Okay, I'll take you up on that. See you up front."

Sarah walked around for a few minutes, stopping for words of welcome and congratulation as she made her way to the food table. People from all over the community were there. Most were friends of the brides, but there were also people who were curious about Lavender Meadows and those who wanted to see actual lesbians get married. She smiled to herself, thinking how many of the guests were wondering about what lesbians do in bed.

Jen grabbed her up from behind in a big hug. "Hey, Ms. Mother-of-the-Brides!" she said. "All your little chickens, safely married. And everything came together so beautifully!"

"Yes! That Savannah – she could have been a wedding planner."

"Yes – she is incredibly organized. I could never do that!" Jen said, admiringly.

"And Reverend Leah – that was a beautiful ceremony, wasn't it? And quite the speech!"

"Yes!" Jen cleared her throat. "Maybe, someday, she could do a ceremony for us!"

"Who knows? Maybe someday," Sarah whispered, lifting her face for a kiss.

≈≈≈≈

Vick and Gayle sat on the bench facing the lake, smoking. Vick looked down at the ground, not watching the guests walking around the lake, not paying attention to the music coming from the white tent.

"It sure was a beautiful wedding," Gayle said. "I've never seen anything like it."

Vick grunted.

"Honey, are you hungry?" Gayle asked. "Do you want me to get you something to eat?" She put her hand on the back of Vick's neck.

"No," Vick answered. Her body was tight, ready to spring.

"What is it? Are you angry?"

"No," she said again. She rested her arms on her knees, her hands clasped tightly in front of her.

"Everybody loved the flowers. You did a beautiful job. You have such a good eye, and you can make everything come together so it looks graceful. I could never do as well, even though you've taught me so much," Gayle said.

Vick stood abruptly and started walking toward the lake. Gayle hurried after her. "Honey, where are you going?"

"Leave me alone!" she shouted. "Stop talking! Leave me alone!"

Gayle stopped, stung. "Hey, girl," she said angrily. "I didn't do anything! Don't you yell at me!"

Gayle jumped back quickly as Vick took a swing at her. "Hey! Stop that!"

Vick burst into tears.

Gayle realized what was happening. "Oh, no, sweet girl. I'm sorry. All this stuff going on, all these people, all this noise. Too much for you, too much. I'm sorry." She reached into her pocket, pulled out a black bandanna and dabbed at Vick's eyes. "C'mon, let's walk," she said. She took her arm and they started on the path, keeping well away from the other women strolling around the lake. After a few minutes, they came to a secluded, shady area with a picnic table. They sat down, stretched out their legs, and lit cigarettes, admiring the big rhododendrons that grew along the edge of the clearing.

"Hey, look, what's that?" Gayle said, catching a glint of sun on metal. She got up and looked more closely. "Oh, look, it's a little statue of a woman," she said. "Isn't she pretty! She looks a little like Sarah Chase. I wonder who she is!"

Vick came up behind her and looked at the little figure too. "Pretty," she said. She took a deep breath, feeling calmer in the quiet. She reached up and snapped off a spent rhody blossom, then another and another. Gayle started deadheading flowers too, and tossed one at Vick, who immediately fired one back. In moments, they were pelting each other with flowers, chasing each other around the picnic table, and laughing, laughing.

༄༄༄༄

"I'm worried about Vick," Gayle said to Sarah later. "She had a big meltdown today."

"I'm sorry to hear that," Sarah said. "There was so much going on, I'm not surprised she was upset. You know, people with Alzheimer's can get overwhelmed if there's too much stimulation."

"I know, and I didn't realize it was happening until it was too late. It's easy to forget that sometimes she's different than she used to be."

"I know. It's very hard on her, and I know it's hard for you too."

"Knowing that she's here is such a load off my mind, though. I know you're all keeping an eye on her. I was so worried that something would happen to her, that she would have an accident or something when I wasn't around."

"We're doing the best we can to keep her safe and calm," she said, and told her about the rummage box they had set up for her in the dining room. "It keeps her occupied for a while at night if she can't sleep."

"Thanks for doing that," Gayle said. "She's always liked to be busy."

"Speaking of busy, you two did an incredible job on the flowers. They are gorgeous!" Sarah said.

"Thanks!" Gayle said. "It was mostly Vick's ideas. The woman has the touch. And I thought the rest of the wedding was beautiful, and the food was wonderful." She laughed. "I didn't think we were going to get any because Vick and I ended up goofing off and chasing each other around a picnic table in this place across the lake. Where the little statue is? But then finally, Vick got hungry and we made it to the tent just in time for the last of the food. Yum!" Gayle said.

Sarah smiled too. She had good memories of that very place herself.

※※※※

It took a while for things to get back to normal after the excitement of the wedding. Of course, there was a lot of clean up to be done, equipment to be stored, and trash to be picked up. Lee was not looking forward to participating in that process – she had already put a lot of energy into the setup, and she had a ton of other work to do besides.

So she was very glad when Sarah asked the Sanchez family to stay around, help them around the place, and stay in the old caretaker's cottage. Rosa and Marie seemed to hit it off pretty well when they worked together in the house, probably because they didn't understand each other that well. The two little girls, Carmen and Francesca, enjoyed running around on the lawn, playing and giggling, and Miguel, the baby, got passed hand-to-hand to anyone who needed a baby fix. It sure beat staying in a storage unit, she thought. She knew about that from her own experience.

※ ※ ※ ※

Paula's shirt was twisted at an awkward angle from her frantic attempts to scratch that spot on her back she could never quite get. She used to be able to get it with a ruler, a back brush, or a long spoon, but now she could only scrape it against the back of her wheelchair, looking for some relief. She looked at her twisted fingers and sighed in frustration.

"What's the matter, dear?" Clarisse asked from across the room. "Itchy?"

"Grrrr!" she answered. "I'm all right, thanks."

"Here, let me help you," she said, putting down her counted cross-stitch. She hiked herself out of the rocker and went right to the spot that she knew drove Paula crazy.

"Oh, oh, argh, ah, ah…" she groaned in relief. "Thanks! Oh my Lord."

Clarisse chuckled and straightened Paula's shirt.

"There now."

She sat up in her chair. "Honestly, Clarisse, I think you'd have better things to do than scratching my damn back. Or picking up my book, or my fork, or holding a glass of water for me. You are here for yourself, not to wait on me."

"No, really, I don't mind," she said mildly. "Besides, I know you would do the same thing for me."

"Maybe!" Paula laughed. "Maybe I'd just let you suffer!"

"Ha!" Clarisse said.

They heard footsteps in the hall, then Lee's voice. "Lunchtime, girls!" She stuck her head into the room. "Ready, Paula?"

"Yes. I don't know how I can be hungry, though. I haven't done anything all day!"

"Me too," Clarisse said. She picked up her sweater. "I wonder how many calories cross-stitching burns off!"

Lee moved Paula's wheelchair out to the landing and positioned her by the stair climber.

"Race ya down," Clarisse said, starting down the stairs.

"We're having chicken burritos today," Lee said. "And Reverend Leah is joining us for lunch."

"Oh good. Someone new to complain to," Paula said.

"Are you feeling grumpy today?" Lee asked.

"Of course!" she said. "How else should I feel?"

"Goodness!" Sarah said, meeting her at the bottom step. "What's wrong?"

She sighed. "I'm just so tired of feeling stuck. I am stuck! I can't do anything for myself!" she said as Sarah moved her to the table and put a napkin around her neck. She pulled out a chair beside her and put a burrito and some salad on her plate.

"Everybody here?" Sarah looked around. Grace, Edna, and Carrie were already in their places. Vick lumbered in from the porch and sat down next to Clarisse. Reverend Leah came out of the kitchen, carrying a pitcher of lemonade, and pulled up a chair next to Vick. Jen came in, carrying a bowl of salsa and some tortilla chips warm from the oven. Marie started passing around plates of food and Lee sat beside Edna to help her eat.

"Happy happy, joy joy, everyone!" Grace said.

For a few minutes, the clink of forks on plates and hums of appreciation filled the air.

"So, Leah, what are you up to? What's the news from the outside world?" Clarisse asked finally.

"Well, let's see. Roseanne, my partner, has planted some new rosebushes in front of the house. Chrysler Imperial, a lovely red, like the color of our front door. And our cat Sadie has dragged home a little calico kitten from somewhere – I don't know if she found it or stole it – she's not talking!"

"It's not her kitten, though," Paula said.

"Oh, no, we like to keep everyone spayed or fixed or whatever. Too many hungry strays!"

"It's hard not to keep them all," Clarisse said, remembering generations of cats she had shared her home with over the years.

"Yes, and the shelters are so full. There aren't enough people to foster, and some of those poor critters get put down for no good reason!" Vick said gruffly and sniffed.

Sarah looked at her in surprise. It wasn't very often that Vick showed a tender side.

"It's true. We should do something!" Grace said.

"Like what?" Leah said.

"I know – let's have an adoption day! We can raise some money for the shelter and help some of the animals find new homes!" Lee said, excited.

"What a good idea! Let's see what we can do," Jen said.

"Great! I nominate Jen to head up the Pet Adoption Day!" Sarah cried. "All in favor?"

"Aye! Aye! Aye!" came a chorus of voices.

"Uh, uh, what just happened?" Jen said.

After lunch, everyone scattered, to the porch, to the lake, to the bench for a smoke.

"Where do you want to go, Paula?" Sarah asked, pulling her back from the table.

"Oh, I don't care – it doesn't matter," she said truculently. "It's all the same."

"What's the matter? Are you hurting?" she asked.

"Always," she said. "I just get so sick of it. It never ends." A tear slid down her face, surprising her. "Oh, damn," she said, dabbing at her face with a twisted hand. "I'm sorry."

"No need," Sarah said, and took her hand gently, looking at her pale ragged nails. "Hey, how about a manicure!"

Paula looked at her hand and laughed. It was too absurd. "Sure, why not? Mud on the rose."

"Why don't you wait here and I'll get the stuff," Sarah said, moving her in front of a sunny table in the living room.

Paula looked out the window at the trees waving gracefully in the breezes and the ducks floating through the sunny glints on the water. Margret strolled in and draped herself across Paula's knees, purring warmly.

"You have a perfect life, don't you?" she said, running her hand over the smooth brown head. "You go where you want, you sleep wherever you want, and everybody loves you!" She smiled bitterly. "And you can reach to scratch whatever itches!" She rubbed her back against the wheelchair.

Sarah came back in, hands full of manicure implements and bright bottles of polish, followed by Leah. "Itchy, Paula? Here, let me help you," she said, somehow hitting the exact spot.

Paula groaned in relief.

"Look, I found another manicure customer," she said.

Leah pulled up a chair. "Hope you don't mind if I join you," she said. "I never seem to get around to my nails."

"Oh, no, the more the merrier," Paula said. "I thought all you clergy types were supposed to have nice soft hands."

"Not with the amount of time I spend in my garden," she said.

"Or fixing your shed, or painting, or doing your pottery," Sarah said with a laugh.

"I never was one to sit around."

"Me either. Now that's all I do," Paula said.

Sarah clipped off rough edges and smoothed Paula's nails with an emery board. "What color polish would you like?" she asked.

"Oh, I don't care," she said. "Pink, I guess."

"Sarah! Sarah!" Lee came trotting into the room. "Could you come see Edna? She's not feeling well. Urpy."

"Oh, I'm sorry, Paula. I hate to run out in the middle…"

"Oh, that's okay. Go be a nurse."

She got up and followed Lee out of the room.

"I can finish up," Leah said. "Promise not to tell anyone, but I used to work in a beauty parlor when I was in college. I've polished a few nails."

"Multi-talented woman, huh?" Paula said.

"You bet," she said. "So, Paula, you and I have never really had a chance to talk. Where did you live before you came to The Meadows?"

"I lived over in West Seattle, over near Alki Point," she said. "My daughter and her husband have a house there, and I lived with them for the past couple of years."

"Oh, that's nice. It's great to be with family."

"Yeah, up to a point. They have two boys, five and seven, and my daughter is pregnant, due in about six weeks. But she can't take care of a new baby, and the rest of her family, and me too." She sighed. "It's gonna be a girl this time, thank goodness."

"That'll be nice. I have a couple of girls myself, and one boy – he's the youngest, and he keeps us all on the run." She finished up Paula's right hand, and reached for the left. "So what did you do before you went to live with your daughter? If you don't mind me prying, that is."

"Oh, no, you're not prying. I was a home ec teacher for years and years, taught cooking and sewing and such in a high school, and a little child care too."

"That must have been fun."

"Oh, it was, especially back in the sixties before women started going back to work in droves. They didn't have so much time to fuss around the house then, started looking down on housewifey things."

"That must have been hard to see."

"It was, in a way, because I always liked to do things, projects and stuff, and I love to cook. Loved to cook. I was like an early-day Martha Stewart. But now cooking is chic again, even though the way people cook and eat is a lot different now. And finally boys want to get more involved now, not just sit around and wait for their wives or mothers to make dinner for them."

"It's about time," Leah said. "It's a survival skill, after all. All my kids know how to change their oil, and to sew on buttons, too. Everybody should know how to do things."

"I agree," Paula said. "Of course, I can't do anything anymore, just sit here and wait for people to do things for me, and complain."

"How long have you been in a chair?" Leah asked gently.

"Almost ten years," she said. "It started when I was in my thirties. My mother had bad arthritis too, and I remember what she had to go through. I knew the life I was looking at, and it wasn't pretty. I worked for as long as I could, but I couldn't do much with my hands anymore, and it was hard to stand. Robbie had to do everything for me. So one day I sat down, and that was it." She sniffed angrily.

"Who is Robbie?"

"My girlfriend." She sighed, a single tear running down the side of her face. She brushed at it jerkily with her bent hand. "More than that. She was everything to me. I would get out of work before her, and when she got home, I had dinner ready. She loved my cooking, would complain about how I was making her plump. Womanly curves, I said. In the evenings I would sew, or knit, and she would do the crosswords. We went to the movies a lot too. She knew everyone who'd been in every movie since the beginning of time."

"What kind of work did she do?" Leah asked.

"She was a bus driver. One of the few women on the line." Paula laughed. "They wore these uniforms, unisex, I guess you would call them, and a baseball cap. She would get so mad when people thought she was a guy, call her sir or man or something. They just weren't used to women drivers." Her eyes lit up. "She always looked like a woman to me, though, cute as can be, with the bluest eyes. She loved helping people get on and off the bus, and she was so patient. Not a mean bone in her. Sometimes she would end up holding babies while the moms got their strollers tucked in. A couple of times she got peed on for her trouble, too." She laughed again.

"She sounds really sweet. Do you get to see her very often?"

"Only in my dreams," Paula said sadly. "She passed about three years ago. That's when I went to live with my daughter." She tried dabbing at her tears again. Reverend Leah pulled a tissue from her pocket and held it out; Paula looked at her and nodded, giving permission for her to wipe her face. "Thank you," she said.

"You're welcome," she said. "Ministers always carry tissues. Part of my job description."

"Hell of a job," Paula said.

"Sometimes," Leah said.

Paula paused and looked at her. "Let me ask you something, Reverend," she said finally. "Do you think God punishes us for our sins? Not just in the next life – in this one?"

"Do you?" Reverend Leah asked.

"I don't know. I was raised Catholic, and it

seemed to me that you got payback pretty quickly if you stepped outside the lines. And I went to parochial school, and so talking about sin was a big part of our lives. Pretty scary stuff," Paula said, shaking her head.

"Yes, really," she said.

"Especially when I realized that I really liked Helen Stasio, a girl in my third-grade class. I mean, I *really* liked her. She was beautiful, with this long black hair and green eyes. I couldn't help staring at her all the time. She was perfect. And her clothes were perfect. Even her lunch was perfect. Her mom would cut her carrot and cucumber slices into little flowers and cut the cheese on her sandwiches into kittens and stars. And I could imagine doing that for her." Suddenly she laughed. "Hey! Maybe that's what started me off on my home ec thing! And to think, I might owe my whole career to Helen!" Just as quickly she stopped, got serious. "Maybe she started me off on the whole gay thing too!"

Leah laughed. "Now Paula, surely you know by now that if you're gay it's because you were born that way. You can't blame some little girl in your third-grade class!"

"I guess not," she said sadly. "She's probably fat with thin hair and nineteen grandchildren by now. And she probably cuts cats and stars into their cheese sandwiches too."

"Maybe so."

"But seriously, Reverend. Do you think God is angry with us? Do you think he punishes us for being lesbians?"

Reverend Leah thought for a minute. "This is a big discussion, Paula. I think I need a cup of tea."

"Me, too," she said. "If you can spare the time."

Leah thought for a moment before answering. "There's no easy answer, Paula. Everybody has their own ideas about this, I think. I can only tell you what I believe."

"That's okay. I've certainly spent enough time thinking on my own. I just wanted your opinion."

"All right then. Be right back." Leah went back to the kitchen, lit the burner under the kettle, and rummaged around in the tea cupboard. She picked up a few different tea bags and put them on a tray with a sugar bowl, a honey bear, and some packets, and took a little cream pitcher out of the fridge. She found some lemon slices, then noticed a plate of cookies and put them on the tray as well. She sat down as she waited for the kettle to boil, and sighed. She'd had conversations like this before with different people, and it was never easy.

She returned to Paula's table and put down the tray. "Sorry, I don't know how you take your tea, so I brought everything I could think of," she said.

"Goodness," Paula said. "How about some lemon ginger tea and some honey?"

"Easy enough," Leah said.

"For you," she said.

"True," she said. "Sorry."

"That's okay," Paula said. "It's just me being crabby. What kind of cookies are those?"

"Oatmeal raisin, chocolate chip, and it looks like molasses cookies."

"Mmm, that's my favorite," she said.

Soon they were settled, Leah holding tea and cookies for Paula as they talked.

"So, what are you thinking?" she asked.

"I don't know," Paula said. "I see everyone

else running around, having their lives, and I just sit here and watch everything go by. I can't do anything for myself, and I get so bored I could scream. It's embarrassing, too. If I have to go to the bathroom, I have to wait for someone to help me. I can't even scratch my own damn back!" She took a deep breath. "It's just not fair!"

"True," Leah said. "I can see why you're angry."

"I was pretty happy growing up," Paula said. "I was pretty athletic – I loved to run and ride my bike and play volleyball. My parents were nice, kind of strict, but reasonable. My mom was pretty into the church thing, and we went every week, Sunday school and all that. I liked it, too, all that magical stuff, incense, and communion, and I loved the music."

"Me, too," Reverend Leah said. "The church I was raised in had lots of singing."

"While I was growing up, I had lots of crushes, usually on girls, starting with Helen, of course. I'd heard lots of stuff about homosexuality being a sin, but I didn't really connect that with how I was feeling toward those girls. I thought only boys were gay. Then when I was about twelve or thirteen, I started to realize that I was one of those people, and I went into a big funk. Of course, I couldn't tell anyone how I felt, and I started keeping more to myself. My mom kept encouraging me to do things with friends, join church groups and stuff, but I felt like I couldn't trust myself. What if someone found out? I tried talking about it in confession once, but he shut me down really fast. I must've said a million Hail Marys, asking God to make me normal, but it didn't change anything." She sighed. "Then I met Stacy."

"Hmmm," said Reverend Leah. "And how old

were you?"

"I was a junior in high school, about sixteen. She was new in town, and when we looked at each other, we just knew."

"Lightning strikes."

"Yes," Paula said. "We hung around together all the time – we were inseparable. I went to her house every day, or she came over to mine. We had a couple of classes together, and we worked on our homework together. And of course, one thing led to another. We couldn't keep our hands off each other."

"Wow, that must have been a very exciting time for you both," Leah said.

"Oh, it was. Of course, our parents encouraged us to go to parties and date, but we weren't interested. We just wanted to be together. But at the same time, the whole sin thing really tore me up. I worried about going to hell. Stacy and I talked about it, but her parents were both doctors, and they had talked about it with her starting when she was pretty young. They belonged to a church that was more open. But she didn't talk to them about her feelings about me because I was so freaked out, didn't want anyone to know. So we kept it a secret."

"That's a big burden," Leah said.

"Yes, it was," Paula said. "Then one day we were over at my house, just sitting around on the couch, reading. My mom was out shopping, and we didn't hear her come in. Stacy had her feet in my lap, and I was rubbing them." She paused, and swiped at her teary eyes. Reverend Leah reached up, dabbed her face with a napkin, and held it while she blew her nose.

"Ew, sorry, thanks," Paula said. "That's above and beyond the call of ministry, I'm sure."

"Don't worry about it," she said. "So what happened then?"

"Well, my mom got really upset. She said, 'What are you doing? Are you two lesbians?' I didn't know what to say. Her face was all twisted up and she was crying. In a way, it was almost funny, the way she was carrying on. We weren't really even doing anything! But I guess she'd had her suspicions for a while."

"So what happened then?"

"Well, my mom yelled for her to get out. Stacy got up, grabbed her things, and headed for the door. 'Bye,' she said. 'Sorry! See you tomorrow!'"

"'Never!' my mom said. 'Never again!'"

"Whew!" Reverend Leah said. "That must have been awful!"

"Oh, it was. I'd never seen my parents so angry. I tried to tell her that we weren't doing anything wrong, that we loved each other, but that just made things worse. They dragged me to church, made me talk to the priest, that wrinkled old man, and pulled me out of school. They stuck me in a Catholic school across town, and my mom drove me there and back every day. And I had to go to church every day and pray for forgiveness. It was awful!"

"Oh my goodness! I bet it was! No wonder you feel so conflicted about it!" Reverend Leah shook her head. "So what happened with Stacy?"

"Well, she tried calling me, but my parents wouldn't let me talk to her. They kept really close tabs on me, so we didn't really see each other anymore. Every now and then, I would catch sight of her in the mall or in the grocery, but we never got to talk to each other again. I was so sad! And I missed her terribly."

"So sad!" Leah said.

"I know," Paula said. "When I got to college, I tried to be normal. I didn't want to be a sinner anymore. But you know how it is – I couldn't stop the kinds of thoughts I had. But I tried dating some guys, and it was okay, I guess, but I didn't ever feel how Stacy made me feel. Then I met Stan."

"So then what?"

"Well, Stan and I really hit it off. He was sweet and funny, and he was like me. We understood each other. My parents liked him, and they were relieved that I'd found someone. They didn't know that he was a sinner too, like me. We managed to have enough of a relationship to have a couple of kids, but the physical stuff was never much to us. We both had our own things going on."

"That must have been very stressful for both of you, though."

"I guess it was, in a way, but at least we weren't hiding anything from each other. But we did agree to keep it from the kids, and that was hard in a way."

"Why did you do that?" Leah asked.

"We wanted our kids to grow up normal. We didn't want other kids to tease them, and we didn't want our parents to know, either. So we were very discreet."

"Our sad little secrets," Reverend Leah said. "The pain we give ourselves, and each other."

"Yes. And so we went along like that until Stan met someone at work and really fell for him. He didn't want to live a lie anymore, so finally, he moved out, and he and his boyfriend were together for a long time. He died a few years back."

"So how did you deal with your family? Did you ever actually come out to them?"

"Yes, to our kids. After all those years of hiding who we really were, we had to come clean with them, and they took it pretty hard at first. It took a long time for them to come to terms with it, and with our lies. And of course, we'd brought them up in church too, and then we had to admit that we were the people that they'd been warning them about. It was very hard."

"What about your parents?"

"We never did come out to my parents – they'd both passed away before we divorced. I'm glad I never had to deal with them on that – they tried so hard to get me straight. All in vain!" Paula laughed bitterly.

"So what happened then?" Leah asked.

"A couple of years after the divorce, I met my girl. It was a rocky road, believe me, but eventually my kids got to where they could accept us, sort of, anyway. They were grown and going off to college, and finally we moved in together. We had a sweet few years, but during that time, I started having trouble with my hands, and my knees, and my back. I was still teaching, but it was hard for me to stand in the class, and hard for me to get around. I started thinking more and more about how maybe I brought the pain on myself through my actions. Maybe if I had overcome my feelings about women I would have had a more normal life, a healthier life, a better relationship with my kids."

"How did your partner feel about that?"

"Well, it hurt her feelings. You can imagine."

"Yes, I can. But generations of people have felt that way about themselves, made themselves miserable for the same reasons."

"Yes, I know. But I still can't shake it off, not completely. What do you think?" Paula asked.

Leah sighed. "I had a pretty conventional

upbringing myself, and I was fed the same lines about being gay. It was a sin, end of story. I felt like a bad person, someone who could never be accepted by God, who could never be admitted to heaven."

"So what changed your mind?" Paula asked.

"Well, when I was in college, I studied science, biology and botany and such, and started looking at the world in a different way. Everything that was possible existed in the world, an infinite variety. Of course, scientific thinking made the idea of God seem kind of silly, a made-up story to explain things we couldn't understand. But I couldn't believe that the universe started with a spontaneous big bang, and from that we have oceans and birds and flowers and sheep in the meadows and cows in the corn, la la la!" She laughed.

"But seriously, the more I studied, the less a closed scientific description of the world made sense. How could the salmon know where to go to spawn, and the migrating birds find their way? How could the animals whom parents did not nurture, like turtles or butterflies, be born with a full set of knowledge, everything they needed to know for their survival? How can cats know to grow more fur when the winter is coming? How could such amazing complexity and connectedness exist in a world without some kind of divine plan, for a lack of a better term?"

"True – but what about religion? What about all the rules? What about sin?" Paula said, shaking her head. "Is it all a lie?"

Leah shook her head too. "I don't know. I wish I knew! Or maybe I don't!" she said. "I think these things were developed to make it possible for people to live together, in whatever crazy way. Infinite variety! Inexplicable!" She laughed. "Maybe if we all knew the truth, we'd be like lemmings, unable to handle it. Maybe we'd be molecules of water, now rain, now rivers, now the ocean! Whew!" she laughed. "Sorry, I'm getting a little carried away here."

Paula laughed. "Reverend Leah, you're a poet!"

"No, not really," she said, grinning. "I just get lost in the everythingness of it all."

"So what about sin?" Paula asked.

"Well, take homosexuality, for example," Reverend Leah said. "If there wasn't homosexuality present in the world, there wouldn't be laws and rules against it. It exists! Often the very people who preach against it practice it. But you don't see them exploding or lightning striking them. And the same is true of many other things we call sins."

"True. But what about the commandments? And what about hell?"

"I don't know. Maybe there is a heaven, maybe there is a hell. The idea of a place to go after you die has always seemed a little farfetched to me, but that's my own opinion. I think that the real sin is causing harm, to other people and beings, to the planet. I think that we are part of a central consciousness that includes everyone and everything, forever and ever, amen. But again, that's my own opinion."

"But what about the Bible?" Paula asked, anxiously.

"Well, there were lots of fingers in the Bible pie. Some things were added or subtracted according to the politics of the time, sometimes hundreds of years after events happened. There are lots of things in the Bible that just don't work for Western civilization anymore, like slavery or polygamy, or an eye for an eye, for that matter. Our society has evolved, not always for the better, perhaps. But there are many lessons to be learned from the Bible."

"And what about God?" Paula asked. "And Jesus? Do you believe that he was the Son of God?"

"I was raised with the vision of an old man with a long gray beard sitting on a throne up in the clouds, passing judgment. That doesn't work for me anymore. To me now, God is that central consciousness, that central truth of the universe, the Great I AM. And as for Jesus, he was a great philosopher, and the son of God, as we are all children of God."

Paula took a deep breath. "So why is it that I am sitting here in this chair while people who kill and steal and abuse run around free?"

"I don't know," she said sadly.

❦❦❦❦

Jen surprised everyone by stepping up for the Animal Adoption Day. Not only did she arrange with the Animal Rescue and shelter people, she also called the local newspapers and radio station to generate some publicity for their event. She got Zoe and Carol to put together some art for posters, a Web site, ads, and invites, and got Lee and Willow to distribute some of the materials around town.

The residents were excited about the prospect of a day with the animals, too. Most of them had had cats and pups in the past, and they enjoyed Margret and Ralph and Won Ton and Bad Lily, but the more the merrier. Some of the residents who had pets at home prevailed upon their families and friends to bring them, too, so they could all enjoy a day together in the sun.

The day dawned soft and bright, perfect for both

people and animals.

They rented a big white tent where the animal staffers could sit and make out paperwork, and where the refreshments could be served. Lee, Rosa, Marie, Savannah, Carrie, and Ginny participated in making dog-and-cat-shaped cookies for people and bone-and-mouse-shaped treats for dogs and cats, while the other residents watched and cheered on their efforts. Grace, Gayle, and Vick bagged up the cookies and pet treats and sold them for a dollar each, with the money going to animal rescue. They also cooked and sold meat hot dogs and veggie hot cats with all the trimmings as well. Rachel even sewed little bags of catnip for the feline guests.

Even Isobel, the Montessori teacher, got her students involved. They had a coloring contest and prizes were arranged for the best, most colorful, and most unusual animal pictures, and they also had the kids make costumes they could wear for an animal parade with some help from Rachel.

"It was such a good idea to have the kids out here, honey," Sarah said to Jen. "What made you think of it?"

"Well, you know a lot of the ladies miss having kids in their lives," she said. "Some of them have grandkids they don't get to see too often, or they don't have kids at all. I heard them talking about how much they enjoy kids, and it just seemed like a great match. I talked to Isobel about it, and she's always been interested in intergenerational stuff. Our families have changed so much, we don't see extended families as much as we used to. In my family, we always got together with my grandparents, aunts, and uncles on holidays and got to know each other, but that doesn't happen so much now. People live so far away, and everybody is so busy. So Isobel and I thought it might be fun to let the ladies interact with the kids. They have a lot they can teach each other!"

"So true," Sarah said. "I'm excited to see how this works out!" She grabbed Jen around the waist and gave her a big kiss.

So on Animal Adoption day, eight kids, ages four through six, joined in the festivities at Lavender Meadows. Some of the parents who were not working that day came along with the kids to help out and join in the fun. Isobel even brought along her sixteen-year-old daughter, Elaine.

All in all, there were twenty-five animals up for adoption – eleven dogs, including two Labs, one yellow and one chocolate, three poodles, two Chihuahuas, and four mutts of various sizes. Eight cats included two calicos, a mother and daughter, a big black-and-white tuxedo boy, a Siamese mix with two white feet, one longhaired red girl with many toes, and three young tabbies. In addition, there were two brown-and-white lop-eared-bunny brothers and a pair of box turtles.

Ralph and Won Ton ran around, talking to all the animals in their pens and carriers, while Margret and Bad Lily watched from the sidelines on the porch with Edna and Clarisse.

All the animals were nervous, but the animal rescue people were good about helping them calm down and show their true personalities to the surging crowd, to give them a better chance of being adopted.

At the end of the day, nineteen of the animals had been adopted, leaving only the two turtles, the chocolate Lab, and the black-and-white cat. Gayle opted for the Lab, promising Vick to bring her when she came to visit, Jen fell in love with the tuxedo cat (so formal! so elegant! she said) and Lee scored the turtles and took them back to her little house with Elaine's help.

"They're so cute!" Elaine said. "What are you going to name them?"

"I don't know," Lee said, looking at Elaine with a shy grin. "Why don't you think of some names?"

"How about Patience and Sarah?" she said. "It's my favorite book."

"I like that book too," Lee said. "A lot!" She hesitated for a moment. "But I don't even know if they're girls or boys."

"I don't think they care," Elaine said. "But we can look them up on the Internet and see if we can figure it out. If you want."

"Sure, that would be great," Lee said.

"And can I come back to visit them?" she asked.

"You bet," she said.

So at the end of the day the animal rescue people made some much-needed money, twenty-three animals found good homes, and other wheels were set in motion.

~~~~

"That's so lovely, but you know I can't just leave you girls all alone," Sarah said. "Who knows what kind of trouble you'll get into!"

"Well, you need to have some time off. You haven't been away from here except to go to the store since this place opened," Grace said briskly.

"That's true," Sarah said thoughtfully. "When I was going to other adult family homes, I talked to one of the owners who said she hadn't been to a movie in seven years!"

"No, we don't want you to do that. I can take over when you're away," Marie said.

"No, Marie, you can't do that. What if something happens? And what about the meds that need to be given? And you are still doing most of the cooking. It's too much! And with your heart…" Sarah trailed off as she saw the thunder clouds gather on Marie's face.

"Hummph! I was taking care of Grace and this house long before you showed up, Missy. And we managed perfectly well!"

"Now Marie, you know that Sarah didn't mean to hurt your feelings. But there's more to do now, and you can't be awake all the time. And doing so much of the cooking and cleaning up the kitchen too!" Grace soothed her.

"But I'm used to doing all that kind of stuff. I took care of Annie, and you too. And when we had the bed and breakfast running, I always did the cooking. And we had those two girls who came in to do the cleaning. Now what were their names?" Marie fumed.

"That was a long time ago, Marie. Things have changed. This isn't a bed and breakfast anymore. You took great care of us, but you can't keep things going like that, around the clock. And you have to take good care of yourself, you know…your heart."

She got to her feet. "Heart shmart!" I'm as good as I ever was!" Her breathing quickened and she clutched at her chest.

"Yes, my love, I know – but we have more people to help you now, and you need to let them do that. Now please sit down!"

Marie sank back into her chair and caught her

breath. "You're not the boss of me, Grace Meadows!" she muttered.

"Oh, but I am, at least about this."

"About a lot of other things, too," Marie said.

"That's right," Grace said, and winked.

They both laughed.

"Yes, Sarah, I think this would be the perfect time for you two to get away." She counted on her fingers. "The wedding is over, Lee is everywhere, Willow is settled in, Rosa and the other Sanchezes are here, Rachel's baby is not due for another few weeks. Everything is under control. And the weather is still pretty nice. Take advantage, girl! Get out of here!"

"Okay, I'll talk to Jen," she said doubtfully.

Later that day Sarah brought up the subject.

"Grace and Marie said we should take a few days off and get away," she said. "What do you think?"

"Are you kidding? What a great idea!" Jen said. "We hardly ever get to do anything anymore, and we never get to have any time for ourselves..."

"I'm sorry," Sarah said. "You know I've been busy, and there's always so much going on."

"Now, I'm not criticizing you, love," Jen said soothingly. "But really, when is the last time we went to the movies? Or out to dinner? Or curled up in bed together without getting called because someone was sleepwalking or throwing up or something?"

"True," Sarah mused. "Now that you mention it, I do miss that." She put her arm around Jen's waist and nuzzled her neck. "I could do with some us time."

"When we wouldn't have to be quiet," Jen said. "Or dressed!"

"Bad girl!" Sarah said, and pinched her. "So – where should we go?"

"How about the ocean?" Jen said.

"Or the mountains?"

"Or to the city? Seattle or Portland?"

"Or the San Juan Islands?"

"Whoa, too many choices! I won't ever want to come back!"

Sarah stopped. "I hope you don't really feel that way," she said. "I know you got more that you bargained for when you met me. Your whole life changed!"

"For the better, honey. You know I love our home and our ladies and the garden and everything. And I don't know what I would have done if you hadn't been around to take care of me after I fell. But it would be nice to get away for a few days. Wherever we go, I just want to be with you."

They finally decided on a little cabin by the ocean, over near Westport. The beaches were beautiful out there, and Jen could do some fishing. "It's a long time since I've been on a boat!" she said. "I've missed it!"

"If I let you out of bed," Sarah teased.

So finally, they were packed with every possible thing they could want for three days in a cabin (or for a month, Jen said. That's why I have a van and not a motorcycle, Sarah said.) Sarah wrote notes and lists and reviewed every contingency plan until everyone rolled their eyes. Dr. Emily also knew they were going and promised to help keep an eye on things, especially on Rachel and her monitoring. "Don't worry, everything will be fine," she reassured them.

Grace, Marie, and the rest of the ladies lined up to give hugs and wave good-bye.

Sarah felt a little prickle of tears start as her eyes swept over them and over the house. "Don't forget to call us if you have any questions!" she said.

"Go, go, get out of here!" Grace called, waving them off.

"I feel like I'm forgetting something," she said as they pulled away.

"Don't worry, honey, they'll figure it out," Jen said, and gunned the engine.

The cabin was everything they'd hoped it would be – clean, comfortable, with a nice fireplace and a great view of the ocean. There was a little kitchen where they could cook lazy breakfasts and lots of snacks and a little porch where they could watch the sun go down.

"Whoohoo!" Jen yelled, and threw herself down on the bed. "Alone at last!"

"You fool!" Sarah laughed. "Honestly, you'd think we never saw each other."

"It feels that way sometimes," Jen said. "C'mere, you, let's get this vacation started!" she said, patting the bed beside her invitingly.

"But we have to get the stuff out of the car!" Sarah protested weakly.

"Later, later – much later..." Jen mumbled. She reached for Sarah's hand and pulled her down beside her.

The wind picked up as the late afternoon sun threw long shadows across the beach. Jen shook Sarah's foot gently. "Hey, lazy," she said. "Let's take the kites for a spin!"

They threw on their clothes, got out Jen's green dragon and Sarah's long-tailed purple cat, and raced down the beach, their kites lifting and tumbling in the breeze, silhouetted against the copper sky.

"You know, I have to figure out about work," Jen said later that night as they lay in front of the fireplace,

Sarah's head on her stomach. "I think I'm as good as I'm going to get."

"No room for improvement," Sarah teased. "You're stuck."

"You know what I mean," Jen said. "Everything's a big joke with you."

"That's right. I crack myself up all the time. Now could you please tell me what you're talking about?"

"I have a physical coming up next week. They want to see how my leg is doing, to see if I can go back to work."

"But it's only been a couple of months," Sarah said. "You had a really bad break!"

"Three months. Almost four."

"No way. It can't be!"

"It is! And I've been out of the chair and off the crutches for weeks! I don't use the cane too much either."

"I know," Sarah said. "Not as much as you should be!"

"I don't want to depend on it," she said. "Not any more than I have to!" she sighed. "And I've been doing the physical therapy with Carol, and trying to move around as much as I can, but I'm still having a lot of pain. Not as much as I did at first, of course, but I worry about whether or not I can do my job."

"I know; you've been working really hard since the beginning."

"Yes, but my ankle is still pretty stiff, and I still walk funny. I don't know if they'll want me back." She sighed again. "And there's another thing."

"What is it, honey?" Sarah said, tenderly, running her hand through Jen's brushy hair.

"I'm kind of scared, you know? What happens if

I fall again? Or if someone gets hurt because I can't do my job right? I don't want to be a cripple!"

"Of course not," she said.

"I've always been active, you know? I don't want to sit on the sidelines!"

"You're just worried about whether you'll be able to play softball."

"Bat girl, maybe. I'll just pull the team down," she said sadly.

"We'll just have to wait and see what happens, honey. Let's send some more healing thoughts to your leg, okay?" She sat up and stroked Jen's leg gently from the foot upward, noticing again that the ankle was still swollen.

"You are just looking for an excuse to play with my leg, ma'am."

"Maybe so," she said with a grin. "But since when do I need an excuse?"

❧❧❧❧

Sarah hated to see the time pass. She'd been more relaxed in the past few days than she'd been in months. She and Jen had more time for leisurely meals and beach walks. At night, they held each other close and talked about Lavender Meadows and all the things that were going on there. But most importantly, they had some time where they did not need to talk at all except for those little sounds and half-words that meant whatever they were needed to mean at that particular moment, as the sound of their breaths mingled with the sound of the waves.

Reluctantly they gathered up their stuff and packed up the van on that last afternoon, then rode home slowly, the long way, trying to stretch out the time as much as they could.

"Really, it'll be good to be home," Sarah said as they drove up the last few streets. "I've missed Margret and everybody."

"Yeah, me too," Jen said, pulling up to the driveway, then stopping suddenly at the gorgeous horror of the police car's lights blinking blue and red, blue and red.

☙ ☙ ❧ ❧

Sarah raced up the front steps and flung open the door, narrowly missing the officer. "What is it? What happened?" she cried.

The house was all in an uproar, and he had to speak loudly to make himself heard over the din.

"May I ask who you are, ma'am?"

"I'm Sarah Chase, the director of Lavender Meadows. Now can you please tell me what's going on?"

"And where are you coming from?" he asked.

"We're just back from vacation," she said, indicating Jen, who had just made it to the door. "What difference does that make?" She looked around frantically until she caught sight of Lee's stricken face.

"Wait! Stop! What happened? Tell me right now!" She reached out and grabbed Lee's arm. But one look at her twisted face told Sarah that there was no information to be had from her, not yet.

The officer cleared his throat. "Ma'am, my name is Officer Joseph Wendell. You can call me Joe. I'm afraid I have some bad news for you," he said. "Here, why don't you sit down?" He indicated the wooden armchair beside the door.

"No, I'm fine. Please just tell me!" She couldn't control the sudden flood of tears. "Is it Grace? Marie?" Jen came up behind her and put her arm around Sarah's waist. Suddenly, she realized that she hadn't seen an ambulance when they pulled in, only the police car.

"Um, one of your people..."

"Residents," Lee piped up.

"Yes, residents, uh, had an accident tonight. A serious accident."

"Who? What happened? Where is she?" Sarah cried.

"It was a motor vehicle accident," he said. "Motorcycle. Victoria Williams."

It took her a moment to realize who Victoria Williams was. She'd never heard her full name. She shook her head. "What? How could that be? She doesn't even drive. She never leaves this place alone!"

"Well, she did. And I'm sorry to say she did not survive."

A sudden burst of sound came from Lee's mouth, the sound of an animal in pain, in grief. Sarah and Jen put their arms around her and held her, rocking her and each other.

The other residents gathered around them in the hallway, standing or in wheelchairs, looking shocked and dismayed. Carol picked her way among them, administering pats, squeezes, and tissues. "Come on now, ladies, let's go into the dining room and let the police do their work. We'll have some tea. This is a terrible day."

Grace and Marie joined them in the living room and Sarah introduced them. Everything felt so surreal, and she knew she was running on autopilot. She couldn't believe this was happening.

"So what happened?" she asked. "Where was it?"

At that moment, Lee came into the room. "It was all my fault," she said. "I did it. She's dead because of me." She scraped the tears off her face with her arm.

"What do you mean?" Jen said. "How could that be?"

"Well, you know how she is about bikes. She really misses – missed – riding. She loved when Gayle would come and take her for a ride. She loved to go out to the garage and stare at your bike, sit on it sometimes."

"I didn't know that," Jen said thoughtfully. "How sad." She paused. "So it was Gayle and Vick who were in the accident? Where is Gayle now?"

"Ms. Williams was alone when she had the accident," the officer said.

"How could that be?" Sarah said.

"We thought the door from the kitchen to the garage was locked, like usual," Lee said. "We were just finishing up after dinner, and I was going to take Vick out for a smoke, but I couldn't find her. I figured she went up to her room. I heard an engine start, but I didn't pay attention. I was pretty busy around the kitchen by then."

"So it was my bike?" Jen said, horrified.

"I'm afraid so," he said.

"How did she get the fob?" she asked. "I always keep it on my key ring." She patted her pockets, frowning.

"No, honey, you didn't need it because we were taking the van," Sarah said. "You hung the fob on the key rack."

"Oh, no," she said. "I never should have done that, leave keys to anything around this place. I knew how light-fingered she was getting. It's my fault!"

"I don't think it's helpful to place blame," Joe said. "It was a combination of a lot of things, I guess." He cleared his throat. "It sounds like Ms. Williams was not in full possession of her faculties," he said delicately.

"No, she had Alzheimer's Disease. She would get confused, and we did whatever we could to keep an eye on her. Lee, here, or one of the other staff members, was usually with her when she would go out for a smoke. She was starting to wander a bit, but just in the house. We kept the doors locked at night."

"But the house hadn't been locked up yet," Jen guessed. "It was still early."

"So she came riding through town," Joe said. "I was parked over by the Day Rise Market, having my dinner, when she went by, going pretty fast. I went after her, put on my lights, but she didn't slow down. She started to swerve, take the turns wide. I put on my siren, but she just kept going, crossing the center line, speeding up. It's a good thing nobody was coming the other way. I radioed for backup, but as we were going along the big curve over by Miller's Bay, she kept going straight. Just sailed out. Like Thelma and Louise." He shook his head. "It was awful! I couldn't stop her!

"It was dark by then, of course, and I heard the bike hit, but it was hard for me to see where it landed with just a little flashlight. I called for help, and I started trying to get down the cliff face. I could still hear the engine sputtering a little, and I could smell it smoking, and that's how I found it. She'd been thrown off the bike, maybe twenty feet or so. She didn't have a helmet on. I checked to see if she was alive, but her head was a mess. I could see that she was gone. There was nothing

I could do." He paused. "I'm so sorry."

For a few moments, there was only the sound of muffled crying as each of the women ran the images in their heads. Sarah and Jen gathered Lee in their arms, and the three of them rocked and cried, rocked and cried.

Minutes passed before the crying slowed long enough for them to catch their breaths, but they continued to hold Lee in the circle of their arms. "How did you know Vick lived here?"

"Well, she had her bracelet on with her name and the name of this place on it," he said.

"Of course," Sarah said. All the residents wore similar bracelets.

"We also looked in her pockets and she had her wallet on her. We called her emergency contact, Gayle, and she's on her way over."

"Oh, no, poor Gayle," Lee said. "She's gonna be devastated."

At that moment, they heard the rumble of a distant motorcycle headed toward them. Sarah, Jen, Lee, and Joe went outside to meet it.

Gayle sat on the back of Vick's bike behind another woman. Her eyes were red and swollen. She slid off, went to Lee, and put her arms around her. "Oh, honey, I'm so sorry," she said.

"No, I'm sorry! I didn't watch her enough! She just got by me! I didn't know she was gone till it was too late!"

"No, Lee, if she was bound and determined to get out, there wouldn't have been anything you could have done to stop her. You know she was stubborn, and sneaky too!"

Lee laughed and hiccoughed at the same time,

thinking about all the times she'd caught Vick hiding cigarettes and candy in her pockets and under her mattress, too.

The other woman on Vick's bike slipped off her helmet and came up to them. She stuck out her hand. "Hi, I'm Merrill, Gayle's sister. You must be Sarah, and Jen. And of course, you're Lee," she said, shaking all around and nodding at Joe.

Sarah looked at her and nodded. "Of course you are! You look just like her!" She wiped her eyes. "I'm so sorry. She was such a good woman, and a really fun addition to our family." She took her arm. "Come in now and have some tea with us."

They went inside and more tea was poured and more cookies were produced. A golden bottle of sherry and some glasses materialized on the table and were passed around. Gayle told silly stories about Vick and her exploits. Clarisse told about how Vick had frightened her the night she could not get back to her room.

Gayle sat on the couch next to Merrill, her head on her shoulder. "I could see how much she was changing just in the past few weeks," she said sadly. "Sometimes she didn't even know me. That just about broke my heart." Merrill handed her another tissue and she wiped away a few more tears. "I know she didn't remember everything, but sometimes I would look at her and she looked so scared. She knew things weren't the way they should be."

"She really missed you, too, Gayle," Lee said.

"And I missed her, but I couldn't keep an eye on her all the time. Even though she was standing right here in front of me, she was already gone. She wasn't the girl I knew anymore!" She blew her nose, and

Merrill gave her a big hug.

"I know you're right, Gayle. You know how Vick liked to have things on her own terms. I don't think she would have wanted to live that way."

"I'm sorry, I have to get back to the station," Joe said, and handed Gayle and Sarah his card. "Come down to the station in the morning and we'll help you with your arrangements."

"I'll be there," Gayle said.

"I'm sorry for your loss," he said. "For all of you."

"Thank you," Sarah said, walking him out to the car. "And thank you for your kindness."

~·~·~·~

Word traveled quickly through the bike and leather community, and they decided to have a gathering at Lavender Meadows for people who wanted to get together and honor Vick. Carol and Zoe did up poster-sized pictures of Vick and Gayle, their friends and family, and of course, her bike. Marie, Lee, and Rosa put together trays of finger foods and treats and they set up a keg of beer in the yard.

"I sure like the party kind of food better than the funeral meats," Lee said darkly.

"Whatever the occasion, your food feeds the body and the spirit," Reverend Leah said, carrying platters out to the garden.

A somber crowd of biker women dressed mostly in black leather lined up their bikes in the driveway, many in tears. They eyed the residents and the staff members, who eyed them back. Gayle and Merrill took Lee around and introduced her to many of the women. She looked around, her eyes big. Even Joe the policeman showed up on his own bike to pay his respects.

"I hear you hung out with Vick quite a bit before she passed," a gruff-looking woman said to Lee. "She was a good friend of mine, and I want to thank you."

"I liked her so much. She was very special to me, too," Lee said.

"Gayle tells me you're a baby biker," she said. "If you ever want to come out riding with us, you would be welcome."

"Thank you! I would love that!" Lee said, excited. "That is – it would be cool."

Many of Vick's family showed up as well, and Lee was glad to meet the people she had only heard stories about from Vick. She couldn't help picture what her own funeral would look like – no family to cry over her, that was for sure.

Sarah was glad to see lines crossed after a while, like kids at a high school dance, and the family, the bikers, and the residents started mixing over stories, beer, and music until long after dark.

Finally, the last bike pulled out of the driveway, and they looked at each other, exhausted. The evening had taken its toll on everyone. There was hardly any food left, and once they put that away, they decided to leave the rest of the clean up until the morning.

The day dawned brightly, in sharp contrast to the gloom of the day before. Most of the ladies were still asleep, and after a quick cup of coffee Sarah, Jen, and Lee went outside armed with garbage bags and cardboard boxes to make quick work of the mess.

They worked in silence for a few minutes, then Lee called out to them, excitedly. "Hey, come look at this!" She waved them toward the garage, where she stood in front of Vick's big black Harley, tears streaming down her face.

※ ※ ※ ※

Zoe and Carol drove up in the truck and stopped in front of Sarah and Mr. Sanchez, who were nodding and smiling and shaking their heads at each other, both obviously frustrated.

"Hi there!" Carol said, jumping out. "What's going on?"

"Hiya, girls," Sarah said. "I thought you were off today, Carol!"

"Oh, I am, but we thought we'd come up here and get some measurements for Zoe's stuff. What are you guys doing?"

"Well, we're having a little communication problem here, as you could probably guess." She waved her hand at Mr. Sanchez, who nodded and smiled at them all, saying nothing.

"Maybe I can help," Zoe said. She smiled at Mr. Sanchez. "Buenos dias," she said, and introduced herself.

His face instantly cleared, and he let loose with a rapid stream of Spanish. Sarah's eyes widened, and she smiled, sincerely this time. She and Carol looked from one to the other, trying to follow what they were saying as the conversation went back and forth.

At last, they paused. "Hey, Zoe, I didn't remember you spoke Spanish," she said. "Sure am glad you came along! We can usually manage pretty well when we have things to point at, obvious things, but we're short on concept words. And nouns, too."

"I can imagine," Zoe said with a laugh. "My

grandmother – abuela – is from Mexico, and my mom was born there. We spoke half-and-half growing up."

"That sure comes in handy. I didn't know you were part Mexican. I took French when I was in school. Fat lot of good that did me." She shook her head. "So can you help us out here a little?"

"Sure, sure," Zoe said. They pulled up some rockers on the porch.

"I'll go find something to drink," Carol said, disappearing into the house.

A few minutes later, she reappeared with some lemonade and slices of cake to find them hunched over some papers, drawing madly and talking at once.

"So what's going on?" Carol said.

"Well, Mr. Sanchez has some ideas about getting the lavender beds and the strawberries back in shape for next year. You know that this place used to be a little farm, and they sold the lavender, berries, and some vegetables at the farmers' market in town. But they had to let everything go after Annie got sick," Zoe said.

"I know," Carol said. "I often thought how sad it was that all that work just went to waste. Everything is so grown over in the back fields."

"I know. It is sad," Sarah said. "I fixed up that little garden, and Lee and Jen help me with it some, but I don't really have time to do much more than I'm doing."

"No, I know how busy you are," Carol nodded. "Even so, it's a shame."

At that moment, Jen strolled out of the house. "Hey, is this a party?" she said, looking around. "Hi, girls, Mr. Sanchez," she said, nodding to all. "Can I join in?"

"Sure, honey, pull up a chair," Sarah said.

"Thanks!" she said, helping herself to a glass of lemonade and a slice of cake. "So what's happening?"

Sarah quickly filled Jen in on the conversation. "Hey, that's great! I didn't know you speak Spanish, Zoe. There's lots of things we wanted to talk to Mr. Sanchez about, and Rosa too. And the kids! We're definitely gonna have to take advantage of you – you can be our official translator!"

"I'll be glad to help out when I'm here," she said. "You know I was in the Peace Corps in Mexico for a few years, teaching English to kids and their families too. I really enjoyed it!"

"Oh, my goodness! Well, we could really use some help around here!" Sarah said.

Zoe and Mr. Sanchez talked for a few more minutes. "He wants to tell you how much he appreciates you letting him and his family stay here, especially with the baby. They love staying in the house."

"Oh, they've helped us so much! It's been great for us, too," Sarah said. "All that stuff with the wedding, and cleaning the place up, and Rosa's been so much help with Marie and Lee – we've loved having them around. And the ladies like playing with the kids, too."

Zoe shook her head, confused. "He's saying something about a storage unit, but I don't understand what he means."

Sarah laughed, then quickly filled her in about how they'd met Mr. Sanchez and his family through Lee when they were all staying in the storage place.

"Oh no! I can't believe they were all living out there!" she said.

"Better than in a car," Jen said. "I'm just glad we have a place for them to stay."

"Well, that's the thing," Zoe said. "He wants to know when they are going back."

Sarah and Jen looked at each other.

"Well, I don't know," Sarah said. "We haven't talked about it. And we haven't talked to Grace and Marie about it lately. It seems to me that if they want to stay around, they would be a pretty good fit here."

"So what do you want me to tell him?" Zoe asked.

"Let's tell him we'll talk to Grace and Marie and see what they have to say. Maybe we can offer them all a job!"

Zoe spoke to him for a couple of minutes. He looked down, obviously moved. He looked up again, swept his hat off with a nod and a smile to each of them. Then he spoke to Zoe again.

"What did he say?" Sarah asked.

"He says his name is Felipe."

"Welcome, Felipe!" Sarah said.

"Bienvenidos!"

"No penis envy here," Jen said.

❦❦❦❦

The mood was quite different than it had been the last time they'd sat down together to discuss the fate of Lavender Meadows. Back then, Grace and Marie had been almost ready to let go of the big white house that had formed so much of their lives for over forty years. It had seemed so hopeless then. Now it looked like it would keep going for many years to come.

Savannah straightened up a sheaf of papers covered with spreadsheets, projections, and scribbles. "Well, ladies, things certainly look better financially than they did the last time we talked about it. I have to say I'm impressed with what you've done with the place."

Marie laughed. "Hear, hear," she said, raising her half-empty glass of golden liquid.

"And we owe it all to Sarah," Grace said, raising her glass too.

"No, I think Sarah owes it all to you. None of this would have happened if you hadn't come up with the idea of bringing in other women, taking a chance with her."

"Well, that's true," Grace said. "But it was almost like it was meant to be. The bed and breakfast, the flowers, the berries, now the ladies living here, and the parties, and the wedding – and of course, Rachel and her baby—this place has a life of its own again!"

"Here's to Lavender Meadows!" Savannah said, raising her glass too. "A life of her own!"

≈≈≈≈

Rachel was glad that things had quieted down. She didn't get to be physically active, and she didn't get to participate in the everyday goings on at Lavender Meadows as she had when they were preparing for the weddings, but she valued the opportunity to do her own fiber work, check out music and movies, read, and tune in to the life growing inside her.

Not that she was neglected. If anything, she sometimes felt overwhelmed by the attention. Sarah or Willow came up to talk, and to monitor the baby every couple of hours, and Rachel was reassured to hear his steady heartbeat. Then Luanne came in three times a week to give her a massage to help her relax and keep her from getting sore muscles from lying in bed.

("Relax?" Rachel laughed. "If I was any more relaxed I'd be a puddle of goo!")

The ladies stopped in to see her at different times during the day, to see how she was doing, tell stories, and have snacks. Sometimes Lee and Marie sent up an indoor picnic so the ladies could eat lunch together. Emily popped in and out as her schedule permitted, and of course, she had Pee Wee, Bowser, and Margret and Fido, the tuxedo cat, sleeping, bathing, and occasionally squabbling on the bed.

"I think I'm getting jealous," Sarah complained to Jen. "Margret doesn't care about me anymore!"

"Of course she does," Jen said. "It's just that she has a captive audience now. You have other things to do than pet her all the time. Once Rachel has the baby, you'll be right at the top of her list again."

Rachel and Emily had hoped for a home delivery. "I planted the seed that gave you life," Emily said to the baby. "I want to be the one who helps you get from the inner to the outer universe." But things had changed when Rachel started bleeding, and reluctantly they'd changed their plans to avoid complications from the placental separation. "It's not worth taking chances," Emily said.

Rachel looked forward to the end of each day when Emily would come in after a busy day at the office and the hospital, crawl into bed beside her, and kiss and run her hands over Rachel's growing belly. They loved talking and singing to him, and he would kick and jiggle his appreciation while they laughed.

Rachel loved Emily telling her about the stages the baby was going through, and what he was doing. "Yes, he's floating around in there, comfortable as can be, waiting and growing," she said. "As he grows more, his head will move down into your pelvis, getting ready to be born. He won't be moving around quite so much once his head is engaged, and there won't be as much room for him to move around. It won't be long now," she said. "Soon he'll be out here with us, our little boy, and we'll do so many things together."

So when Rachel felt a twinge low on her belly, she didn't think much about it. She'd been having them occasionally, but had no signs of active labor. She was still early, four weeks from term, and the baby was doing fine. She hadn't had any bleeding since she'd been in the hospital months ago.

Sarah came upstairs right before lunch to monitor the baby. She hooked up the monitor, turned it on, and watched the screen for a minute.

"Uh, Rachel, let's see if this thing is hooked up right," she said. She adjusted the monitor belt and checked out the screen again. "Hmmm," she said. "Are you having any contractions?" she said.

"No," Rachel said. "Is something wrong?"

"I don't know," Sarah answered. "It looks like the baby's heartrate is going down a little. It's probably nothing." She reached for the bed control. "I'm going to put your head down, and I want you to lie on your left side," she said.

Rachel turned quickly. "Is it back up? Can you tell? Is he all right?" she asked, her voice rising.

"It's coming back up a bit, but I want to be sure," she said. "I'm going to call Lee." Quickly she dialed Lee's cell number. She could hear the sound from the stairway.

"Lavender Meadows, this is Lee," she said.

"Lee, could you bring up the oxygen set-up from the cabinet in the kitchen to Rachel's room?" she said.

"Sure thing. What's the matter?"

"Just come," Sarah said, her eyes on the screen.

In moments, Lee came crashing through the door, dragging the green oxygen tank behind her. "I'm here," she said breathlessly. "What should I do?"

"We're going to give you some oxygen to help the baby," she said, slipping the tubing over Rachel's head. "Try to breathe normally."

"What's going on?" Rachel cried. "Is the baby all right?"

"His heart rate is going down a little. Try not to panic!" Sarah said. "Lee, please get me some gloves and some lubricant from the bathroom."

Sarah slipped on the gloves and Lee opened the packet of lubricant, her hands shaking.

"I'm going to have you stay on your side while I check you," Sarah said to Rachel. "Lee, can you support her leg"?

Gently she slipped her fingers in. The cervix felt closed, and she did not feel any umbilical cord or see any blood or fluid.

They heard the door open downstairs, and the sound of whistling.

"Emily! Emily! Hurry!" Rachel cried.

The whistling stopped, and they heard footsteps pounding up the stairs. She burst into the room. "What? What is it?"

The unflappable Emily was shocked to see Rachel on her side, wearing an oxygen mask, Sarah and Lee holding her.

"The baby is having some heart rate deceleration," Sarah said. "I was just doing some routine monitoring when I saw it."

Emily glanced at the monitor and saw the tracing

of the baby's heartrate slowly climbing up from the valley of squiggles on the screen. Quickly, she changed places with Sarah. "Are you having any contractions?" she asked Rachel.

"No, I don't think so," Rachel said, starting to cry.

She looked over at Sarah. "Any bleeding? Fluid?"

"No," Sarah said. "And no cord."

Emily ran her hands over Rachel's belly. "He's still floating," she said. "His head is not down in the pelvis yet," she said to them. "But he could still be putting some pressure on the umbilical cord, or it could be twisted up." She locked eyes with Sarah and shook her head slightly. "Let's check her out," she said.

Lee got some more gloves and lubricant from the bathroom and handed them to Sarah.

"Stay on your side, honey," she told Rachel. "Try to breathe normally. I'm just going to examine you real quick."

The beeping of the monitor slowed again. "Uh oh," Emily said. She pushed her hand up slightly to change the baby's position and the rate of the beeps began to increase. "That's better," she said. "But let's not take any chances here," she said. "Lee, could you call 911 and tell them we have an obstetric emergency?"

"I need to go to the bathroom," Rachel said.

"I'm sorry, honey," Emily said. "Try to hold it. Your bladder will give the baby some support and keep him from pushing down on the cord."

Rachel sniffled. "I'll try," she said. "Tell them to hurry, please," she entreated.

"The ambulance is on its way," Lee said. "They should be here soon."

"Good," Emily said. "Are you comfortable? Can

you stay like that?" she asked Rachel.

"Yes, I guess I'm okay," she said.

"Lee, could you clear the way for the ambulance? And make sure nobody is blocking the driveway," Sarah said. "And tell Grace and Marie what's going on."

Lee ran down the stairs.

"When's the last time you ate, honey?" Emily asked.

"I had some toast and some ginger tea for breakfast," she said. "Why?"

"I'm not sure yet, but we may have to do a Caesarian section," Emily said. "It looks like the baby is having some distress, and we might need to get him out before he gets into real trouble."

"But he's so early!" Rachel cried. "He's a whole month premature!"

"Yes, but he could certainly make it if we can get him out quickly," Emily said. "He's strong! And we want to give him his best chance to be healthy."

They could hear the ambulance pulling up in the driveway, and moments later, they heard the EMTs coming up the stairs with the gurney.

"Hi, everybody. My name is Julie and this is George." The young woman nodded toward her partner as they set up the gurney and pushed it toward the bed. "What's going on here?"

"Hi, Julie," Emily said. "Hi George."

"Dr. Emily! What a surprise!" George said.

"This is my wife, Rachel. She's about thirty-six weeks along, and she's been on bedrest due to partial placental abruption. The baby's having some fetal distress, with cardiac decelerations. Her membranes are intact and she's not having any bleeding," Emily said.

"Okay, we'll get her out of here in a minute," Julie said. She looked at the decelerations on the monitor. "It's lucky you were here, Dr. Emily."

"Actually, it was Sarah who noticed the decelerations, and got her positioned to take the pressure off the cord," Emily said.

"Good catch," George said. "Do you want us to start an IV real quick before we go?"

"Sure, let's do it," Emily said.

"I was surprised when we got a call for an obstetric emergency from this place," Julie said. "I thought this was a nursing home!"

"It's more than that," Rachel said. "It's like a family home. They've been keeping an eye on me and the baby for months."

Emily let go of Rachel reluctantly as they prepared to go. George and Julie eased Rachel onto the gurney, still on her left side, and headed toward the stairs, watching out for the IV and oxygen tank. Lee and Sarah followed behind, carrying Rachel's things, including the stuffed orange kitty that had been sitting on the bottom of the bed all these months.

A little crowd was gathered at the bottom of the stairs, standing back out of the way of the little procession, and there was a chorus of voices.

"So long, Rachel, take care!"

"Don't worry, everything will be all right!"

"We love you!"

"Good luck!"

"We're praying for you!"

"Hey, what's going on? What happened?" Jen said, coming up from the garden. Marie told her about how Sarah saw the baby's heart rate decreasing, and how Emily had come along just at the right time.

Within just a few minutes, she was on her way to the hospital.

Rachel waved as they loaded her into the ambulance. "Thank you!" she called.

"I'll let you know as soon as we know anything," Emily said, and climbed in behind her. The door closed with a thunk and the ambulance pulled out, sirens and lights going.

Grace and Marie stood on the porch, watching the ambulance go. Sarah looked at them inquiringly, and Grace waved at her. "Go! Go, you two!" she said.

Jen and Sarah raced for the van.

※ ※ ※ ※

A couple of hours later, Sarah called Lavender Meadows and spoke with Grace.

"Rachel had the Caesarian section, and she's doing well. Benjamin was born at 2:10 PM, and he weighs five pounds, eight ounces. They're going to keep him in the Intensive Care Nursery for a few days, but they say he's doing well."

"It's a blessing!" she said. "Wonderful news!" Sarah could hear Marie and Lee cheering in the background and telling the rest of the ladies.

Emily came by the next day, filled everyone in on the details, and showed lots of pictures. It was hard to make out Benjamin's features in the incubator, but everyone declared that he was the cutest baby ever.

"Rachel's going to stay in the hospital for a couple more days, get her strength back," Emily said.

"I bet she's not gonna want to stay in bed, though." Lee laughed.

"No," Emily said. "No more bedrest for her! The first thing she wanted to do when she could move around was get up and go to a real bathroom!"

Emily and Lee packed up Rachel's things and Bowser and PeeWee and loaded them into the car. "I never realized she had so much stuff here!" Emily exclaimed.

"That's what happens when you have a crafter in a confined space for a long period of time. It starts looking like a combination yarn, bead, and fabric store!" Sarah said.

"We appreciate all your good care," Emily said. "But I have to say, it'll be good to get home again to our own bed." She smiled. "I sure will miss the food, though."

"You'll miss the quiet when that baby comes home, too," Sarah said.

"When he gets too noisy we'll just bring him over here to hang out with his aunties," Emily said with a grin.

"Can't wait!" she said.

※※※※

The phone rang just as they were finishing dinner. "Thanks for calling Lavender Meadows Family Home. This is Sarah Chase. How can I help you?" she said.

"Oh, hi, Sarah. This is Ro. I hope I'm not interrupting your dinner," she said.

"Oh, no, we're just about done," she said, wiping Edna's mouth with a napkin. "How are you two?" she asked. She didn't know Ro very well. She usually dealt with Luanne about scheduling massages, so she was curious.

"We're doing great, busy as usual. Actually, I was wondering if you could help me out with something."

"Sure, what can we do for you?"

"Well, I have a client, a woman with two young boys, three and five years old, and she's in a really tight spot."

"Why, what's going on?" Sarah asked.

"She's been living with a very abusive husband. He's an alcoholic, uses some drugs too; I don't know what. He beat her up earlier today, who knows why. It doesn't matter. Anyway, he's been beating her for years, but she's been afraid to bring charges against him. She's tried to leave him a couple of times, but he's come after them and brought them back. Now he seems to be escalating, and she feels like he's a danger to the kids, too, even though he hasn't actually hurt them yet."

Sarah shook her head. "At least not physically, right? Poor things! Of course the kids are hurt, too. How could they live in an environment like that without damage?" She felt a sudden chill.

Jen looked at her inquiringly. "It's Ro," Sarah said to her. "She's having a problem with a client." She spoke into the phone again. "Okay, I'm back with you now. What can we do?"

"I've been trying all day to find a safe place for them to stay until I can help her make some arrangements. The shelters are all full, she has no money, and the husband is on the loose. We don't know where he is."

"I don't know what we can do," Sarah said. "Let me talk to Grace and Marie and see what we can come up with. I'll call you back in a little while," she said.

"What's going on?" Grace asked.

"Well, that was Ro, and she's having problems getting help for a client of hers who's been abused. She has two kids, too, and she has no place to go."

"That's terrible!" Grace said. "What can we do to help? Maybe give her some money for a motel for a couple of days?"

"I don't know," Sarah said. "It's hard with kids. And Ro said she thinks the husband is pretty dangerous."

They sat quietly, lost in their own thoughts.

Marie came in from the kitchen and started clearing the dishes. She looked around for a moment. "How come you are so quiet? What's the matter?"

"Oh, we just got a call from Ro, and she's having trouble with one of the clients," Grace said. Quickly she filled in the details.

Marie scowled. "That's terrible. What can we do?"

"We don't know. We were just thinking," Jen said.

Grace cleared her throat delicately. "Um, you know, we do have that empty room where Rachel and Emily were," she said. "We gotten some calls about it, but we don't have it booked yet. Maybe we can let them stay there for a couple of days."

"What a great idea!" Jen said. "Nobody would think about looking for a runaway wife and kids in a place like this!"

"What about the other ladies?" Sarah said. "You know, two little kids could cause quite a ruckus. They might disturb everyone."

"Well, we're all here, I think. Why don't we talk about it?" Savannah said.

"Okay!" Carrie said.

Everyone looked at her in surprise. She was usually so quiet.

"All right. So," Grace said. "There's this woman and her kids, she needs our help. We can keep her here until Ro makes some arrangements for her, either for a shelter or to get out of town."

A murmur of assent greeted her words.

"Does anyone have a problem with this?" she asked.

Lee came in from the kitchen to get more dishes. She looked around at the group. "Hey, what's going on here? Are you having a meeting?" Her voice started to spiral down to a whine. She hated to be left out of anything.

Sarah brought her up to speed. "We were just getting ready to take a vote, I guess. How would you feel about having them here for a few days? Maybe not even that long, just until Ro can find a place for them."

"That's fine with me," Lee said. "I hate that kind of shit—whoops, sorry," she said to the ladies.

"Ok, I'll give Ro a call."

About an hour later, Ro showed up with their guests. They all looked extremely stressed, and had all been crying. The little boys held on to their mother, looking down shyly. The little one sucked vigorously on his thumb.

"Hi, Sarah, Grace, everybody," Ro said, nodding at all the women. "Thanks for helping us out. This is Ellen, and these two fellows are Matthew and Teddy." They looked around them, big-eyed.

"Nice to meet you." Grace stepped forward and held out her hand. Ellen took it and squeezed it gratefully. She was too overcome to talk.

Sarah looked over Ellen's face, saw the black eye, the swollen cheek. "Are you hurt anywhere else?" she asked.

Ellen shrugged. "I don't really know."

"Well, I'm a nurse; let me take a look at you. Have you gone to the hospital? Did you call the police?"

Ellen shook her head. "I just called Ro. I had her card from the last time."

"When was that?" Sarah asked.

"About a week ago," she said. "He's been drinking a whole lot lately. But he doesn't mean to act like this. He loves us."

Sarah and Ro shook their heads.

"Hmmmph," Marie said. She gently peeled the youngsters away from their mother. "C'mere, boys, I'm going to give you two the best cookies you ever ate!" Their mother nodded encouragingly, and they went off, holding Marie's hands.

Sarah shook her head in surprise. You never know, she thought to herself.

Sarah looked Ellen over carefully, noting the bruises on her body ranging from purple to green to yellow. She knew that the newest bruises would not show up for a couple of days. "Did you lose consciousness after he hit you?"

"No," Ellen said.

"Well, I'd like to have our doctor take a look at you. Is that okay?"

"Yes, I guess so," she said.

"Did he hit the boys?" Sarah asked.

"No, thank God." Ellen said. "He's pushed them a few times, and he screams at them a lot, but I don't think he's ever actually hit them."

"Good," she said. "Why don't you come sit down

and we'll get you some tea while I call the doctor," Sarah said. She also put in a call to the police.

Sarah put in a call to Dr. Emily while Lee fixed the tea. The boys sat with Marie at the kitchen table and she fed them cookie after cookie. She also pressed a golden glass of sherry into Ellen's hand, and she sipped it gratefully.

"Let me show you your room, Ellen," Sarah said when she was done. "Do you have any things with you?" she asked.

"No, we just ran, got in the car, and drove away as fast as we could. He's gonna be so mad!" The tears started down her face again. She looked around the room, at the pink flowered couch and the cushy beds. "This is really nice. Is this a hotel?"

"No," Sarah said. "It's a family home." Quickly she explained about Lavender Meadows.

"I never heard of a place like this," she said. "You know I'm a Christian," she said warily, clutching the crucifix around her neck.

Sarah grimaced a little. People could be so weird sometimes. Here she was, hiding from the man who beat her and threatened her kids, and she was worried about being in proximity to a bunch of old lesbians. "Don't worry," she said. "You're safe here."

Joe Wendell and his partner Gwen Phillips arrived in short order, and Lee refilled the kettle. "Hello ladies," he said. He introduced himself and Gwen to Ellen and shook her hand. He got out his notepad. "So why don't you tell me what happened," he said.

"Oh, just the usual. My husband Freddy was drinking, and when he has a little too much he gets kind of angry, you know?" Ellen shook her head. "And things haven't been going so well for him the past few months. Lost his job from the drinking, so he gets mad a lot."

Joe made some notes. "Have you ever called the police?" he asked.

Ellen shook her head. "No, our neighbors did a couple of times when they heard us yelling."

"Did you ever press charges against him?" Gwen asked.

"Oh, no, then he'd really be mad!" she said.

"So what do you see happening here, Ellen?" Joe said.

"Well, he'll cool off. He always does," she said.

"And what about your boys?" Ro said. "Doesn't it bother you that he could hurt them too?"

She began to cry again. "Of course it bothers me," she said. "But we have no place to go."

"Do you have any family?" Joe asked. "Friends?"

"I have a sister," Ellen said. "But she has a full house, husband and kids of her own. And besides, she lives right down the road from us."

"So do you want to press charges now?" Joe asked.

"No, I can't," she said. "I just can't."

"You know that this kind of thing will just go on and on," Ro said. "It won't stop. Maybe someday he'll even kill you, or the boys."

"He would never do that," Ellen said.

Dr. Emily came by and looked Ellen over. "I want you to come in for an x-ray at the office tomorrow," she said. She basically asked her the same questions that Sarah and Joe had already asked, and encouraged her to press charges.

"Okay," she said. "I don't think you have a concussion, but you let me know if you have any dizziness or nausea."

She gave Sarah some instructions and she walked back downstairs. "I don't get it," she said. "I want to understand, but I just don't."

"I don't either, but then again, I make less violent choices in partners apparently," she said, looking over at Jen, who was helping Lee with the dishes.

"We're all lucky," Emily said. "Oh, and speaking of lucky..." She pulled out her phone and showed Sarah a bunch of Ben and Rachel pictures. "Isn't he just the sweetest! I miss them already."

Sarah looked at the pictures, passed the phone over to Grace and the other ladies for a quick oohing and aahing session before she retrieved it and passed it back to Emily.

"Go home, then," she said, giving her a quick hug. "Thanks for coming out. We'll let you know if anything happens."

Joe and Gwen prepared to leave, too. "Thanks for coming," Sarah said.

"Sorry we couldn't do more. Our hands are pretty much tied if people won't press charges."

"I know," Sarah said. "I don't get it."

"Neither do we," said Gwen. "If anyone tried to treat me like that I'd..." Words failed her.

"I know," said Sarah.

"Keep reminding her not to tell anyone where she is," Joe said. "We don't want him tracking her down. That means no cell phone calls, notes, emails, nothing."

"Okay – but surely she'd have better sense than that," Jen said.

"You'd be surprised," Joe said.

Next day, Ro and Sarah helped Ellen change her appearance in borrowed clothes, including sunglasses, a baseball cap to cover her dark hair, a sequin sweatshirt, and Jen's old leather motorcycle pants. They set out for Emily's office at lunchtime, when there would be the fewest patients and staff members around. The boys were worried about the change in her looks and reluctant to see their mother leaving, but she explained that she would be back with them soon. Jen and Lee volunteered to hang out with them, and when they left, they were happily watching Sesame Street and eating grilled cheese sandwiches.

They looked up and down the street before they went into the office, but there was no sign of Freddy.

Dr. Emily checked her over and took a couple of x-rays. Ellen assured her that she was not dizzy and was able to breathe without too much pain.

"Do you have any idea what you're going to do now?" she asked.

Ellen just shrugged. "I don't know. I don't have a job, or any money, really, and the kids are in school, so we're pretty much stuck," she said.

"Well, I'm still looking around for a place for you to go," Ro said. "But it's important for you to stay out of sight for now. We don't want him to know where you are. And remember, don't contact anyone!"

"But what about my sister? She must be worried to death!"

"No, if she doesn't know where you are she can't tell him, right? Just be patient for a little bit longer," Ro said.

"And of course, you are welcome to stay with us

until you get squared away. And safe!" Sarah said.

"Thank you so much!" Ellen said, looking around at the three women. "I can't tell you how much I appreciate your help!" She paused. "But what about my car? I can't leave without my car."

Sarah, Ro, and Emily looked at each other in dismay. "Where is the car now?" Sarah asked.

"It's still at our house, I guess." she said. "Right next door to my sister's."

"Oh no," Sarah said. "That certainly makes things more difficult."

Sarah waited with Ellen while Ro ran across the street to the Goodwill to pick up a couple of changes of clothes for Ellen and the boys, as they'd left their home with only the clothes on their backs.

The boys were happy to see their mother when they got back to Lavender Meadows, but they were all still jumpy. They went out to burn off some energy, playing with Rosa's kids while Ellen went upstairs to lie down. Sarah sat in the kitchen with a cup of tea while Sarah filled Jen, Marie, and Lee in on their visit to Dr. Emily.

"Tell you the truth, I hope Ro finds some place for them to stay soon," Lee said. "I don't feel comfortable having that skunk prowling around. I'd like to kick his ass!" She yelled suddenly, then executed a couple of quick karate moves.

They all jumped, then laughed. "Hey, Bruce Lee," Jen said.

"Yeah, right," Lee said. "Scary moves can come in handy when you live on the street."

"I bet," Jen said. "What else can you do?"

"Oh, panhandle, shoplift, break into places, jack cars, get tons of samples at Costco, which you know, some unmentionable things, which you don't know..."

"Wait! Did you say you could jack cars?" Jen asked, excited.

"Uh, yeah, I've done a few...why?" Lee asked.

"Maybe you could help Ellen get her car back!"

"Hmmm...maybe...where is it?"

"It's at her house, but she can't really just go over there...and she doesn't have a key...she ran out without any of her stuff."

"Let's see what we can do," Lee said, proud that she could use her special skills to help the Lavender Meadows crew.

※※※※

"Wait a minute," Sarah said. "Are you talking about sending that child over there alone to commit crimes and to put herself in danger?"

"Well, not alone, I'd go too!"

"Okay, good idea. But I want to go, too!"

"Safety in numbers, I guess," Ro said doubtfully. "But I can't officially condone this, you know."

"No, of course not," Sarah said. But Freddy couldn't take them all on. Unless he had a gun, of course, but Ellen assured them that his deer rifle was at Ace Pawn.

So in the end, Lee, Jen, Sarah, Zoe, Willow, and Ellen piled into the van with ropes and a bunch of tools and headed over to Ellen's house to get her stuff.

Freddy was out drinking most nights, so they decided to go over there at around midnight, before the bars closed. They made sure that they all wore dark clothing and caps so they would be inconspicuous. They didn't want anyone to see them sneaking around.

Especially Freddy.

Zoe stifled a laugh. "What's so funny?" Jen asked.

"We look like clown-car ninjas," she said. Jen poked her as the van filled with nervous laughter.

≈≈≈≈≈

They pulled up as quietly as they could, headlights off, staying close to the shadows, and cut the engine. Two cars were parked side by side in front of the dark, quiet house.

"The green one is mine," Ellen said, pointing to the beat-up Ford Fiesta.

"Not worth stealing," Lee mumbled under her breath.

Sarah opened the van door and left it open a bit so it wouldn't make noise when she closed it. Jen did the same on the other side, but there was no way to muffle the sound of the sliding van door. Willow laughed shakily and Zoe punched her on the arm. "Shhh!" she said.

"Sorry," Willow whispered.

Lee got a flashlight and looked the car over while the others unloaded some tools from the van. Jen took a screwdriver and tried to pry the door of the house open, but it would not give. "I'll look around the back, but we may have to break a window," she said to Zoe.

Ellen jumped from the van. "Oh, no, wait," she cried. "Just a minute now. Here. I think..." And with that, she bent down, felt around the bottom of the porch post, and came up with a fist-sized rock, which she waved triumphantly. "Look, it's still here!" And with that, she opened the rock and dumped the house and car keys into her hand.

Jen looked at her in disbelief. "So we don't have to break into the house after all, and we don't have to steal the car," she said, disappointed.

"No, I guess not," Sarah said.

"Guess what else," Lee said.

"I don't know. What?" Willow asked.

"This car is unlocked. And it's warm."

They all froze.

"Maybe he walked over to my sister's house," Ellen said hopefully.

"Maybe he killed himself," Lee offered.

"No such luck," Zoe said.

"Oh, no, do you think he's in the house?"

"I doubt it," Sarah said. "Surely he'd have heard us and come out by now."

"Maybe he's passed out upstairs," Ellen said. "He sleeps like the dead when he's been drinking."

"Well, let's get her stuff and get out of here," Willow said. "This place gives me the creeps."

"Me too," said Ellen. "I never want to see this place again."

As Ellen inserted the key into the lock, the door swung open.

"Unbelievable," Jen said. "It's not locked."

There was no sign of Freddy inside, so they rummaged around as quietly as they could, filling big plastic bags with clothing, shoes, and some of the kids' favorite toys. Ellen found her purse with her cell phone, checkbook, lipstick, and key ring and clutched it to her chest. She took a few things from the kitchen too – her mom's teapot, her favorite kitchen tools, her big spaghetti pot, her cast iron skillet.

They loaded the stuff into Ellen's car, and Jen got behind the wheel because Ellen was still feeling shaky, then everybody else got back into the van. They were very pleased with how things had gone. They'd accomplished their mission without causing any real damage, and Ellen was able to get her stuff back. She could start a new life.

"Hey, we might have a real future as burglars," said Willow.

Lee shook her head. "Yeah, right," she said.

There was a soft groan and the squeak of a rocker as they stopped at the end of the driveway, preparing to turn out onto the road. He sat in the dark for a moment, then grabbed the porch rail to heave himself up. He squinted as he watched them pull away.

"Lavender Meadows," he read on the back of the van. "Family Home." He shook his head, belched loudly, and turned back to his chair.

"Dumb bitches," he said.

They were all pleased and proud of themselves when they got back home, strutting around and talking tough. They danced around the room gleefully, working off the adrenaline from their adventure.

"Yeah, we sure took care of business tonight."

"Slicker than owl shit!"

"That man's in for a big surprise when he gets home!"

Only Ellen remained quiet. She was glad that she would be able to give her kids back some of their things, but her heart ached. Her life as she knew it was over. She knew she could never go back. Everything was up to her now, for her and for her boys.

Sarah noticed her silence and sat beside her on

the couch, tucking her feet under her. "How're you doing?" she asked.

Ellen plucked a teddy bear from the top of one of the plastic bags, smiled wanly, and shook her head, saying nothing.

"You have to forgive the other girls – they feel like they accomplished a successful scouting mission or something, but none of this is funny to you, I know."

A small sob escaped Ellen's lips, and she buried her face in the bear's worn fur. Sarah put her arm around her thin shoulders, and Ellen leaned into her, releasing a torrent of tears.

Jen came in and looked at Sarah questioningly. Sarah shook her head slightly, and Ellen continued to cry as Jen beat a retreat to the kitchen to put the kettle on.

After a while, the tears slowed, and finally stopped. Marie stuck her head in and Sarah nodded. In a few moments, she came in with tea, rugalach pastries, and the sherry bottle. Grace joined them too, carrying some delicate glasses and a big afghan, which she draped over Ellen's lap, even though the room was not cold. Ellen wrapped it around herself gratefully with a hiccoughy sigh.

Grace handed around glasses of golden liquid and raised hers in toast. "World peace," she said.

Ellen laughed ruefully and raised her glass too. "Amen," she said.

They sat there in the living room for a while, talking story, until the sherry began to work its magic. Ellen was exhausted, began to nod off.

"Come on," Sarah said. "Let's get some sleep. It's very late."

They walked her up the stairs to her room and

gave her gentle hugs at the door. The boys breathed softly, flushed with sleep, their blankets tossed every which way. Ellen pulled them up around their shoulders and climbed in beside them, wanting the comfort of their warm puppy bodies. She sighed as she relaxed, her muscles aching.

Grace and Marie headed toward their room, stopping for a hug from Jen and Sarah before they went back downstairs to their own room.

"You two did good things tonight," Grace said.

❦❦❦❦

Marie was exhausted, stressed out from the whole business with Ellen. She hated to hear about things like that, hated even more to see it. She'd have loved to get her hands on that miserable worm.

Grace was already in bed when Marie slid between the sheets and cuddled up next to her. Grace rubbed her back gently, humming tunelessly in her reedy voice. "My girl," she said. "Don't worry; we'll make sure they'll be all right. You're so soft-hearted."

"Hmmmph," Marie mumbled softly, and snuggled in closer as she drowsed off.

She was sitting at the kitchen table, slicing up green and yellow squash with the long black knife when she heard the creak of stealthy footsteps coming toward the back door. She thought it was one of her brothers trying to scare her, and she laughed and said, "Get out of here, now, I know it's you!"

The door swung open, and James filled the doorway. "Ah, so you were expecting me!" he said.

She yelped in surprise. "Get out of here! Right now!"

He stepped inside and grabbed her arm. His breath reeked of alcohol, a smell she remembered from their last encounter, and his body was sweaty and unwashed. She pushed at his chest, but he was too strong, and pulled her against him. He held her tight with one arm and pawed at her clothes with the other while she screamed and struggled.

"You hurt me, you bitch," he said. "But you won't get away with it. I'll fix you good!"

He backed her across the kitchen, pulling up her dress. He tried pushing her down on the floor, but she grabbed at the kitchen table...and the knife. She slashed at him, catching his cheek, and he yelled and loosened his grip. She pushed him back, then drove the knife deep into his chest, still screaming. He gasped and lurched forward on top of her, crashing to the floor.

She fought for air, but he was a dead weight across her chest, and she could not breathe, could not breathe, the pain like a crushing band.

She struggled to sit up and catch her breath, clawing the blankets off her, sweat pouring down her face. She reached for the brown bottle of nitroglycerin next to the bed, opened it with shaky fingers, and slid one under her tongue.

After a moment, her breathing slowed a little. Grace stirred and reached for her. "What's the matter, honey? Are you okay?"

"I'm fine, Grace, go back to sleep," she said, sinking back onto the pillows.

But she could not get back to sleep. After a little while, she crept quietly down the stairs to make herself a cup of tea.

Sarah flopped down on the bed, exhausted. Jen kicked off her shoes and lay down beside her. "Some night, huh?" she said.

"Really. I don't want to have any more like this, ever!" Sarah said.

"That poor girl! And those kids! It's just awful. I can't imagine what their lives are gonna be like now, starting from scratch."

"I know. I understand a little about starting from scratch, but I've been so lucky," Sarah said thoughtfully. "I have an education, and I could get a good job anywhere...I found Grace and Marie, this place. And poor Ellen. No job, no skills, two kids..."

"And the worst part of it is she's got that crappy car," Jen said.

They laughed.

"So many women were raised to think that a husband would provide and take care of them and tell them what to do. Thank goodness that's not so common anymore!"

"Really," Jen said. "I can't imagine! But the older women in my family were all like that, then when they got divorced or their husbands died, they were screwed. Of course, you're preaching to the choir. If I ever had a child, I would make sure that she would be educated to take care of herself in the world!"

"And what if you had a boy child?" Sarah asked.

"I would make sure that he knew how to cook... and sew on his own buttons...and whatever!"

Sarah laughed. "I pity the child who would learn to cook from you, Ms. Potluck McDonald Cheeseburger!"

Jen joined her. "You're right about that! I guess

I'll have to leave that part to you," she said slyly. She paused for a moment. "The things that you were grateful for when you were starting over – I noticed that I was not on your list."

"You're at the top of my list," she said. She rolled over and put her arms around Jen. "Did I mention that I love you, butchy girl?"

"Me too, you," she answered.

≈≈≈≈

They awoke to the sounds of Ralph barking and growling and Freddy yelling, "Get away! Get away!" He kicked at Ralph, who was snapping at his arms and legs. Ralph yelped, but continued his attack.

"Open the door, you fucking bitches! Open the door! I want my wife! I want my kids!" Freddy yelled, trying to fend Ralph off. "I'm gonna kill all of you, and this fucking dog too!"

Jen and Sarah jumped out of bed and raced toward the front door as he kicked it in, yelling in pain as his foot hit the wood.

"Where is she?" He looked around wildly. "Ellen!" he yelled. "Boys! Come out here. Right now!"

Lights went on around the house as women were awakened from their sleep. "Somebody call 911!" Sarah yelled.

"Got it!" Clarisse yelled from upstairs.

Ellen came out of her room in a panic and leaned over the railing. "Freddy, no! Get out of here! Leave us alone!"

He raced up the stairs and grabbed her by the hair. "You're my wife, and you're coming with me!" He shook her while she screamed.

Matthew and Teddy came running out of the room. "Daddy, no! Don't hurt Mommy! Don't!" they yelled. Matthew grabbed at his father's legs and bit down deeply on his thigh. He tried to shake him off and still maintain his grip on Ellen while he yelled in pain.

Then they were all on the stairs, trying to move in different ways – Freddy trying to drag Ellen down, his sons trying to hold him back, Ginny swinging Edna's cane and yelling like a banshee, Grace hitting Freddy in the head with her slipper. Savannah stood a step above Freddy, her arm looped around his neck. They all got tangled up in the stair climber rail as Sarah and Jen tried to pull Ellen and the boys away from him. Lee ran from her room, waved her arms, and gave a couple of karate yells, but she couldn't get close enough to Freddy to do any damage. Margret yowled and scratched her way through the knot of people, then slowly, slowly, they rolled down the stairs together like an old cartoon, landing at the bottom in a big heap.

Marie ran out of the kitchen, her old iron skillet in one hand and her long black knife in the other. "Let me at the son of a bitch!" she yelled. "I'll kill 'em!"

Just then, Joe Wendell and Gwen came racing in, guns drawn. They pulled up short, stunned by the pile of yelling, squirming arms, legs, and other body parts at the foot of the stairs, some naked and some clothed. "What the hell is going on here?"

Everyone started talking at once, and the police stood there, shaking their heads, trying to make sense of what they were seeing. Those who could unwound themselves from the pile and stood, trying to explain their version of what happened as loudly as they could. Those who couldn't stand lay there, including Freddy, who was out like a light.

Then Grace looked over and screamed as she saw Marie go down. "Marie! Help Marie, Sarah," she yelled.

Sarah raced to Marie. Her eyes were open, but she was gasping, barely breathing. "Lee, get the nitro! Get the oxygen!" she yelled.

Joe shook his head, and put his gun away. "I'm calling for backup and some ambulances," he said.

❦❦❦❦

The ER was crowded, especially after the ambulances from Lavender Meadows arrived. Freddy was just starting to come around, although nobody was in a hurry for that. Gwen had handcuffed him to the gurney, and stood guard in his room. She added up the assault, breaking and entering, and attempted murder charges in her head, and nodded, satisfied. He'd be out of their way for quite a while. He had a broken leg, scratches on his face, bite marks on his arms and legs, and several bumps on the head from a cane and a pink shoe. In addition, he was still very drunk.

Ellen had some new bruises and a bloody patch where she'd lost some hair. Matthew had knocked out a tooth that was almost ready to come out anyway, and between bouts of tears, he was proud to show the gap to anyone who would look. His mom could hardly stop hugging him and telling him how brave he was. Teddy was okay, too, sound asleep with his thumb in his mouth on the bed next to his mom. Joe stood beside her, taking her statement so she could press charges against him for all the harm and havoc he had created in their lives.

Marie had spent just a very few moments in the ER

before being whisked off to the cardiac catheterization lab for an angioplasty, and possibly, bypass surgery.

"What is an angopulsty?" Lee asked.

"They put a balloon up into your heart and blow it up to unblock the arteries," Sarah answered.

"Sounds like fun," Lee said.

"Not to me," Grace said, snuffling and dabbing at her nose with a balled up Kleenex.

"Oh, Grace, you know she's a tough old bird," Jen said.

"I know. That's the only thing that keeps me from wanting to kill her," Grace said angrily. "What was she thinking?"

❦❦❦❦

Sarah, Jen, and Grace sat in the waiting room of the Cardiac Care Unit for news of Marie's condition. Finally, the doctor came out and sat beside Grace.

"We've finished the procedure, and Ms. Meadows came through it pretty well, considering," he said. "It's a good thing you had a nurse there, or she might not have made it."

"That's Sarah Chase over there," Grace said. "Our shero!"

The doctor looked puzzled for a minute, then laughed. "Oh, I get it!" He cleared his throat. "Well, she had quite a blockage, but we were able to get enough blood flowing to keep her going for a while. We might need to look at doing a bypass down the road in a while, but she's very strong…"

"Ornery," Lee said.

"Mean," Jen said.

"Stubborn," Sarah said.

He looked at them in surprise. He turned to Grace.

"I'm glad your sister is doing so well," he said.

"She's not my sister – she's my wife!" she said proudly.

❧❧❧❧

Later that day, Marie woke from a troubled sleep. She'd had terrible nightmares for so long, but this one seemed different. There was a lot of screaming and shouting and people running. She sighed. She heard all kinds of beeps and clicks around her and realized that she was in the hospital, and that Grace was beside her in the bed.

"Hi, honey," Grace whispered into her ear. "I know you're awake. How do you feel?"

"Tired," she said. "And sore. But I feel like I can breathe a little better."

"Thank goodness," said Grace. "You gave us quite a scare!"

"Why? What happened?" Marie asked.

Grace filled her in briefly on the evening's events. "And then everybody fell down the stairs, and you came running out in your nightgown with your frying pan and your knife, and then you fell over! What was all that about?"

Marie didn't answer for a few minutes. Big, silent tears rolled down her face and splashed onto the blanket, unheeded. Grace just lay there with her and held her hand, giving her space until she was ready to talk.

Marie started the story slowly with the first time James had come to the house, and how she had grabbed the frying pan and threw it at him.

"I've always wondered what happened to your hand," Grace said. "You just said you burned yourself, but you never told me how!"

Gradually, Marie kept going, filling in the details about how he had broken into their house and tried to rape her, and how she had stabbed him.

"Oh, no, love. I can't believe it! My poor girl!" She blew her nose, took a deep breath, and tried to hug her as much as the monitors and IV tubing would allow. "So what happened then? Was he dead? Did you kill him?"

"He was. I did. Just a couple of gasps like a fish on the bank, and then he was gone. And then my parents came in and saw us, and my mother was screaming, and my father pulled him off me, and he was yelling and crying and he sat on the floor with me and rocked me in his arms, and there was blood all over my dress..."

"Oh my God," Grace gasped. "So then what happened?"

"Well, the police came, and I was arrested, and there was a sort of trial, but everyone knew what happened, and after a while they let me go. They said it was self-defense. But a lot of people thought it was my fault, that I was a murderer."

"Unbelievable! So then what?"

"My dad and mom sat me down and told me that they thought I should leave town. I could never have a normal life there, with everyone knowing what happened. I would always be that girl who did that awful thing. I was afraid to go, but they were right. They sent me off to my mom's sister in Tacoma, and that was that. And the rest you know," Marie said.

"So all those years, all those terrible nightmares

you said you never remembered! How could you keep that to yourself all that time?"

"Hmmmph," she said.

❀❀❀❀

Sarah lay in bed, naked, waiting for her honey to bring in the goodies, Margret curled up at her side.

Jen came in, set the tray next to the bed, pulled off the beautiful batik robe Sarah had given her, and climbed in beside her. She leaned over and gave Sarah a lingering kiss. Sarah sighed and ran her hand lightly over Jen's spiky head, then her arm, then her back...

They took their sweet time until finally they were both thirsty and sat up. Jen lifted the tray from the table and place it between them. Sarah looked at it and laughed. There was tea, an enormous plate of cookies, and two delicate crystal glasses of golden sherry.

"This has certainly been an eventful couple of weeks," Sarah said. "Rachel having the baby, then Ellen showing up, and that whole business with the break in..."

"And Marie's angerplasty, as Grace is calling it..." Jen laughed. "And getting the Sanchez family settled, and helping Ellen find a new home..."

"Tell you the truth, there hasn't been a dull moment in the whole time I've been here," Sarah said. She poured herself a cup of tea and one for Jen. It was barely warm now, but neither of them minded. "Hey, pass me an almond cookie, wouldja?" She dipped it into her cup and bit down happily. "Finding Grace and Marie, and you, of course, and getting Lavender Meadows started, and finding the other ladies, and Lee, and Vick too..."

"It's been amazing, all right," Jen said. "My whole life has changed because of you and this place."

"Mine too," Sarah said. "And I've learned so much here."

"Yeah, like what?"

"Like accepting people and being accepted. Connecting with people, and really listening to them. Seeing people for who they really are."

"Like families," Jen said.

"Like families are supposed to be." She took a deep breath. "I also learned that you can choose who is part of your real family. You don't have to be limited to the family you were born into!" She laughed as Margret nosed between them. "Or even your own species!"

Jen handed Sarah a glass of sherry, and raised her own for a toast.

"To the Lavender Meadows family, and to their future!"

"And ours!" Sarah said, and tinked her glass.

About the Author

Diana Sue Wellspring is a registered nurse and technical writer who lives with her wife, Gay Dawn Wellspring, and cat, Pokadotsi, in Lakewood, Washington.